AWAKENED

Also by Kate Douglas

INTIMATE

REDEMPTION

Available from St. Martin's Paperbacks

AWAKENED

KATE DOUGLAS

St. Martin's Paperbacks

This is a work of fiction. All of the characters, organizations, and events portrayed in this novel are either products of the author's imagination or are used fictitiously.

AWAKENED

Copyright © 2016 by Kate Douglas.

All rights reserved.

For information address St. Martin's Press, 175 Fifth Avenue, New York, NY 10010.

ISBN: 978-1-250-06478-3

Our books may be purchased in bulk for promotional, educational, or business use. Please contact your local bookseller or the Macmillan Corporate and Premium Sales Department at 1-800-221-7945, ext. 5442, or by e-mail at MacmillanSpecialMarkets@macmillan.com.

Printed in the United States of America

St. Martin's Paperbacks edition / July 2016

St. Martin's Paperbacks are published by St. Martin's Press, 175 Fifth Avenue, New York, NY 10010.

10 9 8 7 6 5 4 3 2 1

32020 9750

Finishing *Awakened*, the third and final book in my Intimate Relations series, has been a bittersweet experience. As always happens with a series, I've grown really attached to my characters. With this book, I'm telling them goodbye. They've lived in my head, been a huge part of my writing life, and whispered their secrets to me when I'm lying in bed, trying to figure out what they're up to next. Their voices aren't even whispering to me at this point, and I already miss them. I know, however, there are always more out there!

This book is dedicated, with much appreciation and not a little bit of humility, to the amazing women who helped me bring this series—these characters—to life.

My agent, Jessica Faust, president and owner of BookEnds Literary Agency, has been my guiding light in this often convoluted world of publishing almost since the very beginning of my career. She has helped me grow my career over the years, and there aren't enough superlatives to describe her skills. (For a writer, that's admitting a lot.) St. Martin's Press editor Eileen Rothschild saw the potential in my wine country series, and helped me create much better stories than if I'd been left to my own devices. Thank you, Eileen, for your insightful edits and your patience. My thanks also go to Amy Goppert, my SMP publicist, who has done her best to let all of you know about my books, and hopefully entice you to buy them.

These three amazingly talented (and very busy!) women are a major part of the team that helps me bring my stories to life. I owe them a huge debt of gratitude as well as my sincere thanks.

ACKNOWLEDGMENTS

When I realized that Marcus Reed, my male protagonist in *Awakened*, had to recover memories lost during a traumatic childhood event, I went to Roger Dent, MBA, CCHt, a Master Hypnotist and Certified Clinical Hypnotherapist (CCHt) (www.rogercdent.com). He freely shared his experience and knowledge of the field of hypnotherapy, which helped me create the character who is my Master Hypnotist in *Awakened* as well as figure out how I was going to help Marc discover what had been haunting him throughout his adult life. Please note that any mistakes or misinterpretations you might note in the book regarding the hypnotic process are entirely mine.

I also want to acknowledge and thank my intrepid beta readers for once again finding the time to read my work before I ever send it to the editor. They have saved me countless times from making a complete fool of myself! (Editor Eileen Rothschild owes them, too . . . if not for my betas, she'd know what my writing is really like!)

Jay Takane, Ann Jacobs, Karen Woods, Sue Thomas,

ACKNOWLEDGMENTS

Kerry Parker, Lynne Thomas, and Rose Toubbeh, you have made this job so much more fun, and my stories better. Please know I am more appreciative than you can possibly imagine. Thank you!

And as always, a big thank you to my husband, who actually seems to understand how to deal with marriage to a writer—and who does it so well.

CHAPTER 1

He'd been here so many times before, this room that was almost familiar, the wall of mirrors reflecting an image he'd tried to forget. He didn't know the woman who struggled. Couldn't see the face of the man whose hands encircled her throat. Marc didn't know who they were or when this happened. Not until they turned. He watched her slim body sag and disappear from view. Raised his head and gazed in horror at the man in the mirror.

Marc stared into the eyes of a killer. His very own dark brown eyes.

"Marc? I've got honey oat muffins just out of the oven. Are you awake?"

Mandy. He rolled to his back, sucked in a deep breath and concentrated on slowing his racing heart. "Be out in a minute. I overslept."

"Don't worry. I'll keep them warm for you. Not gonna let you starve."

He heard her laughing as she went back down the hall. The last remnants of the dream faded away, but Mandy was in the kitchen and the muffins were warm.

All was once again right with the world.

* * *

"Hey Marc! Your cell phone's calling you."

Marc reached into his pocket and laughed. "Crap, Ben. Where is it? I thought I had it."

"Sounds like your bedroom."

With a half-assed salute, Ben Lowell threw his military duffle over his shoulder and headed for the front door. Marc raced down the hall to his bedroom and grabbed the phone off the bedside table. It stopped ringing the moment he reached for it, so he glanced at the caller ID before returning the call.

No. On second thought, he wasn't about to return this bastard's call. A notification popped up, telling him he had voicemail. He deleted the message without listening, shoved his phone in his pocket, and went back to the front room.

It looked like the cab was here for Ben and his fiancée, Lola Monroe. "This your bag, Lola?" When she nodded, he said, "I'll take it down." He picked it up and pretended to fall over. "Pack the set of horseshoes for the trip? Gonna play a game on the mall in DC?"

"Of course." Lola's expression never wavered. "Thank you. Tell Ben I'll be there in just a sec." Then she went back to her conversation with her sister Mandy, an extension of what the guys had been calling *the long goodbye* over the past few days. The girls were close. He wondered how Mandy was going to handle the two of them being apart for at least a week.

Though his biggest concern was how *he* was going to handle being alone with Mandy. Worrying about it had kept him awake nights for most of the week, but there was nothing he could do about it now. Hauling Lola's suitcase, he headed down the front stairs to the waiting cab.

* * *

The moment the door closed behind Marc, Mandy remembered. "Don't go yet, Lola!" She raced back into the kitchen and grabbed the bag of chocolate chip cookies off the kitchen counter. She caught her sister as she was reaching for her new carry-on bag.

Lola paused at the door. "Okay. What'd I forget now?"

"You didn't. I did. I forgot to give you the cookies I baked for you and Ben to munch along the way."

"Yum! Thank you." Laughing, she took the cookies from Mandy. "You realize, I actually hope we'll both be sleeping. I can't believe my first trip in an airplane's going to be in the dark. I won't get to see anything." She stuck the cookies in her bag. "Thanks. I'm going to miss you."

"I'm going to miss you, too. Now hurry. The cab's here."

Lola gave her a tight hug and whispered in her ear, "You just want me out of here so you can finally get Marc all to yourself."

"Yeah. Like that's going to do any good." Mandy exhaled. Loudly. Frustration was too simple a word, especially when Marcus Reed and his lack of interest wasn't the only thing that had her upset tonight. "Text or call me when you two get to your hotel, okay?"

"I will. Love you, sis." Lola winked and added, "Good luck."

Smiling, because that was the best she could do, Mandy merely shrugged. "One can hope. You, too. Have a safe trip. Let me know when you get there."

"Promise."

One last hug, and then Lola was practically skipping down the stairs. Ben grabbed her bags and stuck them in the trunk while Marc helped Lola into the back seat, leaned in to kiss her cheek, and then shook Ben's hand before Ben got in beside Lola. Mandy waited beneath the porch light and waved as the cab pulled away from the curb, heading to San Francisco International Airport.

Silly, how she actually felt sort of weepy, standing here on the top step, watching Lola leave with Ben. She and her sister had never really been apart, but they'd been alone so much as kids, they had practically raised themselves. Now Lola was headed to DC with Ben while he testified at a pretrial hearing in a case against a powerful senator. They'd be gone at least a week.

Yeah, she was going to miss Lola, and Ben, too, but not for the obvious reason. Their absence meant she'd be here alone with a man she'd lusted after for years.

One she'd fallen head over heels in love with when they'd finally met.

A man who'd been one of their roommates for a little over two months now—sixty-three days, to be exact. The only problem? Marc didn't notice Mandy at all. Why should he? The guy was gorgeous, brilliant, rich— the list was endless—while Mandy was nothing but the ex-barista for a now defunct coffee shop. She'd still had a job this morning, but she hadn't quite gotten around to telling any of her roommates she'd suddenly joined the ranks of the unemployed.

Standing alone, watching Marc as he said goodbye to Ben and Lola, she wished she were something better, someone more. A woman Marc might look up to and respect. A woman he could love.

He turned then, glanced at the house, and actually made eye contact with her for one brief moment. Then he bowed his head and, with both hands shoved deep in his pants pockets, walked slowly toward the front steps.

He couldn't have made his feelings any more obvious. It was clear he was dreading the idea of the two of them alone together for however long the hearings in Washington, DC lasted. Sighing, Mandy turned away and went inside. Marc walked slowly up the steps and followed her into the living room.

She'd wondered for weeks what it would be like, finally to be here alone with Marc.

Now she knew. It was going to be absolutely heart-breaking.

"Seems really strange with them gone, doesn't it?" Staring at Mandy's slim back as she walked through the front room and into the kitchen, Marc wondered how he was going to handle the next week. Damn, he hoped the hearings didn't last any longer.

Mandy opened the cabinet over the sink and grabbed a bottle of gin. "You have no idea," she said. Turning, she held up the bottle. "I think it calls for gin and tonic. You want one?"

She looked stiff and uncomfortable. Mandy was usually so laid back, relaxed, and cheerful. She always managed to make him laugh, and he enjoyed being around her. He'd worked really hard at keeping his feelings buried, and she'd made it easy. She hadn't come on to him the way so many women did—especially the ones who knew what he was worth.

He'd never realized what a problem having money could be, but Mandy wasn't the least bit impressed. She teased him the way she teased her friends Kaz and Jake, and Ben and her sister. She treated Marc exactly the same as the ones she thought of as her family, and yet she had no idea how much that meant to him.

Tonight though, she really wasn't acting like herself. He had no idea at all what was going on, but a drink sounded like a good place to start. "Yeah," he said. "I'll get the lime and tonic water."

"Thanks." She set the bottle on the counter, paused there for a moment, and then bowed her head. "I'm sorry. I'm not going to be very good company. I already miss Lola." She raised her head and sent him a sad little smile. "We've never been apart more than a couple of days. Not ever."

"She said this is her first flight."

Mandy nodded. "It is. I'm still waiting for my turn." She sighed and handed the bottle to him when he reached for it.

"Sit," he said. "I'll make 'em."

"Thanks." She took one of the stools at the counter, propped an elbow on the granite, and rested her chin in her palm. She looked absolutely lost.

This went way beyond her sister going on a trip.

He kept glancing her way as he grabbed two glasses out of another cabinet, found the tonic water in the refrigerator, and snagged a lime out of the basket on the counter. She hadn't budged, hadn't said a word. "Cheer up, Mandy. She'll be back before you know it."

Mandy nodded and stared out the back window.

He added ice and mixed the drinks, but it was weird with Mandy so quiet. She usually had something funny to say about everything. Not tonight, but he wondered if it might be something else—her gloomy behavior seemed a little excessive just because Lola had taken off on a trip.

Maybe she just needed to relax. He knew he did. Ever since he'd learned that Ben and Lola were going to make this trip, that he and Mandy would be here alone, he'd been a wreck.

He finished making the drinks and topped them off

with an extra shot of gin. Then, squeezing a slice of lime into each of the glasses, he handed one to Mandy.

"Thanks." She took a sip and sighed. "Tastes good. How come we never put you in charge of the drinks?"

"All you have to do is ask." He took the stool beside hers and sipped his drink. Maybe he was taking a risk, sitting so close, but something was wrong and it wasn't in him to ignore a friend. Especially Mandy. "Okay, Mandy. Are you going to tell me what's really bothering you?"

She shook her head, but at least she smiled. "How'd you know?"

"Big block letters scrawled across your pouty little face."

This time she laughed. "You are such a charmer."

"Perceptive, too, I think." He wished he could tell her how many nights he'd fallen asleep, imagining her above him, beneath him, her honey-blond hair framing her beautiful face.

No way was that going to happen. Not with Mandy.

She was much too special, and he cared for her too much to take the risk. He never touched Mandy, never allowed himself the luxury, but for whatever reason, he reached out and used his fingers to push her long bangs out of her eyes.

Her head snapped up at his touch, her lips parted. Her brown eyes, so unusually dark with all that streaky blond hair waving this way and that around her face, had filled with questions.

He ignored them. "Talk to me, Mandy. Tell me."

"I lost my job today." Her lips trembled, she rubbed her hand over her eyes, and Marc wanted to hold her so much he ached.

"What happened?"

Mandy let out a slow breath, but she wouldn't look at him. "My boss shut the coffee shop down without any notice or warning. I've worked there for seven years, and there was nothing, no 'thank you for all your help,' nothing. I went in this morning to work and she handed me my final paycheck and said she'd decided to close this one because the new shop was doing so well. When I think of all the hours I've worked without overtime, all the days off I've given up . . ." She raised her head and her expression was bleak. "I feel used, Marc. Like I never mattered to her at all. I thought we were friends. I watched her kids for her when she was in a bind, took her soup when she was sick, but she opened a new shop downtown, hired all new people, and closed this one without even warning me."

"That sucks, Mandy. Damn. I am so sorry." He wasn't sure how, but in a heartbeat she slipped past his defenses. He had his arms around her, holding her the way he'd dreamed since the first time he met her a little over two months ago. She felt even better than he'd imagined. Her cotton knit dress hugged her curves, and once he held her, he knew she wasn't wearing a bra. Everything about Mandy felt soft and warm and so wonderfully feminine.

Her hands slipped over his waist, slowly crept around him, almost tentatively, as if she wasn't sure of his response, so he hugged her tighter. She needed it right now, needed him.

And damn it all, he needed her. Needed Mandy Monroe more than he'd ever needed or wanted anyone or anything in his entire life.

She'd wondered what it would feel like if Marc ever hugged her. She'd imagined all the bells and whistles, the thrill of their bodies coming together, the shivers and fireworks of sexual awareness she'd read about but had never experienced. Now? As she nestled close to his broad chest, heard the steady beat of his heart beneath her ear, felt the warmth of his breath on her cheek, she felt none of those things. What she felt was something so much stronger, so powerful, it left her stunned.

For the first time since she was a little girl growing up with the world's most dysfunctional mother, Mandy felt as if she'd truly come home. Sighing, she allowed herself this one moment in time and held on to Marcus Reed as if she'd never let him go.

But the most amazing part of his simple hug given for comfort? It didn't feel like Marc wanted to let go of her, either.

Long minutes later, he sighed. "You okay?"

Well, she knew it had to end at some point. "Yeah." Drawing in a deep breath, she straightened. "Thanks."

He smiled as he released her; she sat straighter on her stool in front of the counter. Took a sip of her drink. Stared at the lime slice floating on top of the ice. It was easier than looking at Marc, easier than seeing that "I'm your good buddy" look on his face.

His drop-dead gorgeous face. And the best thing about all that absolute deliciousness? He didn't have a clue how attractive she found him. He was naturally classy, his body trim and toned, not muscle-bound, but all lean strength and almost patrician good looks. His short, thick hair was so dark brown it was almost black, and he wore it neatly trimmed most of the time. Only on a few occasions had it come even close to touching his collar the way it was now. Marc looked like an aristocrat—it was easy to imagine him in a sleek, black tux, sipping a martini in a classy nightclub somewhere.

Not here in her kitchen wearing a ragged T-shirt that fit like a second skin, and faded black jeans resting low on his hips, hugging his perfect butt.

Even his bare feet were sexy.

"I've got an idea." He stood and held out a hand, bringing her back to reality.

Raising her head, she grinned at him. "What? Besides getting blitzed on gin and tonic, that is." She took his hand. They never held hands unless he was tugging her somewhere, but she'd never been so aware of being alone with him before. She glanced at their clasped hands. He must really be feeling sorry for her.

His fingers tightened around hers and he laughed. "Well, we can do that, too. I unpacked a couple of boxes I hadn't emptied since the move and found the six-episode set of Star Wars movies I thought I'd lost. How's that sound?"

He leered at her. Mandy giggled. Marc didn't strike her as the leering type, but then she wasn't much of a giggler, either.

"I promise to continue refreshing your drink."

Actually, that didn't sound like too bad an idea. "Be still my heart," she said, reaching for her gin and tonic. Laughing as he tugged her along behind him, she followed Marc into the front room. "A Star Wars marathon while being plied with cheap gin sounds like a marvelous way to spend a Saturday evening."

Sliding Rico, her basset hound, to one side, Mandy got comfortable on the couch while Marc stuck a DVD in the player. When he walked back to sit, she thought he'd take the recliner, but instead he slid Rico a little bit farther along the leather seat and sat between the old dog and Mandy.

He put his bare feet on the coffee table. "You're not going to yell at me, are you?"

"No. What for? You're not wearing shoes." Lola had strict rules about feet on furniture with shoes.

He grinned at her, and damn but he had the sexiest

smile. "Not the feet on the table, silly. This." He settled close beside her on the well-worn couch and wrapped his arm around her shoulders. "You've gotta have an arm around the girl if you're at the movies."

He had to be kidding if he thought she'd yell at him for this. Kidding or just terribly dense. She welcomed the weight of his arm resting over her shoulders. Snuggled close and inhaled his scent, subtle but so very much his own. "No," she said. "Not gonna yell." Then she sighed. "Too bad we're out of popcorn."

"So we drink instead." He raised his glass as he settled back. Rico grunted and resettled himself closer to Marc, and the only sound was the DVD cycling through the legal notices before the opening credits to the first movie started. That, and the pounding of Mandy's heart.

It took her only a few more heartbeats to relax against Marc. He was warm and solid and strong, and so welcome, tonight of all nights. He was offering friendship and comfort, but she was greedy. Mandy wanted more. Tonight, if Marc seemed willing, she'd take whatever she could get.

He knew the moment Mandy finally let go and fell asleep. She sort of nuzzled his chest and the next thing he knew she was all scrunched up against him, her lips slightly parted, taking slow, even breaths. He carefully lifted her and settled her slight frame in his lap with her head tucked up against his shoulder.

She was so much tinier than Lola, barely five three to Lola's five eight, her slight but perfectly proportioned frame giving her a pixie quality that hid what Marc and Ben privately referred to as a personality that was a force of nature, and a spine of pure steel. Mandy might be kind and loving, a truly good-hearted soul, but he'd heard tales of her bravery that gave him chills. The thought of her calmly facing down Lola's crazy ex-boyfriend when the guy barged in armed with a gun made Marc really glad he and Ben had decided to put better locks on the doors, even though they'd done the upgrade a couple of years after the actual event.

Of course, that hadn't been the entire reason—when Ben showed up in search of his brother Jake a few months ago, he'd unknowingly brought a whole lot of unexpected trouble home from his tour in Afghanistan, including some scary guys with guns trailing him.

Putting extra deadbolt locks on the bedroom door had been Marc's suggestion. In case anyone actually managed to break into the house, he'd said. He hadn't been able to explain the real reason—that it was a way to keep him out should he ever be the source of danger. Until he knew the truth about the old nightmares that had returned in full force, Marc preferred to keep that fear to himself.

Still, it was better to keep future bad guys out rather than worry about Mandy playing heroine. The locks on the bedroom door were for Marc's peace of mind, but that thought slipped into the ether as Mandy twisted a bit in his lap and curled against his chest. The first movie ended but he didn't get up to slip in another. Both their drinks were empty—they'd each quit after a second one—but he wasn't willing to let this evening end.

He'd wanted to hold her since the first time he'd seen her—his best friend's girlfriend's roommate, the cute little barista with the perpetually optimistic outlook on life.

Except for today, when she'd confided in him. She hadn't wanted anything but a hug, but that didn't mean he couldn't do something to help her out. Maybe she'd like to have her own coffee shop. One of the units on the bottom floor of his building was going to be empty in a few days. A coffee shop would work perfectly in there, but only if he could figure out a way to approach the subject without it sounding like charity.

That was the problem with having a shitload of money when your best friends were still earning their way. There was a fine line between helping, and looking as if you were trying to control things. He didn't want to be that guy, but he did want to help.

He sat there a while longer, holding her. Realized it might be hard to explain if he fell asleep and they both woke up out here in the morning. It wasn't worth the risk. He hadn't had any blackouts for quite a few years now, but he wasn't up to taking any chances. Not with Mandy.

He tightened his hold on her and stood with her in his arms. She blinked and focused on him as he walked with her around the room, turning out lights and checking the locks.

"What'cha doing?"

He kissed her forehead. Imagined tasting her lips instead. "Turning things off. Checking the locks. Making sure Rico's dog door is unlocked. And then I'm carrying you into your bedroom so you can get some sleep. It's late."

"Oh. Okay." Her arms went around his neck and she held on.

He got to Mandy's room and shoved the door open with his hip, carried her to the bed, and carefully placed her in the middle. She sat up, blinking, still half asleep, her hair all tousled, full lips soft and inviting. Damn, she was sexy as hell.

Then she looked at him like a tiny waif, reached out, and took his hand.

"Stay with me tonight. Please? I don't want to sleep alone."

He hadn't expected that. He sat on the edge of the bed. "Do you think that's a good idea?" He hardened against his jeans. His cock thought it was an amazing idea. He'd managed to keep his arousal under control all evening long. One simple request from Mandy and he was glad he was wearing snug jeans that hid the evidence. He hoped.

She tilted her head and studied him. He met her gaze and held it, because there was nothing he wanted more than Mandy in his arms, no matter how bad a move it might be. His good intentions only went so far.

"Yeah," she said. "I think it's an excellent idea." Then she frowned, but she looked so cute he almost kissed her. "Unless, of course, you're not attracted to me."

How could she possibly think something like that? He cupped her face in his hands and drew her close for a kiss. Of course, there was no reason to think otherwise. They'd lived two months in the same house and he hadn't touched her, much less kissed her.

Their lips met and she tasted sweet, an alluring combination of the drink she'd had earlier and a flavor that had to be all about Mandy. Her lips were soft, parting just for him. The tip of her tongue touched his, and it was all the invitation he needed. Still holding her face, he explored the contours of her lips, the sharp edges of her teeth, swept into her mouth and tasted all of her. Her hands were in his hair, her fingers sliding from his neck to his crown and raising shivers along his spine. It was embarrassing, how quickly his good intentions shattered and fled.

As long as he left her satisfied and sleeping. That's all that mattered. He couldn't risk spending the night. It was too damned dangerous, but he knew there'd be no stopping now. Not tonight, no matter what he knew he should do.

Finally, when he was nowhere through with wanting the taste of her, Marc slowly ended the kiss. So caught up in the dazed look in Mandy's beautiful brown eyes, in the soft sweep of her tongue as if she tested her lower lip and then the upper, searching for his taste, that it took him a moment to find his voice.

"I hope that takes care of any doubt about my being attracted to you. I swear, Mandy, you're like a lodestone, drawing me to you no matter where you are, what you're doing. From the first time I met you . . ."

She smiled, remembering. "That night Jake and Kaz got back, after Jake saved her from the kidnapper. You came over to go out to dinner with us. I'll never forget the first time you walked in our front door."

"Neither will I. When Kaz opened the door and invited me in, she introduced herself first and then Lola, but when you walked into the room . . ."

"You were the only one I saw." Mandy's eyes sparkled and he realized she was fighting tears. She reached for him, ran her fingers across his eyebrow, down the line of his jaw. "I already knew you."

No, she didn't. He would have remembered her. "How? I don't remember. I would never have forgotten you."

"I knew you, but you didn't know me. This guy used to ride by the coffee shop when I was working, but it was years ago. I didn't know who he was on an old beatup Schwinn, but I'd watch him go by." Laughing, she glanced sideways at him.

"I had an apartment out on Irving for a couple of years. Not far from the coffee shop. I was probably riding home from buying groceries. It was a while before I got around to buying a car."

Mandy laughed. "Well, I thought this guy was so hot, and I wondered who he was. A couple of years later, I saw a picture of Marcus Reed in *People* magazine, an article naming him as one of the year's 'sexiest young multi-millionaires,' and I thought he looked like the guy on the bike, but I figured Reed was really rich and wouldn't ride an old Schwinn."

She laughed self-consciously. "I cut it out, though." Blushing, she lowered her head and covered her eyes. "It was on my bulletin board for a long time. I took it down when we met you so you wouldn't see it and think I was some kind of crazy stalker, but I still wasn't sure the guy on the bike was you. Then, when you moved in here, I saw you putting that old Schwinn in the garage. That's when I knew for sure you were the one I'd had a crush on, and I wasn't quite sure how to deal with it."

He laughed and pulled her into his arms. "I will keep that bike until I'm old and gray. I paid for it myself, with money I earned tutoring kids in my computer class in high school. My first job."

She gave him a deadpan look. "You've done well, Mr. Reed."

"I've done okay. So, you thought I was hot, eh?"

She rolled her eyes. "Oh, yeah."

"I never knew." He held her face in his hands, kissed her quickly, ending it before he got carried away. "Mandy, I've wanted you since the first time I saw you, but I can't make any promises. There are things about me that you don't know, that I'm not sure I'm ready to share with anyone, that . . ."

She covered his lips with her fingers. "It's okay. We can do this and know that we're friends, first. Nothing will hurt that, Marc. We won't let it."

"Do you think we can we do that?" He traced the line of her jaw with a single fingertip. "You're special to me, Mandy." He laughed, knew he sounded self-conscious, but didn't try to cover it up. "More special than you can possibly know."

She pressed her hand against his chest and her eyes twinkled. "Thank you. But I just had a thought that could screw up any plans we might be considering. I'm not using birth control, and I don't have any condoms. Do you?"

He tried not to. There was no stopping it. The laughter exploded out of him, and once it started there was no stopping. At least not right away. When he finally got it under control, he was lying on his back on Mandy's bed, staring into an expression he wished he could capture.

"Are you okay?" She tilted her head and stared down at him, but from the way her lips were twitching, she was fighting a smile. "I had no idea there was anything remotely funny about not having condoms."

He reached up, wrapped his hand around her neck and pulled her down for a kiss. When he turned her loose, she had a wonderfully glazed expression in her eyes. "Mandy, if I had any condoms they would be out of date. I haven't had sex with anyone other than my right hand for so long it's not even funny."

Her frown was actually kind of cute, and he waited for the questions. When they didn't come, he sat up and wrapped his arm around her. "I do, however, have an idea. I bet Ben has a stash in his bedroom."

"Are you sure? Lola's on the pill. At least she is now. Why would he need condoms?"

"When they first hooked up, I know he bought condoms. I was at the store with him."

"Yeah, but . . ." Shrugging, she just watched him.

"Trust me. Ben bought a couple of economy packs. He can't possibly have used all of them." He stood and reached for Mandy's hand. "I mean, I know he's got it bad for your sister, but there have to be a few left. C'mon.

It's almost midnight. Their plane left at eleven. Even if he needed them, he won't be coming back for any tonight."

His giggling co-conspirator let him drag her down the hall to Ben and Lola's room. They tiptoed in as if Ben might pop out of the shadows at any moment, and Marc went straight for the bedside table. With all the drama he was capable of—which wasn't much—he held a finger to his lips and cautioned Mandy to be quiet. Then he slowly opened the drawer.

It was filled almost to the top with little foil packets. Dozens of them.

Deadpan, Marc glanced at Mandy and whispered, "I was right. He does have a few extras. I doubt he'll miss any if we take a couple."

Mandy slapped her hand over her mouth. When Marc grabbed three of the packets, Mandy reached inside the drawer and took three more. He turned to her and raised his eyebrows.

"One can hope," she said. Then she grabbed a couple more.

So did Marc. "Just in case," he said.

This time it was Mandy grabbing Marc's hand, dragging him back to her room, and tossing the condoms on top of the bedside table. He added his handful to the pile.

For a moment, they merely stood there, staring at each other. Mandy made the first move. She slipped her hands beneath the hem of his long-sleeved T-shirt, ran her fingers over the sensitive skin above his waistband, and Marc knew there was no fighting the inevitable.

CHAPTER 2

The first time he saw Mandy, Marc thought she was adorable, a cute little blond-haired, brown-eyed pixie with a twinkle in her eyes and a perpetual smile on that sexy mouth. She wore her hair fairly short, and no matter what she did with it, it always had that tousled *just-out-of-bed* look. She was petite—slim and fit looking, yet rounded in all the right places—but still an adorable pixie.

His physical reaction to her had been a lot more down and dirty. He'd wanted her. It had been a visceral punch to the gut, so unexpected that he'd actually tried to avoid her the first few times they were all together.

Avoidance hadn't worked when, less than a week later, a fire in his apartment building had coincided with the girls and Ben asking him to move in. Ben didn't want Mandy and Lola left here alone when he reported for duty at Camp Parks across the bay.

They knew by then that someone had targeted them, but they'd had no idea who it was or what it was about. Since Marc's apartment had been damaged by the fire and Ben worried about leaving the two women alone, Marc had agreed to make the move permanent.

The danger was over, the perpetrators in jail, but Marc was still here, an accepted member of this loosely knit family of old and new friends.

A win-win situation, right? He'd had no idea at the time how much Mandy was going to come to mean to him, not a clue what kind of effect she would have on his life.

He'd been here a little over two months now, and it hadn't taken him long to figure out he was in big trouble. Lola had Ben, Kaz, the woman who had once been the girls' roommate, had Marc's oldest, closest buddy, Jake Lowell. Jake and Ben were brothers, once estranged, now rebuilding a relationship they'd lost almost twenty years ago, and they'd drawn Marc in, even closer, as part of their family. Jake and Ben had accepted him as if there was something even more binding than their life-long friendship. He was their brother—and by virtue of their relationships, Kaz and Lola's as well.

Then there was Mandy. They were the only two of their group who weren't attached to anyone, and while no one had actively tried to throw them together, the couples dynamic had paired them up whenever they did stuff as a group—which was quite often. It hadn't taken long for Marc's physical craving to develop into something so much deeper, a longing for so much more. While it was natural to think of Kaz and Lola as the little sisters he'd never had, there was absolutely no way he could ever see Mandy in that role.

Beautiful, adorable, funny, sexy Mandy. She was everything he could have asked for in a woman, a wife, a partner.

Exactly what he couldn't risk having, because keeping her safe was more important than anything else. So far, and he fully intended to keep it that way, none of the others had any idea that he was the greatest danger among them. If only he knew for sure, but the memories were merely fragments of dreams, his fear of the horrible thing he might have done so many years ago literally the stuff of nightmares.

Except he knew in his gut that the nightmares were based on truth. If only he could remember, maybe then he might understand. Might learn why he'd done what he thought he had.

For now, though?

He had to live one day at a time. Keep a close watch on his thoughts, his behavior.

And hope like hell he was wrong, that he hadn't killed a woman on a night he couldn't remember anywhere but in the terrors that struck while he slept.

Maybe, if he and Mandy just took things slowly it would be okay, but as her fingers traced ribbons of fire along his ribs, he knew his resolve was crumbling. He fisted his hands in her hair and bit back a groan.

Obviously, Mandy wasn't on the same page—she'd missed that part about going slow. Instead, she slipped his shirt up over his back and he almost laughed at how easy it was to switch gears and help her get it over his head. She took the shirt from him and tossed it on a chair in the corner of the room.

Then she just stood there, staring at his chest. He wondered if she'd expected some guy who waxed, because he sure didn't. Not that he had a lot of hair, but there was certainly enough for her to run her hands through, should she choose.

She chose. He sucked in a breath as her fingers parted the springy mat across his pecs and circled his nipples. Damn. He'd had no idea those things were erogenous zones on a guy, but if his cock got any harder, he was going to bust through the zipper on his jeans.

Mandy's eyes had a glazed look about them. He wondered if she focused as much on the crisp hair on his chest as he'd suddenly focused on the paths her fingers made spearing through it. Standing there, rock hard and still as stone, he fought every base male impulse he had to grab her up and tear her clothes off her and just take her. Now.

"Mandy. Babe." He sucked in a breath, but it wasn't enough. She ignored his soft plea, leaned close to his chest and ran her tongue over that damned nipple. "Holy shit."

His balls sucked up even tighter and he was so close to coming. He felt as if the last two months of behaving himself around her had never happened, but he'd been lusting after her since that first night when he'd been shocked into an awareness he'd never felt for another woman.

Now, body trembling with need, he reached down and grabbed the soft fabric of her dress in his hands, tugged it up over her hips and finally over her head. He missed her fingers, missed her touch as she raised her arms so he could whisk the dress away to join his shirt on the chair.

His reward was Mandy, wearing nothing but a tiny pair of silky pink bikini panties.

Mandy, with her perfect breasts bare to his avid gaze, her dark nipples already puckered into tight little buds. She started to cross her arms over her chest, but first she raised her head and looked at him. She must have seen what was in his eyes because she dropped her hands to her sides and stood there, so perfect, so open that the potential to screw this night up had him breaking out in a cold sweat. More than two months now since that first day, since she'd totally blown him away merely by walking into the room. He'd wanted her. Dreamed about her.

Hidden his feelings, his desire under a flimsy façade of mild disinterest. As if any of his feelings for her could ever be classified as mild. She was here, now, almost entirely naked and waiting, a tiny smile teasing her lips, her eyes focused solely on his. He wanted to be so much more for her, more than the guy who didn't know what a woman really wanted. He'd had so little normal experience with girls. He'd missed out on dating entirely in high school and even during his short months of college, first because he had never really gotten over his self-image as an incompetent nerd, and then after the blackouts happened, after the nightmares took hold, there'd been too much fear. He was afraid of what he might have done. What he might do.

His short burst of *People* magazine fame hadn't been at all helpful in fixing things. In fact, that period in his life had been an absolute nightmare. In spite of all he'd done, inside he knew he would never succeed enough, earn enough, achieve enough to feel as if he had value.

The women who'd suddenly flocked to him had definitely reinforced that image—they hadn't cared about Marc Reed, but they were sure as hell interested in his net worth.

Tonight, though, Mandy was looking at him as if he were the answer to every dream she'd ever had. It was an unfamiliar feeling, to look into a woman's eyes, a woman he found absolutely fascinating, and see that emotion returned. Unfamiliar and terrifying.

"You are so beautiful." He reached for her and again he wished he could be what she needed, what she wanted. "Ah, Mandy. So perfect. You have no idea . . ."

She stepped into his embrace, wrapped her arms

around his waist, lay her head against his bare chest, and mumbled, "No, Marc. You have no idea."

He felt her shudder. Was she crying? "Mandy?"

When she raised her head, she was smiling, her lips twitched and thank goodness it was laughter, not tears. He didn't get it. Not at all, and his frown must have told her exactly that.

"What?" She rolled her eyes in a most dramatic fashion. "Marc, I told you. Six, maybe seven years ago at least, I was watching you. I had the biggest crush on that hot guy on the bike, kept waiting for him to come in for coffee, but he never stopped. I wondered where he was going, who he was, what he did. Then when I saw the picture in *People* of Marcus Reed, I thought that must have been you in spite of the old bike, but I realized that if it was you, you were so far out of my league that there was no way in hell we'd ever end up . . ." She closed her eyes and shook her head. "But here we are, so let's just stop talking, okay?"

He tightened his arms around her and held her close. "Works for me. But Mandy . . ."

"Yes, Marc?"

He laughed. "Don't expect a guy with smooth moves. I'm much better with software than I am with women."

"Hmm . . . all that tweaking of code, fingers flying on the keyboard? It's got to be good training for something." She slipped her fingers beneath the waistband of his jeans and he rolled his hips forward without thinking. She raised her head and stared at his mouth. "Your sexy lips pursed in concentration, working on some tough code. Yeah. Definitely good."

"Oh. Yeah. Sexy lips?" He sucked in a sharp breath. "One can hope."

She glanced up, smiling, and then focused on his pants again. She flipped the metal stud free at the waistband and lifted the tab on his zipper. Slowly, with both of them watching the snail-speed progress, she drew the tab down, unzipping his pants one set of metal teeth at a time.

The sound echoed in the room, or at least it sounded that way to his heightened senses.

By the time she reached the bottom, his cock was pressing against the fly of his cotton knit boxers and he had to grab her hands.

"If you so much as touch me, the party's going to end right here."

"Really?" Eyes wide, she stared innocently up at him. Innocent like a barracuda . . .

He leaned close and kissed the big grin off her mouth. Damn, but her lips were so good, full, and warm, and when he lifted her against him and felt the soft press of her warm breasts against his chest, his whole body shivered with the shock of connection, the full knowledge that he needed to be inside Mandy now. He broke the kiss, inhaled, exhaled, sucked in another deep breath, and turned them both toward the bed.

When he fell, it was with Mandy on top of him. She landed with her knees to either side of his thighs, her hands grasping his shoulders. He lifted just enough to grab the nipple on her left breast between his lips, sucking it into his mouth, pressing the tautly furled tip with the flat of his tongue.

Her body was sleek and warm, her nipple a hard knot of puckered flesh between his lips, and he couldn't get enough of her.

She moaned and arched her back, but then she was scrambling out of his reach, grabbing the waistband of his jeans and tugging them down his hips. His boxers went with the denim, though she had to pause and lift the elastic over his erection. Biting back a terribly unmanly sigh of relief, Marc raised his hips so Mandy could pull all the offending cotton over his ass, down his legs, and off.

She sat back on her heels and stared at him. His cock twitched, standing there between his thighs, leaning most obscenely in Mandy's direction. He thought of it as a homing device and almost laughed when that simple thought had him swelling harder, larger.

Raising her head, Mandy made eye contact and then slowly shook her head. "I can't believe you've been hiding this from me, Mr. Reed."

He laughed. It was so simple—she made him happy. He'd enjoyed her friendship from the very beginning, but this? He'd been afraid to even dream of something like this, but he grabbed Mandy at the waist, rolled with her, and held her down with his cock planted firmly against the silky, sexy, pink panties.

So close, but he had to know. "Promise me this won't change us? That you won't be angry and want me out of your life? I'm so afraid of ruining what we have."

"You sure you're not just concerned about missing out on Lola's cooking if we screw this friendship up?"

He really did have to bite his lip to keep from laughing. "There is that, and yes, I've taken it into consideration. I'm her boss. I can always install a kitchen at the office."

"I see." She ran her fingertip along his jawline and sighed dramatically. "Then I guess we'll just have to wing it." The laughter, the twinkling humor in her eyes sort of faded away as she studied him. "I want you now, Marc. I can't imagine this being anything but wonderful."

There really wasn't a response for that. Not verbally, anyway. He dipped his head and ran his tongue around the nipple on her left, the one on her right. Suckled that taut bud between his lips, tugging enough to wring a moan from Mandy. He repeated the process on the left one, used his lips and teeth this time.

Her short, sharp pants had to be an affirmative response. He hoped.

He kissed his way down her ribcage, mouthing each rib's rise and fall until he reached the sleek skin over her stomach, tasting her, not following any rules or thoughts beyond what felt right, what he wanted, what he hoped Mandy wanted. Inhaling her subtle fragrance, tasting the unique flavors that were all Mandy, exploring freely after so many nights of needing, wanting. Her fingers slid through his short hair as he nuzzled her hip bones and finally moved lower to press his mouth over the satiny crotch of her panties.

He exhaled, a warm, damp breath that had Mandy rolling her hips, tightening her fingers against his skull, holding him in place. He exhaled again and felt her stomach muscles contract.

This was something he'd never done before, had never really thought about until he met Mandy. Since then? He'd fantasized for weeks, tasting Mandy in his dreams, peeling the clothing away from her body, kissing her all over.

Lifting himself up on his elbows, he rolled the elastic band down over her hips, exposing the dark blond curls between her legs and the soft pink folds of her sex already swollen and damp with her arousal. He'd never seen anything so erotic in his life.

"Take them off. Please?" She grabbed the waistband and shoved, lifting her hips. Marc went back on his heels and helped her, tugging the tiny scrap of satin over her long legs. So sleek and muscular—that long walk to and from work every day kept her in excellent shape.

Sometimes she ran with him, and following her had

been its own kind of hell. Watching that perfect ass, those long, sleek legs. He ran his hands from the tops of her thighs to her ankles, feeling the lean strength beneath her silky smooth skin, the firm muscles. She wasn't laughing anymore. There was a dark pink flush to her cheeks, across her chest, over her abdomen.

Arousal had never been so beautiful. Kneeling between her thighs, he slipped his hands beneath her hips, gently palmed her perfectly shaped bottom and lifted her to his mouth, his attention focused on the tightly furled lips of her sex. He glanced up, caught her watching him with a look of absolute wonder in her eyes. "Are you okay with this?"

"Yes. Definitely yes." She smiled and lay her head back on the pillow. Waved her fingers in his direction. "Don't let me stop you."

"Right." How he actually managed a wink, he wasn't sure. His cock had never been this hard, rising up against his belly, fluid already covering the tip, more than ready to find a home deep inside Mandy. Doing his best to ignore the stubbornly persistent thing, he dipped his head and ran the flat of his tongue over her. She was wet and hot, her taste like nothing he'd expected.

He wanted more. He licked her again, going deeper, spearing his tongue between her damp folds, but when he found the taut nub at the top of her sex, she arched into him with a soft whimper. He felt as if he'd found the Holy Grail.

Had he found it on any of the other women? Certainly not with his mouth, probably not even with his fingers. He hadn't taken any of those women to bed. They'd taken him.

That *People* magazine Mandy had saved? He'd been overwhelmed by the sudden feminine interest, women dragging him from the obscurity of his quiet workshop into what had turned into almost two months of constant but meaningless sex with the most predatory females he'd ever met. He really had gone a little crazy.

At least he'd finally come to his senses, but not until he'd had sex with close to a dozen women—never anyone more than once—and it had been some of the worst times he could remember. He never, ever wanted to feel that way again. A commodity, somebody one lucky girl hoped to snag, at least long enough to get her hands on his rapidly growing income.

He didn't remember any of their names, didn't care to see any of them ever again. Each and every single one of them had been a beautiful, intelligent predator. He'd come to his senses after one particularly bad evening and hadn't been with a woman since.

Mandy was more than making up for all those terrible nights. As her body writhed in his hands, he grew more confident with each lick and stroke. When he thought she might be close to coming, he concentrated on her clitoris—such a technical name for that small nub of nerves at the top of her sex—ground zero for all those wonderful sighs and whimpers she was making. He held her bottom with his left hand, teased along her cleft with his right, entering her with two and then three fingers.

He was fairly big and he didn't want to hurt her, but this he'd actually researched, proof Mandy was right—computer skills weren't all about the software.

He wrapped his lips around her clit and tongued, then suckled that sensitive bit of flesh. Thrust deep inside her with his fingers. Her knees clamped the sides of his head, her vaginal walls clamped down on his fingers, her body arched, and she screamed.

He'd never imagined Mandy as a screamer, but he couldn't stop grinning as he slowly brought her down and then reached for one of the condoms on the bedside table. He had himself sheathed and back between her knees in a heartbeat. Carefully he took himself in hand and pointed his erect cock at Mandy's center with his eyes locked on hers, on the dreamy look on her face, the sparkle of tears in her eyes.

She wanted him, Marcus Reed. The man, not his money, not his name. Just him. He pressed forward, she lifted her hips, he pushed harder and filled her, and it was unlike any other time with any other woman. He was meant to be here, with Mandy. She was beyond unique, and she was his. He'd never wanted anything or anyone this much. Somehow, some way, he had to figure out how to keep her—and keep her safe. He leaned forward and kissed her. Put his heart and soul in his kiss, hoping like hell he didn't screw this up. Not this, not when, for the first time in his life, he knew exactly how coming home should feel.

Still in shock when Marc's lips met hers, Mandy opened to him. His lips were damp, even his chin, and she knew she tasted herself in his kiss. It was wonderful and raw, and so erotic she trembled. He filled her, so completely, so perfectly, she almost cried. Maybe she would. Later.

She'd never once been with a man who'd gone down on her. For that matter, she'd never gone down on a guy, either, but she wanted to. With Marc, she wanted to do everything. His lips parted over hers, his tongue swept boldly across her teeth, tangled with hers before he gently ended the kiss. She arched to the stretch and burn as he thrust deep between her legs, slowly pulled out, and then tilted his hips and just as slowly filled her again.

"More," she said, and wondered who this woman was, asking Marc for more. "I want all of you, Marc. Harder. Faster."

He sucked in a breath. "I don't want to hurt you, Mandy. I'm big. You're tiny." His laugh sounded beautifully strained. She liked that. A lot.

"Not that small, and I'm a lot tougher than I look." She raised her hips, meeting him mid thrust, felt the thick head of his cock slide across her cervix. "So good. More."

"Greedy, aren't you?"

"Only for you. I've waited so long." She wrapped her arms around his waist and palmed his taut butt. The man had an exquisite body, toned and sleek, and while he'd said he wasn't good with women, she wasn't sure how he could get any better. "Unrequited lust isn't all it's cracked up to be."

"Truth," he said, and he rolled his hips, thrust harder, faster.

Her body was already spiraling high, finding that peak once again. Another first. She'd never come with a man during sex. It always took a little help, if not from the guy, then she'd do it herself, but tonight—with Marc—it appeared that wasn't going to be a problem. Not at all.

He went back on his heels, taking Mandy with him. She wrapped her legs around his waist, her arms around his neck, and her heels pressed against his butt. He pounded into her, deeper, harder, so much deeper than before. From this angle, he managed to connect with her clit on every pass, but when he leaned close and took her nipple between his lips and teeth everything connected—a super-charged bolt of sensation linked her breasts, his mouth, her womb, his cock.

She cried out as his thrusts went from long and hard to short, fast, and wonderfully deep. His arms tightened around her as all her internal muscles clamped tightly around him, her back arched and Marc's primal groan sent shivers racing across her skin. They collapsed together, the two of them in a wet and sweaty heap, trembling with the aftermath of orgasm.

She'd never experienced anything even remotely this amazing. Not that she'd had all that many lovers—there'd actually been very few—but having a mother who changed boyfriends the way most women changed their clothes had deeply affected both girls. Lola had been every bit as choosy, especially after one of her exes turned out to be totally psycho.

Now Lola had Ben, and Mandy hoped like hell she had Marc, because that crush she'd carried around with her for so many years? After tonight she knew it was so much more.

She didn't want to risk their friendship, but she wasn't about to give up on love, either.

Marc awoke with a start, and realized he'd fallen asleep in Mandy's bed, which was exactly what he didn't want to do. It was too dangerous. At least there'd been no dreams, but they needed to talk about what had happened, figure out a way to do this again that wouldn't put Mandy's safety at risk. That meant telling her everything, stripping himself bare. So that she would at least have the chance to tell him to leave, before this went too far.

But not tonight. She was exhausted. And he was selfish enough to hold on to the fantasy for just a little bit longer.

Carefully, he slipped his arm out from under her and rolled away. She came with him, wrapping her arms around him, nuzzling his throat, kissing his shoulder as she came awake. Then she was kissing her way down his side, pausing over his hipbone. Her hair tickled the root of his cock.

She hadn't said a word, hadn't made a sound, but he was rising hot and hard against her cheek when she turned toward him and unexpectedly licked the full length of his cock from root to tip. His hips bucked and he went from semi to full-blown erection in the course of a couple of heartbeats.

Mandy rolled to her knees and took him in her mouth. The firm pressure of her lips, the wet warmth of her mouth enfolding him as she sucked him deep and then slowly slipped back to the tip before sliding down again, was unbelievable. Looking into her dark eyes in the soft glow from the nightlight in the hallway, her lips stretched around the thick girth of his cock as she rhythmically glided her mouth up and then down over his length was a visual he'd never forget.

The other women, every single one of them, had performed oral sex on him, but that's all it had been—a performance. This—what Mandy did—was something else. The intimacy of her lips on him, the way her mouth stretched around his thick length, the tip of her tongue sweeping over him when she reached the end and, holding him in her fist, used her tongue to lick across his slick, plum-shaped glans? Heaven.

She took him to the edge. When she cupped his balls in her hand and her mouth tightened around his entire crown, he groaned. There was no stopping a sound he hadn't consciously made, but as he reached for her, she turned him loose, backed away, and grabbed a condom. Kneeling between his legs, she carefully placed it over the broad tip, shiny now from her mouth, and rolled it down his shaft.

Her touch almost took him over the edge. He'd been hanging precariously since she first turned to him in her sleep, but now he fisted his hands around the blankets twisted beneath him, and held on. Barely.

"I know in theory how this is supposed to work." She studied the way the sheath covered him. "I've never done this before, so tell me if it's on right. I'm not ready to be a mom."

"It looks perfect." He lay back. "For what it's worth, when you are ready, you're going to be a perfect mom. Now straddle me. You be on top this time."

"What? No control issues? You'll let me be in charge?"

He laughed. "Actually, I'm letting you do all the work."

"I should have known you'd see it that way."

But she crawled closer, planted her knees on either side of his thighs, lifted herself over him, let him grab hold at the base of his cock and aim while she positioned herself until she could just sit down on him. Only she did it slowly—much slower than he'd expected—forcing him deep, but moving at a snail's pace until he was gritting his teeth by the time she settled herself against him.

Her feminine muscles rippled over his shaft, a subtle, rhythmic pulse of surprising strength. He lay there a moment, absorbing the feelings, the sense of connection that was so new, so unbelievably powerful.

Watching as his thick shaft disappeared between her thighs, watching the way her body spread and stretched to accommodate him, had been absolutely fascinating. Now, the almost delicate waves of tiny contractions—a precursor to climax, maybe a sign of her arousal—held him immobile.

"Thank you," he said. When she cocked her head and sort of frowned at him, he couldn't stop smiling. "It's amazing," he said. "The way it looks when I fill you up, how your body opens for me." He focused on her eyes—such a beautiful shade of brown, yet they looked almost black in the low light. "I've never seen that before. I think it's my new favorite visual."

They both laughed as he raised his hips and bounced her a couple of times.

This time, the frantic edge was missing. Marc loosely cupped her hips in his hands and knew they had discovered a perfect meeting of two bodies. He couldn't imagine ever growing tired of this, of Mandy, and yet, until he figured out the meaning of those horrific dreams, he saw no way to make this wonderful connection growing between them work.

This time, at least, he didn't try to sneak out. Lying there with her head on Marc's shoulder, her body still quivering, she turned to him, wondering if he'd fallen asleep.

He lay beside her, eyes wide open, his forehead creased in thought. Raising up on one elbow, she leaned close and kissed him. "What's wrong, Marc? I'm lying here feeling as if my whole body is still soaring, and you look like you've just lost your best friend."

He turned to her with a hint of a smile. "I did lose my best friend one time," he said, referring to the five years Jake Lowell had spent locked up in a juvenile detention center for a crime he didn't commit. "This is actually more difficult to deal with."

She shifted until she was sitting cross-legged beside him. "Sex with me is that bad?"

He rolled over and sat facing her. "Far from it. Pretty damned wonderful. I've been trying to figure out how to tell you that I can't stay with you, here in your bed, overnight." He leaned close and kissed her and then slipped off the bed before she could stop him. Searched for his boxers in the tumbled pile of clothes and slipped them on.

"I have to stay in my own room, Mandy. There's a lot

I need to think about before I can talk to you about it, but remember when I said there were things you didn't know about me? They're important things, and one in particular is probably a deal breaker." He shook his head and stared at the open bedroom door. Then he held out his hand.

She took it. What other choice did she have? He tugged and she stood beside the bed, naked, but for all the attention Marc paid to her body right now, she might as well have been wearing sweats and a T-shirt. She followed him to the door. He wrapped his arms around her and kissed her, but there was no joy in his kiss. No sense of anything other than despair.

"Lock the door behind me. If I come back to your room tonight, don't let me in. We'll talk in the morning."

She forced a small laugh. "What? Are you a vampire? A werewolf that changes at the full moon?" She shrugged. "The full moon is over a week away. Just a tiny sliver out there, now." Except her voice broke on the last words. When Marc closed his eyes, looking like a whipped puppy, she let it go. Let him go.

She gave him a quick kiss. "Go," she said. "I care enough about you to do what you ask me to do, even though it doesn't make sense."

He sucked in a ragged breath, stepped out of her embrace and out of her room. Then he closed the door behind him. It was a heavy door, very old and solid wood, but she still heard him. Figured he must be leaning against the other side.

"I want to hear you lock this. Please, Mandy? Do it."

She turned the deadbolt, turned away, and walked back to the bed, but she crawled under the covers on the side where Marc had been. At least it smelled a bit like him. Maybe she'd even be able to pretend he cared enough to stay, except she didn't think caring had a damned thing to do with his leaving. There was something tearing him up inside. Something horrible.

Did a woman who loved a man let him work things out on his own, or did she go to him, help him carry the load? He'd been adamant that she stay away. If only she knew for sure.

The last time he'd cried had been the day the bailiff marched his closest—hell, his only—friend, Jake Lowell, out of the courtroom wearing handcuffs. Marc hadn't even made it to the car. No, he'd stood there in the hallway outside the courtroom and he'd cried like a baby. Cried for Jake, for the end of Jake's amazing Olympic career, and he'd cried for himself.

The only friend he had in the world, the only person he'd ever thought of as family, had just been sentenced to eight long years at the California Youth Authority. Marc was terrified of making it without Jake's steady presence beside him.

But he had made it. He'd survived and prospered, and eventually Jake had come home, almost three years early for good behavior, and he'd prospered as well. But this? This was something Marc couldn't solve on his own, but he was afraid to risk Mandy's safety by asking her to help him through it. Whatever it was.

He didn't deal well with hopelessness. And with the image of Mandy's concerned face in his mind, Marcus Reed, successful young entrepreneur and software wizard worth somewhere in excess of seventy-five million dollars, buried his face in his pillow and wept like a child.

Mandy stood it as long as she could—which probably wasn't very long at all, even though it felt like forever—but when she got out of bed, pulled on her ratty old bathrobe, and unlocked her door, she knew it was the right thing to do. She paused a moment in front of Marc's bedroom door and hoped he hadn't locked his.

When she tried the handle, it turned easily, but the sounds coming from the bed were wrong. Wrong, but somehow not unexpected. She walked across the room, dropped her robe to the floor, lifted the covers, and crawled into bed beside Marc without saying a word. When she wrapped her arms around him, he turned and held on to her just as tightly.

He didn't speak and neither did she. All she did was hold him. Whatever was tearing him to pieces, they'd figure it out, but there was one thing he was going to have to accept—she wasn't going to let him deal with whatever it was on his own.

He was family. Her family. And he'd damned well better get used to it.

CHAPTER 3

He hadn't expected the overwhelming sense of relief he'd felt when Mandy crawled into bed beside him and wrapped him in her arms. For a little thing, she was strength personified. It only took him a minute or two to get his act together, but she never said a word, not a thing, though her warmth and steady presence spoke volumes.

Finally he rolled away and grabbed a couple of tissues from the box on the bedside table, blew his nose, wiped his eyes and tossed the tissues in the wastebasket. When he lay down beside her, she snuggled close against his side, but all she did was hold him.

After a couple of minutes, he cleared his throat and spoke into the darkness. It was somehow easier with Mandy's arms around him and her head on his shoulder. Peaceful, in fact, in spite of the visuals he'd never forget, the horrible sense he'd never be free of the nightmares.

Or even worse, proof that somehow, at some point in his life, he'd done something terrible. "When I was a freshman in college," he said, almost as if he were merely telling a story about someone else, "I started tinkering with some software ideas. I was on scholarship to Stanford, but it didn't cover everything, so I worked an outside job, too. My father had already lost at least two fortunes and was dealing with what he called 'another financial setback'—which meant there was money for his playboy lifestyle and his scams, but not for my education. The stress of trying to keep up my grades, working nights doing website work for a couple of businesses, and using whatever time I could find to work on my own projects was killing me. My grades were suffering and I was falling apart.

"It was hard to see a logical application of some of the required courses to my overall goals, which meant the work just wasn't getting done, but I didn't want to fail because I knew I'd lose my scholarship if my grades dropped. I loved Stanford. I didn't want to leave school."

He turned his head far enough to kiss Mandy's forehead. For whatever reason, that brief connection made it easier to talk. "Then I had a blackout, at least that's what I think it was. I remember coming home from work around midnight and I still had to study for an English exam. Next thing I knew, it was hours later and I was wandering through a park not far from campus. I had no idea how I got there. I went home and slept, and flunked the test the next day."

He sighed and Mandy merely held him tighter. "That was the beginning of my downward spiral as far as grades. I had at least three more blackouts that I recall. Once I sort of woke up while walking in Golden Gate Park. The last thing I could remember, I'd been leaving an evening class on campus, and Stanford is a long way from San Francisco. I have no idea how I got there. It was scary as hell, but I attributed it all to stress.

"Then the dreams started. Nightmares, really. Horrible nightmares where I heard a woman screaming, and each time I dreamed, I saw more. Her face was bruised, her blond hair matted with blood, but I couldn't tell who she was or who was hurting her. I saw hands around her throat, and then the dream would end."

He realized he was talking faster, starting to hyperventilate. Mandy hadn't moved, except she was stroking his chest, her hand warm and comforting. He took a couple of slow, controlling breaths, enough until he got it back together.

"The thing is, each time I dreamed, I saw more. The images would be clearer and I finally thought I recognized the room. I knew it was her room, the woman in my dream, but I didn't know who she was or who was hurting her. The thing is, once the nightmares started, the blackouts ended, which makes me think they had to be connected."

He lay there a moment, remembering, trying to recall the small details, but so much felt scattered. He wondered if he was subconsciously trying to forget what really happened, except . . .

"One night, just before I was going to meet with the administrator dealing with my scholarship, knowing I had to tell her that I hadn't been able to keep my grades up and couldn't qualify for more funds, I had a different version of the same dream. This time I realized I wasn't really seeing the woman, I was seeing her reflection in a mirror, just her face and what looked like a man's hands around her throat. Her body had gone limp. She wasn't struggling anymore."

He lay there, remembering that awful moment when the dreams and the blackouts suddenly came together, and he couldn't lie there anymore. Couldn't have Mandy touching him when he finally told her the truth. He pulled away from her warmth and her loving embrace.

Gave her distance. Stood beside the bed staring down at her, at the confusion in her gaze.

"I saw more in that mirror, Mandy. Everything shifted. I saw the face of the man who'd killed her, as clear as can be. It was my face. It was me."

She was out of bed in a heartbeat and he knew she'd be running far and fast to get away from him. He'd move out in the morning. Not tonight. He was just too damned tired tonight.

Except she wasn't running. She wrapped her arms around his waist and buried her head against his chest, and then she held him. Just held him, as if to protect him from . . . what? From himself? If anyone needed protecting, it was Mandy. She was a beautiful, caring, loving woman.

While he, Marcus Jerome Reed, was a murderer.

There was absolutely no way in hell that Marc had killed anyone. He was the kindest, gentlest man she'd ever known. There wasn't a mean bone in his body, not a single part of him that felt at all dark. If anything, he'd always seemed a little lost, as if he never quite knew how to fit in or what to say, though he'd definitely loosened up over the past few weeks.

And he'd really loosened up tonight. She'd never imagined sex as good as it had been with Marc. She'd loved him for so long, and there was no way she'd ever fall in love with a murderer. He had to be wrong, believing his dreams meant he'd killed someone. She was a good judge of human character. It wasn't in him to do something evil.

"Marc?"

He cupped her face in his big hands and gently kissed her. "I don't know why you're still here, but thank you."

"What do you mean, 'why I'm still here?' You are my

friend and so much more, Marc. I'm going to help you figure out what the hell is going on in your head, because I know for a fact you've never hurt anyone, much less killed anybody."

"You can't know that."

"I can. I know you. You, Marc Reed, are not a killer." She grabbed his hand and tugged. "We're going to get back into bed, together, and sleep, and I will be here if you dream."

"Mandy." He exhaled. Loudly. "I don't know if it's safe for you. Those blackouts happened, and I have no idea what I did while I was out of it, but I was conscious enough to travel around the city, and quite possibly I killed a woman during one of those lost periods. What if I have one while you're here with me, what if . . ."

She pressed her finger to his lips. "No more, Marc. Get into bed. I'm tired and so are you. We both need to sleep."

He stared at her for what felt like a very long time, and she knew the moment when he gave up the battle, gave in. "Your bed." He looked resigned more than happy about it.

She shrugged. "Okay." Holding his hand, she leaned over and grabbed her robe off the floor, before leading him out the door and into her room. "But why mine?"

He tugged her close beside her bed and kissed her. "Because the condoms are in here. I don't want to risk being in a bed with you without protection handy. Your protection, Mandy, because someday, if we can solve this, if somehow we can prove I haven't killed someone, there's nothing I'd love more than seeing you with my child. But now isn't the right time."

"Oh, Marc." He really was breaking her heart. She kissed him, hard and too fast for him to kiss her back before she broke the connection. "I love a man who thinks ahead."

He swatted her bottom as she turned to crawl into bed. The stinging slap was so unexpected she dropped her bathrobe and practically leapt into the tumbled bedding.

"Wow." He stared at his hand and laughed. Then he looked surprised that he was actually laughing, but he grinned at Mandy and said, "I had no idea how effective that could be."

"In. Now." Biting back a smile, she pointed at the space beside her. He got in without any other comment, but he was definitely more relaxed.

He was also noticeably aroused. The moment she saw his erection, Mandy's body reacted. She glanced at the pile of condoms.

Marc caught her looking and raised a terribly expressive eyebrow.

She shrugged and reached for one of the packets. "Once more, okay? It'll help us sleep."

He laughed out loud. "If you say so."

"Oh, I do, Marc." She paused, amazed by his sudden change in mood. He'd been horribly upset, and they still didn't have any answers. Not really. "Are you okay?"

"Do you have any idea what it feels like, after so many years living with this horrible thing, to actually tell someone? To have that someone believe in me enough to want to look for answers? Even if I find out I'm guilty of a terrible crime, I'll have that, Mandy. The fact that you're at least willing to believe I'm a better person, that I didn't do something that is so abhorrent to me I can't even comprehend how or why I could have done it."

"You didn't. All we need to do is find out what actually happened. I know there's an answer. It might be something as simple as your having seen it in a movie and, with all the stress in your life, turning that visual into a dream that's haunted you. But not tonight. Make love to me, and then you are not allowed to think about it or to leave. You *will* stay here with me. I don't want to sleep alone." She kissed him. Slowly, gently, before pulling away. "Not after fantasizing about you in my bed for way too long."

He touched her everywhere, fascinated by her body's reaction to him, the way she shivered when he kissed her breasts, how she arched into him when he put his mouth between her legs, the way her sex plumped and her juices flowed. He loved her taste, her sounds, the scent of her arousal, the fact she seemed to welcome whatever he did with her, to her . . . whatever he tried.

It was all so new, this making love to a woman he actually loved, one he'd wanted and never hoped to have. When she was there, waiting at her peak, so close to coming that merely looking at her had him on the edge, he grabbed a condom with hands shaking so badly that Mandy took it from him, ripped open the packet, and rolled it on over his erection.

He filled her in a single thrust.

She cried out, her fingers scrabbling against his thighs. "More," she said. "Harder. I want more of you!"

Exactly what he wanted to hear. Thrusting hard and fast, he knew he'd never gone this deep, experienced this powerful sense of connection, been so fully aware of the feel of his cock sliding across the solid contours of a woman's cervix. Across Mandy's.

Her inner muscles clamped down on his erection and her fingernails scored his flanks. That sharp burst of pain was all it took, setting off a shockwave of sensation that raced from his spine to his balls and beyond.

Throwing his head back, his harsh groan practically echoing in the small bedroom, he came as if he'd not climaxed in years, as if the times earlier tonight had never happened.

Panting, gasping for breath, he held his weight off of Mandy as she rode out her own climax, but when her arms came around him, he slowly lowered himself, covering her as she held him close against her.

Long moments later, she opened her eyes. Blinking owlishly, she stared at him. "Marc?"

He leaned close and kissed her. "What, babe? God, that was so amazing." He kissed her again. "You're beautiful when you come."

She licked her lips. "So are you, but Marc? Does anything feel different to you?"

Different? He grabbed his cock at the base and, holding the end of the condom so it wouldn't slip off, pulled slowly out of Mandy. Her muscles still rippled around him, but something did feel different. He wasn't sure what, but . . . "Crap. The condom broke."

Mandy started laughing. She lay on the bed, laughing until tears ran down her cheeks. When she finally got it together, after Marc had disposed of the rather messy condom, he crawled back into bed beside her and, propped up on one elbow, stared at her until she took a deep breath, blinked, and then smiled at him. "For what it's worth, this isn't the right time of the month for me to get pregnant. It's okay, Marc."

"Why the hysterical laughter, then?" He brushed her tangled hair back from her face and kissed her.

"Because I think this has probably been the very best and very worst day of my life. The broken condom was sort of the candle on the cake."

He nodded. "Yeah, one of those trick candles you can't blow out?"

She smiled. "Exactly. I'll stop by the pharmacy to-morrow. There's stuff I can take that . . ."

"If you think the risk is low, I'd rather you didn't. I'm a wuss, but there must be side effects with stuff like that. I don't want you to take anything to make you feel bad."

"The risk I'll get pregnant really is pretty low," she said. Then she kissed him, just a short, sharp reminder of her taste. "So, unless you have mega powerful little marathon swimmers that can hold their breath for days and days, I think we're okay."

He pulled her close for a long, very satisfying kiss. Satisfying for him, definitely. From the look on Man-dy's face, okay with her, too. He rested his forehead against hers. "We can talk about it in the morning, okay? For what it's worth, if by chance you do end up preg-nant, I will be here for you and whatever little whatsit we end up with. I promise. You okay with that?"

"Definitely okay. G'night, Marc. And don't worry. I feel very safe with you. I always have."

He awoke once during the night, momentarily disori-ented when he realized he wasn't in his own bed. Then Mandy moved in her sleep. He identified the slight weight of her snuggled close to his chest. She rubbed her face against him, sighed, and settled back into sleep. He lay there a moment, going over the night they'd had, the things he'd discovered about Mandy.

About himself.

He had definitely fallen hard over the past weeks. Fallen hard and figured it was just something he'd have to deal with, because he couldn't risk Mandy's safety. But lying here with her cheek resting on his chest and her fingers curled against his belly, he realized that hold-ing her like this, having her close to him, his body sated from their lovemaking, was the closest thing to perfec-tion he could imagine.

She was willing to fight for him. The least he could do was fight just as hard.

He heard the front door, whispered voices, recognized the soft sound of his best friend's familiar voice. What the hell were Jake and Kaz doing here? He'd thought they were headed to Italy early this morning for a photo shoot—at least that's what Jake told him when they'd talked yesterday.

Careful not to disturb Mandy, Marc slipped out of bed, grabbed his pants off the floor and headed out to the kitchen. He glanced at the clock—it was well after nine. He never slept this late, but then he'd never had a night like last night.

Intense didn't even come close. Intense and satisfying on so many levels.

He heard them in the kitchen. Kaz had lived here for a couple of years before she and Jake hooked up, and now, because of Kaz's hectic modeling schedule, Mandy and her sister were deep into plans for Kaz and Jake's August wedding. He hoped there weren't any problems with the Italy trip—Kaz was calling it her pre-honeymoon—because they should already be in the air.

"Good morning. I thought you two would be on your way by now."

"Hey, Marc." Jake laughed. "The place is so quiet, I wondered if anyone but Rico was here. Your vicious watchdog, by the way, didn't even wake up when we walked in. Our flight got delayed, and then Kaz remembered a scarf she left here yesterday that she wanted to take."

It was hard to picture Kaz as the stunning model gracing the latest cover of *Vanity Fair*, not when she was standing here in the kitchen in worn yoga pants and a long-sleeved tee, but she was gorgeous even when she wasn't wearing make-up and half a million dollars in jewels. Marc slipped an arm around her waist and kissed her cheek. At six-two, she had him by a good inch in height, but she was a perfect match for Jake, who was taller than just about everyone. "So, did you find it?"

With a sheepish look, she held up a beautiful hand-dyed scarf in shades of blues and greens. "I remembered hanging it on the back of the chair. Jake bought it for our first shoot."

"That's the one Jake used in the photos for the Intimate debut." He'd never forget the way that scarf had looked, artfully draped around Kaz's amazing body, showcasing the jewelry designs that were now adding to his fortune. The exquisite photographs Jake had taken during their week in wine country had pushed his newest company into a phenomenally successful launch.

Jake and Kaz had also launched a romance that was every bit as beautiful.

Jake slipped his arm around Kaz's waist and hugged her close. "I actually bought it for Kaz. I wanted her to think it was merely a prop to set off your jewelry designs." He kissed her. "It was all about seducing the sexy model."

Kaz rolled her eyes. "I was so easy."

"You still are, darlin'. It's part of your charm." Jake ducked when she took a swing at him.

They were all laughing when Mandy walked into the kitchen in her ratty old bathrobe. Marc turned and held his hand out. She took it. He pulled her close and, without thinking, kissed her. "Morning, sleepyhead."

She groaned and leaned close. Marc raised his head and caught both Kaz and Jake staring at them. "Um . . ."

Mandy shook her head. "S'okay, Marc. I'm not about

to try and hide anything from Kaz. She's got roomie radar like you wouldn't believe."

Except Jake was the one laughing. "You mean you finally did it? Hallelujah! Ya know, when Ben first showed up, he asked me if you were gay. I swore you weren't, but man, after so many weeks and no action, I was beginning to wonder if I'd missed something important."

Marc merely shrugged. "I didn't want to rush Mandy." He pulled her into his embrace, wrapped both arms around her waist and tucked her back against his chest. "She's much too important."

"You're darned right she is." Kaz planted her hands on her hips and stared at Marc, but there was a definite twinkle in her eyes. "So you'd better treat her right. Lola's not here to protect her and I won't be either. Mandy, you be careful while I'm gone. You know the rules. Always use protection, don't let him boss you around, and don't forget a single detail so we can drag them out of you over margaritas."

Marc kissed the top of Mandy's head, though his mind was spinning over the protection issue, which had, for the moment at least, totally eclipsed his other problem. He and Mandy really needed to talk. "Hopefully, Kaz, the details will be good ones."

Jake and Kaz left with hugs, good wishes for their trip, and a lot of congratulations in return. Mandy felt like she deserved an Academy Award for her performance, or at least an Emmy. She closed the door, leaned against it, and exhaled in relief. When she raised her head, Marc was staring at her, his face a study in conflicted emotions.

She held out her arms. He stepped into her embrace and she hung on for dear life, but at least this morning she had an idea.

Marc nuzzled the top her head, snagging strands of hair in the bristles on his unshaven cheek. She rarely saw him with anything more than a light shadow at the end of the day, and she liked this look. A lot. Tilting her face to his, she kissed his scruffy chin.

"You okay this morning, babe?"

She loved the way he cupped her face in his hands, the way he looked at her as if she were someone special. "Better than fine, Marc."

"Aren't you worried about . . . ?"

"That's just it." She went up on her toes and kissed him. Hard. "I know how we can find out what your dreams are about. I've got a great idea!"

"Dreams? I'm thinking about the broken condom. You've said more than once you're not ready to be a mother, but the risk . . ."

Shaking her head, she wrapped her arms around him, hugging as tight as she could. "I told you it's highly unlikely, but I also thought about it last night, and I realized that I've always figured I'm not ready because there was no one I knew whose child I would want. That changed when you moved in, Marc. No, I don't choose to get pregnant now and the odds are that I won't, but if I do, I can't think of a better man than you to have as a baby's father."

She saw a flicker in his eyes, knew what he was thinking. Realized how well she knew this man after only a couple of months. Before he could speak, she covered his lips with her finger. "No. Don't think it, don't say it. It's not because you have money. You could be dirt poor and I would still be thrilled to have a baby with you. You're a good man. I keep telling you that, and wondering how I can make you believe me. I can't imagine you not being there for your child. You know what it's like to have been abandoned by your parents, and that's going to make you a really good father because you will never let that happen to your own children."

He lowered his head and rested his forehead against hers. "Thank you. I really hope you're right." Because he'd been worse than abandoned. He'd been used. Was still being used.

Smiling, she said, "Of course I'm right. I hope you can learn to deal with that, because I generally am. Just ask Lola."

"Okay. I just might do that. So what's the big idea you've got?"

"C'mon. I'm going to fix us some breakfast and then I'll tell you all about it."

Mandy had eggs and toast ready in just a few minutes. She loaded their plates at the stove while Marc filled a couple of bowls with sliced melon and set the table. When she'd finished, Mandy carried the plates over, and sat across from him.

It felt sort of weird to be the only two here. They generally had a crowd at meals, but that was usually Lola's doing. She always planned on leftovers, but generally had extra bodies show up at the table and rarely had anything left over.

Marc gave Mandy time to eat most of her breakfast before he finally nailed her with that intense gaze of his. She took her last bite of egg, wiped her lips, and set her napkin aside. "Okay. I will tell you my idea. I met a lot of interesting people while I was working at the coffee shop. Lots of our customers stopped in almost every day. One of them is a really interesting man who came by around mid-morning every few days and would get a double-shot espresso and a muffin.

"I used to tease him about his wake-up coffee, and he said he thought of it as his 'keep awake coffee,' because that's what his wife called it. His name is Alden

Chung. Turns out he's a hypnotherapist, and he has an office not far from the shop. One day when it was really slow, I asked him about hypnotherapy, and he was really forthcoming about what he can do and how he uses it in his practice."

Marc steepled his fingers beneath his chin and shrugged. "So how does this very interesting man who hypnotizes people affect me?"

"He does a couple of things that might apply. He told me once that he can help people interpret their dreams, but he said that it's sometimes part of a therapy they call 'age regression.' Essentially, he takes you back in your memories to uncover things your conscious mind has forgotten. He told me we don't really forget things, we just don't have the ability to retrieve them consciously. The hypnotherapist helps the client recover those memories that are lost."

Marc shrugged. Clearly she hadn't convinced him. "Is it real?" He was shaking his head and smiling, but at least he didn't look totally shocked. "When I think of hypnotism, I get the visual of those old cartoons with a magician swinging a ticking gold watch in front of a guy; you know, making some poor shmuck sing or cluck like a chicken. Guess I associate it with stage magic."

"It's a lot more than that. One time when he was in, I'd lost my cell phone and I asked him if he could help me find it. I was just teasing, but the place was empty so Dr. Chung hypnotized me—he said I was barely under, but he asked me to walk through my paces to when I remembered having it last. I found it. Turns out I'd carried it out in back to look at some of the pruning Ben had done, and I'd set it down on the back steps to help Lola move a heavy flower pot. When I was hypnotized, I vividly recalled setting it down and actually reminding myself not to forget where I put it. Which, of course, is exactly what I did."

Marc still looked a bit dubious. Then he reached for her hand and wrapped his fingers around hers. "Not to put down your experience, but strangling a woman until she's either dead or unconscious is a little more than a lost phone."

She rolled her eyes. "I know. I just wanted to let you know that it's not scary to be hypnotized."

He laughed. "And for that, I thank you. I'm not sure it's real, though. I guess I keep thinking it's some kind of scam, but if you'll promise to go with me and stay with me, I'll make an appointment with him. Will you do that?"

"Of course I will. And I can't imagine sending you to do something like this on your own. I want to be there with you, Marc. It's not at all scary, though. At least the process isn't."

She squeezed his hand. "I can't promise what it will feel like, to unravel the story behind your nightmares, but I will be there. And if it's the worst possible thing you can imagine, I will still be there." She stood and grabbed her plate and coffee cup. "That's what friends do. I'm going to get the dishes done, but first I'll go find his card. You can call and leave a message. Maybe even set up an appointment."

She went back to her room and found the card stuck to her bulletin board. "Here," she said, handing the card to Marc. "You'll probably get an answering machine. It is Sunday, after all."

"Thanks." He gave her a quick glance, then leaned over and kissed her.

She kissed him back, and then held up her own phone. "I've got a voicemail from Lola. I'm going to call her while you make an appointment. Then you can help me with the dishes, okay?"

He nodded and walked into the front room. Mandy called Lola, and sat down to hear all about her sister's very first flight across the country.

But when it was Mandy's turn, she left out all the details of her night with Marc.

Marc ended the call and wondered just how ready he was to find out the truth. Dr. Alden Chung sounded like an okay guy, and he said he could see Marc this afternoon, that he worked weekends and took days off midweek. There was no reason not to trust Mandy's take on the man, and the conversation Marc had just had with him had been informative.

Besides, Mandy seemed to be a pretty good judge of character, and he loved her. He wished he could tell her how he felt, but it wouldn't be fair. He was only just figuring it out for himself. If Dr. Chung helped him decipher his dreams and they turned out to be every bit as bad as he thought they might be, he'd never be able to tell her.

He didn't want Mandy to have the added burden of his love if that was the case. Even so, he trusted her to stand by him as his friend, no matter what he learned.

If you couldn't trust the ones you loved, then who could you trust?

In his world, there were very few people. He'd trusted Bill Locke, his head of security at Reed Industries, and look where that had ended up. The bastard had kidnapped and tried to kill Lola. It wasn't until later that they'd discovered Locke was working for the wife of a famous senator—the same senator recently indicted on a number of charges ranging from racketeering, money laundering, and obstruction of justice, to tax evasion. Ben and Lola were in Washington, DC now, giving preliminary testimony for the prosecution on the senator's case, since notes Ben had kept while stationed in Afghanistan had become evidence crucial to the government's case.

Marc had trusted his parents, and they'd both screwed him over. His father was a scam artist and an absolute jerk who appeared to have made it his life's goal to get money out of Marc, and once his mother had lost the custody case, she'd completely abandoned him. The one person he'd ever been able to count on, Jake Lowell, had done a job on him as well when he'd pled guilty to a crime he didn't commit out of some misguided loyalty to his older brother, Ben.

Except it was hard to think something was misguided when it was done out of loyalty and love, so Marc held no animosity toward Jake. Blood didn't matter; Jake was his brother.

That line of thought led him to wonder just who he could trust. Mandy, of course. Jake, Kaz, Ben, and Lola were the siblings he'd never had. He would trust any of them with his life. Theo Hadley, his business manager. They'd known each other for years now; Theo's kid sister had graduated from the same high school with Marc, and the two men had a good working relationship. He trusted Theo to keep his various businesses running and his money safe, and so far he hadn't been disappointed. Ted Robinson, the FBI agent they'd all gotten to know while trying to figure out why someone was after Ben. Definitely him. Ted was good people.

And that was about it—a pretty short list. Short, but comforting. He wasn't alone. He stared at the business card with Dr. Alden Chung, licensed psychologist and certified hypnotherapist's address on it, and went in search of Mandy. They needed to get moving if he was going to make that appointment.

CHAPTER 4

"No wonder he's a regular customer. His office is really close to the coffee shop." Marc's arm slipped around her waist as they walked by the place where she'd worked for the past seven years.

"Was." Mandy stared at the closed sign on the door. "He was a regular customer. I wonder if he knows it's closed for good? There's no other place nearby that sells good coffee."

Forget poor Dr. Chung. She wished she had some idea what she was going to do now. So far? Not a clue. It wasn't like there was a huge shortage of baristas in San Francisco. The job didn't pay nearly enough, but there always seemed to be plenty of people willing to do it.

Marc didn't say anything. She knew he was apprehensive about the appointment. She was, as well. Worried for Marc and what he might learn today. It could be anything, but she was positive he wouldn't discover he'd murdered anyone.

"This way." He pushed open a door and they took the stairs to the second floor. Dr. Chung's office was the first door past the stairwell. There was an open sign in the frosted window, and they stepped through into a small office with a front desk but no receptionist. A small brass gong on the desk had a note that said to ring for Dr. Chung. Marc tapped the gong with a tiny brass hammer on the plate beside it.

The sound was such a pure note that Mandy stood perfectly still so as not to miss the final tone as it gently faded away. When she glanced at Marc, she realized both of them were smiling.

Squeezing his hand, she whispered, "If he's as good as his gong, this will be a successful visit."

Marc barely bit back a snort as the door beside the desk opened.

The middle-aged Asian man stepped into the room and focused on Mandy first. "Mandy! I had no idea you were the one Mr. Reed mentioned. Welcome. And you must be Mr. Reed. I'm Alden Chung. It's a pleasure to meet you." He shook hands with Marc and smiled at Mandy.

"Now, before we begin, what happened to the coffee shop? I went by this morning as I always do and it's closed. Will it be open tomorrow?"

"I'm afraid not." When his shoulders slumped, Mandy could only shrug. "I went to work yesterday and the boss was there ahead of me. She gave me a final paycheck and essentially told me not to let the door hit me on the ass on my way out. Said the new store near Union Square is doing so well that she decided to close this one. No warning, nothing."

"I'm sorry. That's not a good way to end an employer-employee relationship. It's sad the way this old neighborhood is changing. I'm going to miss the shop. I'll miss you, too, Mandy. You have always been a bright spot in my morning. I wish you luck in finding a new position."

He smiled and turned to focus on Marc. "Now," he said, with a quick glance at Mandy, "Mr. Reed asked that you be present during our session. I need to be certain you're all right with that. I don't want you to be uncomfortable should anything highly personal come to light. Will you be able to sit quietly and listen without judgment, not participating unless you are specifically requested to do so?"

She glanced at Marc. "Are you okay with me hearing anything you might say, Marc? Is that all right?"

He took her hand and squeezed it. "There's nothing you don't know already, and we both want to find out what I might know. I have no secrets from you, Mandy. Nor do I want to keep any."

Mandy smiled. "Looks like we're good to go, Dr. Chung."

"Excellent. And, in case I didn't explain my credentials when you called, I'm a licensed psychologist as well as a board-certified hypnotherapist."

Marc leaned close to Mandy and, in a stage whisper said, "I think that means he knows what he's doing."

Dr. Chung laughed. "One can only hope." Then he opened the door and waved them both into a small but beautifully furnished office. Forest green walls with natural wood trim, dark brown leather furniture—a couch, a recliner, and a matching office chair on wheels in front of the therapist's desk—set off by a large turquoise ceramic pot of live bamboo growing beneath a light in one corner. Shades darkened the one large window in the room. There were a few framed diplomas and certificates on one wall along with a photo of Dr. Chung with people Mandy figured must be his family—an attractive woman and two teenaged children.

Everything about the office was aesthetically pleasing, designed to put a person at ease. Mandy glanced at

Marc. He looked outwardly calm, but she sensed the tension seething just beneath the surface. It was time to get him parked and on to business.

She'd quickly learned that Marcus Reed wasn't a man who waited patiently for much of anything, which was why it had bothered her so much that he appeared to have limitless patience while waiting to show any interest in her. Now that she knew why he'd hesitated, Mandy realized she loved him even more. He'd been protecting her. Misguided, as far as she was concerned, but it had to mean he really did care for her.

Dr. Chung stood beside his desk. "Mr. Reed. Would you prefer to lie down on the sofa, sit in a recliner, or possibly sit on the sofa with Ms. Monroe beside you?"

"Sofa." Marc flashed her a nervous smile and tugged her hand. She'd never really seen him act nervous before. She squeezed his hand. He smiled, more relaxed this time, and squeezed hers and they both sat.

"Excellent." Chung took the office chair and then rolled it across the hardwood floor until he was in front of them. "With your permission, I'll record this session, Marc, and the recording will be yours to keep. I find that my clients are more comfortable when they can replay everything they've said and know that the words they recall are their own." When Marc agreed, Dr. Chung flipped on a recording device and spoke into it, giving the date, Marc's name and Mandy's as well.

Mandy sat quietly beside Marc, still holding his hand.

Then Dr. Chung returned his attention to the two of them. "Call me Alden," he said. "There's no need for formality. Are you comfortable with your given name?"

"I am. Marc works."

"Have you had hypnotherapy before?"

Marc shook his head. "No, sir. This is a first."

Alden smiled and clasped his hands in his lap. "Even better," he said. "Starting with a clean slate. To explain, hypnotherapy is the method used to take advantage of the mind and body connection to accomplish certain goals, or, as in your case, to uncover memories long buried. The therapist—that would be me—helps you achieve an altered state of consciousness, a trance, which you will consciously allow yourself to enter. I'll be your guide. I'll help you tap into your mind's poten- tial to find that state yourself. Once you're there, my job is to guide you in the hope of finding the answers you're searching for."

"I need specifics," Marc said. "All I know about hyp- nosis is what I remember from cartoons—swinging a gold watch in front of someone and then making him do stuff."

Alden laughed. "I hate to disappoint you. No gold watch. I'll speak to you, help you relax your muscles by virtue of the cadence of my voice, the speech patterns I've been trained to use. The goal is to relax your con- scious mind in order to let your subconscious take over. The conscious mind forgets, the subconscious never. To get there, where you can tap into those memories, I'll try a few things to see what works best for you. Some- times it's as simple as having a client count backwards or imagine a number or picture, something you like looking at."

"Mandy." Marc was smiling when he added, "Stay right there."

She laughed.

Alden nodded. "Exactly. Think of something pleas- ant, or an image you can focus on. Probably not Mandy, because I have a feeling that might push other parts of your brain to the forefront. And I'm not talking about the one between your ears."

Mandy squeezed Marc's hand. "The man already knows you."

"Ya think?" Marc smiled at her but then focused once again on the therapist.

The hypnotherapist smiled, but then he got very serious. Mandy could easily picture him in front of a class of students when he said, "There's an important point I want to make—you never can be made to do something in hypnosis that is inconsistent with your beliefs. If at any time you feel uncomfortable, you can bring yourself out of the trance. Now, we're going to be working with the subconscious mind, so we'll rely on what we call *ideomotor* signals where you'll tap into your subconscious and decide a specific finger to mean yes, another to mean no. We'll also establish a signal to indicate if you are uncomfortable with my questions or just don't want to answer, and by using signals, we can determine those things while you remain in hypnosis. I can't force you to answer something you don't want to talk about, but if it's the reason you're here, we'll need to set up some parameters. You mentioned you were hoping to retrieve memories. From childhood, or are you thinking of a more recent time?"

Marc exhaled and glanced at Mandy. "More recent, I think, though I can't rule anything out. Finding the time frame for the dreams I'm having will help me narrow down what I appear to be recalling."

He squeezed Mandy's hand. She glanced at him and then spoke to the therapist. "Alden? Would it help if you knew what Marc's trying to find out? Would that help you direct your questions?"

"It could, though I don't want to lead you in a predetermined direction. Can you tell me what you hope to learn without too many specifics?"

Marc stared at him for what felt like a very long time,

but Mandy knew the moment he came to his decision. He glanced her way before speaking to Alden. "My re-occurring dream is a violent one. I need to learn the identity of the man who might have murdered a woman. I don't know when it happened or who she was, but somehow I know I'm involved. I need to find out if my dreams are telling me the truth, or totally confusing the issue."

"Fair enough. Let's try a simple session this first time. See how difficult or easy it is for you to reach a state of altered consciousness. We might not even get into the dream this time, or we could find all the answers you're hoping for. Honestly?" He chuckled. "Sometimes it's a lot like life—an absolute crapshoot."

Marc shrugged and took a quick look at Mandy. "You'll be fine," she said. "I'll be right here with you." She was surprised when he visibly relaxed, as if that was all he needed to hear.

"What do I do?"

"Get comfortable." Alden adjusted his position in his own chair and waited while Marc settled into a spot on the sofa. He didn't let go of Mandy's hand.

"Now, I want you to close your eyes and think of a number. Just one. Concentrate on the shape of it, the color as you see it, what it makes you feel. Does this number have a particular meaning for you?"

Mandy had to force herself to concentrate on Marc, not on Alden's voice. His rich baritone seemed to shiver over her nerve endings, made her want to fall into the sound of his words as much as what he was saying.

She watched Marc, wondered what he was thinking. The man was undeniably brilliant. He was thirty-five years old with only a few months of college education, yet his net worth was already in excess of seventy-five million dollars, all on the basis of the software he'd

developed and his business acumen in investing his
original earnings. His mind fascinated her. Beyond his
intelligence, it was the way he still cared so deeply about
his friends, even while he carried this horrible burden.
She hoped Alden Chung could help him. Wished she
could help him, somehow ease the load.

Alden continued to speak, but Mandy knew the moment Marc went into a trance. It hadn't taken long at all
before his grip on her hand relaxed and he settled against
the pillow-soft back of the sofa.

Dr. Chung stopped speaking and studied Marc for a
moment. Then he nodded as if to himself, and said,
"Marc? I want your subconscious to choose a finger to
indicate yes. Show me which one means yes with a small
movement."

Marc's right forefinger tapped the arm of the sofa.

"Good. That's very good. What finger would you like
to use to signify no?"

Marc's middle finger tapped the sofa.

"Excellent, Marc. Very good. Now, if you become uncomfortable with my questions and want me to stop, I'll
need a signal from you, maybe . . ."

Before he'd finished, Marc lightly drummed his three
middle fingers against the arm of the sofa.

Alden smiled. "Perfect, Marc. There will be no confusion on my part at all. Now I'm going to ask you a
few questions, Marc. Indicate yes or no with the appropriate finger. First of all, I want to remind you that you
are safe here. Do you understand that?"

Marc's forefinger tapped the sofa.

"Excellent. Marc, we're going to talk about dreams.
I want you to feel safe when I ask you questions. Please
indicate no if you feel at all uncomfortable, or if any of
my questions are inappropriate. Can you do that?"

Forefinger. A single tap.

"Marc, sometimes you have dreams that make you uncomfortable. Do you remember them?"

Forefinger again.

"You don't like to talk about the dreams, though, do you?"

Marc shook his head and tapped his middle finger.

"Marc, I need to know if it is safe and appropriate for you to recall this information."

Forefinger. A light tap.

"Is it safe and appropriate for you to feel the emotions associated with these memories?"

Forefinger. Mandy noticed his movement was a bit hesitant this time, not much more than a twitch. She glanced at Alden, but he merely nodded.

"Very good, Marc. I'm going to touch your shoulder so you'll know that you're not alone, that it's safe here to talk about your dreams." He leaned close and did just that. "Mandy is with you, too. She's still holding your hand. We're both here to help you. I want you to think about your most recent dream. The one you described to Mandy. You can use your voice now. I want you to think about how you feel when you have this dream."

Marc's foot began tapping against the carpet. Alden touched his shoulder again. The tapping stopped. "Let's do this a bit differently. It's a scary place inside the dream, isn't it."

"Yes."

"I think it might be better if you were to step back. Maybe go someplace safe where you can watch. Does that sound like a good idea?"

"Yes."

"Why don't you watch your dream in a movie theater? The seats are comfortable and Mandy can sit beside you and hold your hand. You can watch the movie together. Does that work?"

"It's still scary."

"It's just a scary movie, Marc. It can't hurt you. Do you remember how you felt when you watched it?"

He took a couple of short, sharp breaths. "Afraid. I was afraid."

"You don't have to be afraid now, Marc. The theater is a safe place. Mandy's with you and nothing can hurt you here. Do you feel safe now?"

"Yes."

"Look at the screen, Marc. What do you see on the movie screen?"

"A little boy. I see a little boy." He was whispering now, his voice so low that Mandy could barely hear him.

"Where is he? You can speak to me. No one but Mandy and I can hear you. It's okay." He touched Marc's shoulder again. "We will both keep you safe."

Marc sighed softly. "He's behind the bed. He's afraid, and he's hiding."

Mandy realized she was staring at Marc. His voice had changed, not the adult depth of it, but the cadence, his manner of speaking. As if he were that little boy. The therapist didn't miss a beat, and she wondered if this was common.

"Do you know what room he's in? What house?"

"He's in my house. In Mommy and Daddy's room. It's too far away from mine."

"Do you feel alone at night, in your own room?"

"Sometimes. I'm a big boy. I'm not supposed to be afraid at night. That's what Daddy says. But the little boy heard shouting and it scared him. He came to find his Mommy."

"How old is he, Marc?"

"He's four. His mommy calls him her little man, but he's going to be big someday."

"Yes, he is. He will grow to be a big, strong, man. What do you see on the movie screen now?"

"I see Mommy and Daddy in the mirror."

Marc sighed again, and Mandy's heart went out to that little boy afraid at night, feeling so alone. But then he said, "Mommy and Daddy are fighting."

Mommy and Daddy? Was that what he saw? His parents fighting? Mandy clung to Marc's hand, starkly aware of the tension in his grasp, the sheen of perspiration on his forehead.

Her inability to do anything but hang on to his hand.

Alden's voice slipped into the quiet. "Are you still in a safe place?"

"I'm still in the theater, and I'm being quiet like a tiny mouse. That's what Mommy says to do when Daddy's angry."

"You have a very smart Mommy."

"She left me and never came back. She left me with Daddy. He's not a nice man."

"What is Daddy doing?"

"He has his hands around her neck. He's hurting her, but she's not crying anymore. She isn't moving. The little boy is still hiding. He doesn't want to go where he can really see them. He's afraid."

"Can't he see them on the movie screen anymore?"

A frown wrinkled his forehead. "No. But he can hear Daddy breathing real hard. He's really angry. I don't want to watch this movie anymore. I want to leave."

"That's a good idea, Marc. I want you to leave the theater and go someplace even safer. You're a grownup now, Marc, but little Marc is still afraid. Do you want to comfort him? You can make him feel better."

Marc nodded and tapped his finger at the same time.

Alden reached behind him and grabbed a soft pillow. He placed it against Marc's chest. "Maybe he needs a hug, Marc. He needs to know that he didn't do anything wrong, that he was a very good, very brave boy. What his father did is something only a very sick person would do."

Marc wrapped his arms around the pillow and held it against his chest, but he didn't let go of Mandy. Carefully, she switched hands, grasping his left with hers. Then she moved closer so he could hold the pillow and still hold on to her hand, but she wrapped her other arm around his back, holding him.

His body trembled. She pressed closer, with her cheek against his shoulder.

Alden nodded and smiled. "This is a good place, Marc. You're safe here. Mandy is with you, and I'm here. What you saw was frightening, but you were very brave. You didn't do anything wrong, but what your father did was wrong. When you awaken, I want you to remember everything you've recalled today. It's all over. Nothing will hurt you. Now Marc, I'm going to count slowly from one to five. As I do, you'll become more awake and aware with each number. When I count five, I'll touch your shoulder and you will be completely awake and aware. Your eyes will open, and you'll feel very good."

Alden counted, touched his shoulder, and Marc's eyes flew open. He turned and focused on Mandy. She reached for him and he grabbed for her at the same time, holding on to her, his entire body shivering as she held him close. Alden left the room for a moment. Then he was back with two paper cups of cold water. Marc took the one he offered.

Mandy took the other and held it while Marc emptied his. "Thank you," he said, when she handed hers to him. He drank it down as well. Then he stared at the paper cup in his hand as if he had no idea what to do with it.

Mandy took the empty cups and set them on the table beside the sofa. "Do you remember what you saw?"

He nodded, but it took him a moment before he spoke. "I do. It wasn't me in the mirror at all. It was my father. He would have been twenty-eight when she disappeared." He raised his head and stared at Alden. "When he killed her. That's what I saw, isn't it? He strangled her in their bedroom. I must have been asleep in my own room and heard them fighting. They had one of those closet doors that was all mirrors, and I saw him in the mirror, strangling her."

"You didn't say, but I assume you originally thought you were the man in the mirror?" Alden took his glasses off, wiped the lenses with a tissue and then put them back on. "You realize now that you were entirely innocent, a child, who was an unfortunate witness to a terrible act."

Marc frowned, gazed a moment into the distance. "I guess I do. What I saw today looked enough like me that I thought I saw myself doing this horrible thing." He ran his hands almost frantically through his hair. Mandy wondered if he might be in shock. She certainly felt a little out of it after his revelation.

Alden nodded. "But you didn't recognize your mother in the dream, not until today?"

Marc shook his head. "I've seen very few pictures of her, but when I saw her today, I remembered her immediately. It's like my father scoured her from my life. He taught me to hate her. When I think of the way he lied to me . . ." He raised his head and stared at Mandy. "He said she fought him for custody, and he only got to keep me because he offered her a huge payoff. She took the money and left. He said all she wanted was his money and she didn't want to see me again. I've believed that my whole life, when all along the bastard killed her. I can't believe I watched him kill her and couldn't remember."

"That's most likely how you survived this terrible incident with your mind intact." Alden sighed when he added, "You were protecting the child. Now, though, you'll need to deal with this. It's a horrible thing, but something that cries out for closure. How do you remember your mother now?"

Marc's eyes filled with tears. The panic-stricken look he gave Mandy spoke volumes, but he took a deep breath, closed his eyes a moment, and then exhaled. "I loved her. More than anything, and I know she loved me. I think she protected me from him, telling me how to hide, how to be like a tiny mouse. She was afraid of him." A hard glance at Mandy.

She squeezed his hand when he added, "As she had every right to be."

"Is your father still alive?"

Marc's entire expression changed. Mandy didn't think she'd ever seen him like this, so angry he was shaking. "Oh, yeah," he said. "He called me a couple of weeks ago, wanting more money, but I didn't give him any. I made the mistake of loaning him money once before, a fairly large sum that he neglected to repay. He seems to think I'm his personal bank, because he called again yesterday. I didn't take his call and erased his voicemail without listening."

He focused on Mandy. Intense—she'd seen him working on a problem he couldn't solve, and he'd had this same look, as if he'd find the answers he needed or die trying.

"What now?" Mandy rubbed her hand over his shoulders, down his back. "How do we prove that he killed your mother? And what do we do with the information?"

"We'll find a way to prove it, and I know just the man to put in charge of the search for evidence." The look on his face would have scared her silly if she'd thought his anger was aimed her way, but she knew exactly who he was talking about without Marc saying another word.

The man who'd come to San Francisco with the goal of keeping her sister's fiancé, Ben Lowell, alive long enough to testify—a job he'd performed admirably—while proving he could be as good a friend as he was an FBI agent. "Ted? Ted Robinson? But he's FBI. He's not going to want to . . ."

"I think he is. I haven't said anything, but Ted called me a couple of weeks ago, said he's had it with Washington, wants something new. He really loved it out here, said he felt a connection with us that had him thinking of making a major change, and wondered if I knew of anyone hiring. I told him Ben's got the security spot but that I was sure I could find more than enough work with Reed Industries to keep him busy. I've been waiting to hear back from him, but I'll call him once we get home."

He turned to Alden and held out his hand. "I can't thank you enough. I have a feeling I'm going to need to see you again. I'm wondering if there's anything else I can remember from that night, anything that will help me find the details of what he did with my mother, maybe where she's buried. I really want to nail the bastard's ass to the wall."

Alden nodded. "Sometimes after a session, the memories that you've recalled can jog a lot of others loose. Don't be surprised if you have new dreams, every bit as vivid though not as frightening because you'll experience them with the recovered knowledge you have now and the distance of your maturity. They'll make sense to your adult mind as they might not have to the child. And another thought—and this is my psychologist side speaking—I'm wondering if the fact you saw your own face in the mirror could be a reaction to guilt. You were just a child, but you clearly loved your mother very much. She had protected you from your father as best she could, and yet you couldn't save her. Possibly that four-year-old boy felt guilty enough to blame himself for her death."

Marc shoved his hands in his pockets and gazed at the wall covered with diplomas. Mandy wondered what was going through his mind, how he was going to deal with everything they'd discovered.

"I do feel guilty," he said. "Guilty for hating her all these years, for believing the lies he told me. That bastard." He glanced at the clock. "Is that the correct time?" When Alden nodded, Marc turned and gave Mandy a lopsided grin. "I can't believe we've been here for over two hours. It feels like maybe half an hour since we walked in the door."

"Hypnosis can be like that, stepping out of what is in everyday perception, the real world, and into a world that's filled with more truth than we thought possible." Alden glanced away, and then turned his attention back to Marc. "I'm curious. I thought you would have more trouble finding the trance state, but you slipped into it quite naturally. What number did you focus on?"

Marc shrugged. "The only one that matters. Zero."

"Interesting. And why is that?"

"It represents infinite possibilities. There's no beginning, no end, merely an infinite loop." He laughed. "When I can't sleep at night, I merely imagine a large zero. Works every time."

"I'll have to remember that. Good luck to you, Marcus Reed." He shook Marc's hand. "I will mail a recording of our session to you—it will be on a locked DVD for privacy. I'll email the password later this afternoon and you should have the recording by the end of the week. And please keep in touch. I'm going to want to know what comes of this."

When they pulled up in front of the house a few minutes later, Marc was still thinking of Alden Chung's words, of finding a world inside his own mind with even more truth than the reality he lived every day. He'd gone inside that place for such a brief period, and in that short time, his entire life had changed.

He'd learned more about himself and his dreams today than he'd believed possible, but he'd learned something even more important. He never would have done this without Mandy. Mandy, who was his friend and his lover and more. With his feelings all over the map and his world quite literally turned upside down, the one thing he was most certain of was the fact that he loved her.

She was everything he wanted in a life partner—a lover, a steadfast friend, the light to take him through whatever darkness cursed him. He was certain she cared for him, but after today's revelations he wasn't ready to pressure her for more than she was willing to give.

Would Mandy stick around to see this thing through with him? That was going to be asking a lot, because he fully intended to make his father pay. He'd never thought of himself as a vengeful person. Today, everything had changed.

He couldn't explain it, the almost visceral need to get back at the man who had lied to him, who had used him, who had killed the mother who loved him. That was what hurt the most, the fact Steven Reed had taught Marc to hate his mother, a woman who had only ever done her best to protect her son.

For that alone, the man had to pay.

Marc only hoped Mandy understood. He couldn't lose her. Couldn't give her up. He needed her so much it was almost frightening when he thought of the power she held over him. He glanced her way, caught her watching him, and returned the quick smile she shared. Then he backed the Tesla into the driveway and parked close to the charger. Mandy was out before he could get her door, so he went ahead and plugged the car in and then followed her up the steps. Rico greeted them as if they'd been gone for days, and then settled down as soon as the front door was closed with both Mandy and Marc inside.

It was almost five, but Marc went into his bedroom and took his clothes off, rummaged around for a pair of old sweats and put those on, along with a truly ratty looking T-shirt. As he headed back to the kitchen, he ran into Mandy heading for her room.

"You beat me to it. I want to get into something comfortable, and then I'm going to sit down with a glass of wine and see if I can decompress." She took both his hands and wrapped them behind her. He took the hint and held her close.

"There's so much I want to say, and I don't know where to start."

He laughed softly. "I know. I feel like a balloon with all the air let out. It's going to hit me really hard before too long, when everything sinks in. My first reaction was absolute rage, but I can't live like that. I can, however, do everything in my power to find out exactly what happened. More than anything, I need to know what he did with her. I have the strongest feeling that I might actually know where her body is buried, but nothing concrete."

He leaned close and kissed her. The taste of her mouth, the warmth of her body next to his. Damn. He wanted her now, but he forced himself to end the kiss, to wait. "I'm going to sit and have a beer while you have your glass of wine, then let's just fix breakfast for dinner. I know we've got everything here to make omelets. You okay with that?"

"Perfect." She stood on her toes and kissed him one more time.

He watched her walk toward her room. Tried to imagine dealing with this alone, and knew he couldn't. He hadn't. No, he'd been willing to live half a life rather than find out what the hell was going on in his dreams. One night with Mandy, and already he was finding answers to questions he'd never even considered, much less imagined.

The smell of bacon led Mandy back to the kitchen in record time. Marc was flipping a potato pancake of shredded russets, the bacon was already in the toaster oven keeping warm, and he had all the ingredients on the counter for omelets.

"Ya know, there's nothing sexier than a man in front of a stove with a spatula in his hand."

Marc turned and cocked one eyebrow. "Last time you said there was nothing sexier than a man doing dishes. Make up your mind, woman. Which is it?"

"Both. Kneeling in front of a toilet with a scrub brush is hot, too." She slipped her arms around his waist and hugged him from behind.

"What about kneeling in front of the pot tossing his cookies?"

"No. Definitely not sexy." Laughing, she stood on her

toes to kiss his shoulder and then turned to grab silver-ware for the table.

Marc had dinner ready and on the table a few minutes later. Mandy grabbed the last of the sliced melon out of the refrigerator and took her seat across from him. She watched as he put his napkin in his lap and then sat and stared at his plate.

"You look exhausted," she said. Reaching across the table, she wrapped her fingers around his hand.

Marc nodded. "I am. Physically and emotionally. I don't get the physical exhaustion. Emotional makes sense. Today was absolutely intense and I'm still getting hit with fragments of memories, things that have been totally hidden, wherever those sort of memories go to hide." He smiled, but while his lips tilted in the required direction, there was no laughter in his eyes.

"So does the physical exhaustion." When Marc cocked an eyebrow, she laughed. "Sex, Marc. We both burned a lot of calories last night. Good sex is hard work." She pouted. "How quickly he forgets. No wonder you can't retrieve your memories. We had absolutely exquisite sex just hours ago, and you can't remember?"

This time the smile hit his eyes. "Oh, I remember it. I just don't recall it being work. Not work at all."

They ate and cleaned up the kitchen. Marc called Theo Hadley, his business manager, and told him he might be late coming into the office Monday morning. Mandy heard Marc's end of the conversation as she headed to the bathroom for a quick shower.

Marc was in the middle of another phone call when she got out. She kissed his cheek, whispered, "I'm going to bed," and went back toward the bathroom. She took a quick detour into Ben's room and grabbed some more condoms.

Just in case. Then she went into Marc's room and

crawled into bed. Knowing Marc, he'd feel so guilty about the broken condom that he wouldn't want to sleep with her tonight.

That wasn't going to happen. Pulling the covers over herself, she punched her pillow a couple of times and then snuggled under the covers.

CHAPTER 5

Marc ended the call to Ted Robinson, and sat back in his chair, wondering at what he'd just put in gear. Ted's shock over Marc's story had quickly given way to a list of questions that would allow him to start his search for information long before he made it out to San Francisco. Marc had asked Ted if he had any family—a wife or kids who'd be coming out. He'd said no, just him, and that he was looking forward to seeing everyone again.

And he fully intended to be here by the end of the month—just three weeks away. All he'd asked was that Marc find him a place to stay—preferably a furnished apartment somewhere that was priced within reason.

That was simple enough, especially if Ted was on his own. Marc had made an offer on the house he shared with Ben, Lola, and Mandy. He'd not talked it over with them in the beginning because he honestly didn't know if the landlord was willing to sell or not, but the elderly man had been satisfied with the offer and the terms, and relieved not to have to deal with new renters. He'd told Marc he'd been planning to list the place since the long-time absentee renter in the second half of the unit had recently moved out of state.

Escrow was due to close in about a week. Marc planned to let everyone know what he'd done once it was signed and sealed. It was all good. He only hoped that they'd all be okay with the purchase. The second unit was a little smaller than the one he and the others lived in—two bedrooms rather than three—but he'd thought of offering that one to Kaz and Jake, which would free up Jake's apartment for Ted.

They'd both said how much they wished they lived closer—the running joke was that they wanted in on meal times because Lola was such a good cook, but he knew it was more than that. This group of friends was closer than most families—they'd been tested in horrible situations and had come through stronger than ever. They needed each other—at least Marc freely admitted that he needed each of them—but it would be a lot of fun if Jake and Kaz were close enough to pop in on occasion, yet still had their own space.

At least it all sounded good on paper. He wondered if Jake and Kaz were at their hotel in Italy. He had the number, but the least he should do was tell Mandy first. He wasn't really used to considering anyone else when he made financial decisions. He'd always just gone ahead and done things on his own. Well, with Theo Hadley's help. He trusted Theo's business sense, and Theo had agreed that purchasing this duplex was an excellent decision. Still. . . .

Having a family, formal or otherwise, changed the dynamic. But it must be in a good way, because just thinking of the way his own, small family had grown made him feel better. Relaxed, even. In spite of what he'd learned. In spite of what he hoped to find out.

All because he was no longer in this on his own.

Humor much improved, he went in and took a quick shower. Wrapped a towel around his waist, grabbed his clothes, and turned off the light. Then he stopped in front of Mandy's door and wondered if he should join her. He stood there for a moment, considering, but he knew she was exhausted, and there was no way he'd be able to keep his hands off her.

It wasn't easy, but he walked away and quietly opened the door to his own room. Luckily, light from the hallway slanted across the bed before he flipped on the bedroom light and woke her. Mandy was in his bed.

Not only was Mandy in his bed, there was a small pile of condoms on the bedside table.

Smiling, he set his clothes on the floor, dropped the towel, and crawled in beside her. Just holding Mandy was enough. She curled into his embrace with a soft sigh. The last thing he remembered was the scent of the shampoo she'd used, and the slight tickle of the damp strands of her silky hair against his chin.

The gray light of morning barely filtered through the closed window blinds when Mandy opened her eyes to the fact that she'd slept through the night without waking, that the hair on Marc's chest was tickling her nose, and she really had to pee. Now.

Carefully she disentangled herself from his loose embrace and crawled out of bed. It was just a little after five, but she used the bathroom, washed her face and brushed her teeth, and then tried to work the tangles out of her hair.

She knew better than to go to sleep when it was still wet, but waking up in Marc's arms trumped wrinkled hair any day of the week. She went straight to the kitchen and put on a pot of coffee. Then she turned and went back to Marc's bedroom and slipped into bed with him.

He pulled her into his arms and buried his face in her hair.

"You through wandering the halls yet?"

"For now. I put the coffee on."

"Um."

"Real talkative guy in the morning, aren't you? I didn't mean to wake you."

"S'okay." He hauled her over on top of him until she was sprawled across his body like a rather lumpy blanket. "That's better."

"I'm glad you think so. Are you going in to work today? I heard you talking to Theo."

He sighed and blinked slowly. "You're not going to let me go back to sleep, are you?"

"Of course not. It's after five. I'm usually up by four, and I went to bed before nine. This is when my day usually starts."

"Hmmm. I wish you'd mentioned that before crawling into my bed."

"You're avoiding the question. Are you going in to the office?"

"Eventually. I need to hire a temp while Lola's gone. Totally forgot to do it, and I told her not to, that I'd find someone. It sort of got away from me."

"I can do Lola's job while she's gone. It's not like I have to be at the coffee shop."

He blinked. More than once. "You know office work?"

"Uh, yeah. I've worked in an office before. Besides, I have a business degree."

He frowned. She could almost see the wheels turning.

"Then why the dead-end job in a coffee shop?"

Shrugging, she smiled. "Because I like people? I love the work, and I always wanted my own coffee shop. As you can see, that hasn't happened. Yet."

"Well, since you're currently unemployed then yes, I would love for you to handle Lola's work while she's away. But only if you don't call me Mr. Reed."

She kissed him. "Why not? Lola does."

"Yeah, well after the revelation yesterday, I don't want the same name as my father. At least not from you."

"Oh, Marc." She kissed him again, and this time he kissed her back. "You've made that name your own. You are not your father. For one thing, I'd never be lying on his naked body, trying to figure out how to get him to screw me silly."

"You've got that right."

At least he was laughing when he rolled her over. And Mandy decided this was definitely how she wanted to start every single morning for the rest of her life.

First, though, she had to help Marc figure out the answers to the questions that had to be driving him absolutely crazy.

He'd been taking Lola into the office with him for the past couple of months, but it was a whole new feeling to have Mandy beside him in the front seat. Especially since they'd spent all morning making love. He'd never known anything as amazing as sex with Mandy. She had no inhibitions and no problem telling him what she wanted him to do, but the best part of it all was the way she responded to everything he tried with her.

Marc figured he'd learned more about pleasing a woman in the past two days than he'd ever expected to learn, and it was all good. Better than good—it was absolutely amazing.

"So," she said, turning in the seat and studying him. "What kind of boss are you? Demanding? A pushover? Do you expect me to make coffee? Have sex on the desk in the back office? I need to know my parameters, ya know? Limits? That sort of thing?"

"I have no idea how you managed to say that with a straight face." He glanced sideways and then returned his attention to the busy street in front of him. "Sex on the desk in the back office? I don't have a back office. That's Theo's space, and no, you are not having sex with Theo. Besides, Theo's gay. He wouldn't be interested."

She snorted. He wasn't sure if he'd ever heard Mandy snort, but he didn't crack a smile, at least not until she rolled her eyes and calmly said, "Theo's too old for me, besides the gay thing. I just don't think he's my type. Of course, he might be Lola's, but I really think she's hooked on Ben."

"There is that." He smiled her way. "It would be awesome if you made coffee, but that's not part of the job. Mainly I want you to keep the bills and statements straight and make sure anything that's due gets to Theo. I own a lot of different companies. Lola organizes the paperwork by business and Theo handles the payments. She also makes sure that all the legal stuff is up to date, but she's got a handy calendar that will keep you organized. I don't think there's anything major due right now."

"Lola's always very efficient."

"That she is." He stopped at a red light and had enough time to give Mandy what he hoped was a meaningful look. "But she's not you. I don't think there's anyone like you."

He liked the fact she was still smiling when he pulled into the small garage that was part of his building.

Lola really did keep things organized. Mandy slipped into Lola's chair and into her job without any trouble at all. It was actually sort of fun to be dressed in a classy pantsuit, sitting at a desk instead of standing behind a counter, but she missed the people she saw at the coffee shop every day.

Theo was nice enough, but Marc had disappeared into his office as soon as they'd arrived, and he'd hardly come out. It was almost eleven before the door swung open and he stopped beside her desk. "I've got an appointment I need to go to. Totally forgot about it, but I should be back in time for lunch. There's a really good restaurant not far from here where I'd like to take you. Okay?"

"Sure." She reached for a stack of invoices from Intimate Wines. "I'm just getting ready to go through these. That should take me close to an hour. I'll see you when you get back."

"Theo's here. He usually brings his lunch, so he'll be in his office if you need anything."

"Go. I'll be fine."

"Mandy?" He leaned close and kissed her. "Thank you for doing this. I really appreciate it, and I know Lola will, too. Otherwise she'd be coming home to a huge mess."

"Marc, you really do have to get over this issue you have with hiring people." She laughed and waved him off. "Now go!"

He saluted. "Yes, ma'am."

And then he was out the door. She spent the next half hour checking the invoices, figuring out what needed to be paid now and what could wait, and then packed everything up and took them into Theo's office. She'd never met Marc's business manager before this morning, but she liked the man. He was quiet and undemanding, but appeared to love his job. So, being Mandy, she asked him.

"You look like you really love what you're doing. Do you? Or are you just a really good actor?"

He laughed and leaned back in his chair. "Marcus Reed is one of the best men I've ever met. Unfortunately he's straight, or I would have pounced on him years ago, but he's a fantastic guy to work for, and, I think, a good friend. And where do you fit in?"

"I'm Lola's younger sister, and I told Marc I'd cover for her while she's in Washington."

He nodded. "She told me a little bit about the deposition she and Ben have to give. He's another good one, and so's your sister. I think that's part of Marc's appeal. He seems to attract really terrific people. It's hard not to admire that."

"I know. I need to get back to work, but I'm glad I finally got to meet you. I've heard about you from Lola."

"Ah, the crazy nerd in the back who's glued to his computer?"

She laughed. "Actually, no. What I heard about was the sexy Shemar Moore lookalike who runs the place and lets Marc think he's in charge. Don't underestimate yourself, Mr. Hadley."

They were both laughing when she left to go back to the front office, but a few moments later, Mandy heard the front door open. The man who walked in looked so much like Marc that she finally understood how his dreams could have confused him. Like Marc, but not. Where Marc was warm and loving, his father struck her as a man without a soul. There was something about him, a sense of cruelty and dissipation, depravity, even, that immediately made her nervous. She couldn't help but wonder if she would have felt the same way if she hadn't known Marc's story.

The minute he opened his mouth, she knew she would have disliked him even without the backstory.

"Where's Marc?"

Rude and demanding, his tone lacked any pretense of

manners or class. "Mr. Reed's not here right now. He had an appointment."

The guy looked around and then glanced toward Marc's office. The door was ajar. "I'll just wait in his office."

"No, sir. You won't. What can I help you with?"

"Look, missy. I'm Marc's father and I have every right to be here." He started toward Marc's office. "When's he due back?"

"I really don't know." She found the button under the desktop, the one Marc had installed after all the problems they'd had with the senator's wife and Marc's last security chief. Giving it a quick press, she maintained focus on the senior Mr. Reed.

Mere seconds later, Theo wandered out into the front office, carrying a couple of folders. He stopped, blocking entrance to Marc's private office. "Ah, Mr. Reed. Marc's out for a couple of hours. I'm afraid you'll have to come back later."

"I'll wait for him."

Theo's smile looked flat-out deadly. "I don't think so. Mr. Reed gave me specific instructions that you were not to have access to his office or be allowed to intimidate his staff."

Mandy noticed how Reed's hands clenched as he focused on Theo. Evidently Theo noticed the shift in stance as well.

He stood straight, made eye contact with Reed. "Now, I'm not the least bit intimidated by you, sir, and I won't have you upsetting Ms. Monroe. She has work to do. Please leave. We'll be sure and let Mr. Reed know you stopped by. He'll call you if he feels a need to get in touch."

Theo merely stood there watching while Steven Reed glowered at the two of them before he turned away and stomped out the door. Mandy turned to Theo and held up her hand. He high fived her and they both laughed. "Damn," she said. "You're good. And you look like such a mild sort."

"It's the glasses," he said. "I think I'd wear them even if I didn't need any. They make me look nerdy enough and intellectual enough that I don't look like a guy that can kick ass. But I can." He winked. "And I have. On more than one occasion."

"That's good to know. I'm glad Marc has you here." She glanced at the closed door. "I'm really glad I have you here. His father scares the crap out of me."

"He's an odd duck. How'd you know he was Marc's father? Have you met him before, or did he tell you?"

Mandy shook her head. "He didn't have to. Don't you see the resemblance? He looks like an older, psychotic version of Marc." She rubbed her arms. "He makes my skin crawl."

"That he does. You might want to call Marc, let him know his father was here in case the bastard decides to wait by the door to catch him."

"Good idea." Mandy grabbed her phone and sent a quick text. *Your father just left. Theo asked him to go when he insisted on waiting in your office. We didn't let him in.*

The phone rang seconds after she sent the message. "Hi," she said. "Thought it might be you."

"Thanks for the warning. Do you think he might be waiting outside for me? I really don't want to talk to him. At least not yet."

"He might be. It's almost noon. Are you free?"

"Just left the meeting."

"Perfect. Why don't I come and meet you for lunch? Where are we going?"

He named a restaurant a couple of blocks away, one

Mandy had been to ages ago. "I know right where it is. I'll let Theo know I'm leaving. Give me ten minutes."

"Do you feel safe walking over here? He could be outside."

"I've got my cell phone. Don't worry. I'll close up my work and be out of here in a minute."

"Okay," he said, though he still sounded worried. "Be careful. I'm headed to the restaurant now."

She stopped off in the restroom, refreshed her lipstick and ran a comb through her hair. Then she poked her head in Theo's office. "I'm meeting Marc for lunch. Should I put up the closed sign?"

"Yeah. I've got some stuff I have to get out today. I'll lock the door behind you." He stood and followed her back to the main office. Mandy shut down her computer and grabbed her handbag.

Theo paused at the door. "Be careful," he said. "If Marc's father is still hanging around out there, come back inside and we'll call Marc. The guy really is creepy."

"Thanks, Theo. You don't have to convince me. I'll watch for him."

She didn't see any sign of the elder Mr. Reed as she walked the two blocks to the restaurant. Marc had walked to his meeting at a building not far from there, and was already waiting in front of the restaurant when she turned the corner. She loved the way his eyes lit up when he saw her, the smile that changed his entire look.

He grabbed her hand, pulled her close, and kissed her. Quite thoroughly. She had to catch her breath when he finally broke the kiss. After waving her hand in front of her face as if to cool herself down, Mandy covered her heart. "My goodness, Marcus. I never saw you as the PDA type."

"I know that one," he said, leading her into the restaurant. "Public displays of affection. And no, I am not a man known for PDAs. Not unless I want the public to know who my affection is for." He squeezed her hand.

"I'm flattered."

"You should be." They followed the *maître d'* to a quiet booth at the back of the restaurant. "Until you, I've never participated in a single PDA. Not one."

"You're admitting that I took your PDA virginity? Me?" She slapped a hand to her chest.

"I am." He stood while she slipped into her seat.

"Well," she said, gazing up at him. Falling more in love with the man every moment she spent with him. "It's only fair. Because you took mine, too."

When he slipped into the seat across from Mandy, Marc pictured the two of them doing this years from now, maybe with a couple of kids wanting to play with the silverware or fussing about being hungry. He had no memories of doing anything so perfectly average like that with his parents.

A few memories had resurfaced, though he hadn't had the time to really dissect them. A day at the beach, though he only remembered his mother holding his hand, walking with him through the sand. His father wasn't part of that memory at all. Nor was he part of the other snips and fragments of a past long gone—a day in the park, playing on the swings. Walking outside in the rain wearing rubber boots and a bright yellow slicker. His mother had been the focus of those memories, too.

But the bulk of them, of days at the park or walking in their neighborhood, were spent with nannies. The upside was that he spoke more than one language. The downside? His mother had been gone, and all that time he'd believed she hated him so much that she'd taken the money and run.

The waiter stopped and took their orders. "Have you been here before?" Marc asked when the young man had moved on to another table.

"A couple of times, but it was years ago. I think I've spent so much time in a restaurant environment that I usually prefer eating something at home, but this is special. It feels like a date." She made a face. "In case you haven't noticed, I don't date much."

"Actually, I have noticed. I've been wondering how I would deal with it if some guy came to pick you up at the house and I had to make nice with him. I didn't think you'd approve of my punching him in the face."

She laughed. Damn, but he loved the sound of Mandy's laughter.

"No, that wouldn't have gone over well, I imagine. Especially since you'd never asked me out yourself."

Her grin was beyond cocky when he took her hand. "I plan to remedy that, beginning today."

The color washed from her face and Marc spun around to see exactly what had upset her. His father was crossing the restaurant, coming directly for their table. "Don't worry," Marc said. "I'll handle this."

Mandy nodded.

Marc stood, blocking Mandy from his father's view. If he'd disliked the man before, he truly hated him now, but he couldn't say anything. Not until they had proof. Ted had been adamant that he not let his father know he remembered what happened.

It wasn't going to be easy. Not when that was all he could think of.

"So, you're dating the help now, eh, son?"

Steven Reed had once been a handsome man. Time had not been kind to him. His florid coloring and heavy jowls gave him a dissipated look that was anything but attractive. And along with that thought, Marc imagined how satisfactory it would be to see the bastard keel over right here in the restaurant. Heart attack? Stroke? It really didn't matter. He ignored his opening insult. "What do you want?"

"You might answer my calls, for one thing. And show a little respect, because that's not a respectful way to speak to the man who raised you."

"I have nothing to say to you. I've told you not to come by my home or my office. I don't want you calling me. Get a clue—I don't want to see you anywhere. I don't want you bothering me. Not me, not my friends, and especially not my employees. Now go."

"I'm not going anywhere."

He moved closer, slipping well into Marc's personal space. Marc glanced at the *maître d'*, who appeared to realize there was a problem brewing.

"I think you are." Marc turned away to sit just as the neatly dressed *maître d'* reached their table. Steven Reed's hand snaked out and he caught Marc's arm in a powerful grasp. Marc bent his elbow and twisted his wrist free.

The simple but effective move was one Theo had taught him.

At the same time, the *maître d',* now accompanied by a couple of burly waiters, reached the table and focused on Steven Reed. "The police have been called, sir. If you wish to leave before they arrive, you might want to go now. Otherwise, I have the authority to press charges."

"Son of a . . ." Reed shot a hate-filled look at Mandy, turned away, and stalked out of the restaurant.

The waiters had already gone back to their stations when Marc stood and shook the *maître d's* hand. "Thank you. I didn't realize he'd followed us."

"My apologies, Mr. Reed. He should have been

stopped at the door. We will, of course, comp your meals and beverages. I'm very sorry this happened."

"Absolutely not." Marc sat down again as the waiter brought their meals. "That was, unfortunately, my father, and trying to stop him would have only created a huge scene. I'll expect my bill. Thank you again for your help."

After the man left and Marc realized the adrenaline rush had apparently settled into a low hum, he took a sip of water and glanced Mandy's way.

She was shaking her head. "Do you have any further entertainment planned for the day?"

He almost snorted his water, while she calmly attacked her sandwich. After he'd finished half of his, he remembered a call he'd had earlier. "Jake called while I was walking over here. I totally forgot to tell you. He and Kaz are going to stay an extra week. She's very popular in Italy, and there are two different companies who want her to pose for them, with Jake doing the photos. He said the contracts should pay for the entire cost of the wedding, and he asked if we could take over some of the legwork. When I asked for an interpretation, he said that means they want us to check with the various caterers they've got on their list and let us know which one we like the best."

"Wow! Kaz trusts us to do that?"

"Jake said it was her idea. She's loving Italy, and I don't think she wants to come home. Even for her wedding."

"I can understand that. I've always wanted to see Italy. The northern part, up where the Dolomites are. I used to watch a bike race called the *Giro d'Italia,* just for the scenery. A lot of the courses went through those mountains. They don't even look real."

"I've never been there either." He shrugged, tried to

play it cool while imagining making love to Mandy in a beautiful Italian villa in the mountains. "Maybe that's a trip we can do together one day."

"I wish." She laughed and checked her watch. "I need to eat and get back to work. I hear the boss can be a real pain in the ass."

"That's true. But before we go, there's one more thing I need to tell you, and I also want your opinion. I don't know if I've overstepped my bounds or not."

Mandy finished her sandwich and folded her hands on the table. "Okay, what did you do now?" At least she was smiling.

"I bought our house."

"You what?" Her eyes went wide. "You mean the place we live in? Our house?"

He nodded. "I did. I checked with the landlord. He was thinking of selling because the renter next door, you know, the guy you've never met? Well, he'd not renewed his lease because his temporary move out of state turned permanent, and the landlord didn't want to deal with new renters. It's been empty for a couple of years now. The owner's quite elderly, I made a good offer, and he accepted. Theo's the one who told me I should invest in some smaller rental properties, and that seemed like the perfect place to start."

"Wow. Are you going to have strict new rules? I hope there's not going to be a no pets clause, because Rico would not approve. And what about the empty unit?"

"Well, see, that's the deal. Jake and Kaz hate living so far away. Jake said he has so little free time that he wished they were closer so he could get to know Ben better. Twenty years is a long time for brothers to be apart. Plus, Kaz misses hanging out with you and Lola in the little bit of free time she has. I thought I'd offer the unit next door to them and then pick up the lease on

Jake's apartment for Ted Robinson. He's moving out here at the end of the month."

"I think it sounds like a great idea. I imagine Jake and Kaz will love it. She doesn't really like Jake's place very much. He's got a furnished one like your old apartment. She says it has no character, that it's like living in a showroom."

"Well, the place next door definitely has character. One of the bedrooms is painted bubblegum pink and the other one has striped wallpaper that makes my eyes cross. I know they'll want to have it painted and it'll probably need some serious remodeling, but I'll wait until I know for sure if they want it. If not them, then Ted, I guess, though I think he'd prefer Jake's. It's closer to things in town. It's almost impossible to find rentals in this city, which is why I'm trying to work this out in a way that makes sense for everyone."

"I'm actually excited about seeing Ted again. Do you think he can help you find out more about your mother?"

"I'm sure he can. He's starting at the beginning, learning what he can about her background, where she was from, her age. I don't know any of that, but he's got access to records most of us can't get into. I can't approach my father with anything until I have proof. I have to believe Ted will find something."

"Do you plan to see Alden again?"

"I do. I'm getting little snips of memories. I think I'm going to give it at least a week or so, keep taking notes, and then see him again. I really need to get this settled, Mandy. I have to know what happened to my mother. I keep thinking, all these years and no one has mourned her. She had no family that I know of, no brothers or sisters, her parents were gone. At least that's what my father told me. I could have cousins, grandparents. I just don't know."

Mandy stood and held out her hand. "C'mon. We need to get back to work. Call Jake and tell him we'll go to Healdsburg and check on caterers and florists and whatever, and tell him about the house. Give him time to get used to the idea before they come home. That's not something you really want to spring on a couple, ya know?"

He sighed. He could be such an idiot sometimes. "I kind of figured that after I'd already made the offer, but then I didn't want to say anything until I knew for sure that the deal was going through. In hindsight, it was pretty presumptuous of me to make a decision like that without consulting all of you."

"Actually, Marc, it was thoughtful and very generous. You're truly one of the good guys, ya know?" She hugged his arm close to her body. It took all the willpower he had not to kiss her senseless, right there in the restaurant. Mandy gave affirmation so easily, and yet Marc couldn't ever recall anyone other than the occasional nanny saying anything positive about him or to him while he was growing up.

Probably why he felt like wallowing in her kindness.

They stopped at the register on the way out and the cashier found his bill. He showed it to Marc—nothing but a large zero with a slash through it. "There's no charge, sir. Ian, the *maître d'*, said to comp your meals. He feels badly that you were bothered by that man."

"Let me at least leave a tip, then." Marc pulled out his wallet while the cashier made out a charge tag. Marc handed over his credit card and took the receipt showing nothing in the total. He signed, and added a thousand dollar tip. "This is for the staff," he said. "That was handled really well."

The cashier looked at the tag and then gaped at Marc. "Of course, sir. Whatever you say. And thank you."

As he and Mandy left the restaurant, he saw the cashier racing over to the *maître d'*. As the door closed behind them, there was a very loud shout. More like a war whoop.

Some days, having all that money was really worth it.

CHAPTER 6

There was a moving van parked in front of his building when they got back from lunch. Mandy paused while a couple of men passed in front of them with a dolly loaded with filing cabinets. "You're losing a tenant?"

"I am." Marc laughed. "Two of them, actually. A couple of women opened up a temp agency, providing secretaries and other office workers, and they've been so successful they're moving to a new, larger location. They've been in this building longer than I have—I inherited them along with the purchase."

Mandy stuck her head in the door and sort of checked out the space. "What are you going to do with it now?"

Marc grabbed her hand and dragged her inside. It was probably much too soon, but this was the perfect time to show the place to her. "I've had this idea for quite some time, which is why I haven't advertised the space as available. What do you see when you walk along this stretch of Battery Street?"

"Office buildings, some apartments." Pausing, she smirked. "No place to park."

He leaned close and kissed her. He couldn't help

himself. "There is that," he said. "Unless you own your own parking garage."

"I imagine that was a selling point with the building, right?"

"It was. Definitely." Still holding her hand, he walked to the back of the almost empty space. "Now, more specifically, exactly what do you see when you look out this window?"

She stared a moment. "Mostly apartments, I think. Or offices? Can't tell. Why?"

"It's what you don't see that matters. There's no coffee shop in this area. No restaurants for a couple of blocks. The one we went to is the closest, and it's pretty pricey. But there are apartments and lots of people. I've been thinking of searching for a tenant to either put in a small café-style restaurant, or even a coffee shop, similar to the one you worked in. You know, a place where you can grab a quick breakfast or lunch and coffee or tea?" He shrugged. "When you lost your job, I immediately thought of you, but I wanted to be able to show it to you first. Would you be interested in a partnership? Silent partner for me, though." He laughed, realized he sounded nervous and bit back the sound.

Glancing away, he said, "I'm not much of a cook, and I doubt I'd make a very good barista. You'd have to be the brains of the operation." He hoped he'd been subtle enough, that she wouldn't see this as a way to bind her to him even more, but it was such a perfect idea. Mandy would have her coffee shop—and he would have Mandy. It was the only way he knew to keep her close and happy. He couldn't tell her how he really felt, that he loved her, not while this mess with his father was hanging out there. Not until he knew where his mother's body was buried.

It wouldn't be at all fair to her, tying her to a guy

whose life was totally in flux right now. But business? Business was different. Straightforward, with contracts that kept things organized.

Contracts kept people together. Forced them to work things out.

He understood contracts a hell of a lot better than he understood women. Though Mandy wasn't like any other woman he'd ever known. He glanced her way again. She was beautiful. She was kind, and so smart and funny. She was everything he wanted, but she didn't look at all happy with his suggestion.

In fact, she looked absolutely furious.

Damn. He was so screwed.

She watched the conflicting emotions flying across Marc's face and honestly just wanted to slap him. She was not a charity case, nor was she a gold digger. She wanted Marc, not his money. Not what he could give her or make happen for her. Just Marc. So why'd he have to go and screw things up by trying to buy her?

That hurt. She straightened her spine and let go of his hand. "I'm not for sale, Marc. It's a great idea, but I imagine it's also an idea you came up with about ten minutes ago, if even that long. You're better than this, Marc. So am I. Right now? I have work to do."

Turning away, she ignored Marc's protest and walked back to the entry that would give her access to either the stairs or the elevator to his third floor offices.

She took the stairs, hoping she'd get a chance to work off that unexpected burst of anger. Her unwanted disappointment in Marc.

It was sort of anticlimactic that she had to knock so Theo could let her in. She stood tapping her foot impatiently, hoping like hell Marc wouldn't catch her standing in front of the locked door to his offices.

She was still seething when she settled herself at her desk to go through the rest of the mail that Theo had brought in. Marc didn't come in for another ten minutes, and by then she was deep into work. She didn't look up.

Until she had to. He stopped in front of her desk and waited. She was pissed, but she couldn't be rude. It wasn't in her nature. Hell, she'd even been polite to Lola's idiot ex when he showed up at their place with a gun. It had worked, too. He'd put the gun down and surrendered even before the police arrived.

She might not be rude, but she wasn't usually a push-over, either. She raised her head and looked into those dark brown eyes of his and practically melted. He looked horribly sad, but he'd still really blown it.

"We need to talk," he said. "Will you come into my office for a minute?"

She nodded, saved her work on the computer and fol-lowed him into his office. She sat in one of the comfort-able chairs in front of his desk, expecting Marc to go around to his chair behind it. He didn't. Instead, he sat on the edge of the big desk in front of her and stared over his shoulder, gazing out the window with its view of Yerba Buena Island and Treasure Island just north of it. Then he stood, shoved his hands in his pockets, and walked over to the window. He looked terribly lonely standing there, his back to her.

But then, Marc had always appeared to be alone, even when they were together as a group, as if he sat apart from the camaraderie, the connection that came so nat-urally to the rest of them. That sense had totally dis-appeared over the past couple of days, but now it was back.

She'd brought him out, watched him come alive, and now it appeared she'd sent him back to that same place in his head. Even so, as much as she thought she needed to say something, anything to make him feel better, she managed to keep her mouth shut. It wasn't easy.

After a moment, he turned around and faced her, but he was on the opposite side of the room, almost as if he were afraid to come closer. "I want to apologize. And explain." He shook his head and shrugged. "I really have been thinking about you running a café or coffee shop for me for quite some time, but you already had a job and the space was leased. The tenants just asked if they could break the lease a few days ago when another space opened up that would fit their business better. Of course I said yes. It's not hard to find a tenant in this economy, but I really did already have the idea I tossed at you today."

"Marc, I . . ."

He held up a hand. "No. I need to say this. Please." He sighed, glanced away, and then focused on her again. "This past couple of months have been the best in my entire life. I've had Jake for years, but I never expected the rest of you." He walked across the office, stopped in front of her chair and squatted down until they were at eye level. "I never expected you, Mandy. The first time I saw you, I was totally blown away, but I had all this crap in my background. I still do, which is why I haven't been totally honest with you. I love you, Mandy. I think I've loved you from the very beginning."

She sucked in a breath. This wasn't what she'd expected him to say. Not this at all, but he was slowly shaking his head, looking away now.

He turned back to her, took her hands in his, studied their entwined fingers for a moment before raising his head, looking into her eyes. "I love you so much it just fills me up, but I only realized it after the hypnosis therapy. It was too soon, my mind was a wreck . . . I couldn't say anything. I've been afraid you didn't feel the same way, that you wouldn't want to hang around until I got this crap in my life all straightened out. But I thought that if you had a vested interest in something of mine, in a business here in my building, that you'd at least have to stay until we got all the questions answered. That's why I brought it up today. I was hoping you'd agree so that you'd have to stay."

He laughed, but there wasn't a bit of humor in the sound. "I'd have your name on a contract. I thought that would keep you here even if you didn't want to stay for me."

She thought of that little boy in his parents' bedroom, what he'd witnessed. The lonely, horrible life he'd led, and all of it made perfect sense. Jake had made a similar comment, how Marc had convinced him to invest in the Intimate Winery. It wasn't because Marc needed the money. He needed to know that Jake had a reason to stick around other than their friendship.

Still hanging on to his hands, Mandy stood, pulling Marc to his feet. "Marc, I love you so much, but I couldn't understand why you were interested in me at all. I'm just an unemployed barista with nothing to of-fer. You're . . . you're Marcus Reed—you have every-thing going for you. I'm . . ."

"You're the most important thing I don't have, Mandy."

"Marc, you've always had me." She laughed at the look on his face. "When you moved in, I had the feeling everyone was pushing you at me and you weren't inter-ested, so I backed off. I hated to think they were mak-ing you uncomfortable, but you know how it is when couples are all paired up. They want everyone in pairs."

He wrapped his arms around her and pulled her close. "I wondered if that's what was going on, but you were really good at playing my FWB."

"FWB?" She laughed. "As much as I wanted it, we were not 'friends with benefits.'"

He laughed and kissed her. "No, it also means 'friends without benefits.' That's changed, but I wasn't sure how you felt about me. I really do want you to manage a coffee shop downstairs, Mandy, but now, knowing what I know about my mother, what happened to her, I want to do it a bit differently. The ladies who run the temp service train and hire women from a shelter. I'd like to do that same thing—hire women who need work because they've been in a bad situation. I know you and Kaz and Lola have looked into various shelters, researching the memorial for the woman and her child who were killed in Ben and Jake's accident so long ago. Now that I know what happened to my mother, I have a vested interest in getting even more involved with anyone trying to protect women in danger. I want to lend my support to whatever shelter you choose, but I would also like to have a business that could offer employment to women in an abusive situation. Maybe even childcare here as well. There's a lot of this building we're not using. Think about it, please? It really would mean a lot to me."

"So it's not an offer you made because you feel sorry for me?"

He shook his head and pulled her close. "Far from it. Why would I ever feel sorry for you? You're the strongest woman I know. You have everything that's important. A great attitude, a sister who loves you, friends who love you just as much. You give so much joy to everyone around you, just by being you."

There was no stopping the tears. Not when he looked at her like that, when his voice sounded so deep and emotional—when his dark eyes glittered as if maybe he was dealing with a few tears himself.

A few moments later, he cupped her shoulders and

held her away, far enough to look into her eyes. "What do you say we take a few days and head up to Dry Creek Valley to the winery? Take care of some of that stuff that Jake and Kaz want us to do? I'll check with Cassie and Nate, make sure we can use either the apartment above the tasting room or Cassie's little guest cottage. We'll check with some of the caterers, look into booking a musician, maybe even a small band or a deejay for music for dancing. Does that work for you?"

"Can you just leave?"

"I can. I pay Theo well and I think he prefers it when I'm not here." He glanced over her shoulder as if checking to make sure his business manager wasn't lurking. "He says I tend to meddle."

She didn't even try not to laugh. "Ya think? Personally, I think it's a great idea. I'll see if Jasper and Abdul can take Rico. They live a couple of doors down and they've watched him before. He even has his own pillow in their sunroom, so it shouldn't be a problem. When do you want to go? I can be done here by about three."

"That works. I'll let Theo know he's captain of the ship. And I think I'll have him set up Ted's office. I have a feeling Agent Robinson will be here sooner rather than later."

Mandy had Rico settled with Abdul and Jasper and their calico cat, Sheba, on the pillow in their sunroom by three thirty. She and Marc were packed and on the road by four, though the traffic was awful. Mandy called while Marc drove to let Cassie, the winemaker, and her husband Nate, the vineyard manager, know when to expect them. She caught Cassie as she was making a run into town for groceries.

"Your timing's perfect," she said. "I'll stock the refrigerator in the cottage so you'll at least have snacks and breakfast stuff. In fact, I'll make you a deal—I'll even add real food if you guys will pick up Mexican on your way out here. Can you do that?"

Mandy laughed and turned the phone on speaker. "I can hear you salivating. Are chili rellenos good for pregnant moms to be?"

"They are for this one. You know what we like, right?"

Mandy went over the list of their favorites, wrote everything down to make sure she didn't forget, and settled back in her seat while Marc dealt with the late afternoon traffic from San Francisco to Healdsburg.

She'd only met Cassie a couple of times, but she and Nate were already a couple of Mandy's favorite people. Cassie's father was the one who'd started the winery Marc now owned. It was originally called Tangled Vines back in the mid-eighties, but advancing Alzheimer's had led to some bad financial decisions, and by the time Cassie realized the trouble her father had gotten them into, they were verging on bankruptcy.

That's when Marc had stepped in and bought the vineyards and winery, renaming it Intimate Wines, but keeping Cassie on as winemaker. He'd hired a new vine-yard manager, Nate Dunagan, from a large winery along the central coast of California. Nate was now Cassie's husband, and they were expecting their first child.

Marc had deeded a small plot of grapes and both the family house and guesthouse back to Cassie when she and Nate were married, which kept the Tangled Vines wines alive.

Marc wasn't able to spend much time at the place, not as much as Mandy was sure he wanted, so this totally unexpected visit was a rare chance for both of them to enjoy the beautiful wine country and actually relax for a few days. Relax while checking out caterers, bands, and anything else Kaz and Jake needed for their wedding.

"We're going to have to look into security, too. Ben's going to be busy as a groomsman." Marc smiled when he said that. Jake had asked Marc to serve as best man. Even Ben had agreed. Marc had been here for Jake while his older brother Ben was soldiering around the globe.

"We'll need someone to deal with the paparazzi." Mandy cracked up when she said it, but it was true. Kaz's fame had exploded across the country with two high-profile advertising campaigns, her nationally covered kidnapping and heroic rescue, and her sassy sense of humor. She'd become quite a media star in a very short time, with talk of movie deals and lots of gossip mag coverage. "I never once imagined having to worry about paparazzi," Mandy said, "but I bet they'll be even worse after this Italy trip."

"You never know. Just be glad we don't live in LA." Marc glanced at Mandy and she laughed at the forlorn expression on his face.

"I take it you had to deal with that after the *People* article came out?"

"Oh, yeah. Like an idiot I agreed to go down for a couple of interviews. Never again. I like my peace and quiet—and anonymity—a lot."

By the time they reached the vineyard with a couple of bags filled with Mexican food—which Mandy thought looked like enough for an army but Marc assured her was just about right for the four of them—the sun had gone behind the western hills and the valley was bathed in shadows.

Marc opened the car door for Mandy and helped her carry the bags up the steps to the house. Cassie met

them at the door—a much larger Cassie than when he'd
seen her last month. "Wow. You've grown."

Laughing, she opened the door wide and stood aside
for the two of them. "That I have, and no, there's only
one in there. A very big one, I think."

Nate walked out from the back of the house, grabbed
a beer out of the refrigerator, and handed it to Marc.
"What's scary is that she's still got three months to go."

"It's going to be a long summer, my love." She tilted
her head and kissed his chin, and then she and Mandy
got the food out of the bags and the silverware on the
table.

Nate handed a glass of wine to Mandy. "Since the
pregnant lady isn't drinking, she wants all of us to
suffer."

"Thank you for the rescue." Mandy held her glass
high. "Here's to little whatsit and a perfectly wonderful
future for the entire Dunagan clan."

Marc and Nate raised their bottles of beer, Mandy
sipped her wine, and Cassie merely sighed and stared at
her glass of ice water. Then she glanced at Nate. "Birth
control, Nathan. That's what this no-drinking policy is.
It's a subversive form of birth control."

It was a long time before Marc fell asleep. Mandy slept
soundly beside him, her nude body warm and damp
from the sweat of their exertion, while his mind spun its
usual circles as he wound down before sleep. He'd learned
he couldn't force memories, but he wondered if thinking
about things before he fell asleep might help push his
dreams in the direction he wanted them to take.

Mandy turned toward him in her sleep. She tucked
her cheek against his throat and curled her fingers in the
trail of hair heading downward from his stomach. Her

intimate touch brought a bit of life back to his neglected dick. He lay there, sort of reveling in the knowledge that he loved Mandy, that she loved him, and they could make love anytime they wanted.

Well, any time within reason. She was absolutely exhausted tonight, but she'd caught up on everything in the office, and they'd had more than enough emotional stuff over the past twenty-four hours to wear anyone out. He needed answers and he wanted them now—patience was definitely not one of his better qualities. He wasn't going to learn anything new unless he actively went looking for it. With that thought in mind, he drifted, forcing himself to think of that last night in his parents' bedroom. Wondering what happened next.

The dream was so vivid he thought he was awake and actually remembering something he'd thought forgotten. At some point his conscious mind surfaced enough to convince him that no, this was merely a dream, but a dream he'd requested, in a way.

And once again he was that terrified little boy trying to understand what was happening.

He'd been hiding behind the bed for so long, but he thought now might be a good time to sneak back to his own bed. Mommy would come in and wake him in the morning, and everything would be okay. Well, as okay as it could be with Daddy so angry all the time. He started to crawl out of the room when the worst thing ever happened.

"Where the hell do you think you're going, Marcus? Get back in here. Now."

He was shivering. Shivering and shaking so hard he could barely stand, but he knew better than to disobey. Daddy had started spanking him a few weeks ago with his big leather belt instead of his hand, and it hurt. A lot. But he stood very still while Daddy stared at him.

Well, still except for the shaking. He waited for Daddy to start yelling but when he talked, he was even scarier. His voice was really quiet and sort of flat, but he told Marcus to get dressed and wait in his room. Even though it was the middle of the night! Then he said, "We have to go for a ride."

He remembered getting in the back seat of Daddy's big car, but he must have fallen asleep, because he thought he heard Mommy talking to him, but all she said was that she loved him and that she would always love him. He already knew that. Silly Mommy.

The next thing he remembered, Daddy was turning the car onto another dark road, but this one was bumpy. When they stopped, there weren't any lights or houses around. There was barely any light from the moon, and he was afraid. Was Daddy going to leave him here? He'd been asleep on the back seat, and he didn't even have his seatbelt on. Mommy never let him in the car without it, but he heard a noise and peeked out the back window. The trunk was open and the light inside it was on. He saw Daddy take a shovel out and lean it against the car. Then he lifted a bundle of something heavy over his shoulder that was wrapped in the comforter off Mommy and Daddy's bed. He picked up the shovel too, and walked down a little trail. Marc watched him through the side window, but it was steamy, so he rolled it down, but Daddy heard him. He stopped, turned around, and stared at Marc. "Stay in the car," he said. "Roll that window up, and don't get out."

Marc waited in the car for a long time. He must have fallen asleep again, because he heard the trunk slam shut, and then Daddy was getting back in the car.

"I have to go peepee," he said. "But it's dark."

Daddy said a bad word, but he got out and opened the door for him and told Marc to go right there. There was enough light from inside the car to show that he peed on the side of a big rock that had a tree growing out of one side. Then he got back into the back seat, but this time he put his seatbelt on. He felt a lot braver, now that he wasn't worried about wetting his pants, so he asked Daddy a question. "Why did we come here?"

"I had to take care of some garbage," his father said. "I buried some stinking garbage."

They drove again, and the road was really bumpy. Then they turned onto a smoother road. Later, he remembered a bridge that was way up high, and lights in a valley that seemed a lot lower than the bridge they crossed, but it was dark out here on this road. He must have fallen asleep again, because he didn't have any more memories. None at all.

Marc thought he'd only slept for a few minutes, but when he blinked and finally opened his eyes, sunlight was streaming through the blinds over the bedroom windows, and Mandy was coming out of the bathroom. Her hair was all wet and slicked back from her face and she didn't have on a bit of makeup. She wore one of his T-shirts, but nothing else.

His heart thudded in his chest, but he figured it had to pump like crazy to fill up his suddenly engorged dick. Amazing how that worked. Just like that, he was horny and hard and almost desperate to hold her. She could do all that to him with nothing more than a smile.

Mandy was amazing. She was absolutely beautiful, and she was smiling just for him.

She crawled across the bed, leaned close, and kissed him. She tasted of toothpaste and sex, and he wanted her. Now.

Straddling him, she leaned forward and kissed him again, this time with tongue and teeth and lips, with her hands stroking his chest, her thighs clasped tightly against his hips, and the hot center of her planted firmly on his erection.

When he finally came up for air, they were both grinning like fools. "Can we arrange for this kind of wake up every morning?" he said. "It works really well for me."

She raised up and set his cock free before settling back down with it rising between her legs. "I sort of got that feeling. It looks a bit naked, though." She reached for a condom, stared at it a moment, but then she handed it to him. "The last time I put one on you, it broke. I think you better do the honors. Which reminds me. Saturday it'll be a week since that sucker broke. I'll do a pregnancy test then to be sure, but I think we're fine."

He kept his mouth shut, though in the back of his mind he kept imagining her with his child growing inside. She'd stay for sure, then. He raised his eyes and watched her watching him when he grabbed the packet, opened it, and suited up. No. He wanted her to choose to stay with him out of love, not because of a child. And not because of some stupid business contract, but because she loved him too much to leave.

Still, the thought of one day making love to her without any barrier between them was his greatest fantasy of the moment, but neither of them was ready for that yet. He knew that time was coming, though. He could wait until it was the only choice they had. For now, this was truly amazing, and once he was covered, he palmed Mandy's butt and slowly settled her back over his highly impatient dick.

She wiggled a bit to get everything where it belonged, and then she just sat there. Clenching and releasing her inner muscles.

Damn. She felt absolutely wonderful, her sheath warm and so tight, the rippling clench of all those feminine muscles doing absolutely amazing things to him. He groaned and raised his hips, lifting her, going as deep inside her as was physically possible, and then he just held her there with his back arched and his dick planted. Mandy supported herself on her knees, but those rhythmic contractions never ceased.

They weren't moving their bodies at all, but his balls had clenched up tight between his legs and a sheen of sweat covered his body. Then an absolutely magnificent thing happened. Mandy climaxed. He hadn't moved, but she'd climaxed merely from flexing those amazing muscles around his erection. Her back arched, her fingers tightened on his forearms and she cried out as he clasped her hips and drove into her, thrusting hard and fast, following some inner need to claim her now, to remind her that she belonged to him.

That she would always be his.

His own climax hit harder than he'd ever experienced, a deep welling of sensation, a shocking connection that shot from his spine to his balls and practically exploded from him. Mandy folded over, bending at the waist and lying across his chest while his hips continued an involuntary thrust and retreat long after he'd reached his own peak and moved well beyond.

He wrapped his arms around her, held her close against his thundering heart, realized he'd started to doze off, that Mandy was still limp in his embrace. He kissed her lips, her cheek, the curve of her jaw. "You okay, babe?"

"Hmmm. Oh, yeah. Definitely okay." She raised her head and he had to admit, the glazed expression in her eyes, her lips swollen from his kisses, the rosy flush across her breasts and throat, were a rush all on their own.

She certainly looked like a well-loved woman.

He hoped she felt that way as well, because every

time they came together, he knew it would never, ever be enough.

Mandy left her window down, well aware that her hair was going to be a mess by the time they got where they were going, wherever that was. Marc had said he wanted to take a ride this morning, but instead of heading toward town, he'd taken the road that curved up the hill just west of the dam at Lake Sonoma.

In fact, he took it quite fast in his sleek little Tesla, while wearing a huge grin on his face, but there was no traffic and the sky was a perfect robin's egg blue. They reached a point where a left would eventually take them to the coast, and straight ahead would go out Rockpile Road.

Marc paused at the stop sign, then went straight.

"Where are we going?"

He shook his head. "I'm not sure, but I had another dream last night, a really different one, and something about this road feels familiar to me."

"Why didn't you say anything?"

Just then the road straightened out ahead of them. Mandy realized they were approaching a long bridge that appeared to cross an arm of the reservoir behind the dam. Marc pulled to the side of the road and drove a short way to a vista point overlooking the bridge and lake. He stopped the car, turned it off, and rested his forearms on the steering wheel. "I didn't say anything because I didn't remember the dream until we got to the stop sign back there. That's when I realized why I felt as if I needed to come this way.

"This is just so weird, Mandy." He opened the door and got out of the car. So did Mandy, and she walked around to the front of the vehicle and slipped an arm around his waist.

"What do you remember?"

"I was four in the dream, and I was in my parents' room that same night, after it had gotten quiet. I tried to sneak out and my father caught me. I was terrified of him. In my dream, I remembered that he had beaten me recently with his belt." He shook his head. "I don't know if that's true or just something I imagined, but the sense of terror was real."

He stared toward the bridge, his arm draped over Mandy's shoulders, a stance that would appear relaxed to anyone who saw them. He was anything but. She felt the tension in his muscles, in the shuddering flex of his biceps against her neck, in the defensive way he held himself. She wrapped her other arm around his waist, hugging him close, pressing herself against him. Telling him without words that she was here for him, that she wasn't leaving.

"I think she's buried somewhere out near this road." His voice cracked, emotion evident in every word he spoke. "No. I don't just think it. I know she's here. He took me with him and we drove a long way. I fell asleep, but I remember stopping in the dark while he got a shovel out of the trunk along with something heavy wrapped in the comforter off their bed. I remember wondering why he'd brought it. I fell asleep again, but when I woke up he was putting the shovel back in the trunk. I had to take a piss and he let me out of the car. The dome light was on, enough for me to see what I was doing. I remembered peeing against a big rock with a tree growing out of one side. That was over thirty years ago, but I remember the tree and the rock. And I remember when we left, we crossed this bridge. Most of all, I remember what he said when I asked him what we had come out here for."

Marc's shoulders slumped. He turned and wrapped

his arms around her, hugging her so tightly she could barely breathe. "He said he had to bury some garbage. In my dream, his words were, "I had to bury some stinking garbage."

Mandy leaned away so that she could see his face, his ravaged face, eyes filled with tears, lips pressed tightly together.

He inhaled deeply, slowly let it out. "She's out here, somewhere. He killed her, and he buried her body where no one would find her."

"I don't know, Marc. You saw the rock in your dream. You saw the tree. It's mostly oaks out here, and while thirty years is a long time for us, it's not long at all for an oak tree." She tugged his hand. "Let's take a drive. See if anything looks familiar."

He glanced at their linked hands, pulled Mandy close, and kissed her. "Thank you," he said. "I love you, and that sounds like a terrific idea."

CHAPTER 7

They'd gone all the way to the end of the road—around ten miles before it became a private dirt road—without any luck. There had been so many changes to the rolling, tree-studded hills. Vineyards grew where sheep had once grazed, and vines marched in neat, trellised rows across the landscape. Marc drove slowly, studied the terrain to the right, since he remembered his father making a left turn from a dirt road to pavement when they left, but there was no sense of familiarity at all.

Mandy reached across the console and took his hand. "It's been over thirty years, Marc. A lot of changes have been made. Cassie said the vineyards up here are relatively new."

He nodded, staring at the hills rolling off into the distance. "Once they started putting vineyards in up here in the 1990s, all kinds of changes could have been made. The tree could be long gone and even the rock might have been moved. What good are a little kid's bad dreams?"

"Don't give up. Cassie mentioned the museum in town. They're doing a history of this area since the dam was built. It's not open until later in the week, but if we're still here, we can stop by. You might see a photo that jogs more memories, might run into someone who remembers a big oak tree growing out of a rock. Were you right on this road when your dad stopped the car, or did he pull off on a side road? Because there aren't too many of those. That might help you narrow it down."

He shook his head. "I remember there was a long stretch of bumpy road, so it might have been a dirt road. Then he turned left off the bumpy stretch to go home. I was a little kid and scared to death. He could have been making a U-turn for all I know."

"But you might know." She squeezed his hand. "Maybe that's something Alden can help you recall."

"Maybe," he said. But he didn't sound convinced.

They had the list of caterers Kaz had emailed to Marc. Mandy called as they headed back into town, setting up brief appointments for the rest of the day. By five o'clock, they'd narrowed the list down to three. One of them was a Thai restaurant in town that Kaz loved.

Mandy called Cassie. "Okay, we're in town and picking up takeout. Do you like Thai?"

"Love it. Buy everything on the menu."

"We're in Marc's Tesla, not a U-Haul." Laughing, she added, "Get specific, preggo."

She had a long list by the time they pulled into the little restaurant. Marc ordered a beer for himself and a glass of wine for Mandy while they waited for their food. He sat there staring out the front window for at least a full minute, sipping his beer. "Would you be averse to driving back to the city if I can get in to see Alden tomorrow? I have a feeling I could remember more with help. We could go down in the morning, have the appointment, and come back tomorrow evening." He turned and smiled at her. "We still need to check on bands and security."

"Sure," she said. "I don't mind going back in. What kind of music?"

"Kaz likes blue grass, Jake likes jazz."

Mandy laughed. "Jazzy bluegrass? Is there such a thing?"

"Ya never know." He pulled out his cell phone and typed it into the search engine. "Yep, there is, but I might have to fly them in from New Orleans."

"I doubt that's in Kaz's budget."

"Kaz doesn't have to know. Neither does Jake." He glanced away and blushed.

Mandy reached across the table and tapped his chin. "You're blushing." She laughed. "You have to tell me."

He shook his head, laughing. "Yes, ma'am. The thing is, Jake's the closest friend I've ever had." He took her hands in his and stared at their fingers. "Well, before you, that is. I guess that sort of moves him back to number two, but now that he has Kaz, that's only right. Anyway, they don't know that their wedding is my gift to them."

"That's a pretty special gift, but why aren't you telling them?"

"Because then Kaz would want to cut corners, and so would Jake. They'd feel like they were taking advantage, but they're not if they just plan what they want. They're both making good money now, so I doubt that they're at all concerned about cost. I don't want them to be."

Sometimes he was just so thoughtful that she'd forget he was a smart businessman who'd earned a fortune by virtue of brains and hard work. She stared at him for a moment. "You're so busy looking out for your friends, Marc. Who looks out for you?"

The waitress walked out before he could answer and

handed a large cardboard box to Marc. He'd already paid for everything, so Mandy held the door for him and then opened the back door on the car. Marc strapped the box onto the back seat with a seatbelt and then joined Mandy in the car. He backed out of the parking space, drove out of the lot, and took the on-ramp to the freeway that would get them to the Dry Creek Road exit.

Once he'd merged into the heavy late afternoon traffic, Marc said, "You asked me who looks out for me. That's your job." His smile was actually sort of loopy. "Think you can handle it?"

She folded her hands across her chest and said, "I can handle anything you toss at me, Marcus."

"Good." He sighed. His smile had disappeared by the time he checked the rearview mirror and cut over to the right for the exit. "Because I have a feeling I'm going to be tossing a hell of a lot your way before this is over."

Alden said he'd make time to see them if they could get in early, which meant getting up at the crack of dawn and dealing with the commute traffic, but they arrived at his office a little after eight. When they walked by the closed coffee shop, it appeared that renovations were already starting to turn it into something else.

"Wow. It looks like someone else has already taken over." She paused long enough to read a note on the door. "It's going to be a café with a bakery. At least Alden will be able to get his coffee."

Marc tugged her hand and they walked to the hypnotherapist's office. "Does it bother you, seeing it changed?"

"Not really. It's not the shop I miss as much as the people who stopped in all the time. That and the fact that I feel as if the owner treated me badly, but I only have myself to blame. People can't use you unless you let them. I was a class A enabler with her."

She wrapped both her hands around his arm as they paused at the door to the office. "You, of course, may use me as you see fit. I'm all yours."

He raised an eyebrow as they went up the stairs. "All mine? I think I like that." He pushed open the door to the office. Alden was going through a file cabinet, but he turned and greeted them.

"Good morning. I hope the traffic wasn't too bad."

"We gave ourselves plenty of time." Marc shook his hand. "I appreciate your meeting with us on such short notice."

Alden closed the cabinet and led them into his office. "Your dream intrigues me, the fact you suggested that you wanted to dream before you fell asleep, and yet you still dreamt it from the point of view of your four-year-old self. Possibly we can learn even more, now that you're aware that the event wasn't something you did yourself, but rather one that you observed when you were still too young to understand exactly what you saw."

Marc took a seat on the sofa, and Mandy settled beside him. "I thought about that," he said. "I realized that a four year-old-in 1984 was so innocent compared to children today. Kids now are exposed to violence on television and movies, even video games that aren't age appropriate. If I were four now and saw someone strangling a woman, I think I'd know exactly what was going on. I would know my mother wasn't going to come in and wake me in the morning. When I was little, we weren't programmed to think like that."

"Sad but true." Alden glanced at the picture of his wife and kids. "Their childhood was still relatively innocent, but already marred by violence in the media.

Thankfully, not in their lives." He stared a moment longer before turning back to Marc. "Are you ready to get started?"

When Marc nodded, Alden turned on the recorder and focused on Marc. "Are you comfortable? Excellent. Now I want you to close your eyes and think of a number . . ."

Mandy was surprised at how quickly Marc went into his trance. It seemed mere seconds before he was sitting there, completely relaxed, holding her hand. His eyes were closed, but he responded easily to Alden's softly spoken assurances of safety.

"You told me about a dream you had, Marc. Are you comfortable discussing it further with me? The same commands we used in our prior appointment will work."

Marc's forefinger tapped the arm of the sofa.

"Excellent. You dreamed about a ride you took with your father. Just the two of you? You may speak now, to answer me."

"I don't know."

"Who else do you think was with you?"

"My mother. In the dream, I was sure I heard her voice."

"What did she say to you, Marcus?"

He smiled and nodded his head. "She said she loved me. That she would always love me, but I already knew that. Then I went back to sleep."

"Later, when the car stopped, where were you?"

"It was really dark."

"Were you in a city?"

He shook his head. Mandy's hand was sweating where their fingers were clasped. It had to be her. Marc was completely calm, but she wasn't about to let go. Not now.

"Were you in the country?"

"I think so. There weren't any houses around. Not much of a moon, either."

He asked Marc more questions, retracing the dream scene by scene as Marc had relayed it to him earlier. But then he asked Marc to describe what was outside the car.

"But it's dark," he said. "I can't see."

"You have a flashlight, Marc. It's magical, and it shows you what's hidden in the shadows. Do you have it in your hand?"

Marc lifted the hand that held Mandy's. She shot a quick glance at Alden, but he merely nodded.

"Yes. I have it."

"Shine it outside the car. Tell me what you see."

"I see Daddy. He's digging a hole."

"Is there anything around him?"

"The pile of garbage he said he had to bury. It's wrapped in the blanket off Mommy and Daddy's bed. I wonder why he's throwing it away?"

"I don't know, Marc. Maybe he made a mistake. Are there any buildings or trees or big rocks around? Anything that you might use as a landmark to find the hole? What if Mommy wants her blanket back? Do you think you can find it for her?"

"There's a post in the ground where we turned onto this road. It has numbers on it. Would that help?"

"It might. What numbers are they?"

Marc rattled off a string of numbers that Alden quickly wrote down. He read them back to Marc. "Is that right?"

"Yes.

Mandy's gasp startled even her. "That's an address. I saw mail boxes with addresses on them—they're long. All five digit numbers. Fifteen thousand, seventeen thousand. I can't . . ."

Alden held his finger up to silence her. She remembered she wasn't supposed to speak and clamped her lips shut. Marc turned to her, still deeply in the trance state. "Mommy always said I was very smart."

"You are," Alden said. "Marc, is there anything else you remember about your dream?

"No. No more."

"Why don't you close your eyes and rest? I'm going to count to five, and you will slowly awaken until I say five, when you will come fully awake. You'll remember everything we discussed. You've done very well, Marc. Very well indeed." He paused and then slowly counted to five.

On five, Marc blinked and turned to Mandy. After a moment of disorientation, he said, "We need to go back. I want to see if we can find the rock at that address." He stood and turned to Alden. "Thank you so much for agreeing to see us on such short notice."

"Any time." He shook Marc's hand. "Your story is fascinating."

"When Mandy first told me about you, I thought she was nuts." Marc turned to her. She stuck out her tongue, but he just leaned over and kissed her. "I'll let you know what we find."

"Please do. Which winery is yours? My wife has been asking me to take her to Healdsburg. She loves the shops and restaurants, and we'd really like to come out and try the wine at your place."

Marc grabbed one of his business cards and wrote the name and address on the back. "If you come this week, we should still be there. Call me and we can give you a tour. There's a really neat wine cave that's not open to the public."

As they walked back to the car, Mandy tugged on his hand. "I haven't even seen the wine cave. I forgot you had one."

"I promise to give you the private, after-hours tour. Will that make up for my error?"

"Possibly."

She was laughing when he opened the car door and she got in. Marc came around to the driver's side, but his phone rang as he sat down. "Ted. How's it going? Have you learned anything? Mandy's with me. I'm putting you on speaker."

"Hi Mandy. And yes, Marc, I have. I've sent an email to your office account with the details. That was the only one I had, but I can give you the abbreviated version if you like."

"Go ahead." He reached for Mandy's hand and held on.

"Your mother's name was Elizabeth Cole Marchand. Her nickname was Bett. She was the daughter of Marilee Alice Watts and Barnabas, aka Buck, Rogers Marchand." He spelled it out and added, "pronounced *Marshawn*, both from Boston, Massachusetts. Marilee was a young socialite and Buck was pretty much a professional playboy. They both came from money. I can't find any records of either of them ever working. Your mother was their only child. Marilee and Buck—your grandparents—were killed in a plane crash when she was eight years old. Buck was the pilot and they went down off of Cape Cod. The plane and their bodies were recovered—they're buried in a cemetery in Bedford. I'm not certain why, though I think the maternal grandmother's family is buried there. She is as well.

"Bett was raised by her maternal grandmother, Alicia Coburn Watts, widow of Jerome Watts, which I assume is the source of your middle name, Marc. Anyway, Alicia died in 1979 when Bett was twenty-five. Your mother married Steven Reed a few weeks later. I don't know if they'd been dating or had known each other very long, but I did learn that your mother went into the marriage with a very large cumulative trust fund, the only heir of both her parents and her grandmother. I don't know if your father was aware that the way all three trusts were written, she was unable to access the money until she was thirty years old. We also don't know the date of her death, but she was very close to thirty if she died when you were four years old. She would have just turned thirty, or have been about to turn thirty."

There was nothing but silence. Mandy watched Marc, but his face was absolutely blank. She had no idea what he was thinking. Finally, he glanced her way and then stared at the phone. "Were you able to find out anything about the money? Did he get it?"

"No. The three trust funds are still intact. Attempts have been made to access the money on numerous occasions, but the persons claiming to be your mother could not prove their identity to the court's satisfaction. The money is still intact." There was a long pause. "Marc, I know how much money you have, and the amount of funds in these three trusts makes you look like a pauper. I imagine your father thought he would be able to get his hands on it, or maybe he lost his temper and killed her without planning to. Does he have that kind of temper?"

"Explosive. Yes. That makes sense, though. He was so close. Has he ever tried to have her declared dead?"

"Nothing I can find, and there's a provision in the trust that keeps the funds intact for her 'issue.' Her children, and that would be you. Look, I'm going to come out ahead of schedule, if that's okay with you. I'll just get a room at the same extended-stay I stayed in before. My testimony is through for the proceedings here for now, and I'd really like to be closer to this material. How have you done with the memories?"

"So well it's scary, Ted. I think we're close."

"Be careful. Your father is in some serious financial trouble. There might be gambling involved. I'm not positive, but it's not looking good for him. He's got some fairly important people angry with him. He's pulled a few scams that left some really pissed off folks with more power than I think he realized at the time. He's probably feeling pretty desperate about now. Watch your back."

"Advice taken. Mandy and I are making a quick run by my office and then we're headed back to the winery. I want to do some snooping around. Ted, I might know where he buried her."

"How the fuck did . . . ?"

"Call me as soon as you get in."

"Do you mind going by the office before we head back to the winery?" Marc kept his eyes on the road, but his mind was spinning. The bastard. His father might have planned his mother's death from the very beginning.

"Not at all. You need to download the information Ted sent."

"Thank you."

Mandy grabbed his hand and he held on. He'd been holding on to her a lot over the past few days. She'd become his anchor, so solid and strong, someone he'd quickly grown to count on. Did she have any idea just how much she meant to him? Crap, she certainly hadn't signed on for anything like this.

"When do you think Ted will be here?"

"Not soon enough." He tried to laugh. Sounded more like a snort. "I wouldn't be surprised if he shows up tomorrow or the next day."

"I hope so. I'm not used to Lola and Ben being gone,

and with Kaz and Jake out of the country, there's no one else to bounce ideas off of." She shot him a smile. "We're all pretty good at collaborative thinking."

"I don't know, Mandy. You're pretty good all on your own."

"Do you think so? I feel like I'm just dead weight, like I'm not helping you at all."

He didn't say anything. Not until he'd pulled into the parking garage and turned off the car. Then he unhooked his seatbelt, turned, and wrapped his arms around Mandy. "Babe, I can't imagine doing any of this without you. Think about it . . . those dreams have haunted me for years, and then you come along and suddenly I've got answers, I've got a chance to find out the truth about my mother, and maybe even a chance to lead a decent life without fear or guilt or, most important, hating a woman who deserved so much better. Because of you, Mandy. You are the furthest thing from dead weight I can imagine."

He kissed her and wondered just how private this garage actually was, but he quit thinking with his dick long enough to carefully end the kiss and back away. "I hope you appreciate how hard it was not to start unbuttoning and unhooking just then."

She practically exploded in laughter. "And here I thought you were the shy, quiet type."

"A carefully manufactured façade, my dear." He leaned close, kissed her quickly, and then got out of the car, walked around, opened her door, took her hand, helped her out. "Let's go on up, see what we can catch Theo doing, grab the notes from Ted, and get back to the winery. It feels much more sane there, don't you think?"

"Agreed." She grabbed his hand and the two of them raced up the stairs.

As soon as they hit the foyer in front of Reed Industries, they both heard shouting coming from inside. "What the hell?" Marc reached for the door.

"Be careful. That sounds like your father."

"You're right." He paused by the door and listened, but it was difficult to make out what they were saying. "Will you wait here?"

"Absolutely not."

Marc just shook his head. "That's right. I've heard how you faced down a guy with a gun."

"C'mon. We go in like you own the place. Because you do."

He was actually laughing when Mandy shoved the door open. The argument was coming from Marc's office. Clearly, Theo had had enough of whatever Marc's father was telling him to do.

Marc and Mandy paused just outside the door. Steve Reed had his back to them, and Theo never even blinked when the two of them stepped into his line of sight. Instead, he leaned closer and got into Reed's space.

"I asked you, Mr. Reed, how you got into this office. You've been told you're not welcome here."

"I have every right to be here. My son gave me permission to come on the premises to pick up some papers. You are interfering with his orders. Now I am going to get what I came after, and . . ."

"And just what would that be?"

Reed spun around. "What the . . ."

"Get out of here now, before I have you charged with trespassing. As it is, I intend to get a restraining order if that's what it takes to keep you out of my life."

"What has gotten into you?" His father stalked across the room and poked Marc in the chest. "You've always been a prick, but something's put a bee up your ass. Is it her?" He glared at Mandy. "Get a little pussy and you . . ."

"Shut the fuck up." He'd always backed down when his father got aggressive. Knowing what he knew now, it was probably some form of PTSD from being beaten as a child. From witnessing his mother's death. From so many things he might never know, but on some level, Marc realized that whatever had held him submissive to his father, snapped.

He shoved against the man's poking finger, shoved him back and kept shoving, pushing Reed until he was backed up against the desk. Both Theo and Mandy merely stepped back, out of the way. Steven Reed looked perplexed—Marc knew the bastard had no idea what had gotten into his son.

"First, you don't ever speak to Ms. Monroe like that. Never. Do you understand me? And a bee up my ass? I dunno . . . tell me, anything about Rockpile Road ring a bell, Daddy? A long drive on a dark night with a four-year-old boy in the back seat? Something large and bulky wrapped in my mother's favorite comforter the same night she disappeared? She always loved that blanket. And she loved me. She had no need to take the money and run. She could buy and sell you ten times over, so what was it you did that night so many years ago? Don't want to talk about it, eh? Trust me, you will. Now get the fuck out of my office and don't come back. I don't want to see you again. Not. Ever. Got it?"

His father stared at him. The color had leeched from his face, and he looked crazy enough to kill. Marc grabbed him by the front of his shirt, twisted, and lifted him to his toes. Got right in his face, and very calmly said, "Get out. Now. And don't come back."

Reed's hands were clenched into tight fists and he glared at both Marc and Mandy. Then he shoved himself free of Marc's grasp, stepped around him, pushing

Mandy out of the way before she had time to move, and stormed out the door.

Marc grabbed her arm. Steadied her. "You okay? Crap." He sucked in huge draughts of air. Felt as if he'd run a mile, been in a fight. Climbed a mountain. He'd never stood up to his father, but then he'd never known what a disgusting waste of humanity the bastard was.

It took him a few more deep breaths to calm down to a point where he could actually talk without gasping for air. He glanced down and realized he still had such a tight grip on Mandy's arm he'd probably left bruises. He let go as if she burned him. "Damn, babe. I'm so sorry. Did I hurt you?" He brushed his fingers over the red marks on her forearm. "I didn't mean to grab you so hard. I was afraid you'd fall." He shook his head, feeling like a complete jerk. "I'm sorry. I guess I sort of lost it."

Mandy grabbed his hand. "That you did, but you did it with style." She planted an unexpected kiss on his mouth, but she pulled away before he could take it any further, and glanced over her shoulder at Theo. "You might want to explain to Theo what we've found out, just so he knows what kind of nut we're dealing with."

"Good idea. You had lunch, Theo?"

The big man had walked over to the front door and locked it. He turned and shook his head. "No, and I didn't have time to pack one this morning. I was going to order takeout. Get it delivered."

"Whatever you order, get enough for Mandy and me and put all of it on the company account. We have some work to do before it arrives, and then we'll let you know just what the hell is going on."

"What do you want? Mexican, Thai, Chinese, Greek . . ."

Mandy laughed. "What I really want is a hamburger

and fries. After this morning, I need greasy comfort food. Is that okay with you, Theo?"

"American food? I love it." He patted his flat belly. "Unfortunately, it loves me too well, but it sounds wonderful. And you, Marc?"

"Cheeseburger. I haven't had one in ages."

Theo went back into his office to order while Marc grabbed Mandy's hand and tugged her into his office. He found Ted's email and pages of attachments. By the time they had duplicate copies of everything printed, sorted, and stapled, their lunch was waiting by the locked office door. Marc held the door for Mandy while she retrieved the insulated carryall and brought it inside.

Grabbing the bag, he headed toward the rarely used conference room next to Theo's office. Mandy poked her head in the door. "C'mon, Theo. Soup's on."

Marc gave Theo the entire story while they ate their way through way too many French fries and huge hamburgers from a gourmet café a few blocks over.

Mandy cleaned up the trash while Theo grilled Marc on some of the details.

"Marc, I had no idea what kind of shit you've been dealing with. None. This is actually kind of scary, and now the bastard knows what you know."

Marc shook his head. "That was such a stupid move on my part. Ted cautioned me not to tell him I was aware of anything, but I guess my adult brain wasn't in gear."

"It's understandable." Mandy stood behind him and rubbed his shoulders. "Everything we've learned so far is leading to one conclusion, that he killed your mother. Marc, the man is a murderer and a liar. Personally, I think you've behaved admirably. Although, if we'd been smart, we would have held off for a few more minutes and let Theo take a swing at him."

She smiled serenely at Theo. "You did have that 'I'm gonna kill the bastard' look on your face."

"That I did." He glanced toward the door. "I'd gone down to the parking garage to grab my cell phone. I left it in the car this morning, and I felt sort of naked without it. When I got back up here, I caught your father in your office. I have no idea how he got in here, because the door to your office and the front door had both been locked."

"Either he's got keys or he picked the locks. I'd guess the latter. I'll have an alarm put on both the front door and my office. Probably should have the place swept for bugs while you're at it. Do you want to make that call, Theo? I think you have better connections than I do."

"I'll take care of it. You headed back to the winery?"

Marc nodded. "Now that we have Ted's paperwork. You met him last month when all that mess was going down with Ben Lowell and Lola, didn't you?" He stood and began gathering up the papers.

"I did. Hell of a good guy."

"I'm glad you think so." He glanced at Theo. "I told you I've hired him. He'll be starting here as soon as he's ready. Have you had a chance to do anything about his office?"

Theo nodded. "A crew came by this morning to get measurements. They're going to use a prefab setup that's excellent quality. The computer equipment, screens, printer, the electronics and all the surveillance equipment he might need were delivered about an hour ago. Damn." Theo shook his head. "I bet that's how your father got inside. Just followed the deliverymen. They were in and out all morning carting stuff up here. Once in, your father probably picked the lock to your office. I wouldn't have even noticed him because I was working in the back, showing the guys where to set things. Anyway, the entire unit should be installed tonight. It's costing a little extra, but the manager assured me they could have the entire thing up and running by tomorrow morning. I figure it's the least we can do." Laughing, he added, "I still can't believe you're bringing in your own, personal FBI agent."

Mandy brought a damp paper towel to the table and wiped it down. "Why not?" she said. "Doesn't every young entrepreneur have at least one?"

Marc high-fived Theo. Mandy tossed the towel in the trash, and grabbed Marc's hand. "Are you ready? There's a winery calling my name. Specifically a large glass of zin."

"Mine too." He hugged her close. "Call the alarm company, Theo. I want this place covered so that anyone breaking in can't do it quietly, and I'll want it set up to report to my phone and eventually Ted's and Ben's if there's an incident. I really don't want Reed getting in here again. And thanks for moving so quickly on the office for Ted. I have a feeling he'll be here before we know it. If there's anything else you can think of that he might need, get it. Don't worry about the cost. I trust you to do it right."

"Thank you. Works for me. And you can put me on that notification list, too. I really dislike the guy. You sure he's your father?"

"When he was younger, he could have been my twin. But hopefully, the only similarity is our looks."

"He looks like hell now."

Marc wrapped his arm around Mandy and held her close. "Yeah, well, he's definitely earned it."

CHAPTER 8

When Mandy called to ask what they could pick up for dinner, Cassie told them not to stop, that Nate already had something planned, so they drove straight out to the winery. It was almost five by the time they pulled up in front of the cottage.

Marc had added a charging station for the Tesla in front of the cottage as well as one by the tasting room for customers, so Mandy unlocked the front door to the cottage while Marc plugged in the car. Then he followed her inside so they could get cleaned up for dinner. After the episode with his father, he felt dirty. As if the man's touch had somehow tainted him.

While Mandy went in to shower, Marc spread the paperwork across the kitchen counter and tried to make sense of all the info Ted had collected. He tried concentrating on the pages, but the only image he saw was the one in his head—Mandy's sleek body beneath the shower spray.

He held off as long as he could, which wasn't long at all. He stared at one of the pages for a moment, turned and headed to the bedroom, toeing his shoes off, pulling his shirt over his head and slipping out of his pants. By the time he joined Mandy beneath the spray, she was getting ready to wash her hair.

"Hey. Want company?"

She laughed. "Took your time, didn't you? I thought you'd never show up."

"I was trying to be a gentleman." He kissed her shoulder. "My inner horndog won out."

"Wow. I had no idea you even had an inner horndog. I'm impressed."

"As well you should be." He slipped in behind her and propped her hands against the tile wall, gently massaging shampoo into her scalp while trying to ignore her perfect bottom pressing against his erection. "But at least he's a very well-mannered horndog." He rinsed the shampoo out, added conditioner and worked that into her silky strands.

"That's only to be expected," she said, but then she wiggled her ass against him, and her soft moan at the end absolutely blew the overall effect of her snarky comment.

He rinsed the conditioner out of her hair without another word, but he had to admit her moans of pleasure were good for his ego.

She turned off the water and he toweled her dry, starting at her wet head and slowly working his way to her toes. A mere week ago, he couldn't have imagined doing this with Mandy, feeling so comfortable loving her, touching her. He wanted to wallow in their natural intimacy, the fact that this felt absolutely right, but Nate and Cassie were expecting them.

He handed the towel to Mandy so she could return the favor. She started carefully, drying his hair, his shoulders, his back and chest. He noticed she paid close attention to the parts between his thighs. By the time she'd worked her way down his legs, she had to dodge his erection.

When they were together like this, he could forget all the other crap. The fact his father was a class A bastard while he had been a complete idiot. Why had he believed all the lies? Why hadn't he been able to remember the truth about his mother?

Mandy finished drying his feet, stood, and hugged him. "Let it go, Marc. Just for tonight. When you stepped in the shower with me, you were so relaxed, and now that you're out and dry, you're tense as a spring ready to snap." She glanced down at him, at his semi-erect cock. "I don't think that's the whole source of the tension, do you? Stop thinking about your father." She ran her hand over his length and he immediately sprang back to life. "Of course, dealing with this takes care of all kinds of things. Wanna get back in the shower?"

He kissed her. "I wish, but we need to get over to Cassie and Nate's. You're right. I have to quit obsessing over the bastard. I'm sorry. I keep wondering how I could have believed him all my life. I knew she loved me, and yet I swallowed his lies and because of that, I've hated her for years. It doesn't make any sense."

She looped her arms over his shoulders and looked directly into his eyes. There was no hiding from Mandy when she wanted his attention. "None of this makes sense because most fathers don't kill their children's mother, Marc. A good father wouldn't take that trauma-tized child miles away in the dark of night and make him wait in the car while he buried the mother. Your father is an animal. He's a predator. If Ted's informa-tion is true, and we have no reason to doubt it, your father married her to get at that inheritance, which makes him worse than an animal. And think about it— the fact you didn't remember it for all those years is probably why you're still alive. If he'd thought you might have told someone that he killed her, I bet you'd be in the ground next to her."

He sucked in a deep breath, slowly let it out. Then he kissed her. "Thank you. As always, you've nailed something I hadn't even thought of."

"Of course I did. I told you I'm always right." At least she grinned when she said it.

He dragged her out of the bathroom, back into the bedroom. "That has the potential of getting to be a little annoying, you know."

"Oh, I hope so. Makes me unforgettable."

"You're already unforgettable." He kissed her again. He wanted to be doing this whenever he wanted for the rest of their lives. No way in hell would he ever forget Mandy Monroe. No way was he ever going to let her go, either.

He was dressed before Mandy and went into the kitchen to look over the printed pages from Ted once again. His cell was sitting on the counter. "Damn it all." He'd missed a call from Theo, so he called him back without checking voicemail. "What's up?"

"Hey, Boss. You were right. Ted just called. His plane landed about five minutes ago. I'm headed over to pick him up, and I'll help him get settled. There're guys working on his office now and I expect them to have it done ASAP. The alarm system is all set; your phone number and mine have been added. We'll get Ben's in when he's home, and I'll add Ted's today. You want him to have keys, don't you?"

"I do. Thanks for handling this, Theo. I always know I can count on you. Have Ted give me a call once he's checked in. I think he's planning to stay at the same extended-stay hotel he was at last month until we get his permanent housing situation taken care of."

They covered a few more things and then discon-
nected a few seconds before Mandy walked into the
kitchen. Marc walked across the room and wrapped his
arms around her. "Ted's plane just landed and you're in
my arms." He kissed her. "For now, at least, all is right
with my world."

She was laughing when they headed across the yard
to Nate and Cassie's, and the mouthwatering scent of
chicken on the barbecue.

Theo spotted Ted standing in front of the United termi-
nal with two huge suitcases, a carryon, and a bulging
briefcase. He pulled over to the curb, and got out of the
car. "Welcome, Ted." They shook hands. "I understand
you're the new kid on the block. Looks like you brought
everything but the kitchen sink."

Ted glanced at the luggage and laughed. "I think
it's in here somewhere. What's sad is that this is, quite
literally, everything I own. Theo, isn't it? Another The-
odore?"

"No, sir. Thelonious, as in Thelonious Monk. Teach-
ers for some reason had trouble with that and turned me
into Theo. It stuck, but my parents were big fans of both
Monk and Duke Ellington, ergo, I am Thelonious Duke
Hadley." Theo grabbed the largest of Ted's bags and
loaded it in the trunk. There was barely any room for
the carryon.

Ted hung on to the laptop, but closed the back door
after sticking the big suitcase on the back seat. He
glanced at Theo. "Lord, man, I hope you like jazz."

"In that respect, I was a huge disappointment. I actually loved rock and roll, but Dad was a professor at UC
Berkley, and I grew up in Marin. That's what my
friends listened to. I went to the same high school as
Marc."

Ted fastened his seat belt as Theo pulled away from the curb. "You guys were friends in school, then?"

Theo shook his head. "No, I'm ten years older. I have a younger stepsister and she went to school with him. She said Marc was really smart, very quiet, pretty shy. Now that I've met his father, I can understand why. That man's a piece of work. I have a feeling Marc might have been an abused kid. I've never asked him."

"Amazing he's as successful as he is." Ted studied him as if he might be trying to read between the lines. Theo wanted to tell him, there were no lines. What you see is what you get. A forty-six-year-old gay man tired of living alone, wishing there were someone else in his life beyond the man he worked for and the few other employees.

"So, where am I taking you?" he asked. No point in rehashing the crap in his world. "Marc said there's an extended-stay hotel you've stayed in before. That where you want to go until you've got an apartment?"

"That's the plan, but I haven't made reservations. I originally thought I'd just go ahead and rent a car and go there on my own, but I'm pretty beat after packing up and moving out so quickly. I appreciate your picking me up." He gave Theo the address, and they talked a bit about the work Theo did for Marc and the fact Ted had finally left the Bureau after twenty-seven years. "It was time," he said, but he looked out the window, not at Theo.

Made him wonder what was going on in the guy's head, why he'd decided to leave when, from what Marc had said, Robinson was a damned good agent. He dropped him at the hotel and waited until he got his room. Ted walked out a couple of minutes later, but he didn't look very happy.

"Well, that sucks," he said. "No rooms available.

Crap. Tell you what, I'll get a cab and find a room in town. I made the decision to leave so quickly, I was thinking more about getting here than what I'd do when I actually arrived."

"How long since you've eaten?"

Ted frowned. "I dunno. Before I went to the airport. Thanks, but I'm not your worry. I'll be okay."

Except he looked ready to fold, and Theo took pity on the guy. "Come with me. I've got a crew working at the office. They're going to be noisy, so I don't plan to go back tonight except maybe to check on things later. I've got a crockpot full of stew and some fresh baked bread to go with it. I've also got a guest room where you can crash. Tomorrow you'll be in a better position to make decisions like where you want to stay for the next couple of weeks, at least until you get your permanent housing settled."

Ted just laughed. "You've been hanging out with Lola too much. She kept me fed and worried about me the whole time I was out here on assignment. I imagine you've been infected with her caretaker gene. You sure your family won't mind a stranger at the table? In the house?"

"Just me," Theo said. "And I invited you. C'mon. I could use the company."

Mandy held on to Marc's hand as they walked across the yard to the cottage. Dinner had been wonderful, the conversation nothing but laughter and good times, and no mention or questions about the mess with Marc's dad. That was definitely a relief. She hugged Marc's arm and realized she hadn't stopped either laughing or smiling all evening.

"What is it about those two? They're always so much fun."

Marc paused just outside the glow of the porch light. He'd been smiling and laughing a lot, too. She loved seeing him this lighthearted, this relaxed.

"I know. I've thought about them a lot lately. You know how they met, right? I hired Nate as the vineyard manager and Cassie was still totally pissed about losing the vineyard and winery to bankruptcy, and she really wanted to hate him. Obviously that didn't work out." He laughed. "Of course, she wanted to hate me, too, but I'm pretty stubborn. I think she's finally decided I'm not the ogre she originally had me pegged for. Especially since she wouldn't have met Nate if not for me."

"That's their secret, though, isn't it? Why they just radiate contentment. They're so much in love, they have work they enjoy, good friends, they're here in this beautiful valley that seems so far removed from all the crap going on in the world. It's like they have this perfect, protected little bubble."

Marc wrapped his arms around her and held her close. She inhaled, so aware of his scent, of the strong, steady beat of his heart, of the way it made her feel. "I think it's more than that," he said. "They both come from good, solid families. Even though Cassie's mom died when she was young, she never doubted her mother's love, never wondered if she was as important to her father as the work he did. I think that kind of knowledge gives any kid a powerful foundation. The same for Nate. His family was always supportive of every choice he made."

He buried his face in her wind-blown hair and held on to her as if she somehow anchored him. Didn't he realize he anchored her just as well?

"I can't imagine what that feels like," he said, "but I want my child, hopefully our child, to feel the same security. That same sense of unconditional love. I think

I had that from my mother, but it's hard to know anymore. Hard to know what's a real memory and what's merely one manufactured out of wishes and dreams."

Mandy leaned back in his embrace, cupped his jaw in her palm, and focused on his eyes. "The thing is, Marc, you know what you want. You have those dreams, those wishes that are a huge part of who and what you are. You'll make it happen for your children. And, for the record, they'd better be our children. I love you, and I don't doubt you in the least."

He wrapped an arm around her shoulders and they went up the steps to the porch. He opened the door and then paused. "I'm sure glad at least one of us doesn't have any doubts."

"Never," she said. "None at all."

Ted leaned back in his chair and took a sip of wine. "Thank you, Theo. Dinner was spectacular. I don't think I've been this relieved or relaxed since I was last out here." He stared at the dark plum colored Zinfandel in his glass. "The quality of wine with meals is certainly far superior to what I'm used to."

"That's one of the perks of working for Marc Reed. I got a couple of cases from him for Christmas, and we can buy all we want at cost. I tend to keep plenty on hand." Theo stopped talking, took a sip, and then focused on Ted.

Ted had figured there'd be questions. There always were when you met new people, changed situations, made big changes. Lord knew he'd done all of the above.

Eventually, Theo asked. "What made you decide to leave the Bureau after so many years? And don't hesitate to tell me to butt out, but I am curious."

Ted just shook his head. "No, spelling it out is the least I can do, though there were so many reasons leading to this, it's hard to narrow it down to just one. Ben, Lola, Lola's sister Mandy, Kaz, and Jake . . . Marc. Definitely Marc, but it's hard to say which one, or if it was the combination of all of them, but I spent almost two months out here, and when the job was done, I honestly didn't want to go back. Because of them, of the friendship they shared. It was a friendship they pulled me into so easily." He focused on Theo. "It was a harsh reminder just how lonely my life really is."

Theo just shook his head. "I hear ya on that. A little over a year ago, I caught the man I'd been partners with for over twelve years cheating on me. I'm the kind of guy that, when you have a monogamous relationship, you trust your partner to keep it that way. I'm lucky I found out before anything really awful happened, but it's been a tough adjustment. Which is probably more than you needed to know, but it's been a huge change for me, going from being half of a couple to all of a single."

Ted studied him for a long moment. No way in hell would he have ever guessed the man across the table from him was gay, and wasn't that part of his problem? He hadn't recognized it in himself, either. But Theo might understand. "You've touched on another part of my problem," he said. "I signed on at the FBI in 1989. I was only twenty-four, and so deep in the closet, even I didn't know I was gay. The culture there at the time was definitely homophobic, so it wasn't much of an issue. I just figured the right woman hadn't come along yet."

"I think a lot of us have been there. It doesn't always jump out and bite you on the ass."

"Would have made things a hell of a lot easier."

"So how'd you figure it out?"

He laughed. At this point, what else could you do? "Over the years, guys I worked with kept trying to match me up with their sisters or girlfriend's best friends, which is actually quite a compliment, the fact they trusted me enough to want that for me, and I dated a lot of lovely women. It wasn't all that long, though, before I realized that as much as I liked the women, it was the brothers or the sisters' boyfriends I was more interested in."

He still felt badly about all those girls and women. They'd been totally innocent, and in a lot of cases, definitely interested in pursuing a relationship, but he couldn't do it to them. More important? He couldn't do it to himself.

"Is the FBI still down on gays? I mean, I know what the official viewpoint is, but what about the guys you worked with?"

"The culture has definitely changed. They're openly welcome, but I just couldn't come out to the men and women I had known for so many years. I'm fifty-one, and I've never been honest about my sexuality. No one at the office knew, and I had no idea how to tell them I'd been living a lie throughout my entire career."

"So you quit the job, packed up, and left town?"

Ted nodded. "Exactly. Sneaking out under cover of darkness isn't my usual method of operations, but it seemed the best way to leave. I gave notice shortly after I got back from the job here, and didn't even let Marc know at first. I finally called a couple of weeks ago and told him I was looking for a job. I hoped he might have some leads for me, because I really wanted to live out here. I'd fallen in love with San Francisco. I had no idea he'd be able to hire me, but this case he wants me to pursue is fascinating. You say you've met the father?"

Theo seemed to take the change in subject matter in stride. "I have. The guy is scary. In fact, there's something you need to know. I'm not sure if Marc's told you or not, but when his dad showed up here earlier today, it got ugly. Marc is always such a contained sort of a man.

I've rarely seen him lose his temper or even get angry with anyone, but the guy got in Marc's face, called him names, talked down to him, poked him in the chest, and then he insulted Mandy.

"Marc lost it. He told him he knew about Rockpile Road, that something got buried out there the night his mother disappeared. I was watching his father's face. He definitely reacted to that. Not in a good way."

"Holy shit." Damn. This could put Marc in danger. Mandy too, for that matter. "Theo, from the research I've done, I believe Steven Reed is a psychopath. He's killed at least once, and if his back's against the wall, I have no doubt he'll kill again. He's definitely scary, and not someone I'd want coming after me. Marc and Mandy are up in Dry Creek, at the winery?"

"Staying in the little cottage that serves as a guest house at Cassie and Nate Dunagan's. Winemaker and vineyard manager."

"I wonder if his father is aware of that connection. Would he know to look there for Marc?"

Theo shook his head. "I don't know, Ted, but it's not a chance I'd want to take. Marc's made no secret of his ownership of the winery. I mean, he's tied his jewelry company launch to it with the same name, so I doubt his father is unaware of the winery or the location, which I believe is very close to this Rockpile Road Marc was talking about. But there are pictures of the tasting room in the advertising, and they've got a huge website presence with a wine club and scheduled activities." He glanced at his watch. "It's a little after nine. I'm going to call and let him know that he should alert Cassie and Nate to the risk. It might be a small one, but they need to be aware. Besides, Cassie's pregnant. She doesn't need this. Damn it."

"Tell you what, Theo." Ted stood and carried his plate

and silverware to the sink. "Let me call him, tell him I'm here, and that you're babysitting me tonight." He laughed. "For which I am embarrassingly grateful. Anyway, I'll mention the risk. I honestly think he's a bit in shock over the whole thing, to have all of this information dumped on him so quickly. Otherwise, I doubt he would have said anything, no matter how angry he got."

"Sounds good, and you've chosen an amazingly effective way to get out of the dishes."

Ted really did like this guy. "One of my many skills, but dinner's on me tomorrow night, okay?"

"That works."

Ted walked into the next room and called Marc.

Marc rinsed out Mandy's wine glass while she tossed his beer bottles. All two of them, but the place was so small that they needed to stay on top of things, and they didn't want to leave Cassie with a mess. He dried his hands off on the dish towel after drying the glass and putting it in the cupboard.

"So, tomorrow we'll go in search of the address?"

"I think that's a good idea." She stepped close and rested her arms on his shoulders. He loved the way she did that, almost as if she were caging him in, forcing him to focus on her and nothing else.

As if anything else could hold his attention when Mandy was in the room. "You don't plan to do any digging, do you?"

He shook his head. No, Ted had been adamant in one of their discussions that they build a strong enough case and then involve the authorities. Anything else could result in screwing up evidence that might be needed to hold Steven Reed accountable for his wife's death. Ted knew a lot more about the legal end of things than Marc could ever hope to.

"Ted wants us to build an ironclad case against my father and then let the authorities do the digging. So far, we have a lot of circumstantial evidence, but we need specifics. If we can tie this address into the rock and tree, for instance, things that Alden can testify to my having discovered through age-regression therapy, then we have enough to bring in a search team. Did you know there are dogs that can find human remains that have been buried for thirty or more years?"

He rested his forehead against Mandy's. "She's out there, Mandy. Buried alone in an unmarked grave. I never mourned her. I hated her. All those years. All those fucking years when I could have been looking for her. She deserves a decent burial. Deserves a funeral and someone to mourn her."

Mandy's arms tightened around his shoulders. "Think about it, Marc. You've mourned her since you were a little boy. You've missed her. The fact those memories are there, that they're intact? That's proof that you haven't forgotten her. She will be found, and we'll bury her in a beautiful place. That's going to happen because you've never given up. A mom can't ask for more from her child."

He kissed her. "You always know the right thing to say."

"They're not just words, Marc. I mean what I say or I wouldn't say it. Now come to bed. It's been a very long day. I'm exhausted and I know you must be, too."

She took his hand and tugged. His cell phone rang. "Do you have to answer it?"

He smiled. "I have to at least look." He glanced at the screen. "It's Ted."

"Then answer it. And tell him hi from me. I'm going to bed." She kissed his cheek and left the room.

Marc answered the phone. "Hey Ted. You're here?"

"Well, here as in San Francisco. I'm actually at Theo's house. The extended-stay hotel I was planning to crash at was full, so Theo took pity on me and brought me to his place. He's fed me and let me drink some of that wonderful wine. Life is good. Except for one thing."

"Crap. What's that?"

"Theo ratted you out. He said your dad knows you suspect him, that you mentioned Rockpile Road."

"Yeah. I totally screwed up. I just lost it. I'm sorry, Ted. Hope it doesn't mess with your investigation."

"It's not the investigation I'm worried about. From everything I've been reading, I think your dad's a psychopath, and I'm worried about your safety, about Mandy's, and even Nate and Cassie's. It's not like the location of the winery is a big secret, and with your website presence and directions to the property, you are all potential targets."

"You really think he'd come after us?" Crap. This wasn't even on his radar.

"It's a risk. There have been a couple of questionable instances loosely tied to your father. Nothing ever proved, but people who hurt him in business over the years have a habit of disappearing. Are there any people in law enforcement in that area that you know or even someone Nate and Cassie might know? Someone you can make aware of what's been going on? Feel free to make copies of my notes and pass them on."

"I'm sure there's someone. Nate and Cassie know just about everyone around here. Cassie's been here all her life. I'll talk to them in the morning, find out who we can bring up to date on the info I've got and my suspicions."

"Sounds good. And feel free to pass on my name as your investigator. Since I'm an employee, or will be when I sign on the dotted line, I don't need a private investigator's license, but I don't want to step on anyone's toes, either."

"I'm really glad you're here, Ted. Thank you so much for coming."

"I'm glad I'm here, too. You have no idea how ready I was for a change. It was time."

Marc thought about Ted as he headed into the bedroom, about the bravery of a man willing to walk away from everything familiar and reach for something different. Then he glanced at Mandy. She was just coming out of the bathroom wearing a soft bathrobe. She looked absolutely beautiful, and totally approachable, but even so, in a way, he was doing the same thing. He'd stepped out of his comfort zone and taken a chance on love.

Though it wasn't all that chancy with someone like Mandy. He reached out and took her hand. She turned and smiled at him, and he felt it like a punch to the chest, the pure, open joy in her smile. It shouldn't be this hard to believe she actually loved him, but it was. He'd never dreamed it might actually be this way between them. Then she'd smile at him just like this, and he knew.

It was so damned good he could hardly contain his joy.

Then she paused beside the bed, turned, and looked at him. "What did Ted want?"

Four little words, and reality slapped him sharply across the face. "Crap. He called to warn me about my father, the fact I let him know I was on to him. Said it may have put all of us in his sights. I need to call Nate. Look out the window, would you? See if there are still lights on over there."

She walked across the room, peered out through the wooden slats covering the window. "Yep. Looks like.

In fact I see Nate taking the garbage out." She glanced at him. "See? Told you it was a guy's job."

"I already conceded." He walked over to the window and pulled the blinds up as he dialed Nate's number. Saw him reach into his pocket and answer the phone.

"Hey man. What's up?"

Marc chuckled. "Other than watching you do your manly chores?"

Nate turned and waved at him, and then walked across the yard separating the two houses. "How about I meet you on the porch?"

"I'll be right there."

Mandy kissed him. "You go. You really do need to tell Nate. Your father is absolute slime, ya know?"

"Believe me. I know."

Marc opened the door as Nate walked up the steps. He was talking on the phone. "Yeah. Marc had something he wanted to chat about. I'll be home in a few minutes. I love you, too."

He ended the call and stuffed the phone in his pocket. "What's going on?"

"I sure as hell hope you don't regret taking this job from me. This may be a totally false alarm, but I just got off the phone with Ted Robinson."

"I remember him. The FBI agent. He made a trip up here shortly before he left for Virginia. Is there a problem?"

"I told you about the issue with my father, but what I didn't tell you is that we had a run-in today when he broke into my office. Theo had him cornered just before Mandy and I arrived. I don't know what happened, but my father got in my face, started poking me in the chest and I went ballistic. I told him I knew about his trip out Rockpile Road, that I remembered him burying something the night my mother disappeared. He lost it, shoved Mandy out of his way, and left. When Ted found out what happened, he was, to put it bluntly, extremely pissed. Says I painted a bullseye on my ass and one on Mandy, you, and Cassie, too. I am sorry, Nate. I was so stupid, but the guy is psychotic. Ted thinks he may have killed before, not just my mother, but others who've gotten in his way. Right now, I'm the one in his way, but I want you two to be extra careful. Lock up at night, make sure the gates are locked, and stay as close to Cassie as you can. If you wouldn't mind the intrusion, I'll hire security for the property until this is settled."

Nate planted a steady hand on his shoulder. "Thank you. For now I'd prefer not to have to deal with security—I think that would be more unsettling to Cassie than not having someone here, but I'll check. And I'll make sure Cassie's aware of the danger." He paused, shook his head. "Lately she's been going into the cellar early to get work done before the tasting room opens. I'll be sure to go with her. If you can, get a picture of him for me so we know who to watch out for."

"I'll see if I can find one. Picture an older, totally dissipated version of me—jowly, bags under his eyes, about seventy pounds heavier. Hair going gray." He laughed. "Not a promising future look for me, that's for sure."

"One other thing," Nate said. "Cassie's already got a call in to the county sheriff's office. She knows a lot of the guys, and wanted to let them know about the investigation at this point. I'll make sure she updates them."

"Give them Ted's phone number, the one I gave to you earlier. He's going to be handling the investigation for me. And if they want to talk to me, just tell them to let me know when and where."

"You'll get through this, Marc. Thanks for the warning."

"I'm just sorry I have to warn you at all. G'night, Nate."

He watched Nate walk away. Then he turned and went back into the little house. Walked through the kitchen and down the short hallway, straight to Mandy. Everything always looked better when she was in his arms.

She must have known what he was thinking. She was already in bed, naked, arms held wide. There was a large pile of condoms on the bedside table.

CHAPTER 9

There was a breakfast place on the old highway into town that Mandy had spotted on their way in the day they'd stopped to pick up Mexican food, and that's where Marc took her. It was after nine and the place was fairly quiet on a Thursday morning. Marc found a table near the window in front and led Mandy to it.

He checked his phone and found a text from Jake. "This is good," he said. Mandy raised her head from the menu and smiled at him.

"Music is settled," he said. "That band you found on YouTube, the one up in Mendocino County that does a great combo of jazz and bluegrass? I sent the link to Jake and Kaz yesterday and just got a text from Jake with a thumbs up."

She crossed the others off with a flourish. "Excellent. Cheaper than flying a group in from New Orleans, too."

"Very true."

"We might actually get everything done today."

"That would be good. I still want to go out Rockpile Road at some point."

"I know. I'm sorry I didn't want to go this morning."

She reached across the table and took his hand. "Last night with you was wonderful." Her cheeks turned pink. "This morning was even more fun. I wanted to pretend that we were just a normal couple without so much bad stuff hanging over our heads."

"I know. And I think it was an excellent idea." Mandy was the one who'd convinced him they needed to get some of the stuff done for Kaz and Jake, which had been the original reason for the trip. She'd also suggested that it would do him good to get a little distance from all the crap going on, and he'd had to agree with that, too, but it wasn't easy. He wasn't used to having someone looking out for him, someone putting his happiness ahead of everything.

As much as he loved it, it wasn't all that hard to accept, and definitely worth it.

The food came, huge plates of hash brown potatoes and eggs, sausage for Mandy, bacon for him, a big bowl of fresh fruit to share. He dug into his meal while Mandy looked over a few more things. "Eat," he said.

She raised her head, blinking. "Sorry. Got sidetracked." Laughing, she set the notebook aside. "At least we've settled on the caterer. The Thai place. There are enough vegetarian dishes that we can keep the vegans happy while still not allowing the carnivores to starve."

"Excellent. Starving carnivores are dangerous in a mixed group. They tend to feed on the vegans." He took a big bite of bacon.

Mandy nodded. "That would not go over well. Must remember to keep carnivores well fed. One other thing. Cassie said we could hire Lupe and Josie Medino to tend the bar. They'll be serving your wine and a craft beer from a local brewery. Lupe's free that weekend to work."

"They're still living in that little house on the back end of the property, aren't they?" He'd met Lupe when he first bought the Tangled Vines vineyards—the young man had taken on the demanding job as Cassie's vineyard manager when he was barely out of high school, after her father's health had declined. He was a good kid, now studying viticulture at UC Davis, and Nate was managing the vineyards.

"Cassie said they're in the place part time and have an apartment in Davis as well. Josie stays here a lot on her own and helps Cassie in the tasting room. Cassie's hoping Lupe will want to come back to work here. He's really sharp and they work well together."

"Well, if we make it attractive enough, we could probably convince him. He's got family here in the valley and so does Josie. They're all really close." He thought about that, about the fact that Lupe and Josie had worked so hard to send Lupe to school, and how they helped their family members as well. There was a lot to be said for family. The more he saw of loving, functional families, the more he wanted one of his own.

He finished off the rest of his breakfast, his mind going from the trip out Rockpile Road to the list Mandy was working on. List now, Rockpile later.

As long as he remembered priorities, he was okay. Mandy was his number one priority. "Okay," he said. "That leaves security. That's especially important the way things are now. Damn, I wish he were behind bars right now. I hate that he's impacting our friends' lives, too."

"I hate that you don't even have to mention his name, and we both know who you're talking about."

Raising an eyebrow, Marc smiled at Mandy and deadpanned, "Sort of like Lord Voldemort?"

"Exactly. We shall henceforth refer to that man as 'he

who shall not be named.' " Mandy covered her eyes with her hand. "That's just horrible, Marc." Then she snorted, laid her head on her arms, and laughed.

She was still laughing—and so was Marc—when the waitress came to collect their plates and leave the bill. When she gave him a quizzical look, Marc just shook his head. "You really don't want to know."

Mandy had originally felt guilty about dragging Marc into town when she knew he was anxious to follow the lead on Rockpile Road, but they'd both needed to step back a bit. The fact his father was growing more desperate was scary and important, but Marc's life was important, too. She wanted him to experience normal things once in a while.

She didn't think he'd had much normal in his life.

"Okay," she said, buckling her seat belt after leaving the Thai restaurant a little while later. "The paperwork and payment are all taken care of for the catering, and that leaves security. I talked to Cassie last night and mentioned that we needed someone. She texted me a few minutes ago, while you were dealing with the caterer, and said Nate's already arranged for the security guys they use for events—they're legally armed, bonded, and insured, and we can make them aware of any potential for risk."

"Excellent. I didn't even think about asking Nate. Shows you how little I actually do with the winery. Nate and Cassie definitely run the show up here. So, what kind of flowers does Kaz plan to carry?"

She gave him the raised eyebrow. "That's not a guy question. You do realize that, don't you?"

He turned on Dry Creek Road and headed out of town. "Actually, I was thinking of a couple of the pictures that Jake took out here when they did that first shoot for Intimate. Kaz had a bouquet of wildflowers in her arms, but she looked naked behind the blooms, with the slightest hint of the jewelry. The flowers were so pretty, and in the picture, her eyes are sparkling. I think she'd be perfect with wildflowers."

"Marc." Mandy raised an eyebrow and studied him. "No matter what flowers she carries, she will not be naked behind the blooms."

He turned to her with a stricken look. "Really?"

"Really."

He sighed most dramatically. She punched him in the shoulder.

"Ow." He rubbed it, but he was laughing. "It is so easy to get you going."

"And that, dear man, is why you love me. Because I'm an easy target."

"Well . . ." He flashed a bright smile her way. "Among other things." Then he wriggled his eyebrows and she laughed.

This was really enjoyable, she thought. Relaxed, talking, laughing about silly *normal* things. They needed times like this. Time to kick back and not worry about all the serious stuff they'd been dealing with.

Of course, before she was ready, they were climbing the road at the west end of the dam and the bridge that would take them out Rockpile Road.

Marc had entered the address he'd recovered from his session with Alden Chung into the car's GPS system, and it wasn't long before he knew he was close. It had been dark that night so many years ago, but the moment he saw the dirt road leading off of Rockpile toward the lake, he broke out in chills.

For whatever reason, even though he hadn't even noticed it when they were here on Tuesday, he knew exactly where to turn without looking at the GPS screen. There was a gate that would close off the road when locked, but it was standing wide open at the edge of the pavement just before the road turned to dirt. The open gate was practically an invitation to drive past the 'no trespassing' sign. The steel post on the left where the gate would lock had metal numbers screwed into it.

Marc stopped and stared at the post. The gate and the post might be new, but the numbers hadn't changed. Just to be sure, he pulled out the piece of paper he'd written them on when he and Mandy had gone to see Alden. "New post," he said, holding the paper up for Mandy. "Same old numbers."

He stared at the post, the road stretching on ahead, and felt a deep sense of time and place that left him almost dizzy with anticipation. He wanted to get out and walk, but he wasn't certain how far in they'd find the rock, maybe even the tree, if it was still alive.

He was close. Very close. He knew it.

A truck pulled in behind them, just off the main road, and a man a little older looking than Marc got out and walked over to his car. Instead of just rolling the window down, Marc got out. "Hello." He held out his hand. "Is this your property?" The man shook hands and nodded toward the dirt road that eventually led down to the shoreline of Lake Sonoma.

"Good afternoon. It is. This is a private road. I'm sorry, but you can't go down there. I was just getting ready to lock the gate."

"That's exactly why I'm here. I'm Marc Reed. I own Intimate Vineyards. Used to be Colonel Mac Phillip's place, Tangled Vines."

The rancher immediately smiled, and his entire demeanor changed. "Good to finally meet you, Marc. I've heard of you, met your vineyard manager. Nate's a font of knowledge in this business. We've all learned to rely on him. I'm Jeb Barton. I knew Colonel Mac from the time he first developed that vineyard. Beautiful spot. Really something, what happened to him, though. The man went out a damned hero, but we were all real sorry to lose him. His daughter Cassie's still winemaker there, right?"

Marc laughed. "Of course. Only a damn fool would take her out of that job. She's good. Of course, she's also six months pregnant, so we're all hoping the timing works out. You know how we need our winemakers during harvest."

Jeb smiled and nodded. Then he glanced out over the rolling hills that sloped down toward Lake Sonoma. "This property isn't for sale, Marc, if that's why you're up here looking."

Marc shook his head. "I wish that were the reason, Jeb."

Mandy had gotten out of the car, and now she slipped her arm around his waist. "This is my girlfriend, Mandy Monroe. Mandy, Jeb Barton." She shook his hand, but didn't say anything beyond a soft hello.

"Jeb, I have reason to believe my mother is buried somewhere along this road."

"Buried?" He shook his head. "There's no cemetery out here that I know of. We've owned the property since the early 1980s and I've hiked or ridden most of it. Can't recall a marker of any kind that would denote a grave."

"No formal grave. I've recently learned that my father most likely murdered her in 1984. There wouldn't be any marker. I was a four-year-old kid and recall a nighttime ride down this road in the back seat of my dad's car. I remember him digging a hole, saw him carrying a large bundle wrapped in my mom's favorite comforter. We believe my mother was wrapped in that blanket. I know that the grave was close to a big rock—well, big to my four-year-old self—with an oak tree growing out of one side. What I'm hoping to do is find the location. I don't want to do any digging. I just want to find it and turn all the evidence we have over to the sheriff's department. My father has been a free man much too long."

Jeb stared, open-mouthed. "How did you find out . . . ?"

Jeb glanced at Mandy. Marc hugged her close. "I was having some unsettling dreams. I was able to get through the meaning of them with a hypnotherapist. That's how I got the address. I saw the numbers on a wooden post. They were that reflective stuff, which is probably why I even noticed them."

Jeb was shaking his head. "I think I still have that original post, and that's the kind of numbers on it. And if you'll follow me, I can show you a rock with a big tree growing out of one side. Might be the same one, but damn." He was still slowly shaking his head. "That's hard to believe. C'mon. It's not all that far."

If Mandy hadn't been holding on so tight, Marc might have gone over. He actually felt as if he needed to orient himself before he climbed back into the car. He pulled far enough ahead that Jeb could get by him. Then he followed Jeb's big Ford pickup along the well-maintained gravel road.

"You okay?" The soft touch of her fingers against his forearm, the concern in her eyes warmed him. He'd lived his entire life without this kind of support, had never realized quite how empty it had been. How much he needed someone, anyone, to believe in him.

Now that he knew, he realized he'd never survive without it. Without Mandy. "I'm better than I might have been. Babe, I am so glad you're here with me. Thank you. I can't imagine doing this on my own."

"I'm glad I'm here. Though I honestly wish you didn't have this to deal with at all."

"Don't we both."

Jeb pulled to the right and parked. Marc pulled in behind him and got out of the car. Chills raced along his spine, the powerful sense he'd been here before.

With Mandy hanging on to his hand, Marc met Jeb between the vehicles.

"It's over here."

Marc and Mandy followed him around a slight curve in the road. Marc stopped. Stopped dead in his tracks and stared at the massive old live oak tree with a twisted trunk, growing so close beside a huge rock that it looked as if it grew directly out of the rock itself.

"It's the same tree." He walked forward, tugging Mandy along behind him. "No wonder it seemed so big to me. I remember that the rock was taller than me, and the tree was huge." He laughed. "The rock's even taller than you, Mandy."

"And the tree is still huge." She stood on her toes and kissed his cheek. "Where were you parked?"

"Right here. He must have turned the car around while I was still asleep. I got out of the door on this side and walked about three or four steps to the rock and peed on it." He stared at the huge piece of stone he knew as serpentine by its color. It wasn't actually a single boulder as he'd remembered, but instead part of a larger outcropping of the same blue-green stone with darker striations, the glossy, almost waxy look to it he'd learned to recognize. He glanced at Mandy. "I remember that I felt terribly manly, peeing outside on a rock."

She squeezed his hand. "That is such a guy thing. I had no idea it began so young. So where do you think your father was digging?"

"Over here." He held on to her hand and they walked in the opposite direction, away from the big rock.

Jeb had been standing quietly to one side, but then he followed. "Be careful," he said. "There was a slide here a few years ago. I don't know how stable the ground is."

Marc glanced at Jeb, let go of Mandy's hand. "Wait, please?"

She nodded. "Be careful."

He pushed through a thick tangle of deer brush. A few feet in, he stopped. This section of the hill had slipped, and erosion had further gutted the section. If she'd been buried here, her bones could be exposed somewhere below, or buried beneath tons of dirt and rocks.

"Damn. I was four years old and it was dark, but I think he was digging right about where this part slid off the hill."

Mandy came up beside him and took his hand again. "Could he have been closer? Where we're standing now, maybe?"

"Possibly. It's been over thirty years. A lot of these plants might not have even been here then." He'd been so sure they'd find something. "We'll let Ted know, see if he's got any ideas." He pushed the brush aside so Mandy could get through, and then followed her back to where Jeb waited in the shade of the oak.

"Jeb, I'm working with an investigator who mentioned using cadaver dogs if we could get close to where she might be. They're able to find old bones that have been buried even longer than my mother's been missing. Ted, the guy who works for me, is ex-FBI, definitely a professional. If he thinks there's a chance of finding her body, would you be willing to give us permission to search the slide area?"

Nodding, Jeb added, "My only concern is liability. I can't guarantee the stability of this area."

"We'll get it covered, put it in writing in a way that will absolve you from anything stupid we might do, or pay for any damage, however unlikely." He dug in his pocket for his wallet, grabbed a business card and handed it to Jeb. "Is your number listed?"

Jeb grinned. "Got a website." He walked back to the truck and grabbed a card of his own, handed it to Marc. "My wife and I don't live here on the property. We've got a place a bit farther out Rockpile Road. I'd feel more comfortable with something in writing, though I'm certainly not going to stop you from looking."

"Thank you. I'll be talking to my guy tonight, find out about using a dog. I'll also get the paperwork to you before we do anything. I'll definitely be getting in touch with you in the next few days, once I have a little more information."

"Sounds good. I'll look forward to hearing from you."

It was a quiet ride back to the house, but only because Marc's mind was spinning. He'd felt his mother's presence today, as if her spirit approved of his search. All those years and he'd never thought of her, almost as if she'd never existed. Rather than live with hatred for a woman he didn't want to remember, he'd consciously pushed her out of his thoughts. His memories of her were growing stronger each hour, as if he had to make up for so much time wasted.

Maybe he felt her closer for a reason. He hoped it was forgiveness. Did her essence still exist, if only in spirit? He'd never know for sure, but he liked the sense of her nearness. Loved the fact he could now bring those good memories back, and in some small way, bring her back as well, if only in his heart.

Now, if he could just get that same spirit or even his own memories to point the way to her remains, it would certainly make their job a whole lot easier.

Marc was quiet on the ride back. Mandy held his hand, doing her best to imagine what was going through his head right now. She was terribly relieved he hadn't insisted on climbing down that slide to search for his mother. She hoped someone else would find her bones. He was so strong, but in this respect she felt as if he were almost fragile, so deeply ashamed of the way he'd viewed his mother for all those years.

How did you convince a man who had been lied to all his life that he wasn't at fault? He was so open and loving with Mandy, with his friends. His mother's love for him must have been powerful; it had to be her influence that had shaped him and not his father's twisted mind.

She wondered if Ted had found out anything else, if he was getting along okay with Theo. Marc tended to surround himself with really neat people. She liked that he was choosy. Loved that he appeared to have chosen her.

They pulled into the driveway at the cottage and parked under a tree. Marc still hadn't spoken, but he got out of the car and stood there, staring across the vineyard. Gazing up beyond the valley to the hills beyond the dam. The place where Mandy knew he was certain they would one day recover his mother's remains.

She stepped up behind him and wrapped her arms around his waist, felt his ribs expand with his sigh. "Hey, darlin'," she drawled. "Did you throw in any athletic shoes?"

He turned his head, stared at her. "No. Why?"

"Well, I think we need to get you some so we can go

for a run. It always clears my head. Helps me think. Might help you organize your thoughts."

"It does. I might have an old pair of running shoes in the apartment above the tasting room. C'mon."

They sneaked in through the back entrance—the tasting room was already busy, but Josie was there helping Cassie and it looked like they had things under control. Marc found a pair of shoes, ratty but still serviceable, and they went back to the cottage. Mandy had brought running shorts, a sports bra, and tank top along with her shoes. Marc had an old pair of what looked like high school gym shorts, and she was really pleased when he decided against a shirt. He had an absolutely beautiful body.

"Traffic is bad out here—the road is just too narrow. Let's run the service roads in the vineyard. Okay by you?" He finished lacing up his shoes.

Mandy had been so busy watching the bunch and flex of his muscles that she barely registered what he said. "Yeah. Works for me. I don't want to go too far. We're taking Nate and Cassie out tonight, aren't we?"

He stood and held out his hand, pulled her to her feet. "Yep. I really don't want to have to pull your face out of your plate when you hit the wall at dinner."

"Bad visual." She opened the refrigerator and grabbed a couple of water bottles, handed one to Marc and followed him out the door.

It had been foggy this morning, but the sky was clear now with the temperature in the mid-seventies. Absolutely gorgeous. They took off down the driveway to the tasting room and cut off to the left, following a trail that ran north along the creek. Mandy had run a few times with Marc, and he maintained an easy, steady pace that she thoroughly enjoyed. He didn't seem to have that need to show her how great he was, how much stronger or faster. That was a given—he was taller, his stride longer—so it made the runs more fun when he easily accommodated her shorter legs.

After about five minutes, they reached the end of the property and turned left toward West Dry Creek Road. The neighbor just to the north of them had pulled out this section of vineyard and would be replanting before too long. Mandy heard the distant sound of cars on the road and the steady thud of their feet on the packed gravel service road, but essentially it was the rush of the creek and now birdsong that filled her senses. Marc ran behind her, which was all the incentive she needed to pick up the pace a bit.

No pressure, just the knowledge that he was back there, running in time with her steps, teasing her with his nearness. Would she ever grow tired of him? Their love was so new, and they'd been under so much pressure from the beginning. What would it be like when there wasn't some sort of crazy going on in their lives?

They made another turn, and now they were running along the road. Vineyard to the left of them, the road and a vine-covered hillside to the right. Traffic was light, the occasional sound of voices or distant music a reminder that this area was a popular tourist destination.

Mandy noticed a number of cars in front of the Intimate Wines tasting room and a few people out looking at the grapes already hanging heavy on the vines. Marc came up alongside her. "You okay to do another couple of laps?"

"I am. This feels so good, and it's beautiful out."

This had been an excellent idea. After driving all the way out Rockpile Road, finding the address he'd recalled during Alden Chung's session, recognizing the tree in the rock—all of it had been exhilarating. On the flip side, walking to the spot where he was sure his mother's body was buried and finding that the hillside had collapsed into a pile of rubble had been horrible.

Until then, everything had gone too well. He wasn't sure what he'd expected to see, but he'd been so certain he would find something to tell him it was the place where his mother was buried. Now it seemed impossible they'd ever be able to recover anything. He needed to get in touch with Ted, ask him about getting a cadaver dog out here to search the area. He'd also have to get paperwork drawn up to absolve Jeb of liability.

And just like that, with the steady cadence of their shoes against the hard-packed dirt road and Mandy's cute butt in front of him, he felt as if he was back on track. How did she know what would help him focus this way?

Mandy maintained a steady pace and they completed one loop of the property and were nearly through the second, running along the section of service road that paralleled West Dry Creek. They were halfway to the next turn that would loop them back toward the creek when a weird prickling between his shoulder blades had Marc on alert. He'd noticed a few cars passing, thought he'd heard someone turn in at the Intimate tasting room, but he caught up to Mandy so he could run beside her.

"When we get to that big oak up ahead, let's stop in the shade, okay?"

She turned and smiled at him. "What? Don't tell me I'm wearing you out?"

"Dream on," he said, but his attention was faltering. Something was wrong, and he had no idea what it was. His heart rate picked up and his senses seemed more acute, but he slowed his pace as they reached the tree and he pulled Mandy close to him beneath the branches.

"I'm probably totally paranoid, but I've got a feeling someone is watching us."

Her head snapped up, her eyes narrowed and she leaned close. "I'm feeling the same thing. I just thought it was me. That is so weird. And scary, too."

He turned and looked back in the direction they'd come. An older, dark green Ford Bronco was parked alongside the fence, facing toward them, against traffic. There wasn't anyone near the vehicle, no sign of the driver, but he knew it hadn't been there when they'd run by a moment ago. He shoved the paranoia aside. The parking lot to the tasting room was probably just full. That was it.

Still, he'd rather move forward than have to run back by that green Ford.

"Must be an overactive imagination. Let's finish out the loop, okay?"

Mandy nodded, but he noticed she was checking out their surroundings just as carefully. They'd stopped near an older section of the vineyard. The grapes here were dry-farmed without the trellising used in the younger, drip-irrigated section. These vines were gnarled and full, with trailing stems and heavy bunches of grapes, a setting both idyllic and peaceful.

He'd actually been feeling pretty relaxed up until a few minutes ago, but there was still that uncomfortable prickling along his spine, an anxious, uneasy sense of danger without any focus. Mandy shoved away from the tree, turned, and smiled at him. He kissed her quickly and then followed her along the dirt road. She ran a steady pace that he knew the two of them could maintain for at least a couple more miles—if not for that uneasy feeling. He shook it off.

The service road curved back toward the creek another hundred or so yards ahead, but he focused on

Mandy. She had a beautiful stride, long and fluid, especially considering her petite size but her legs seemed so long when she was stretching them out like this. Her arms were sleek and tanned, and she'd tied a folded bandana around her forehead and knotted it in the back as a sweatband. It sent her blond hair bouncing with each step.

His anxiety faded with every step they took. He'd have to let her know she was doing great things for his blood pressure.

The sharp crack of a rifle and the almost simultaneous whiz of a bullet flying by his left ear sent him leaping forward. Marc tackled Mandy without thinking, rolling her to the dirt and covering her body with his as a second shot echoed around the valley. Fire slashed across his left shoulder, his arm went numb, and he tugged Mandy behind a grapevine that wasn't nearly big enough to hide the two of them.

"What happened?" She spun around in his arms, grabbed his shoulder and brought her hand away covered with blood. "Did you get shot? Good God, Marc, somebody shot you! How bad is it? Are you okay?" She went up on her knees so she could see. "It looks like it just grazed you, I think, but damn, Marc. Who?"

They both reacted to the sound of spinning tires, turning toward the road. The Bronco spun away from the shoulder and raced past them. The windows were tinted, but Marc tried to get a good look at the license plate before it sped out of sight.

"Could you see who that was?" Mandy spun around and watched as the vehicle raced away, not an easy feat on such a narrow road. She grabbed her phone out of her pocket and, with her hands visibly shaking, dialed 911.

Marc had gotten a good look at the plate. Mandy

quickly reported what had happened to the dispatcher. Then she handed the phone to Marc and he recited the plate number he'd seen, that it was an older, dark green Ford Bronco. He assured the dispatcher they would be at the house in front of the tasting room to meet with the deputies. Slowly he pushed himself to his feet. The adrenaline was wearing off as quickly as it had hit, and his shoulder hurt like a son of a bitch.

"Marc? What happened?" Nate came rolling up in one of the vineyard 4x4s as Marc handed the phone back to Mandy. "I thought I heard a couple of gunshots. Sounded like a rifle." He jumped out of the rig and ran around the front where Mandy stood with her hands wrapped around Marc's right arm. Holding him up, actually. He wasn't sure she realized how shaky he was.

Nate skidded to a stop. "Geezus, man, you're bleeding like a stuck pig. You got shot? Damn!"

"Sure feels like it. You got any clean rags with you?"

Nate rummaged around in the utility box on the back of the rig and came up with a roll of paper towels. Mandy grabbed them, wadded up a stack and pressed them to the burning divot across Marc's back.

"Shit!" He tried to laugh. Groaned instead. "What are you doing back there?"

"Trying to apply some pressure so it'll quit bleeding." She kissed him. "Don't whimper. It's unmanly."

"Don't whimper?" He loved that she was teasing him. He'd been so afraid for her. "C'mon, Mandy. I just got shot."

"I bet Jake didn't whimper."

"That's a low blow." He waited for her snarky comeback. Silence. "Mandy? You okay?"

Turning around, he caught her staring at the blood-soaked paper towels in her hands. Her face was white as a sheet. "Aw, babe . . ." He reached for her, but with one arm all he could do was keep her from landing in the dirt.

Nate came up behind Mandy and grabbed her around the waist as she toppled. Marc wasn't much help, but Nate got her to the passenger seat of the 4x4, sat her on it sideways, and had her put her head down between her knees. "Deep breaths, Mandy. C'mon. We need to get Marc to the house."

He went around to get into the driver's side.

"I know you're the one who's bleeding here, but can you ride on the back?" Nate had gotten into the driver's side.

"I've got a better idea. Mandy? Honey, can you sit on my lap. Nate's going to take us back to the house."

She nodded and covered her face with her hands. "I am so embarrassed."

She got blood all over her cheeks. He kissed her anyway. She stood while he slid onto the seat, and then she carefully sat on his lap. It wasn't all that far to the house, and he probably could have walked, but he wasn't about to admit he was feeling a bit lightheaded himself. He hugged Mandy with his good arm. She had a fresh wad of paper towels pressed against his left shoulder.

When they pulled into the driveway in front of the main house, Cassie came flying down off the porch. "What happened?"

"Some guy shot at Mandy and Marc," Nate said. "I saw Marc tackle her to get her out of the way, but the bullet grazed his shoulder."

"Ohmygod. Are you okay, Marc?" When he nodded, she said, "I hear sirens. Sounds like the deputy's car." She focused on Mandy. "Did you request an ambulance?"

"No," Mandy said. "Just the sheriff." She pressed a clean handful of paper towels against Marc's shoulder, but at least the bleeding was slowing down. "I was so freaked out when I called 911, I'm glad I could remember the name of the winery." She kissed Marc's forehead. "It looks like the bullet just grazed your shoulder blade. I can't see a hole like you'd get if the bullet went in anywhere. I'll take you into the hospital in town." Then she rolled her eyes. "Kaz said they were really great when Jake got shot."

Nate started laughing, and Marc glanced around to see what was so funny. He was sitting on the top step to the porch, while Mandy held a bloody handful of paper towels against his shoulder. "So," he said, "what's the big joke?"

"Think about it. It was your turn." Nate kissed Cassie. "I am so glad you weren't one of their roommates, babe. I think they're all cursed. First Kaz and Jake. She gets beat up and he ends up with a divot taken out of his arm. Then Lola and Ben, only in his case it was a back full of buckshot, and now you."

Cassie burst into laughter.

Nate glanced her way. "What?"

"How quickly we forget, Nathan." She kissed him. "Bullet? Chest? Saved by the cellphone case?" She turned to Mandy. "When that whole thing with my father's papers hit the fan, the guy trying to steal his briefcase shot at me. Nate jumped between the bullet and me, and he went down hard. I thought he was dead. When the deputy helped me roll him over, he was trying to get his breath, and his cellphone—in a metal case that he'd stuck in his shirt pocket—had a big dent, right in the middle."

"Actually, that's one I'll never forget. The only reason I didn't mention it is because I didn't end up bleeding all over my woman." He looked pointedly at Mandy's blood-stained hands. "Cassie's dad tackled the bad guy. Eighty-six years old with Alzheimer's and he still managed to save both our lives. Hopefully, you and Mandy will be safe from here on out."

Marc raised his head and looked into Mandy's eyes. She shook her head. "I don't think either of us will be safe until Marc's dad is behind bars."

"You think he did this?"

"Who else, Nate?" Marc sighed.

"I can't believe any man would try to kill his own son." Cassie wrapped her hands around Nate's arm and hung on. "That's horrible."

Marc shook his head. "See, that's what scares me the most. I don't think he was aiming for me. I think Mandy was his target." He grabbed her hand and held on. "Ted's right. He really is psychotic." He glanced up as the sheriff's deputy pulled into the yard. "He needs to be stopped, and this is as good a place to start as any."

CHAPTER 10

Theo stood in the doorway watching Ted as he got his first glimpse of his new office. Marc had given Theo carte blanche with the set-up, and Theo hadn't taken any shortcuts. It still smelled of paint and sawdust, but the crew had worked through the past two nights and they'd done a wonderful job.

The room had originally been intended for storage, yet they'd never stored a thing inside.

Now the walls had been painted a deep gray-blue with non-glare overhead lighting. Blinds covered a window with the same view as Marc's office of Yerba Buena Island, but the computer equipment appeared to be what had Ted's eyes glazing over. Theo had chosen a curved wall that now held two thirty-inch computer screens—also curved—across the upper half, and three twenty-inch screens across the lower.

There was a color laser printer, copy machine, desktop computer with a six terabyte hard drive, and all the high-tech toys any one man could want. A laptop was set off to one side, synced to the main system so that Ted could take everything with him when he did fieldwork. The office even had its own gun safe.

Ted turned and stared over his shoulder at Theo. "This is all for me?"

"It is. Those top two screens will give you the same views Ben has in his office—the different screens on the grid are security cams at all of our properties, including the winery in Dry Creek Valley. Use the mouse, click on the screen and in many cases you can get audio, but only if the person on that end enables it. Marc doesn't want anyone to think he's spying on them. This is all about safety."

"Wait a minute. This is real time? That's the winery? Aren't those sheriff's vehicles in front of the house? How can I pull this in closer?"

Theo was there in a heartbeat, grabbed the mouse, and tapped a couple of onscreen icons before bringing the winery image full screen. "Shit. That's Marc, and it looks like he's covered in blood. I'm going to call Mandy." As he reached for his phone, Ted pulled the image up closer.

"Looks like Mandy's holding a cloth to his back, but he's still bleeding. Where the hell's an ambulance? Try Marc's phone, Theo. He's talking, doesn't look like he's hurting too badly, but hell. This is not good."

Marc's phone chimed. "Mandy? Babe, can you get that out of my left pocket."

Holding the blood-soaked paper towels to his back with her right hand, she reached in with her left, found his cell phone in the pocket of his running shorts, and handed it to him.

He glanced at the screen and immediately answered.

"It's Theo. Hey, man. Good timing." He clicked it on speaker.

"Marc! I was just showing Ted his new state-of-the-art office and explaining how the security cameras covered all your places of business, and we look at the one for Intimate and see your skinny ass, half naked and covered in what looks like blood. You're on speaker. Please tell me that's paint."

Mandy grabbed the phone out of Marc's hand and took over the conversation. "Hey Theo. It's definitely blood. A lot of it. Sheriff's deputies just pulled in. Someone took a shot at us when we were out jogging. Ted? I am so glad you're here. You need to get to work, big guy!"

"Give me the phone, Mandy." Marc's comment was dry as dust. He held his hand out.

"Yes, dear." She smirked, but she handed over the phone.

"Older green Ford Bronco." He rattled off the license plate number. "The windows were tinted so we didn't get a good look at the driver. Don't know if he shot from inside the car or if he was hiding in the vineyard, but the thing that scares me is that he appeared to be aiming for Mandy."

"Ted here. What makes you think that?"

"I was behind her and to the right. First bullet whizzed by my left ear, between us, and just missed both of us. I tackled her and we went down, but I was essentially right where she'd been when I caught her. Bullet grazed the left side of my back, barely missed her. Since we know she hasn't got an enemy on Earth, it's got to be the guy we're checking into."

"I have to agree. Looks like the deputies are waiting to talk to you, and you need to get to the doctor and get that patched up."

"Yes dear." He laughed. "You're as bad as Mandy."

"Get used to it. I'll call you later. Oh, and Marc? This office set-up is bitchin'."

"Thank Thelonious. It's all his baby. I have no idea how he managed to get it done so quickly. I'm really glad you're here, Ted. Gotta go." He ended the call and turned toward the deputy who'd been patiently waiting. "I'm sorry. My new security guy was checking out the cameras and clicked on this one." He pointed to a mounted security camera on an overhead light pole. "Got his first view of the area and I was front and center, in living color."

The deputy glanced over at Nate. "Ya know, Dunagan, this used to be a real quiet spot before you showed up. What's going on?"

Nate's hands went up. "Not me, Jerry," he said. "Talk to the owner. This is Marcus Reed, and with him, hanging on to the bloody towels, is Mandy Monroe."

"Good to meet you. Deputy Jerry Russo, Sonoma County Sheriff's Department. Now, first of all, do you need medical attention?" When Marc declined, the deputy grabbed his notebook. "Okay, then. What the hell happened out here?"

"Well, this isn't how I planned to spend the afternoon." Marc slipped a clean T-shirt over his head, and poked his right arm through the sleeve while Mandy helped ease it over the bandage covering the bloody divot across his left shoulder blade. That arm was held close to his body inside his shirt in a sling to prevent movement.

"Me, either," she said. "This is gonna hurt."

"It already hurts." He turned and kissed her. "You realize you're going to have to be on the bottom."

"For a guy who claims he's been celibate for months, you certainly tend to plan your activities around sex."

"I'm making up for lost time." He kissed her again as the nurse stepped into the room with his instructions for caring for his wound, extra bandages, and a tube of antibacterial cream.

She didn't look happy about much of anything. "Your paperwork is at the front window. Take ibuprofen for pain, keep the area dry for a couple of days and if you have any sign of infection, be sure and see your personal physician."

Then she turned and headed back down the corridor.

Mandy watched her go. "She looks like she's ready for some quiet time," she said. "This place is really busy for a small hospital in a little wine-country town." Mandy rinsed her hands off at the sink and then gathered up her handbag, Marc's bloody T-shirt, and his bag of supplies. They'd had to wait almost an hour before the ER doctor could see him because there'd been a group bike ride that had tangled up on one of the back roads. Riders had flooded the ER with a lot of road rash and a couple of broken bones.

"I think I'm the only gunshot wound." Marc walked over and held the door for her.

"You sound proud of yourself."

"Well, at least I didn't fall off my bike."

"No," she said. "You protected the maiden in distress." Laughing, she kissed him on the way out. "Can you drive?"

He reached in his pocket and handed the little key fob to her. "Probably better if you drive. Take it slow."

"I'm ready to take it slow the rest of the afternoon, if it's okay with you."

But when they finally got back to the vineyard, the tasting room parking lot was full and there were cars lined up along the road. Mandy walked with Marc to the guesthouse. He went into the bedroom, slipped his blood-stained shorts off and put on his old sweats, detoured to the kitchen and grabbed a beer out of the refrigerator, and then went straight to the front room. "I think this is as far as I plan to go today. There's a Giants game on. Do you mind?"

"Not a bit. Actually, I'm going to clean up and see if Cassie needs me in the tasting room. They're really busy. She wasn't sure if she'd have help this afternoon and she's been pulling double duty with her winemaking. Triple, when you figure she's doing it for two labels."

"I know. Rub in the guilt. However, you're a lot better person than me, Mandy Monroe." He kissed her before lowering himself carefully onto the sofa in front of the big flat-screen TV.

She stopped between him and the TV and planted her hands on her hips. "Well, I didn't lose a gallon of blood, either."

"There is that."

When Mandy arrived at the tasting room, Cassie looked ready to fold. Both Lupe and Josie had come in to help, but even with the three of them, there were people lined up to taste the wines and try the various cheeses, crackers, and olives set on tables around the room.

Nate was working in the vineyard, and the slow, steady rumble of the tractor as he mowed between the vines blended with all the lively commotion inside. Mandy took a deep breath and waded into the crowd, working her way over to Cassie.

"What can I do to help?"

"Mandy! What a welcome sight. How's Marc?"

"He's fine, staples across his back and his left arm in a sling. I imagine he'll be asleep on the couch in the next five minutes."

And that was all the time they had for conversation

for the next couple of hours. The only bad thing about it? Mandy realized how much she missed working in an environment like this, one where she interacted with complete strangers who were out having a good time. She might have to get serious about Marc's coffee shop-slash-cafe. This was definitely work she loved.

Once they closed the tasting room at 4:30, Mandy took over and sent Josie and Lupe home. They were both always so busy with Lupe in college and Josie working, she knew they wanted some time alone together. There were no arguments when she offered to clean up, but when she suggested Cassie go home and relax as well, Cassie pulled rank.

"When I'm not making wine, this is my kingdom. I'm staying." She opened a can of lemonade and parked herself on one of the stools in front of the granite bar while Mandy loaded wine glasses in the dishwasher and put things away.

Cassie sipped her lemonade and smiled as if this was the best thing ever. "I hope you realize I could get used to this really easy," she said. "I love watching you clean up. You're so efficient!" She laughed. "Must be all that barista training."

"That's got to be it. Did I tell you that Marc's thinking of opening a coffee shop in the bottom floor of his building? The long-time tenants just moved out this week. He asked me if I'd run it. Actually, he wants me as part owner with him as a silent partner."

"You gonna do it?"

"I think so. He wants to hire women from a local shelter. He got the idea after all this business with his mom, and knowing that Jake and Ben want to set up a memorial fund in the name of the young woman and child who were killed in that wreck the guys had so long ago. She and her little boy were victims of abuse long before that happened, which made their deaths even more tragic, if that's at all possible. Marc wants to take the concept of the memorial fund further, and include his mom's name in something. A coffee shop that employs women from abusive relationships, one that offers childcare to employees . . ." She shrugged. "Hard to turn down something like that."

"What would you call it?"

"His mother's name was Elizabeth, but everyone called her Bett. I've been thinking about it while I've been working today, and . . ."

Cassie laughed. "You can actually think when you're in here dealing with a gazillion tourists? I can barely remember my name!"

"Actually, I can. Weird, isn't it? How does Bett's Place sound? Something simple is more apt to stick in a person's mind."

"I like it. Run it by Marc, see what he thinks."

"Yeah, I . . . Cassie, someone's coming up the drive."

"Closed sign is up, darn it. I hate to have to lock the gate but . . . oh, it's Jerry. He's one of the deputies you met earlier." She slid off her stool as the big SUV came to a stop in the lot in front of the tasting room. The deputy got out and, speaking into his radio, walked in.

He ended the conversation as he stepped into the room. "Don't get up, Cassie. Hi, Mandy. Is Marc around?"

"Probably asleep in front of the TV. Want me to get him?"

"Nah. Don't bother him. Hope he's not hurting too badly. I just wanted to let him know we found the Bronco abandoned down past Lambert Bridge. It was stolen from a parking lot in town earlier this morning. The guys dusted for prints but I doubt we'll be able to find much. It looked like it had been wiped clean. We tried to get hold of Marc's father in Marin, but the house is pretty empty. Deputy who checked on the place said it appears that whoever lived there has moved out. Grass is dead, newspapers stacked up on the front porch, most of the furniture is gone."

"Interesting. Marc said he thought maybe his dad was in some serious financial trouble. He's one of those guys who's always running some sort of scam or another, and he's been pressuring Marc to loan him money. Let me go see if Marc's up. He might be able to add some more information."

Marc was just waking up when Mandy got back. He'd slept all afternoon, but he tried to look like he'd been watching TV.

"Busted," she said, leaning over to kiss him. "You've been sleeping, haven't you?"

"Yeah. I think I lasted all of two minutes after you left." He kissed her back. "How could you tell?"

"Sleep wrinkles on your cheek. Go wash your face and grab a shirt. I want you to come to the tasting room. Jerry, the deputy who interviewed you earlier, is here. Said it looks as if your father's house in Marin is empty. Newspapers piled up in front, landscaping dead, most of the furniture gone, from what they could see through the blinds."

"Yeah. Just let me find my shoes." He laughed. "After I wash the wrinkles off my face." He was back in less than two minutes, hair freshly combed, face moderately unwrinkled. He'd put on old sweats and a sweatshirt that had definitely seen better days, but he'd kept his left arm tucked inside in the sling. His running shoes were covered in blood spatters, but he slipped them on without socks before following Mandy. "How'd it go in the tasting room?"

"You made a lot of money on wine today, big guy. The place was really busy."

"Was it hard work?"

She laughed. "I had a blast. I really miss working like that. And yes, that means that I'm in if you still want to do the coffee shop. Wanna call it 'Bett's Place?'"

"Not 'Mandy's'?"

"Not if it's going to be for the women from the shelter. I think we should honor your mom."

They'd reached the tasting room. He pulled her into a one-armed hug and kissed her. "I like that," he said. "I like it a lot."

Deputy Russo questioned Marc for over an hour. "Personally, I think you've got more than enough suspicious information to at least go to the police and tell them what you remember, what you suspect. It would help if we had a better idea where you father might be now."

"I wish I knew, Jerry, but I've had very little to do with him since I left home for college. That was August, 1997. The last time I saw him before this latest run-in was a couple of years ago when he asked to borrow money."

"Was it a large sum?"

"He said he needed fifty thousand in cash, that he'd pay me back by the end of the financial quarter, which would have been the end of June two years ago. I gave him the cash, and that was the last I saw of him until about a month ago when he came to me for more money."

"Did you give it to him?"

"No sir, I didn't. I told him he'd never paid back the first loan and I wasn't an idiot. That's when he pulled the father card and tried to guilt me into it." He shrugged and added, "It didn't work."

"Did you already suspect him?"

Marc shook his head. "No. Not in the least. I just don't like him very much. I'd been having the dreams, convinced I'd murdered a woman, only I didn't recognize her and I had absolutely no memory of doing anything like that at all, other than the dreams. I still don't really remember what my mother looked like, though I now know she's the one I saw. There weren't any pictures of her when I was growing up, and I honestly don't know if there's anything of hers at my father's house. I imagine he's gotten rid of everything associated with her."

"You said there was an inheritance, that you think that could have been the motivation for her murder? There's a lot of money there?"

"More than enough to tempt a greedy man to murder. And I can't help but wonder if that was also the motivation for marriage. She married him just weeks after her grandmother, the woman who raised her, died. I'm wondering if she was his target all along. In fact, I've been wondering what my great grandmother died from. It all feels too convenient. Honestly? I wouldn't put anything past him." He glanced at his hand, tightly linked with Mandy's. She hadn't let go of him once during the entire discussion with the deputy.

Her mere presence, the fact she was there for him, was an unimaginable gift, something he'd never once experienced. While Jake had been there for him over the years as a friend and someone to bounce ideas off of, it had been so much different than the support he took from Mandy. She strengthened him in ways he'd never expected.

Steadied him, enough that he felt totally in control when he focused on the deputy once again. "Where do you suggest I go from here? I've hired an investigator. He's convinced Steven Reed is a dangerous man, possibly psychotic. I'm certain he was shooting at Mandy today, but now that he knows I'm after him, I'm afraid I've put all my friends and employees at risk."

"At this point, it sounds as if you've got enough evidence to get the police interested, especially with the hypnotherapist able to verify what you've told me." Jerry grabbed a card out of his pocket, jotted down a name on the back. "The chief of police in Marin and I have known each other for years. Since the alleged crime happened in Marin County, that's where you need to start. Give him a call. I'll see if I can find out anything to help us focus on Reed as the shooter in today's incident. We really need a good photo of him. Do you know if he's ever been arrested?"

Mandy interrupted. "I'm sure that's information Ted Robinson can find for you. I hate to burden your department with putting manpower into finding something Marc can probably get with his people."

Marc squeezed her hand. "Excellent idea. We're going to be here just a couple more days at the most, Jerry, and then we're headed back to San Francisco." He reached for his wallet, then realized he hadn't stuck it in the pocket of his sweats. "I don't have a card with me. Got something so I can write down my contact info?"

"I've got it. You gave all of that to me after the shooting."

Marc shook his head. "I have absolutely no memory of what we talked about then."

Mandy squeezed his hand. "You might have been just a wee bit rattled, ya think?"

"Yeah. Maybe just a little. And the ibuprofen is wearing off." He shook hands with the deputy. "I guess I'm not as tough as I thought I was."

Nate walked across from the house as Deputy Russo was leaving. The two men exchanged a few words and then Nate followed the deputy as far as the front gate and locked it behind him. They all met on the front porch at the main house.

Cassie sat on the big porch swing and groaned. "Folks, I know the plan was to go into town for dinner, but I'm beat." She glanced at Marc. "And I doubt you're feeling much like partying tonight, either."

"You've got that right. Why don't you go in and relax, and Mandy and I can go pick something up. I promise to get something wonderful."

Cassie sighed. "Really wonderful? Like Italian wonderful?"

"That sounds good." Mandy turned to Marc. "That place in Geyserville, the one Kaz and Jake liked so much?"

"Lasagna. Definitely the lasagna." Cassie moaned dramatically.

"We've got plenty of stuff to make a salad." Nate stood behind Cassie, rubbing her shoulders. "You sure you're okay to drive, Marc?"

Marc laughed. "I've got to prove my manliness somehow." He knew Nate didn't want to leave Cassie alone right now. Not after what had happened.

"We've got a loaf of sourdough French bread." Mandy glanced at Marc. "Unless the wounded one ate it today."

"Didn't touch it." He frowned at Cassie. "Can pregnant ladies eat garlic?"

"Oh, yeah. And lots of butter, maybe a little parmesan cheese on top? I can do that."

Mandy stood. "Cassie, you know the owner. Can you call Luke and order a tray of it? By the time we're cleaned up and go get it, it should be dinner time."

"As far as I'm concerned, it's dinner time now." Laughing, Nate pulled out his phone. "I gave Luke a hell of a deal on wine this year. I'll order the lasagna. I want to make sure we have enough for leftovers."

Dinner was wonderful, but Cassie was exhausted and it was plain to see that Marc was fading fast. The divot across his shoulder blade had been deeper than they'd realized, and he'd lost a lot of blood. Tonight he was hurting and tired, and Mandy sort of enjoyed babying him.

Mainly because it was obvious he still wasn't certain how to handle it when she did.

"C'mon," she said. "Let's go to bed."

He shrugged his shoulders, probably not such a good idea with a back full of staples, and groaned. "I don't think I can sleep right now. I'm really sore."

"Get into bed. I'm going to mix you a hot toddy."

"I don't have a sore throat, Mandy." He rolled his eyes and she laughed.

"Trust me. The way I make them, you won't have a sore anything."

She had him sit on the edge of the bed so she could help him get his shoes off. Then she helped him get out of his sweats and carefully tugged the sweatshirt over his head. He left his knit boxers on, and she knew he must be miserable because he wasn't aroused in the least.

She left him with instructions to crawl into bed and get comfortable. It only took her a couple of minutes to nuke about a quarter cup of honey in the microwave until it was bubbling, add the juice from a fresh lemon, and top it off with a generous double shot of whiskey.

She'd always found the combination to be one of those comfort things that you associated with being a little kid and mom giving you a tablespoon of the sugary stuff that put you to sleep in a heartbeat.

Except it hadn't been her mom. It had been one of her mom's friends, a really wonderful man who'd been their surrogate parent for almost two years while dear Mom was roaming the countryside, following the Grateful Dead. She'd probably still be following them if they hadn't quit performing. Mandy and Lola kept in touch with Ronnie, who had settled in the Castro district in San Francisco back when houses were still moderately affordable. Mandy had thought he was her father for the longest time, until he finally explained that no, he wasn't, but that he loved both little girls as if they were his own.

Their mother might have been a flake, but she usually found good people to care for her girls. It beat being homeless, and it beat being with a mother who really didn't want any part of motherhood. But Ronnie made hot toddies whether they had head colds or bruises from playground booboos, and while the alcohol was most likely so he could get some sleep, Ronnie bringing a toddy was a fond memory for both Mandy and Lola.

She took the steaming mug in to Marc. He was sitting up in bed, checking email on his cell phone.

"I've got texts from Ben and Jake, asking what's up and why we're not checking in or answering texts." He sighed. "I haven't been sure what to tell them."

"Here," she said. "Drink this."

"Wasn't that a line in Alice in Wonderland? And didn't it get her into trouble?"

"I'm thinking it will knock you on your perfect ass so you can get some sleep. The ibuprofen doesn't appear to be getting the job done. As far as Jake, Kaz, Ben, and Lola, I suggest a Skype call tomorrow with everyone on board. I'll send a text and we'll set up a time. The thing is, you getting shot is probably going to hit the paper tomorrow or the next day, and it might make the evening news. You're a somebody, whether you want to be or not. People are going to hear about it."

"Crap. I didn't even think of that, but you're right. We need to let them know before they hear it somewhere else."

"Exactly. So I'll set up something for tomorrow morning. You okay with that?"

"Hmmm, uh, yes." He took another sip of his drink. "This is really good."

"Don't sound so surprised. It's supposed to be. Now drink it."

"Yes, dear."

Laughing, she sent a group text. *I know we're all in different time zones, but Marc and I need to set up a group chat for sometime tomorrow on Skype. Does nine Pacific work? There's a lot going on here, and we want you to be involved. Personally, I don't want to worry alone.*

Before she sent it, she included Theo and Ted. Now that Ted was here, and Theo had protected her from Steven Reed, Mandy figured it was only fair. She looked at the list of names in the group and smiled while Marc sipped his toddy. He'd always said he wanted a big family, and it appeared his was continuing to grow.

She had answers within minutes that the time worked perfectly. Even Theo had replied and said it worked well for both him and Ted. At nine in the morning here in California, it would be noon in DC and six in the evening in Rome, where Jake and Kaz were doing a final shoot Friday morning before flying to Venice on Saturday. She glanced at Marc, intending to tell him they were all set up.

He'd fallen asleep with the empty cup in his hand. Ronnie's toddy had triumphed again.

She lifted the cup out of Marc's lax fingers and helped him turn to his right side to sleep. He mumbled a bit, but didn't awaken. A few minutes later, after straightening up in the kitchen and going through her regular nightly routine, she crawled into bed beside Marc. There was no blood seeping through the bandage, which she figured had to be a good sign.

With a soft pillow against his back so she wouldn't bump into him, Mandy snuggled close, wondering just how the conversation would go in the morning.

CHAPTER 11

Mandy awoke to the dusky gray of early morning. Marc slept soundly, sprawled on his belly with his left arm tucked under him. The bandage was clean with no sign of blood, which meant he hadn't torn any of the staples during the night.

She'd been worried. He'd been restless, and she thought she'd heard him getting back into bed at some point, which meant he'd been up, but he must have gone back to sleep. She certainly had.

The doctor had been worried about bleeding because she was pulling skin together over such a wide area. She'd said it would be painful for a while, but should heal cleanly as long as he took it easy. Mandy tried to imagine Marc taking anything easy. He seemed driven much of the time, as if he always had something that needed to be done yesterday.

Of course, he was a very successful man. She was grinning as she quietly got out of bed. That drive probably had a lot to do with all that success. She pulled on her old fuzzy green bathrobe. Lola insisted it was actually her security blanket, and Mandy knew better than to argue the point. Snuggled up in its fuzzy comfort, she padded out to the kitchen to make coffee. As soon as there was enough in the carafe, she poured a cup and took it out on the front porch.

Mornings here were gorgeous. Fog drifted through the redwood trees on the hill across the road. There was a doe with a couple of speckled fawns tugging leaves off an old apple tree just inside the fence along the front of the property, and she heard wild turkeys up on the hillside. Coyotes had been howling during the night, and she'd heard a great horned owl hooting. Now, as the sun rose over the hills behind her, the musical cadence of workers speaking Spanish out in the vineyard blended with the natural songs of the wildlife.

She checked her watch. It was almost seven. If Marc wasn't up by eight, she'd go in and wake him. She knew he'd want plenty of time to wake up before talking to everyone this morning, and so far, she'd discovered he really wasn't a morning person. She sipped her coffee and felt herself relax even more. It was so peaceful here, such an idyllic setting.

Hard to believe someone had taken a shot at them yesterday. Terrifying to imagine how close she'd come to losing the man she loved.

Marc rolled carefully to the side of the bed and slid his feet off the edge of the mattress. It was the easiest way to sit up, to stand. He'd tried to get out of bed during the night the usual way, and the pain almost flattened him. Dealing with so much discomfort, from what sounded like such a small injury, left him feeling decidedly unmanly.

He should probably take a look at the thing. If it was gruesome enough, he'd feel better about acting like a wimp.

Once he was sitting, he turned toward Mandy, except she wasn't there. He caught the faint scent of coffee, incentive enough to get him up and moving. He managed to clean up in the shower without getting the bandage wet, though washing his hair one-handed and keeping the bandage dry was more than he wanted to deal with. He merely stuck his head beneath the spray and got it good and wet.

At least by the time he finished, he was feeling cleaner and a bit steadier on his feet. He carefully stepped over the raised lip of the shower. Mandy was waiting in the bathroom, holding a big towel.

"I would have helped, you know. Lean over."

"Good morning to you, too." He leaned over so she could dry his hair and then stood still while she wiped down the rest of him. "I hope you realize I could grow used to this sort of service very quickly."

She paused and raised her head. Were those tears? "Babe, what's wrong?" He wrapped his right arm around her and hugged her close.

She sniffed. "I'm sorry. I was sitting out on the front porch having a cup of coffee and thinking how beautiful everything was, when it dawned on me just how easily it could have been me sitting out there planning your funeral. Or you planning mine. It makes me feel a lot closer to what Kaz went through with all those attempts on her life. She's clearly a lot tougher than me."

"Nobody's tougher than you. Help me get dressed, okay? I don't want to have our conversation with the guys while sitting here naked.

"Good point. I would hate to have Kaz and Lola ogling you."

He leaned close and kissed her.

She broke the kiss and glanced down. "I can see how much you love me. Evidence confirms you're recovering.

C'mon. Cover up the goods. I'm going to make breakfast before we call everyone."

Mandy set up her laptop, and Marc took over. He opened the browser and added Kaz, Ben, and Ted, who had said he'd bring Theo into his office with all the cool screens. Within a few seconds, it felt like old home week.

Mandy was so glad to see everyone she was practically bouncing on her chair. "I've missed you guys! Hey, Kaz. Hi Jake. Lola! We're in Dry Creek Valley, Rico's with Jasper and Abdul, and hi Ben and Theo and Ted. And now that I've got that out of my system, I'm going to sit quietly and turn this meeting over to Marc."

Marc sat on Mandy's left so he could put his right arm around her, and he kept his left arm and the sling out of camera range. "Impressive intro, Ms. Monroe. Folks, this is actually a business meeting of sorts. First of all, welcome to Ted Robinson, who is now a full time employee of Reed Industries. He arrived Wednesday and got thrown into the deep end without a life preserver. Details later."

Mandy and Marc were both laughing by the time everyone finished welcoming Ted. The razzing had the new employee trying very hard to keep a straight face. Marc finally interrupted. "Okay. Enough jocularity. We've got some serious business going on. First, I close escrow on the house on Twenty-third next week. I'm your new landlord. The owner wanted to sell and Theo advised me to buy, so if you're unhappy with the new situation, complain to him. The unit next to the one we're living in is vacant and badly in need of renovation, but I'm hoping, Kaz and Jake, that you'll think about moving in. I'll take care of whatever upgrades you want to do. I imagine the bubblegum pink bedroom and nausea-inducing striped wallpaper will need to go. If you're next door, it's a lot more convenient for you to show up at mealtimes, which you generally manage to do anyway. No," he said in answer to their teasing. "Quit making excuses. It's never as much fun without you. And Lola, should they move in, you definitely get a raise."

Mandy shot a quick glance Marc's way. With all the positive comments, there was no doubt Jake and Kaz approved. He glanced at the image of Ted and Theo in Ted's office. "Ted, if it works out, once the place next to ours is done, that might free up Jake's apartment. I'm willing to buy up the lease so you'll have a place to live. It's in a great location and the rent is still fairly reasonable, but we can talk about it later."

"One question." Kaz raised her hand like a kid in the classroom—except she was in Rome. "Why buy that place when you can afford anything?"

He shrugged. "I like it there. It comes with all of you." Before Kaz had time for one of her traditionally snarky replies, he changed the subject. "Okay. Now there's another thing that's been going on." He glanced at Mandy. "Well, two, actually." He leaned close and kissed her. His lips moved over hers as if she were the only woman in the room, which she was, sort of. Though even the power of Marc's kiss couldn't block out the shocked laughter and cheers from the peanut gallery.

When she finally came up for air, Mandy had a feeling she looked very well kissed. She certainly felt that way, so she leaned toward the computer screen and said, "Okay. I think we can end the call for now, okay?"

Marc planted another quick one on her lips before looking at Mandy. "No, Mandy. We can't." Then he laughed and said, "With that visual in mind, you can see that Mandy and I merely needed a little bit of time without the well-intentioned matchmaking that's kept us

apart for way too long. Which actually frees up a bedroom in case you need a place to crash, Ted, until we
get everything worked out."

Theo's laughter had everyone looking his way. "Ted's
already moved into my spare room. I think it's going to
take a forklift and a good pry bar to get him out."

Ted shrugged. "Sorry, Mandy. He's a hell of a good
cook. So are you, Lola, but with just me and Theo, I
don't have to share as much."

"I'm crushed." Lola sighed. "However, I imagine I'll
survive. I'm really glad you're here, Ted." She looked
into the camera. "Okay, Mr. Reed. Now what else is
going on? And is that a sling I see on your left arm?"

"Well . . . yes." He glanced at Mandy. "It appears
I've joined the gunshot club, though I think Ben's still
the only one of us who took lead directly *in*to the body,
and Nate Dunagan's bullet got stopped by his cellphone,
may it rest in peace. But like Jake and Ted, I got grazed
yesterday when someone took a shot at us. The bullet
cut across my left shoulder blade and it hurts like a son-
ofabitch. Jake, I'm not nearly as tough as you."

When the commotion settled, he told them. Everything. Mandy was so proud of the fact he got through
the story without missing anything of importance, and
most of all, without losing it. She wanted to cry every
time she thought of that little boy hiding out in his parents' room, watching his father strangle his mother.

She imagined that at some point the loneliness would
come back to him, the way he'd felt when he realized
his mother wasn't coming back, especially with the horrible story his father had fed him for all those years.

"So," he said, holding tightly to Mandy, "that's going to
be my main focus for a while. Making a formal report to
the Marin police department and then making sure my
father is arrested before he can hurt any of us again."

There was absolute shocked silence while Jake, Kaz, Lola, and Ben absorbed the horror of what Marc had just told them. Theo and Ted knew all the details, but they sat quietly. Then Kaz turned to Jake. "We have to go home. Can you cancel the shoot in Venice?"

"No." Marc held his hand up. "Absolutely not. I don't want any of you coming back sooner than you plan to. Right now, I'm worried sick about Mandy, and I hate to think of Theo and Ted here in danger. I couldn't handle it if any of you were out here, making yourselves targets for the bastard. No matter what anyone says, it's my father who's behind all this, and none of you should be put in danger because of him. I have to agree with Ted. Steven Reed is psychotic. I have no doubt that he would kill any of you to get to me. Please, continue to do what you're doing, and don't come back until you have to. Kaz and Jake, we're taking care of the details for the wedding, so if you come back as planned at the end of next week, with any luck, we'll have him behind bars by then and you can finish up any final wedding stuff with plenty of time before the event."

Ben nodded. "I don't like it, Marc, but I understand." He hugged Lola tightly against him. "I'd hate to be out there now, worrying about Lola's safety and yours as well. I'm really glad you've got Ted with you. It looks like the deposition could go into next week, but if you do need me, just let me know and I can be there in a matter of hours."

"Thank you, Ben, I appreciate that. You can't imagine how much."

They talked a while longer about other things: what they'd gotten done for Kaz and Jake's wedding, the fact that they were talking about opening a coffee shop in Marc's building and hiring women from a shelter, all topics that made this feel more like a regular chat, the kind they had when all of them were sitting around the kitchen table at the house on Twenty-third. It brought a needed sense of normalcy to their lives. Finally, they ended the call.

As soon as the screen went black, Marc slumped against Mandy. "I think I was more nervous making that call than I've ever been at any of my business meetings."

"Why?" She rested her head on his shoulder.

"It's all so much more important now. Every single person on that call means so much to me. I've never had this many people in my life to care about. To worry about. It's a huge responsibility."

She laughed. "No, it's not. Because they care just as much about you, and worry about you even more."

"I doubt that."

"Don't." She shook her head, wishing there were some simple way to knock a bit of sense into the man. "Don't ever doubt any of us. Ever."

He looked at her for the longest time. Finally sighed and said, "I love you so much, Mandy. So much it's scary. And yes, that means I'm paying attention to you and I'm really trying to deal with all this. Okay?" He kissed her. "So, what's on the schedule today?"

"Nothing. Absolutely nothing. I'm going to help Cassie in the tasting room and you are going to heal. Quickly. I don't want to worry about hurting anything next time we, uh . . ."

"Fuck like bunnies?"

She nodded. Barely managed to hang on to her "serious adult" look. "That would be it exactly."

Theo just sat there with a huge grin on his face, staring at the black screen. Ted watched him for a moment until curiosity won. "What?"

"Aw, c'mon. You can see it. I know you can. It's Marc. He's had it hard for Mandy since he first met her. Came to work the next day and talked about all the crap that happened between Jake, Kaz, and that damned stalker, but whenever he mentioned Lola's little sister, his eyes just lit up." Theo waved his hand at the screen. "You look at him now and it's like he's lit up top to bottom from the inside. He's a terrific kid. Too damned smart for his own good, but he's always seemed just a little bit lost, sort of out of step with the rest of the world. Not anymore. I want this to work for him."

"Then we'd better stop the bastard who's after him."

"Agreed. And Ted, I mean what I said. You're welcome to stay at my place as long as you like. You're an easy guy to be around."

Ted caught himself studying Theo, fascinated by the man behind the business manager. Coming to San Francisco had been a huge step, terrifying in a way he'd not really understood. Then he realized what this move had meant—not only was he leaving a job he'd held for twenty-seven years, he was leaving that person behind. The Ted Robinson he'd been—closeted, alone, always wondering what he'd missed—had stayed in Virginia.

This was only his third day in California. He'd spent two days camped out at Theo's, and already felt more at home there, and here in this office built especially for him, than in all those years living in Arlington.

He raised his head and smiled at Theo. "Thank you. But you're pretty damned easy to be around too, Theo. That you are."

Mandy walked in the door an hour after the tasting room closed and flopped on the couch. She sat there a moment, sniffed the air, and sat up as Marc walked in from the bedroom. "What's that I smell?"

"That would be a pot of minestrone soup, courtesy of Nate and Cassie. Nate picked it up for us today. He's keeping the leftover lasagna. They're going to eat it at their place and we're staying in."

"Wonderful. Cassie was beat when we finally closed up. She needs full-time help in the tasting room. She said the crowds this summer are more than double what they saw last year, and she's still doing her winemaking job on top of dealing with the tourists."

"Why hasn't she hired anyone?"

"I think she wanted to be sure you were okay with it, and she hasn't had a chance to ask."

Shaking his head, Marc picked up his phone. "Cassie? Hi. Sorry to bother you. Mandy says you were swamped again today. Look, feel free to hire anyone you need to help you out in the tasting room. Get someone to manage it, if that would help. You're my winemaker—my very pregnant winemaker. I don't want you wearing yourself out. Pay whatever the going hourly rate is, bumped up by a couple of dollars. Yep . . . it makes for a better employee. If you know of someone who can take it over and manage it, run the place entirely, hire them and we'll talk regular salary. In fact, what about Josie? Do you think she'd be interested? Comes with benefits, and she already knows the work."

They talked for a few more minutes. Mandy went in and poured herself a glass of wine, stirred the soup, and went back out to the front room. "How are you feeling?"

Marc stuck his phone in his pocket. "I've decided I'll probably live. I take it you had a busy day?"

"I did. I'm really exhausted, but I think part of that is stress. I keep wondering when your father's going to pop out of the woodwork again."

"I know. I really want this settled." He reached for

her and she tangled her fingers in his. Marc tugged gently and she sat beside him, nestled against his right side. He kissed her slowly, thoroughly, and then kissed her again.

"I called the chief of police in Marin today while you were working," he said. "Told him Jerry Russo had given me the contact info and he said Jerry had already called him, told him to expect to hear from me. I gave him the bare bones story, and he wants us to come in tomorrow. Are you ready to head back to the city?"

She was, but, "I worry about Cassie. She was working her tail off yesterday and today."

"I'm waiting to hear from her. I'm hoping Josie might take the job." He grinned. "It would be a good way to rope Lupe in once he graduates."

She slanted her eyes his way and caught him grinning at her like he'd just pulled one over on everyone. "I like Josie and Lupe," he said. "It makes sense, don't you think? They've both worked here since they were in high school. They already have the house rent free. No reason they can't stay on until they're ready to buy something of their own."

"Right. Just adding to your empire, right?"

"Well," he said, with absolutely no outward sense of remorse, "there is that."

Josie and Lupe showed up later in the evening after Marc and Mandy had finished dinner. Josie was definitely interested in the manager's position. She was looking for full-time work, so she and Lupe both poured over the copy of the employee contract Theo had sent to Marc earlier. After looking at the salary Marc offered, the hours, and the benefits involved, Josie didn't even take it home to sign. In minutes it was a done deal.

"Josie, when Lupe goes back to school, you can schedule your time off with Cassie so you can spend time with him, though we might have to bring in someone to help you in the tasting room when Cassie has the baby."

"It's gonna be crazy," Lupe said. He might still look about sixteen, but he was smart and focused and had been the vineyard manager here while he was still in high school, slipping into Colonel Mac's job once Alzheimer's took its toll. He'd gone to the junior college and then transferred to Davis a year ago. "You'd think a winemaker would know better than to have a baby in October," he said. "She's going to be huge by harvest time."

"Nate may have to lock her in the house to keep her off her feet, and we're all going to have to help get the grapes in this year." Marc grabbed Mandy's hand. "You're going to be working your first crush, babe. You might want to start working out. It's a tough job."

"And you, of course, will still be wounded, and therefore only capable of giving orders, right?"

"Of course."

Later, after Lupe and Josie had gone back to their house, Marc followed Mandy into the bedroom where she was slipping out of her clothes. He paused in the doorway, leaned against the doorjamb and said, "I thought I should let you know that I'm feeling a lot better tonight."

"Oh?" She turned, raised one eyebrow, and studied him. He did look a lot better, even with the sling still supporting his arm. More rested, though she was sure his back was still painful. He moved carefully, and definitely favored his left side.

"How do you intend to do this?" she asked. "You can't be on the bottom because your back's really sore, and you can't be on top because you've only got one functioning arm." She stood there with her arms folded across her chest. Her naked chest.

"I'm not sure, but come hell or high water, we will find a way."

She studied him a moment, and then a slow smile tilted her lips. It was a full-blown grin when she took his right hand and led him over to a straight-back chair with a padded seat. With a few tugs, she helped him take his shoes and then his pants off. Then, much more carefully, she eased his arms out of the cropped sleeves on his sweatshirt. Then she adjusted his sling, made certain his arm was well-supported. "Sit."

Frowning, naked, already getting hard, he sat. She grabbed a condom, knelt on the rug between his feet, and studied his growing erection. He was certain his dick had maxed out in both length and girth when she wrapped her fingers around the base, lowered her head, and took him into her mouth.

He wanted to say something funny, something that would make her laugh, because there was nothing he loved more than Mandy's laughter. Well, almost nothing. The hot suction of her mouth, the sweep of her tongue, the firm grasp of her fingers around his shaft . . . that beat even laughter.

He groaned instead. A low, primal sound that seemed to come from somewhere deep inside, and totally of its own volition. He forgot the damned sling and the ache across his back, forgot his name if he had to be honest.

He tangled his right hand in her hair, needing the connection, the powerful bond he already felt with Mandy, the knowledge that she constantly put him first, did everything she could to make things better for him.

It just didn't get any better than this.

She slowly worked her way up the length of his dick, nibbling with teeth and lips, licking and sucking him until he'd moved beyond conscious thought, into a level of need that defied description.

He'd almost reached the point of no return when she slipped him free of her mouth, sheathed him in a heartbeat, and straddled his lap. When Mandy came down on him, lights exploded behind his eyes, sparks of color somehow linked to the tight glove of her body grasping him. She was so damned tight, so perfectly sized for him that he had to touch, had to slip his arm free of the blasted sling and rest his hands on her strong thighs as she slowly raised and lowered herself over his erection.

He dipped his head as she arched her back, presenting him with the fullness of her breasts, her darkly beaded nipples. He drew first one and then the other between his lips, licking, nipping, sucking hard and deep until he lost himself in the sounds of her soft whimpers and moans of pleasure, in the taste of her, in the intoxicating scent of her arousal.

Lost until Mandy's slick heat and sudden clench of vaginal muscles drew the rush and thunder of Marc's climax, the pounding tempo of their heartbeats thudding in counterpoint, one to the other. Her legs drew up and she clenched his thighs, forced herself solidly down on his erection, her soft cries and wanton gasps blending with his own guttural cry of pleasure.

Mandy collapsed against him, her hands holding tightly to the back of the chair, her inner muscles rhythmically tightening and then releasing, milking him of every last drop. He loved this. Loved her. Loved her so much it terrified him, knowing that his father was out there, that the man was intent on hurting Marc in any way he could. Steven Reed might be crazy, but he wasn't stupid.

The bastard knew nothing would hurt Marc more than losing Mandy.

Somehow, some way, he had to keep her safe.

CHAPTER 12

They were ready to leave Dry Creek Valley a little before ten Saturday morning when Cassie called.

"G'morning, Marc. Josie's already here," she said. "I didn't realize her part-time job had ended last week, so she's ready to start here full time. Timing couldn't have been better. Thank you for hiring her."

One less thing to worry about. "We'll stop by on our way out," he said. "Mandy and I are headed back to the city today." He ended the call, stuck his phone in his pocket, and walked back to the bedroom where Mandy was finishing up putting fresh sheets on the bed. He watched her smooth the blankets, wished he could help. "Do you mind stopping by the tasting room before we go? I want to welcome Josie to the family."

Laughing, Mandy straightened the afghan at the foot of the bed, walked around to his side, and kissed him. "So, you're finally admitting to adding another couple to our growing brood?"

He wrapped his right arm around her and pulled her close for another kiss. "I've decided it's not worth fighting an issue I can't defend. And I really love how you refer to this as 'our' growing brood."

Damn. His throat felt tight. He rested his chin on top of her head and took a few seconds to compose himself. After a lifetime without connections, he suddenly understood what Ben had meant that night when he'd realized how many people in his life actually cared about him. It was wonderful, powerful, in fact, yet in some ways, it was a terrifying burden, made even heavier by the threat his father posed.

He wished the man would just go away, but more than that, he wanted closure. Wanted his father in jail where he belonged, locked away forever so that Marc didn't have to worry about the man hurting the people Marc loved. "C'mon. I've got our stuff loaded in the car. We can drive over, tell Cassie thank you, wish Josie luck, and then leave straight from there."

"That works." Mandy took a quick look around to make sure they'd gotten everything and were leaving the place as clean as when they'd found it, grabbed her phone and handbag, and followed Marc out to the Tesla.

He held the door on the passenger side for her. As she got in, she turned and kissed him before asking, "Are you sure you're okay to drive?"

"I'll be fine, but I'll let you know if I get tired."

Appeased for now, Mandy settled into her seat while Marc carefully got into the car and, driving one-handed, pulled out around the cottage and followed the driveway back to the tasting room. There were already a couple of cars in the parking area. She seemed terribly relieved when he managed not to hit any of them.

Hanging on tightly to Mandy's hand, Marc led her into the tasting room. Cassie was inside, going over inventory, while Nate leaned against the counter with a cup of coffee, laughing at something Josie had said. Cassie turned and waved. Then she walked over, carefully hugged Marc, and then surprised him with a big kiss on the cheek.

He glanced at Nate before asking Cassie, "What was that for?"

"An apology." She laughed and blushed at the same time. "I've owed you one for a very long time. You had to realize, Marc, that I really did not want to like you when you bought Tangled Vines, but if not, I'm sure you figured that out soon enough. I was such a bitch. I hated that we'd lost it, hated the fact Dad was slipping and there was nothing I could do to help him, and I really hated the fact some young guy with too much money had come in and bought the only home I'd ever known and hired a new vineyard manager without even asking me if I needed one." She shook her head and glanced at Nate, then back at Marc.

"Well, it appears I really needed Nate. Marc, I had no idea that you were the best thing that could have happened." She grabbed Nate's hand and he stepped up behind her, wrapped his arms around her waist, and rested his hands on her rounded belly. "Thank you so much for everything you've done for us. And thank you for hiring the perfect man for the job."

He didn't know what to say. Mandy took his hand and squeezed. "No one else knows this vineyard the way you do, Cassie." She turned and smiled at Marc. He was blinking way too fast, his eyes burning and his throat tight. He'd never expected a simple good-bye to turn out so emotional. Thank goodness for Mandy. She always knew exactly what to say.

"Marc's nothing if not a good businessman. Look what you and Nate have accomplished in a very short time."

Marc finally regained his shredded composure. Smiling broadly, he said, "And look what you'll have accomplished in, oh, about three more months." He shook Nate's hand. "Thank you, Cassie. I didn't know you when I bought the property, though I'd always wanted to own a part of this valley. Now, with all that's happened with my personal life, it appears I really needed to be here. I can't imagine anyone better than you and Nate to make this place absolutely perfect. Your love for this vineyard and your skill as a winemaker shows in every wine you create." He smiled at Josie. "And thank you for agreeing to work here, Josie. I think you know this tasting room almost as well as Cassie. You're in charge of keeping her from working too hard. I really don't want her delivering this baby anywhere but in the designated hospital room."

"Gotcha, Mr. Reed. And thanks. I've always wanted to work here. I love this tasting room!" She went back to the four tourists standing at the granite bar, all of them apparently fascinated by the very personal conversation they had just witnessed.

Marc and Mandy stayed a few more minutes, going over some of the plans for Kaz and Jake's wedding just five weeks away, making sure either Cassie or Josie would clear the leftover food out of the refrigerator. There was too much good stuff to let it go to waste. Then more tourists arrived and Cassie and Josie went to work, while Nate walked them out to their car.

He paused next to the Tesla. "I talked to Jerry a few minutes before you got here. He wanted me to let you know that it appears your father slipped into Mexico last night at the San Ysidro border crossing at San Diego. He had a fake passport, but it was good enough to get him through. There's an APB out on him, but they hadn't gotten it in time. He came up on the security video taken at the crossing."

"Any idea where he went after he crossed into Mexico?"

"Not yet. Jerry said they just don't have the manpower to follow up." Nate shrugged. "Maybe your guy can find out something. I'd definitely appreciate knowing if he learns anything." He glanced toward the tasting room. "I worry about Cassie."

Marc nodded. "So do I, Nate." He held tightly to Mandy's hand. "So do I."

Mandy had saved a copy of all of Ted's notes about Marc's mother and father, the information about her inheritances, and the fact there'd been no records of activities of any kind after her disappearance, to a flash drive. They left that with the chief of police in Marin, along with contact info for both Marc and Ted Robinson.

When they walked out to the parking lot, Mandy led Marc to the passenger side and opened the door. "I'm driving. I can tell your back is killing you right now, so get in, relax, and ignore the fact there's a woman behind the wheel of your beloved Tesla."

Shaking his head, he laughed softly. "I'm convinced you can read my mind. I was hoping you'd offer, but I didn't want to blow my tough guy image."

Mandy kissed him and waited until he got into the car. Then she helped him buckle his seatbelt and patted him on the head like a little kid. "For what it's worth, big guy, you don't have a tough guy image. You're much too thoughtful and kind."

He was still trying to think of a comeback when she got into the car, fastened her own seatbelt, and pulled out of the parking lot, but his back really did hurt and his left arm was next to useless. They were just crossing the Golden Gate when Marc's phone rang. He took the call—it was Ted Robinson—and put the phone on speaker.

"Hey Marc. Glad I caught you. I got a call this morning from your neighbor, Abdul. He said he and Jasper spotted lights on in your house Wednesday night when they were out walking Rico. They didn't notice any strange cars in the neighborhood, and didn't think much of it. Abdul said he thought maybe you had lights set on timers, but after reading in the paper about you getting shot, they decided to call your office to let you guys know."

"Great." Marc glanced at Mandy. "That's all we need. Hope no one took anything."

"Actually, it appears they left things. I wasn't sure if you left lights on timers or not, so I took a run by there this morning and did a sweep for bugs. It looks like someone wired your place. It was a sloppy job, actually, but every room was covered. Video cameras in the bedrooms, voice activated recorders throughout the entire house. I've left them all in place, but we'll remove them once you've seen what all is there."

"Wednesday, you say?" Marc glanced once again at Mandy. "That's the day we ran into my father at the office, the day I told him I knew about Rockpile Road. I can't recall if we mentioned leaving that afternoon or not, but if he was watching the house, he'd know we weren't coming back."

Mandy added, "He shot you the next day."

"We don't know for sure it was him," Marc said, even though he couldn't think of anyone else who might be after him. Or Mandy. "Ted, did anyone contact you about the latest on my father, that he was spotted slipping into Mexico late last night?"

"No. Where did you hear that?"

"Sheriff's deputy in Dry Creek, Jerry Russo, told Nate Dunagan, asked him to get the word to me. Said he'd been spotted on a security camera at the San Ysidro crossing in San Diego. He got through shortly before the APB went out. No idea how he got down there so quickly, though they're checking flight records from the Sonoma County airport."

"Let me see what I can find out. Just a minute . . ." Marc heard Ted's muffled laughter, and then he was back. "Where are you now?"

"Just turned onto Nineteenth Avenue."

"Theo and I are almost to your house now. We'll meet you there."

Marc ended the call and leaned back against the seat. His back and arm still ached, but he was already feeling better. Mandy was an excellent driver—normally he was a horrible passenger, and he'd never really been a passenger in his own car—but there was something really sexy about the way she handled the Tesla. Sort of the way she handled him.

He closed his eyes, prepared to take a short nap while Mandy dealt with the stop-and-go traffic.

Mandy pulled into the driveway and turned off the engine. There was a strange car parked in front of their house, but she figured it must belong to Theo or Ted. She hated to wake Marc. He'd fallen asleep almost immediately after talking with Ted, and he showed no sign of waking up anytime soon.

He was so beautiful like this, sleeping peacefully, his features relaxed, long dark lashes underscoring his closed eyes. She rarely had a chance to observe him this still, to indulge herself in looking at the man she'd fallen head over heels in love with.

She remembered all those months of watching him ride by the coffee shop, a tall, gorgeous, dark-haired guy on a beat-up old Schwinn, and she'd spun fantasies about him, about them, never dreaming she'd one day have him in her life.

In her bed. Enough. She really needed to wake him. She leaned close and kissed him. His lips shaped to fit hers and he kissed her back, and then his right hand cupped her skull and he kissed her more thoroughly. Finally she pulled away. "Wake up, sleepyhead."

He blinked, sat up and looked around. Then he kissed her again. "We're home. I thought we were in our bed at the winery. I must have been sound asleep."

"You were. C'mon. I think Ted and Theo are already here." She got out of the car, grabbed her bag and his out of the back and looped them over her shoulders along with her handbag.

"Poor baby. You look like a pack animal." He took the larger of the two bags and carried it in his right hand.

Mandy paused long enough to plug in the Tesla and they headed up the stairs. Theo opened the door, met them halfway, and grabbed the bags from both of them. He followed Marc and Mandy into the house.

"How are you feeling, boss?"

Marc shook his head. "Well, Theo, I've already admitted I'm not as tough as Ben or Jake. This hurts like hell, but I think it's the staples more than the injury."

"You do realize the bullet went deep enough that it shaved off a bit of your scapula, don't you?"

He stopped and stared at Mandy. "I don't remember that."

"I think you were zonked out on pain meds. The doctor said you've got a perfect little divot in the bone. That's bound to hurt, so you're not nearly as big a wuss as you think you are."

"Good to know. I guess."

Ted walked out of the hallway that led to the bedrooms. Mandy dropped her handbag and wrapped her arms around him. "I'm so glad you came back!"

He hugged her tightly. "Me, too, Mandy. Marc, thanks again. I'm going to love it out here." He shook hands with Marc. "But the first thing we need to do is clear this place out. Theo, you have a box?"

"Got it." Theo and Ted went through and removed all the various devices while Mandy followed and recorded the removal of each one. Tiny cameras and electronic bugs so small as to be virtually undetectable—unless, like Ted, you had a powerful scanner that found everything from Bluetooth and Wi-Fi to the more conventional signals.

What was really unsettling was the number of cameras he found—whatever the camera saw would show up on the device screen, and finding cameras focused on all the beds in the house definitely had Mandy rattled.

"How did he get in?" She grabbed Marc's hand while Ted and Theo removed two cameras from her bedroom, along with a couple of listening devices.

Marc tilted his head and stared at her for a moment. "Did we lock the garage before we left?"

Marc's question actually made her feel physically ill. Mandy spun away from him and went back through the house to the kitchen. The back door lock had been jimmied, so she didn't touch it. She remembered opening the garage door so Ben could carry bundles of branches out to the driveway. He'd done a lot of pruning in the backyard and hired a landscape guy to haul off the debris.

She didn't remember locking it. In the past, they'd gotten really sloppy about keeping things locked up around here, but with all the trouble they'd had over the past couple of months, she'd been much more careful. Apparently not careful enough.

Mandy walked back to where the men were finding more devices in Ben and Lola's room. "I think the garage door might have been left unlocked. I didn't go down to check because the door into the kitchen has damage where it looks like someone broke through the lock. I think that's where he came in and I didn't want to mess up any possible fingerprints."

Ted focused on her. "I wonder if we can get prints?"

"Possibly. Whoever it was broke in through the back door. Looks like he used a screwdriver from the tool box in the garage. It's sitting on the kitchen counter, and I know neither of us left it there."

"Theo? You work on these." He handed the scanner to Theo. "I've got an evidence kit in the front room. I'll dust for prints, see if anything comes up. He glanced at Mandy. "Come with me. I need a minion."

Marc had taken over filming the removal of all the devices. He glanced at Mandy. "Minions are us. I'm not sure if I'm been promoted or demoted."

Mandy leaned over and kissed him. "Just do as you're told, dear."

"Yes, ma'am."

"I can't believe that took us all afternoon."

Mandy took the leash off of Rico and flopped down on the couch next to Marc. They'd walked down to thank Abdul and Jasper for watching the beast, and for notifying Theo about the lights on in the house.

Marc wrapped his right arm around her shoulders and pulled her close. "I can't believe how much crap they found. Filling an entire box with miniature listening devices and cameras is sort of mind-boggling."

"I just hope we got everything."

"Theo did a second scan of the entire property, including the yard and garage, and the storage area. It came back clean."

"So did your car and mine, but it still makes me uneasy." She patted the couch on her right side. Rico jumped up and stretched out beside her. "Though if your father really is in Mexico, I doubt he'll be able to get signals from anything this far away. I wonder how long he plans to stay?"

"Not long enough." Marc's arm tightened around her.

Mandy lay her head on his shoulder. "So, what do we do now?"

"Well, Ted called the SFPD to report the break-in and all the bugs, and he actually got hold of José Macias." The officer had been involved when attempts had been made on Kaz's life, and again when Ben Lowell was being followed. At least he was familiar with all of them. "He's supposed to come by tomorrow or Monday to get a report, and hopefully Ted will have some info from the fingerprints. Ted's also researching hiring a cadaver dog, and Theo's having a release-of-liability form drawn up for Jeb Barton. It's going to include a reward, should we find her remains, since I doubt he'll take payment from me for letting us search. In the meantime, I need to get back to work. I've got a lot of businesses that depend on me at least knowing what they're up to."

"Do you actually know all the people who work for you?" She knew he owned a couple of software development companies, the jewelry company, and the winery, but those were the only ones she'd dealt with in her one day doing Lola's job. She didn't know what else there might be.

"Not everyone, though I personally know all the people who run the various operations. I tend to remain as out of the way as I can. There's nothing worse than a manager who inserts himself in every detail of a business that was already doing well. Theo handles the day-to-day contacts for most of them. He's very good, and he likes the challenge."

"It's wonderful of him to take Ted under his wing."

Marc had to agree. Ted seemed so much happier than when they'd first met him. "I'm really glad Ted's here. He fits well with this group. Which reminds me. We also need to come up with a plan for the coffee shop and then nail down which of the three shelters you, Lola, and Kaz think is the best one to work with. We'll have to approach them with the idea of hiring their clients as our employees, possibly through an endowment or trust of some kind, and discuss the kind of funding we can provide."

The three women had actually narrowed it down to the one they felt was best, but they'd decided to wait until everyone was back to tell the guys. They'd chosen a secular group, not associated with any particular religion, so that all would feel welcome, and the emphasis was on giving women the tools to make it in the real world, and to raise healthy children without fear.

Which reminded Mandy . . . she'd picked up a pregnancy test in Healdsburg. She certainly didn't feel very pregnant, though she really didn't know what pregnant felt like, but it never hurt to check. When Marc went into his room to make a few business calls, she headed for the bathroom.

A few minutes later she sat on the bathroom counter staring at the negative test, feeling vaguely disappointed. It had only been a week, but unless her period was late— which it wasn't, so far—she wasn't going to worry

about it. It would be a relief to tell Marc he could probably relax.

Now definitely wasn't the time to be worrying about
a pregnancy.

But she couldn't help but wonder how she would have
felt if the test had been positive.

It was after six before Marc realized he'd spent the last
couple of hours in his bedroom, but he'd had a number
of phone calls to make and a few issues to deal with at
one of the software firms. His shoulder still hurt, but
not as much as it had this morning. Taking it easy this
afternoon must have helped.

He wandered out to the kitchen to see what he could
fix for dinner. It didn't seem fair that Mandy had been
doing so much of the cooking, but she was already pulling something out of the oven.

"Smells good. What'd you make?" He leaned over her
shoulder and recognized meatloaf and roasted potatoes.
"That looks good. I didn't think you liked to cook." He
kissed her cheek as she set the pan on top of the stove.

"I don't. Lola left this in the freezer for us. Now do
you see why I love my sister?"

"I doubt this is the only reason, but it's certainly
valid." He grabbed everything he needed to set the table,
and then got out a bottle of wine. "It seems so quiet here
with everyone gone."

"I know. Kaz and Jake should be home by next Thursday. No idea when Lola and Ben will be back." Without
even pausing to take a breath, she added, "I did the pregnancy test today."

He paused in the process of setting silverware on the
place mats. "And?"

"I'm not pregnant."

She smiled at him, but her lip was quivering. He

dropped the silverware on the table and walked over to the stove. Using his right arm, he pulled her tightly against his chest. "You don't look very happy about it."

She shrugged and then ran her hand across her eyes. "I feel so stupid, but I was actually disappointed. Even though I know the timing isn't right, I've been picturing a little boy like you must have been, imagining what it would be like to hold him in my arms, to love him. I guess I'm not that much against getting pregnant as I thought."

"If it makes any difference, I'm not either. Ever since the condom broke, I've imagined you growing big with our baby. Just daydreams, I guess, but I don't want to wait too much longer."

"Once this mess with your father is over, then maybe?"

He brushed her hair back from her face, circled her skull with his hands, and kissed her. Her lips tasted of salt—the tears she hadn't entirely managed to wipe away. "Definitely then. I love you, Mandy. No matter what happens with him, I'm going to want you in my life. This isn't the time or the place, and certainly not the least bit romantic, but will you marry me? Every day we're together, I'm reminded that I don't ever want to be without you."

"You're sure? We haven't known each other all that long."

"Seventy-seven days, but who's counting?" He kissed her. "Do you love me?"

"More than anything."

"Then say yes. We'll figure out the details later." He kissed her again.

"Dinner's going to get cold." She didn't answer his proposal. Instead, she pulled away from his one-armed embrace and served their plates at the stove. "There's a salad in the refrigerator."

Marc decided to let her think about it, so he got the salad out, grabbed a couple of small plates and filled them with the fresh lettuce and tomatoes. There was homemade vinaigrette on the table, and Mandy set a plate of meatloaf and potatoes in front of each of them.

Marc poured a couple of glasses of red wine, and held his up for a toast. "To you, Mandy Monroe. Hopefully soon to be Mandy Reed. That is, if you actually accept my lame proposal."

She tapped her glass to his. "My answer should have been a given. I love you, but it doesn't feel real. Not yet."

"Probably because I did such a crappy job of asking and you didn't actually verbally accept. Maybe I need to draw up a contract. I'm a lot better at contracts. Jake went down on his knees in a vineyard, Ben knelt in front of Lola by the backyard bench. Even Nate was more romantic with Cassie, down on bended knee. I'm thinking I need a do over. Will you ever forgive me?"

This time her smile was the real thing. "That's not why it doesn't feel real, silly. It's because you proposing marriage has been a fantasy of mine for years, long before you even knew who I was. I'm not concerned about a do over. I'm worried you're going to realize you made a mistake and take it back."

"Never. Not on your life. Now eat your dinner. I'm thinking there has to be a way to celebrate."

She gave him a sexy, pouty glance. "I'm sure we can think of something."

Marc was the first one awake Sunday morning. It was barely dawn, the room filled with gray shadows, while Mandy slept soundly beside him. It was rare for him to be awake in the morning before her—Mandy seemed to have an unlimited supply of energy, though she crashed early in order to be up before the birds. That was something they'd have to adjust to when Mandy crawled into bed before nine and he was up a lot of nights until midnight or later.

So far they'd managed to meet in the middle. They'd certainly managed well last night. He lay there beside Mandy with a stupid grin on his face. This giddy kind of joy had never been a part of his life, not until Mandy. She made everything better, though he still couldn't believe she actually loved him.

And for that he had his father to blame. Growing up unloved had unquestionably done a job on him, but he refused to let that man's failure as a human being define his life any further. With Mandy there was no doubt in his mind—not only was he capable of love, he was loved and he was wanted. In so many ways she validated him, made him see himself as a better man. With that thought in mind, he rolled over and held her close. No point in wasting a perfectly good lazy Sunday morning, especially not when they were the only two here.

He'd just dozed off when his phone rang. Grumbling, Marc reached for it, saw the call was from Ted, and answered. "What's up?"

"I just heard from Jerry Russo. It appears Steven Reed is in a jail cell in Tijuana. No idea how long extradition will take, since he's not yet been charged in Sonoma County, but the authorities in Tijuana are going to hold him for a couple of weeks to give us time to come up with a case. Right now it's on a fake passport charge. Jerry said his people got some good prints off the Ford Bronco, so even if they can't nail him on your mom's case, they can hold him on an attempted murder charge if they come up with a good match."

"I thought Jerry said the car had been wiped down. Where'd they get the prints?"

"On the outside of the driver's side door. A full palm

print, as if he might have stumbled when he was getting back into the car after taking a shot at you two. I'll let you know as soon as I hear."

"What about the prints you got from our house? Anything there?"

"Not your father's. They belong to a two-bit criminal that the SFPD is trying to locate. If we can tie him to your father hiring him, we might have something. In the meantime, I've located a private trainer who has a pretty successful cadaver dog. We'll have to pay for his round-trip flight from Montana, but his reputation is pretty solid. I just need the go-ahead from you."

"You've got it. Give him the info to bill Reed Industries for expenses—you can get that from Theo—but go ahead and arrange for his flight. If he needs a private jet to bring the dog, do that. Theo can help with the details, but you're working under my authority and any expenses will be covered."

There was a long silence. "Ted? You there?"

"Yeah," he said. "I'm here, and I'm trying to get used to doing things without tons of red tape. I think I'm going to like it."

"You'll get used to it. It's a lot more efficient, and actually more cost effective in the long run. Thank you, Ted. Just knowing you're working on this is a good feeling."

He ended the call and glanced at Mandy. She was wide awake and watching him. "Ted's got a dog that can search for your mom?"

"He does. Good morning." He leaned close and kissed her. She wrapped her arms around him, and everything he'd been worrying about quietly slipped away.

Around two that afternoon Mandy wandered out into the kitchen and found Marc working on his laptop. She stood behind him, wrapped her arms around his shoulders, and sighed. "I started my period."

He went absolutely still. Then, without a word, he turned and pulled her into his lap. "I know I should be relieved, but I'm actually sorry. I was kind of hoping the pregnancy test was wrong."

"Me, too." She kissed him. "Things have changed over the past couple weeks or so." She leaned her forehead against his. "At least now I can go on the pill and we can get rid of the condoms."

"For now," he said. But he didn't look very happy about it.

Which, for whatever reason, lifted Mandy's spirits much higher than they'd been.

CHAPTER 13

One week later . . .

Marc checked his phone when he heard it buzzing on the kitchen table, saw who it was, and flipped it on speaker. "Jake! Are you back in town? When did you get in?"

"About an hour ago. Kaz and I are going to sleep for a few hours. Just wanted to let you know we were here, and you can expect Ben and Lola by late afternoon."

"You sure? I haven't heard from them."

"We had a long layover in New York so I called him to check in. He said the prosecution got what they wanted to prepare their case, and that, barring any airline fuck-ups—Ben's words, not mine—he and Lola would be home in time for dinner. Their flight's due in at three twenty."

"Perfect! You and Kaz get some rest and then come over for dinner, too. We have to get together—I've missed you guys."

"Same here. We're anxious to know what the hell's going on with your dad."

"As far as I know, he's still in a Tijuana jail. He can stay there and rot for all I care."

Jake laughed. "Oh, and Kaz wants to know what's going on with you and Mandy."

This time the laughter was all Marc's. "We'll catch up tonight. Later."

"Later."

"Who was that?"

He glanced up as Mandy wandered into the kitchen in her fuzzy green bathrobe with her hair standing out in all directions. It was after eight and she was just now waking up. Totally unlike his early-bird girl. Marc pulled her into his arms for a kiss. "Good morning, sleepyhead. I was going to come in and see if you were still breathing. Have you ever slept this late before?"

She rolled her forehead back and forth against his chest. "No, but I've never worked like an indentured servant before, either. I have a very demanding boss. It was a long week."

"Poor baby . . ." One handed, Marc grabbed a cup off the counter and filled it full of coffee. He'd gotten the staples out of his back just yesterday afternoon, though the doctor had used strips of bandage to continue holding the edges of the healing wound together, but that arm was currently wrapped around Mandy. She took the cup without opening her eyes. Marc led her past the kitchen table and out to the couch in the front room. He took the cup out of her hand and set it on the coffee table, sat on the couch, and pulled Mandy into his lap.

She snuggled against him like a fuzzy green kitten. He grabbed her coffee cup and handed it to her. "That was Jake I was talking to," he said. "He and Kaz got in from Italy this morning, and Ben and Lola will be home before dinner, barring any airline issues. They're all going to be here for dinner. Do you think we should ask Theo and Ted to join us?"

Mandy took a sip of her coffee and then laughed. "Are you cooking?"

"No, but I know an excellent restaurant that will deliver a fully cooked prime rib dinner for eight. It sounds a lot easier."

"That it does." She pushed her arms against his chest and leaned back, making eye contact. "Have you thought about where everyone's going to sit? Our table was maxed out at six, and really tight when we added Ted. You might want to think about that. With Theo and Ted coming, that's eight people, five of whom are not small men."

Marc stood and pulled Mandy back to her feet. "I was going to ask you what all was on the schedule for today. Looks like we add shopping for a bigger table to the list. Let's get measurements to see how big we can go in the kitchen without making it too crowded. One good thing about these older houses. They've got big kitchens."

He led Mandy into the kitchen and dug through the junk drawer for the tape measure. With Mandy on one end and him on the other, they figured what size table the room could easily accommodate. Which reminded him . . .

"We need to work on the design for the coffee shop. I'm having Theo handle the permits and all of that, but we should decide how it's going to look. Have you thought about that at all?"

"One thing at a time." She jotted down the table measurements and then took another swallow of her coffee. "Okay. I've got the numbers for the table. No multitasking until the caffeine starts working, so give me a few minutes on the coffee shop stuff. She took another big swallow, set her cup down and stood. "Be right back." Then she kissed him before sashaying out of the room like she was headed onto a stage.

He waited. Walked back to the front room and sat on the couch, realized he heard the shower running, waited some more. It was a good fifteen minutes later when Mandy walked back out wearing an old cotton maxi dress and carrying a binder. She kept it with her as she went back to the kitchen for a refill of coffee, but when she returned, she sat next to him on the couch and set the binder on the coffee table.

He thought about pouting because he really wanted her back in his lap, but instead she opened the binder and started flipping through pages. Many pages, filled with photos of coffee shops from all over the country.

"None of these look exactly like what I want, but there's at least a little bit of every single one that feels right."

She'd definitely done her research. "I like this. The colors you've got in every one of these are really comfortable." He laughed and glanced sideways at her. "Sort of like Alden's office."

She titled her head and gazed at him with a frown puckering her brows. "There are a few extra things that I think are important, but they'll add to the cost."

"Okay. What?"

"Bulletproof glass for the front windows, a safe room for employees, but big enough for customers if necessary, a way to lock the front door from behind the counter, and security cameras. Everywhere."

"You don't think that's overkill?"

She shook her head. "Women who go to a shelter are generally there because they've been abused. Some of these men are nuts, and way too many of them have guns. If we're going to provide daycare for the kids and a job for the moms, we have to make the place as safe as we can. That means a panic button that goes straight to Ben and Ted, even Theo. The women need to feel safe here while they're working."

"I agree." He leaned back against the couch and wrapped his arm around Mandy. There was only a slight tenderness in his left shoulder when he hugged her close. "Since we've been working on this project, I keep thinking . . . what if my mother had known there was a safe place she could go and take me? Would she have left him? Or was she too deeply involved to even consider getting away?"

"You'll probably never know, Marc. He could have threatened her with any number of things. Maybe even said he'd take you away from her. She was all alone once her grandmother died. No family anywhere, and maybe no money, at least not until she turned thirty. Plus, the laws then weren't as protective of women. It was legal to beat your wife in this country until 1920, but it wasn't until fifty years later that courts actually began to take it seriously, so in 1984, she might not have had much recourse if he was abusive. There are so many possibilities, but from everything your dreams and memories have told you, it seems the most important thing to her was your safety. My feeling is, she was holding out until she turned thirty and could access her inheritance, but she didn't make it."

He thought about what Mandy had said long after their conversation had ended, after they'd had breakfast and gone back to work with the photos and ideas for the floor plan. Finally, when it was almost lunchtime, he stood and grabbed her hand. "You okay going out in that dress, or is that a 'house only' outfit?"

She laughed. "Definitely house only. Give me a minute." She headed down the hallway to her bedroom, but called out, "Where are we going?"

He followed her. There was no point in missing the chance to see Mandy changing clothes. "Well, we need to buy a table we can have delivered today, so let's do that first. Then I want to see the coffee shop in person with your ideas in mind," he said. "Let's take the binder with us, see what might work best."

He was too late. She already had her jeans on and her bra. The shirt went over her head as he walked into the room.

"Sounds good, but only if I get lunch along the way. I'm starving."

"How do you women stay so thin when you eat as much as you do?"

Laughing, she stopped on her way out the door and gave him a big kiss. "It's all that sex. Burns calories."

Ted and Theo were the last to arrive for dinner. When Marc teased them, Theo draped his arm over Ted's shoulders and said, "You do realize we're the only two who actually work around here."

"On a Saturday?" Marc glanced at Mandy and they both shook their heads.

"Yes, boss. On a Saturday." The guys shook hands all around. Ted even got a few hugs.

Mandy squeezed Marc's arm and whispered. Loudly. "I told you I felt like an indentured servant."

"Poor baby." Marc leaned close and kissed her, but then he stood back and watched while the teasing commenced. There was no way in hell he'd be able to wipe the smile off his face—not with this crowd. Jake had his arm around Kaz, and Ben hadn't let go of Lola's hand, except when she'd hugged Ted and planted a kiss on Theo. At which point, Ted pulled the, "What am I? Chopped liver?" line and she'd kissed him as well.

Marc couldn't remember feeling this good about anything, ever. Not of his financial success, not over any of the many material things he'd accumulated, not the businesses he'd added to his portfolio. He tightened his hold on Mandy, just enough to let her know he'd not forgotten her, and sort of basked in the sense of well being, the knowledge he was surrounded by people he thought of as his family.

Raising his head, he caught Jake grinning right back at him. When Jake raised his hand and gave him a thumbs up signal, Marc knew his longtime best friend understood exactly what Marc was feeling at this moment. This was the family both of them used to talk about, one of both blood relationships and friendships, old and new.

People who stood by you, no matter what. Mandy wrapped her arms around his neck, pulled herself up on her toes, and kissed him. "I'm going to get dinner together. It's all ready to go."

"I'll help," he said, though he hated to turn away from the silly quips and jokes flying among the group. But the moment he turned to follow Mandy into the kitchen, everyone else went as well, where an entirely new discussion ensued over the much larger table with eight matching chairs now taking center stage in the kitchen.

Lola cupped her hands around her mouth and called out over the din. "Mr. Reed? Do you want an executive assistant or a full-time chef? This table appears to point toward the chef's position."

Marc never broke stride, slicing the roast. "It adjusts easily to seat four or six. You're safe."

"Good to know."

"But it can be stretched out to feed twelve." Mandy's smirk earned her a swat on the butt from Lola. Then she helped Mandy finish setting the table while Kaz arranged the bowls along the counter—mashed potatoes and gravy, rib roast, green beans, and a big bowl of green salad Mandy had thrown together—and they all lined up to serve themselves. Mandy filled a plate for Marc, who was busy pulling out a couple of bottles of Intimate wine, and it didn't take long before they were all at the table.

Marc raised his glass. "A toast to everyone who's been traveling and made it home safely. I understand many miles were covered and no luggage lost. Congratulations. And to my newest employee, Ted Robinson, who brings his FBI skills on board, and to Theo Hadley, who's always been a member of this family but hadn't been properly inducted before. Welcome Ted and Theo."

He tapped his glass against Mandy's on his right and Jake's on his left, and then turned and gave Mandy a quick kiss, mainly because he couldn't not do it. Which, of course, brought on a round of questions.

Mandy was the one who held up her hand. "Well, for what it's worth, Marc did ask me to marry him." Then she shot a cocky grin his way. "Your turn."

He sort of stared across the room at the wall. "Before she had a chance to answer me, I asked for a 'do over.'"

"What?" Kaz glared at Marc like she wanted to throttle him. Mandy started laughing.

"Tell him where we were and what we were talking about when you proposed."

Marc felt his face flush, covered his eyes with his hands and stared at his plate. He'd sort of been hoping she wouldn't want the details made public. "Well, it all started with a broken condom . . ."

"Which makes it all Ben's fault." Mandy pointed at him.

"What? Me? What'd I do?" Laughing, Ben directed a wide-eyed innocent look to Lola, who merely shrugged.

"You bought cheap condoms." Marc shook his head. "You should know better than to purchase an off brand."

"You were with me when I bought those condoms, big guy. And what does my choice of condoms have to do with your broken condom?"

"We didn't have any," Mandy said, again with the innocent look. "So we borrowed a few of yours."

When Ben opened his mouth to respond, Lola covered it with her hand. "One does not 'borrow' a condom. One may be given a condom, or one may steal a condom, but one does not borrow that which cannot be reused. And there is no way on God's green Earth I'm ever allowing Ben to occupy a previously occupied condom. No matter how good a buddy you are, Marc."

As the dinner conversation deteriorated even further, the food disappeared and the jokes grew rowdier until it was clear the travelers had all hit the wall, but at least the conversation never got back to his horribly inept proposal.

Kaz and Jake were the first to leave, with a promise to be back on Wednesday to see the apartment next door. Escrow was due to close Tuesday, but their three hours of sleep during the day hadn't made up for the twenty-four hour redeye flight from Italy via Germany—with a long layover in New York. Ben and Lola disappeared once the dishes were done, and headed for their room.

Marc and Mandy stayed in the kitchen, talking quietly with Ted and Theo, until Theo glanced at Ted and both men stood.

Ted shook hands with Marc. Theo asked, "Mandy, will you be working on Monday, or is Lola coming in?"

Mandy glanced at Marc. "I hope you don't mind, but I told Lola I had it covered. She's got to be exhausted, and I know she's got laundry to do and unpacking to deal with. She'll need the extra day. Is that okay?"

"Of course it is." Marc shook hands with Theo, but then turned to Ted. "I forgot to ask if you were at all interested in Jake's apartment, since I'm assuming he'll be taking the unit next door once it's refurbished."

Ted's glance at Theo confirmed what Marc had almost thought he'd imagined, and when Theo wrapped his arm around Ted's waist, there wasn't any doubt. Marc slipped his arm around Mandy. "I'd kind of hoped that's how things were going to play out."

Ted frowned. "How could you guess? I didn't even know." He shot a quick, questioning glance at Theo, who grinned right back at him. Ted snorted, then shook his head. "Well, I didn't know for sure. I've been so deep in the closet for so many years, I'd never realized that was the reason for my lack of interest in finding a wife."

"He's a little thick sometimes, but he's cute." Theo laughed, but Ted merely shook his head with a big smile on his face. "We're still new," Theo said. "No pressure, merely a slow and very cautious chance to get to know each other, to find out just how well we do as a couple." He smiled at Ted this time, a warm, affectionate look that spoke volumes. "We definitely work well together. It's almost spooky, how well we can read one another's thoughts, and . . ."

"Finish each other's sentences," Ted added. "Which reminds me. I've heard back from the gentleman who has the cadaver dog, which I learned we need to start referring to as a 'human remains detection dog,' or HRD. They're particular about the appropriate acronym. Anyway, the handler's name is Jenner Don Stirling, a.k.a. JD, and he's from Butte, Montana. The dog, a McNab/border collie cross, is appropriately named Bones. JD can't get here until August 8, but he's flying directly into Santa Rosa. Then he's free for the next couple of weeks after that point. I can't find anyone else who comes as highly recommended for remains this old, but if . . ."

"No. The eighth works." Marc turned to Mandy and kissed her gently. "I think we need a break from all the drama. My father's locked up, we've got a lead on where my mother might have been buried, and we've got a wedding to finish planning. It's been over thirty years. A few more days can't matter in the scheme of things."

"If you're okay with the wait, I'll tell him it's a go."

Marc stood there a moment, so aware of Mandy beside him, of Ted and Theo together. It all felt right, as if everything were coming together the way things were meant to. He had no doubt they'd find his mother. Everything seemed to be leading toward success. "Thanks, Ted, for finding this guy and researching it. You definitely had to hit the ground running. Again, I'm really glad you're here."

"Marc, you have no idea how much this move means to me." Ted glanced at Theo and then returned his attention to Marc. "Which reminds me. The guy whose prints we pulled here at the house? He was a transient. His body turned up last night in Golden Gate Park. Looked like he'd been dead about a week. Apparent drug overdose, but I doubt we'll be able to link him to your father."

Theo just shook his head. "There's no doubt in my mind that there's a connection. From what Ted has uncovered about Steven Reed, bugging your house six ways from Sunday is something Reed's been accused of before. Never convicted, but it sounds as if it's something he likes to do."

Ted nodded toward the front door. "You ready?"

"Just waiting on you. Thank you, Mandy and Marc, for a terrific dinner. I know Marc must have slaved over a hot stove . . ." He glanced at Ted.

"Or a hot mobile phone . . ."

"For at least, oh, five minutes?" Theo said. "Or less?"

"Less." Marc planted his hands on his hips, but it was hard to keep his lips from twitching. "What is this, the Ted and Theo show?"

"Very well could be." Theo grabbed Ted's arm, and with a jaunty wave, the two of them left.

Mandy stood beside Marc on the top step as the men waved once again before getting into Theo's car and driving away. "This was so much fun. I've missed everyone. I think Ted laughed more tonight than I heard from him the whole time he was out here on Ben's case. Theo must be good for him."

"Ted's good for Theo. He's been really down since his partner cheated on him and Theo booted him out. They'd been together something like twelve years. It hit him hard."

"I can't imagine cheating on someone you love. Good for Theo for respecting himself enough to get rid of the guy."

"I will never cheat on you, Mandy. You have my promise." He turned to her and rested his hands on her hips. Leaned close and kissed her. He felt the smile on her mouth as he pulled away.

"Me, you. Not ever." She looped her arms around his neck, her smile wide and free, and her eyes really did sparkle. "Before I even knew you, I had most of my adult life invested in fantasizing over you, that elusive hunk on the old beater bike. Then, when I finally met the man behind all those hot fantasies and the female version of wet dreams, I found out the real Marcus Reed was even hotter and better than the one I'd created. Trust me, big guy. I'm not about to blow a really good thing."

"I like that." He pushed the door open and followed her inside. "But I really want to discuss a couple of points."

"Oh?"

"Can you please describe, in detail, exactly what a female wet dream entails? Inquiring minds want to know."

She glanced over her shoulder. "Absolutely not. Any more questions?"

"Uh, no. I guess not."

"Good. Let's get to bed. I just realized I have a ton of laundry that hasn't gotten done. I know what I'm doing tomorrow."

Mandy lay there blinking in the soft gray of early dawn. Marc slept soundly beside her, on his right side as the left was still tender. The healing wound had left a raw, angry looking scar across his shoulder blade at least six inches long and half an inch wide. The red dots from the staples emphasized the width and length of his injury—the fact it had nicked the bone meant it had plowed pretty deep. No wonder he'd had so much pain.

He still had an absolutely gorgeous back, and the fact that he'd gotten that ugly wound because he'd been protecting her made him even more beautiful in her eyes. She thought seriously about rolling over and snuggling against that long, muscular, naked back.

Except she was already wide awake, and Marc had been exhausted last night. He was still healing and needed his sleep, which was a perfect excuse to take time to catch up with Lola. With any luck, her sister would be up. Mandy crawled out of bed quietly, threw on her old robe, and headed to the bathroom. It didn't take long at all to wash her face, comb the tangles out of her hair, and brush her teeth.

Coffee. She really needed caffeine. Now. She was usually a couple of cups ahead before Marc crawled out of bed. She'd really missed her morning coffee with

Lola, though the two weeks her sister and Ben had been in DC had gone by faster than she'd expected.

She got the beans ground and the coffee going, and had just poured her first cup when Lola wandered into the kitchen.

"I thought for sure I'd sleep later, but guess I'm still on DC time. My brain knows it's only five, but my body is screaming eight."

Mandy poured a cup and handed it to Lola. "Maybe this will help. I've missed you. Was the trip okay?"

"Thanks." Lola held the mug to her nose and sniffed. "Yum. I've missed your coffee." She sat on one of the stools at the counter. "It seemed long. I missed you, too, but I had Ben to myself a lot of the time when he wasn't testifying or explaining his notes to the prosecution team, and it was really special. We'd never had much time without others around who know us. Back there we were able to explore our relationship in a totally unique setting. I loved it."

She glanced away and then focused on Mandy again. "I never imagined I would find a man so perfect for me. It's almost scary how well we click."

"Scary in a good way, I hope. Because that's how I feel with Marc. We had sort of the same thing here. There've been some big changes in my life. I haven't told you that the reason I've been working for Marc is that I got fired at the coffee shop. He hadn't hired anyone to do your job while you were gone, so I volunteered. It's worked out really well."

"You what? You got fired? I mean, I'm glad you were available to help Marc out, and me too, since I know now I'm not going back to a mess, and I really appreciate you're covering for me tomorrow, but what the hell happened at the shop?"

"The day you left, my boss came in and handed me

my final paycheck, said that was the end of it. No notice, no severance, nothing. I wasn't expecting it at all, had actually thought she'd make me the manager and ask me to run this one while she ran the new one in Union Square. Clearly, that didn't happen."

"That sucks." Lola looked like she was ready to chase the woman down and have a few words with her. And knowing Lola, she'd do it if Mandy asked.

"Well," she said, "yes and no. As it turned out, Marc needed me for more than my bookkeeping abilities. We didn't go into all the details at dinner because we wanted to hear what you guys have been doing . . ."

"And if it's a contest, Kaz and Jake win that one hands down. Modeling and photographing said model in the Coliseum in Rome has to beat giving a deposition in a courtroom in Washington, DC, any day."

"No argument from me." Mandy ran her fingertip through a drop of coffee on the table. Their brand new, sturdy, water- and other liquid-proof table. "The trouble with Marc's dad is serious. We really didn't want to ruin anyone's homecoming—figure we've got plenty of time to do that—but like Marc said, his dad's the one who shot him, though he was probably aiming at me. The prints came back a couple of days ago, and there was a good clear one that belonged to his father on the side of the stolen car that the shooter was driving. As long as he's in jail, he's not a threat, but Ted and the deputy in Dry Creek Valley think that all of us are at risk if he gets out."

"Then let's just hope he stays locked up."

"The extradition should be complete in a couple of weeks, and hopefully, with his history of going after Marc, they'll keep him locked up here as well. Ted got prints after the break-in here, but that was a dead end, literally. They found the man's body and he'd been dead at least a week, so a lot of it hinges on finding Marc's mother's remains. Ted has a guy flying in on August 8 who has a cadaver dog, one that can find really old human remains. They're going to go up to that property on Rockpile Road and see if they can find anything."

"That's got to be tough for Marc."

"You have no idea." Mandy wiped her eyes. She really hated Marc's father—even more now that she'd gone through everything that had happened, from Marc's visits with the hypnotherapist to their finding the rock with the tree out on Rockpile Road. "But it was tough," she added, "when Marc walked to the place where he thought she might have been buried and discovered the entire hillside had slipped away. Hopefully the cadaver dog will find something."

"Wow." Lola sat there staring at Mandy, shaking her head. "I really didn't have any idea what you guys have been dealing with."

Mandy just sighed. "It's awful. Think of it—Marc has lived with that fear for years, the mistaken knowledge that he'd killed a woman. He had no idea it was his father and his mother he was remembering. The dreams, coupled with the blackouts he had a few times in college had him convinced he was a murderer."

"Blackouts? What caused that?"

"Stress. The hypnotherapist said we all react to stress differently. Marc was having serious financial issues in college and knew he was going to lose his scholarship. He was overworked and struggling with no support system. He had what he calls a blackout when he awoke miles from campus with no idea how he'd gotten there. It happened more than once. Then he started having the dreams where he saw himself killing a strange woman, except it was his father killing his mother that he was remembering. Once the nightmares started, the blackouts stopped.

"The fact he'd blacked out and then essentially awakened miles from home made him think he could have killed someone while he was mentally out of touch. Dr. Chung said it's extreme, but the blackouts could have been his reaction to stress. An escape mechanism of sorts, tied to his problems in college and repressed memories. As far as the dreams? Who can say what triggered them? He hadn't had them for years, but he's been afraid of what he might do ever since. Now, at least, he knows he's not a killer. Unfortunately, we also know his father is."

Lola grabbed Mandy's hands and squeezed. "I am so sorry, for both of you. What you're having to deal with. But I'm really glad you're there for Marc. He seems so much happier now. More settled, but to go through all of that . . ."

"Yeah, but I wouldn't trade these past couple of weeks for anything. There's so much more good than bad. We'll get through this, his father will end up in prison, and Marc and I will go on with our lives. I love him, Lola. I never imagined what it would be like to have a man you could trust and count on, a guy who's funny and smart and so amazing. And not only that, he was my fantasy for how long?"

"At least the past six or seven years, ever since you started work at the coffee shop. So what about the one you and Marc were talking about? Are you going to do it?"

"We are. It's going to be part of the memorial Jake and Ben want to do—Marc's already set up a foundation to provide funding for the shop once we get it built. We'll call it Bett's Place. Bett was his mom's nickname.

We'll have a small daycare facility and hire women from the shelter. I think it's going to be great."

Lola took a swallow of her coffee. "This will teach me to leave for more than a long weekend."

Mandy laughed. Then she stood as Marc wandered into the kitchen still half asleep. "I'm really proud of us. It's amazing how much trouble we were able to cause in a very short time."

Marc leaned close and kissed her. Then he patted Lola on top of her head. "You have the day off tomorrow, Lola, but only if you promise me you won't listen to your sister when she moans about feeling like an indentured servant."

Lola held up two fingers in a modified salute. "I promise."

"Lola! You're such a traitor."

"I know who signs my paycheck. I hope you negotiated excellent terms before slipping into my desk."

Mandy smiled sweetly at Marc. "I have no terms. None at all." Then she stood and wrapped her arms around his neck and gave him a kiss. When she came up for air, both of them were breathing just a bit harder. She turned to Lola with a cheesy grin. "I do, however, have the boss in my bed, and I'm keeping him. I can't think of anything better than that."

CHAPTER 14

Monday morning arrived long before Mandy was ready. They'd been busy all day long on Sunday, but she and Lola had caught up on laundry and grocery shopping while the guys took care of the yard and cleaned house. They'd all been busy throughout the day, managed to throw together easy meals to keep everyone fed, and still had time to sit out in the backyard with a glass of wine and snacks in the afternoon and take a break.

Marc had wandered out after his shower and brought an extra couple of chairs to put beneath the dogwood tree. Lola and Mandy had grabbed the bench—the one Ben claimed as his since it had been the scene of his infamous meltdown the first night he'd met Lola. Carrying around a huge load of guilt for twenty years had to end at some point, but it had been Lola and Ben's beginning, and the end of a long estrangement between Ben and his younger brother, Jake.

Marc set the chairs across from the bench, put a couple of cold beers on the little round table Lola had dragged out a few weeks earlier, and sat. "I need to go back to the office," he said.

Mandy frowned. "Why? It's Sunday?"

He picked up his beer and took a long swallow. "When you and your sister get together, Ms. Mandy, you are slave drivers."

"C'mon, Marc." Lola leaned over and patted his knee. "You vacuumed, did a little pruning, a couple of dishes, scrubbed a toilet. It can't have been that hard."

Mandy sighed dramatically. "I told him scrubbing toilets was really sexy. You'd think he'd want to work that angle."

"It was work," he said. "Hardest work." Marc glanced over his shoulder as Ben came down the stairs and followed the neatly pruned path to the chairs. "Wasn't it, Ben?"

"Wasn't it what?" Ben took the other chair and the beer Marc handed to him.

"Hardest work. Sunday is supposed to be a day of rest."

"Have you mentioned that to the women?"

"They don't listen."

"Yeah." He sighed dramatically. "But they're real cute. Cute goes a long way, ya know?"

Marc leveled a long stare at Ben. "Lola, you've pulled him over to the dark side."

And then Mandy got the giggles. Sundays would never be the same. Sitting out here in the backyard, laughing over silly stuff with her sister, her future brother-in-law, and her future husband. And one day there'd be kids, and when the fence finally came out between the two units after Marc took ownership, they'd have one big yard with Kaz and Jake thrown into the mix. She wanted to hug herself. It was all better than she ever could have dreamed.

But then Monday morning arrived and she and Marc crawled out of bed and left even earlier than usual. Marc had a number of appointments and Mandy wanted everything caught up when Lola got back to her desk, so it was going to be a hectic day. The drive in was sort of bittersweet—she'd enjoyed going to work with Marc, had loved her time in the office and feeling a part of the excitement of all of Marc's various interests, but Lola would be back at her desk tomorrow, and Mandy wasn't sure where she'd end up.

Someplace where she could work on the plans for the coffee shop, since Marc had told her it was all her baby. She liked that. Mostly, she loved the idea that Marc had enough faith in her to give her free rein on the project.

Marc went straight into his office and closed the door once they got to his building on Battery Street. Mandy went through all the phone messages for Marc that were waiting for her, jotted down the names and numbers along with a brief description of the messages, collated the notes and organized them by order of importance. Then she knocked on his door. He opened it immediately—she'd noticed that when he was on a business call, he tended to pace around his office, or around whatever room he was in at home, and she'd caught him in mid-pace.

He was not the type to sit still when he could stand, or stand still when he could walk. She almost groaned, thinking of raising little boys like Marc, except she could hardly wait for that day to come.

She set the notes on his desk and turned to leave, but he touched her shoulder and motioned for her to stay. She walked over and gazed out the window at Yerba Buena Island, and Treasure Island right next to it, while Marc continued his call.

But her mind was on the man pacing around the office behind her, and it wasn't long before she'd switched her attention from the million-dollar view to the man who had so easily stolen her heart. He was dressed in his usual work uniform of black jeans and a long-sleeved white dress shirt. He'd already rolled his sleeves up, and his hair was mussed because he couldn't talk on the phone without raking his fingers through it. He had a pair of low-top leather athletic trainers on, comfortable shoes she liked to tease him about.

With all the phone calls he took every day, he must walk miles.

Probably why he was in such good shape. Other than running on occasion and disappearing into the man cave in the basement where he and Ben had set up weights and a couple of exercise machines, he didn't obsess about his physique or make a big deal of working out. But whatever he did appeared to do what it was supposed to, at least as far as Mandy was concerned. He had an absolutely perfect body, and when he was focused—the way he was now, with the phone to his ear and his brows wrinkled in a slight frown—he looked absolutely dynamic and so very much in control. There was such a sense of life seething in and around Marc, or as Lola had said shortly after she'd met him, "there's just so much *there*, there."

Whatever it was, it worked.

Marc ended the call, stuck his phone in his pocket, and walked over to stand beside her. "That was Deputy Russo's superior officer—he said Jerry's off on vacation for a couple of weeks, but that he'd keep me in the loop on whatever was happening with my father's extradition. Right now he's in jail and they're holding him there for illegally entering the country using a fake passport, but that won't work forever. He said they're considering deportation rather than extradition. There's a ruling in the treaty between the U.S. and Mexico that can limit what he goes to trial for to the charges that are used to support the extradition. Since they don't have enough grounds to charge him with my mother's murder, deportation would leave them open to add those charges at a later date."

Sometimes the legal twists and turns drove her absolutely nuts. "They have enough to hold him on attempted murder, don't they?"

"They do, but he hasn't been charged yet. The chief of police in Marin has a detective working on a couple of leads that might strengthen the case against him there, and Sonoma County is going to run ballistics tests on the slug. They sent a team back out and found it buried in the trunk of a grape vine."

"That seems apropos."

"Yeah, doesn't it? It appears they got a little more excited about him when Jerry shared the copy of our information with his boss, and he, in turn, had a talk with the chief of police in Marin. It's suddenly taken on a lot more depth now that they're looking at a potential murder and the attempted theft of many, many millions of dollars. The team also went over the Ford Bronco a bit more closely and found a rifle hidden under the spare tire, but I don't know if they got prints off of it or not. All we have now is that one palm print on the door of the car. Neither of us saw him, so we don't have any witnesses to the actual shooting, though the slug could prove to be evidence if it matches the gun, and if the gun has his prints."

"An awful lot of ifs . . ." She wrapped her arms around him and pressed her cheek to his chest, just over his heart. "It's all going to work out. I just wish it wasn't taking so damned long."

His arms tightened around her. "You and me both, babe." He exhaled in a huff. "Anyway, I just wanted to let you know."

"Thank you. I appreciate it. Now I need to get back to my desk." Regretfully, she slipped out of his embrace, but work called. "I really don't want Lola coming back to a mess."

"That reminds me." He took her hand. She smiled. It appeared that Marc wasn't ready to let go, either. "You're going to be busy working on the plans for the coffee shop. I was thinking . . . we've got a small office here that I can have Theo set up for you. Would you be okay with that? Once we get what you need the way you like it, it would mean that when you go home in the evening, or whenever, you wouldn't be tempted to keep working, but when you're here, we can collaborate as needed on whatever you want to do. Think about it, would you? Especially while things with my father are so up in the air. I'd feel safer with you here. It's hard to concentrate when I'm worried about you."

She hadn't even thought of that, of actually having an office here with Marc. Close to Lola and Ben, even Ted and Theo. "I would love it." She wrapped her hands around his neck and hugged him. Hard. "And I love that you're thinking of me. Thank you."

He laughed softly, and rubbed his chin against the top of her head. "I don't think I'm ever not thinking of you, Mandy. You're like an obsession for me. A very good obsession."

"That works." She turned in his arms and kissed him. "I must admit, I love the perks of working in the same building with you. Make sure my office has a comfortable couch and a lock on the door, okay?" Before he had a chance to reply, she ran her fingers across his cheek in a soft caress, turned away, and went back to her desk.

August 7

Marc shook hands with Ben and Jake while Mandy got hugs from both Kaz and Lola. Why he'd thought he could actually stay at home this weekend and then go into his office and work once JD Stirling arrived with his HRD dog was beyond Marc, but it had taken Mandy to convince him that he really needed to be on scene, at least for the first few days.

Ted was already in Healdsburg. He'd found a guest house on a neighboring property for rent so that JD and Bones would be able to stay close to everything. Ted had spent last night in the apartment over the tasting room. He'd wanted to be on-site in order to make sure everything was signed and cleared with Jeb Barton and their use of the dog on his property, and a portable restroom brought on-site for the dog's handler and the potential recovery team. Sheriff's deputy Jerry Russo was due back from vacation today. Marc expected to see him at some point once they started work tomorrow afternoon. JD's plane was due in before noon. He'd told Ted he'd like to go out to the site and let Bones sniff around, that the dog would need a chance to burn off excess energy after being kenneled while on the flight.

There was definitely a lot of interest in Marc's search, though nothing had officially been made public. He was overwhelmingly grateful that Ted was up there handling the details, though Theo had been noticeably grumpy when Marc called him this morning. He wasn't very happy that his roommate was gone.

Marc had told him to feel free to close up shop at the office, bring his laptop, and come to the wine country, that he could stay in the tasting room apartment with Ted if they'd reached a point in their relationship where sharing a bed was okay. If not, and if that's what Ted preferred, Marc would arrange for rooms in town for one or both of them.

He had a feeling Theo might actually beat him there, and as long as he had his laptop, he could deal with any problems that might arise. Besides, Ben was staying in San Francisco to keep an eye on things, and he and Lola could handle almost anything that might need handling.

So that was Ted, Theo, Ben, and Lola, all accounted for. His mind was spinning. There was so much going on, and he didn't want to forget anything. Which reminded him . . . "Jake, you and Kaz are going to keep tabs on the contractor, make sure they get your place the way you want it, right?"

"We're on it," Jake said. "The entire inside is free of striped wallpaper and that hideous pink paint. A huge improvement already. They're working right now—the cabinets are done and they're finishing up the kitchen floor today, putting in the new kitchen appliances tomorrow as soon as they're delivered. It's all supposed to be finished by Friday, so with any luck we'll be heading north and staying at the hotel in Healdsburg so we can make certain everything is good to go for the wedding, which, in case you've forgotten, is exactly two weeks away."

"Smartass." Marc flipped him off. "Like you'd let anyone forget?"

"We're not going anywhere until we shop for furniture." Kaz squeezed Jake's arm and Marc caught himself so he wouldn't laugh. She looked like a little kid in a candy shop. "This will be the first time I've ever gotten to buy furniture for my own place. It's so exciting. We've already picked out a bedroom set."

"Priorities, ya know." Jake's smile was all for Kaz.

"Mandy and I saved the kitchen table and chairs if you want those."

"Yes! I love that set. Like the new one, too, but that

one has memories. Don't need to take anything else, though. I'm looking forward to shopping."

"That's good. Means I get to keep the bed here, right?" Ben slipped an arm around Lola.

Kaz rolled her eyes. "I think you've probably marked that one as Benjamin Lowell territory by now, so yes, it's all yours."

They were all laughing when Marc kissed Kaz on the cheek, hugged Lola, and grabbed Mandy. "We're outta here. We'll pick up something for dinner once we get there, but at least the traffic should mostly be headed in the opposite direction."

Their bags were already in the car, so Marc grabbed Mandy's arm and tugged her toward the door.

Ben stopped Marc with a hand on his shoulder. There was no sign of laughter at all in his dark gray eyes. "You call us, okay? Let us know the minute something turns up."

"I will."

Ben hugged him. Ben usually wasn't a hugger. Then Jake grabbed him in a tight hug. "We're all holding the good thought for you, man. Hang tight."

Marc nodded. He'd actually been holding on really well, putting the reason for this trip out of his mind. If he thought of all the shit he had to do, it was a lot easier to deal with exactly why they were headed to Dry Creek Valley. "Thanks. All of you. Thank you."

Mandy took his hand and hurried him down the stairs. "Do you want me to drive?"

He thought about it for at least a second before handing over the key fob. "Thanks."

He waited until they were well away from the house before pulling out a handkerchief and wiping his eyes. "I was doing okay until those two hugged me."

Mandy reached across the console and stroked his thigh. "I thought that's what did it. They both love you very much. I think this is hurting Jake and Ben more than either of them expected. They have such a crappy relationship with their own mother, and you actually had a mom who loved you, but she was taken away from you. It's got to cause all sorts of convoluted feelings in those two."

"I hadn't thought of it from that angle, but you could be right." He leaned his head against the seat rest. "The really weird thing is, I have such mixed feelings about finding her. I realized that today. If we find her remains, I have to accept that she's really dead, that she's not going to come back. The thing is, over the years, as much as I hated her, I used to have fantasies of her showing up one day, telling me it was all a horrible mistake, that she loved me and wanted to spend time with me. Wanted to make up for all the years we'd lost."

He thought about those years—most of his life, in fact—when he'd believed she'd abandoned him, that money had meant more to her than the child who loved her. It hurt now, to know that was all a lie—one he'd believed without question. On the other hand, finding out what had really happened had allowed him to reclaim her love. Rationally, he'd accepted all along that she wasn't coming back, but he'd never expected to have this feeling, this overwhelming sense of his mother's love. Not ever.

"Sometimes I'd imagine telling her to get lost," he said. "I'd think of all the horrible things I could say when she came back, that I hated her and didn't need her." He'd never really meant it, but damn, remembering that now made him feel like such a jerk. She'd been dead, buried on that lonely hillside, and he'd been thinking of her out living the high life, forgetting him entirely.

And hating her for it.

He turned and gazed at Mandy, the one true constant in his life. He'd never doubted her love, not since that night when they'd made love for the first time. "The thing is," he said, wishing things could be different, knowing they never would, "I never really hated her. I just missed her so damned much. I think I always will."

He was asleep before they got through San Rafael. Mandy wasn't the least bit surprised. He'd been restless almost every night over the past week, wandering from her room into his where she'd find him at his computer, working on a new program. She thought it was most likely busywork to keep his mind off the chaos that defined his life right now.

They'd had regular updates on his father, the fact he was still in that jail in Tijuana, though on the last update they'd learned that the Mexican government was moving forward with deportation proceedings against Steven Reed. Sonoma County was sending a deputy to the border to pick him up when he crossed—an official from Tijuana would hand him over. He'd walk across the bridge where he'd be met by a sheriff's deputy who would handcuff him and put him in the van that would bring him north. As far as Marc knew, it could happen at any time.

They'd all agreed they liked it better when he was locked up in that Tijuana jail.

Traffic was heavy but smooth, the bulk of the vehicles moving in the opposite direction from them, flowing south as the weekend tourists headed home to the city. Even so, it was almost five when Mandy turned off of the freeway into Healdsburg, pulled into the parking lot in front of the Mexican restaurant, and called Cassie.

Marc woke up, blinking, visibly surprised he'd slept

the entire trip. He sat straighter in the seat, stretched his back and arms as much as the space would allow, and then leaned against the door and watched Mandy as she and Cassie talked. After a couple of minutes, Mandy ended the call.

"C'mon. We're picking up dinner for the crew. Cassie's been in the tasting room all day, Nate just got out of the shower, and Ted and Theo are sitting on their front porch drinking wine. We're the only ones who haven't made it in time for happy hour."

"Okay." He unbuckled his seatbelt, got out of the car, and followed Mandy. They'd done this so often, there was no need to even ask what everyone wanted. Except . . . "What are we getting for Ted and Theo?"

"I heard Cassie ask them, and Theo said whatever was good, and a lot of it."

"Sounds like Theo." He opened the door for her and followed her inside. The woman working the counter recognized them and smiled.

Marc waited beside Mandy while she easily rattled off their order. "You sound as if you've done this before," he said, teasing her. He paid the cashier, and then the two of them stepped back outside and sat at a picnic table in front of the restaurant to wait for the food.

Marc suddenly sat up straighter. "Damn it! I swear that silver Lexus that just went by was my father's car. And it looked like my father driving. He's still supposed to be in jail."

"Call the sheriff's office."

"Good idea." He placed the call while they waited. Mandy realized she was sitting there tapping her foot, but all that nervous energy had to go somewhere. After a couple of minutes, Marc got off the phone.

"They're sending a guy down to pick him up late Tuesday afternoon. He's still locked up."

"I'm glad. Thinking of him running around loose is enough to give me a headache."

"You and me both." He glanced up as the waitress walked out with a number of bags looped over her arms.

Mandy grabbed as many as she could while Marc took the rest. This time he drove, so Mandy sat back and enjoyed the ride. With luck, they'd have answers sooner rather than later. It was the best they could hope for.

They moved to the patio behind the house, spread the containers of tacos, rice, beans, chili rellenos, enchiladas, salsa, chips, guacamole, and a platter of heated flour tortillas out on the big picnic table and dug in. Marc took the glass of wine Nate handed to him, held it to the light and then took a sip.

"What is this?" He picked up the bottle, but there was no label, merely a barrel number and a symbol. "It's absolutely delicious." He glanced from Nate to Cassie, who had a devilish grin on her face.

"That's a field blend red from the Mac and Melinda block, the first I've made since you deeded it over to me for our wedding gift."

"It's amazing. I bet your dad had something to do with this."

Cassie blinked away tears. "I like to think so. And Mom, too. I felt them so close when I was making the wine, checking the barrel. We only made one barrel of it—twenty-five cases. The rest of the grapes went into Intimate wines, but I felt like I really needed to keep the Tangled Vines label alive."

"If this is the kind of wine you're going to make with it, I'm glad you did." He glanced from Nate to Cassie and nodded. "Your parents must be so proud of you, Cassie. This is truly exquisite wine. Do you have it in the tasting room?"

Cassie shrugged. "It didn't seem right. It's your winery and your tasting room."

"C'mon, Cassie." He took another sip. "You're doing all the work. Theo?"

"Yessir?"

Theo looked more relaxed and happier than Marc could remember. He was positive he had Ted to thank for that. "Is there a simple way to figure out accounting so we can separate out Tangled Vines and Intimate Wines without creating a nightmare for the tasting room staff?"

"Easy enough. We just designate a key on the register to denote which winery gets the sale. Eventually I want to have barcodes on the labels, and that would simplify things even further."

"For now we could do it with stickers, couldn't we? That way we can print our own for small lots, and . . ."

Mandy reached over and took his hand. Gently squeezed his fingers and smiled at him.

He stopped talking and shook his head. Laughed quietly at himself. "Sorry. I'm doing it again. When I have things I don't want to think about or talk about, I start planning business stuff or creating software. Don't have my computer, so I have to turn a quiet respite from work into . . . uh . . . work."

"S'okay," Cassie said. "We live on a vineyard and work in a winery. Life around here essentially is work, but we love it. And thank you. We'll figure out a system that's easy enough to use in the tasting room, but I like the sticker barcodes just fine."

"Thank you for getting me out of that one." He saluted Cassie with his glass, sipped the perfect red wine, and held tightly to Mandy's hand, while conversation flowed around them. He thought about the changes in his life since the day he'd decided to buy the Tangled

Vines winery and vineyards, and that led to a memory of his mother sitting on the back deck at their Marin home, staring off in the distance with a glass of red wine in her hand.

What was she thinking all those years ago?

He'd been too young to understand, but he knew she hadn't been happy. He remembered an aura of sadness around her; after she left he figured it was because she didn't want him. Not true at all, if his dreams could be believed.

He glanced toward the dam, the huge earthen wall looming over this end of the valley, and wondered when they'd find her. He had no doubt they would find her. She'd drawn him here almost as if she'd personally asked him to search for her. He was doing the best he could, and with Mandy beside him, he felt that he could do anything. It was all coming together, here, this week.

He'd spent such a short time in college, but he remembered something one of his professors had said, that in order to succeed you needed to expect success but plan for failure. Always have a backup plan. Be prepared for anything.

He had no backup plan if they couldn't find his mother's remains. He knew they would find her. They might be using a dog with a really good nose, but as far as Marc was concerned, his mother was guiding him. She hadn't let him down before, even though he'd doubted her. She wouldn't fail him now.

CHAPTER 15

August 8, Dry Creek Valley

It was almost three before Ted pulled into the driveway in front of the cottage with a slightly built dark-haired companion in the front seat and a black-and-white dog hanging his head out the back window. The plane had been late after a mechanical issue in Portland, but Marc was hoping they might still get out to the site today. He called to Mandy—she'd been inside straightening up the kitchen and generally killing time as effectively as she could—and told her they were here.

He grabbed her hand when she came outside, and the two of them went down the stairs to meet the man they'd been waiting for. They got their first surprise when JD opened the car door. He was a very attractive she.

Without missing a beat, Marc grabbed the door on Ted's rental and held out his hand. "JD? I'm Marc Reed. Thank you so much for coming."

JD took his hand and let him pull her out of the front seat. She was a tiny thing, not even as tall as Mandy, with her short dark hair mostly hidden by a ball cap. She wore hiking boots, faded jeans, and a green plaid flannel shirt over a tank top, and the first thing she did after saying hello in a surprisingly deep, raspy voice was to turn away from Marc, open the back door and let the dog out. Bones bounded out of the car and, at a signal from JD, planted his butt on the ground. He quivered, ready to do anything but sit.

Mandy laughed. "He looks like he really wants to run, far and fast. Hi, JD. I'm Mandy."

"It's a pleasure to meet both of you. Is it all right if I let him run? He knows not to get too far from me."

"Please." Marc stepped back and gestured toward the vineyard. He'd started out with thirty-seven acres plus the twelve across the road where the wine cave was, had deeded five acres to Cassie when she and Nate got married, and added some extra land the next-door neighbor had been willing to sell—there was definitely enough room for the dog to run. "The service road is the perimeter of our vineyard, so he's got about fifty acres on this side of the creek where he can go all out."

"Bones, go!"

The dog took off like a shot, head down, body low to the ground, racing across the open ground and then in and out around the vines in a wide circle that brought him back to the spot where the four of them were watching. He made the loop four times before he finally sat at JD's feet.

Marc tried to imagine what he'd look like working. He was definitely a good runner. "Ted said he's a McNab?"

"He is, at least half of him. He was a rescue dog, a McNab/border collie cross. The McNab breed originated up the road from here, south of Ukiah. They're a super intelligent, short-haired, herding breed. He's probably smarter than the four of us combined."

"Is it all right to pet him, or is he working?"

"Thanks for asking, Mandy. Go ahead. He's just

relaxing now. In fact, Ted's already gotten me settled in the residence next door, which is very comfortable, by the way. Thank you. Plus, I made him stop and get me a sandwich on the way here, so if you're ready to head up to the site, we can go any time."

Mandy had knelt down and met Bones at eye level, but she immediately glanced at Marc. "Marc? I need to put on some hiking boots, but I'm ready if you are."

"Works for me. Let me grab my phone. Ted, are you and Theo planning to come up as well?"

"If you don't mind. I'll get Theo. I know he was really interested in watching the dog work. Why don't you go on ahead, and we'll meet you up there."

The ride up to Rockpile Road and then out to Jeb Barton's property took about twenty minutes. Marc handed the key to the gate to Mandy, who got out and opened it. Jeb had told them to leave it unlocked during the daytime if they wanted while they were working, so she pushed it all the way open and hooked it to the post designed to hold it in place. Once she got back in the car, Marc pulled ahead and parked next to the rock with the tree growing out of the side.

JD pulled a heavy plastic water bowl out of her tote bag, along with a jug of water for Bones. She filled the bowl and left it in the shade of the car. After Bones took a drink, he sat, totally alert now that he seemed to recognize it was time for him to go to work.

"Ted told me you have a fairly specific area to search first."

"This way." Marc went toward the edge of the slide. "Between the car and the slide, for now. I'm hoping the area where he buried her wasn't in the section that broke off, so it would probably be best to rule out the easy area first."

"Sounds good." JD watched Marc and Bones watched JD just as closely.

"I've parked about where I remember my father parking his car the night he buried her, but we're dealing with a four-year-old's memories. I really don't know how far away he carried her body, though I can't imagine him going too far from the car. He's not quite my height, and my mother was a fairly tall woman. I'd suggest starting in this area between the car and the slide, and if nothing shows up, possibly on the face of the slide itself. The hillside slipped years ago, so it's probably stabilized by now, but I'd prefer not to have to test it."

"Bones will be okay. I think he's part mountain goat. I'm going to send him out, and you'll know if he gets a hit because he'll lie down until I release him with a command."

Marc nodded, hoping he didn't look as nervous as he felt, but when Mandy reached for his hand, he tightly grasped hers.

"Bones. Find." JD stepped back while the dog shot from his sitting position and went to work, racing around the area with his nose to the ground. He made wider and wider circles without any reaction until he got near the very edge of the slide.

Whining, he turned to JD, almost as if asking for permission. "Find," she said. Bones stared at her, tail wagging and ears up, and then he jumped over the edge.

Marc raced for the edge of the slide, relieved to see that it wasn't as sheer a cliff, as he'd feared. Rocks and trees had tumbled along into a wide swath of rubble. Bones lay on his belly near a ragged bush, panting, watching for JD.

The moment she poked her head over the edge, he barked, but he didn't move. She pulled a wooden stake out of her backpack with an orange flag on the end. "I'm going to mark it and have him continue to search. If this slide occurred long after she was buried, it could have scattered her remains."

Before Marc could caution her, JD was over the edge and moving quickly down the jumbled earth, using dead branches and roots for balance and the occasional anchor.

Mandy grabbed Marc's hand when JD looked their way and said, "You might want to come down here. Be careful because it's steep, but the ground actually feels pretty stable." She planted the stake in the ground and gave Bones his command. "Find."

And he was off. Marc helped Mandy over a couple of the rougher places, but she didn't hesitate to follow him down to the spot where JD waited. They were almost to her when he heard Ted calling. Marc stopped and glanced back the way they'd come. Ted and Theo stood at the top.

"Wondered where you'd gone. We're coming down."

Marc and Mandy reached JD just ahead of Ted and Theo. She glanced at the two men and nodded, but her focus was on Marc. "I think Bones has found something. Didn't you say she was wrapped in a comforter? Take a look."

She brushed dirt away from what Marc at first thought was a pile of dried leaves. A floral pattern, badly faded and the fabric mostly rotted, appeared. "I don't want to pull this out or do anything that might compromise evidence, but I have a feeling this might be what you're looking for."

Bones barked again. About ten feet down the hill this time, the dog had planted himself in a slight depression. JD took another stake out of her pack, threw the pack over her shoulder, and went down to mark that spot as well. Marc turned to Mandy and grabbed her hand just before his legs gave out and he sat, hard.

She knelt beside him, holding tightly to his hand, though, like Marc, she was focused on the faded piece of fabric.

Ted and Theo reached them as he went down. "You okay? Marc?"

He stared at the fabric without touching it. It was faded by time and stained to the reddish color of the soil, but he knew the pattern, knew what the colors had been. Purple flowers—iris? Possibly. He remembered iris in his mother's garden with their long, leathery green leaves and silky purple flowers. The comforter in their bedroom had the same purple iris with green leaves against a white background. After a moment, still hanging on to Mandy's hand, he turned to Ted and Theo. "This is the blanket that was on her bed. The one he wrapped her in."

"I'll call it in." Ted pulled his cell phone out of his pocket and stepped to one side.

Marc blocked out Ted's voice, concentrated on the way Mandy's hand felt grasping his so firmly, the sound of Bones racing across the tumbled ground to JD's commands to "find."

The sound of her pounding wooden stakes into the ground to mark each hit.

Marc had no idea how much time passed. He was still sitting there, lost in thought, caught in the memories that spilled into his mind when he heard cars on the road above them. Ted was waiting to show the deputies where they were.

Marc didn't have to worry. Ted and Theo would bring them down here when they were ready. Mandy was here to anchor him, holding him in the here and now while his thoughts raced through the childhood memories spilling into his adult mind.

Memories hidden for all these long years, images of his mother as she'd looked to his four-year-old self. Tall and beautiful with long blond hair and the same dark brown eyes he had. He felt her close by, his mother's spirit like a warm hug on a very cold night. But then, voices brought him back. He leaned close and kissed Mandy, who somehow must have known he'd needed this time of silence. She stood and tugged, and he came easily to his feet so that he was standing when the four men came over the edge of the slide.

In the background, he was aware of JD's sharp commands to find, of Bones running over the tumbled ground as if this were the greatest game of hide-and-seek in the world. The light was fading, which meant he'd been sitting here for hours at the very least, and more wooden stakes with their bright orange flags studded the hillside. He counted seven of them, all in a line that followed the original direction of the slide.

"Hey, Marc." Jerry Russo shook Marc's hand. "I want you to meet Franklin Emerson. He does a lot of forensics work for the county and he happened to be here on other business when Ted called. When he said it looked like a solid find, I thought we should bring Frank in from the beginning."

After the introductions, Marc squatted in front of the tattered remnants of the blanket and lifted one edge with a twig. "I'm certain this is the blanket she was buried in. The one I remember on their bed was white with purple and green flowers on it. Considering the position of the dog's other finds, I'm guessing the original grave was dug at the point just above us, near where the slide originated." He turned to indicate the area below them. "The dog's had hits on seven other spots, but they're all in a direct line with the slide, as if her bones washed down the hill in whatever storm brought the hillside down. From what I've heard, it happened sometime in the early 1990s. It's fairly stable by now, I think. JD's been all over it with Bones."

He glanced up at Emerson's frown, and shrugged. "Bones is the name of the HRD dog."

"Apropos." Emerson gazed down the slope.

Marc stood and watched the dog working, now far below them on the hillside with Lake Sonoma in the distance. The sun was setting, shadows growing longer.

"It's been over thirty years since she disappeared, right?" When Marc nodded, Emerson glanced over his shoulder as the sun disappeared behind a mountain. "I think I'd prefer to wait, call in a crew in the morning when the light's good. There's less chance of missing anything."

"I understand." Marc glanced at Mandy, wondering if . . .

"Marc and I will stay here tonight," she said. "We can keep an eye on things." She looked his way, as if needing his approval, but there was no need. She always seemed to know exactly what he wanted before he said a word.

Emerson got a few photographs, and then he and Jerry walked down the hill and he took pictures of each one of the marked sites. JD and Bones headed up from the bottom. They hadn't set any new markers.

"If you like, Theo and I can take JD and Bones back to the valley." Ted stared in JD's direction for a moment. "I think Cassie has dinner planned for everyone, so we'll bring something back up here for you two."

"Along with some blankets and pillows," Theo added, glancing at Ted. "We can take my car now, but when we get back let's switch. I'll leave mine, Marc, if you're okay letting me or Ted drive yours. The seats fold down in mine and I have a roll-up mattress in the back, flashlights, a lantern, that sort of stuff. It makes a pretty comfortable camping setup."

For whatever reason, Theo's comment brought Marc out of the fog of memory he'd felt trapped in since Bones had made his first find. He turned to Theo and calmly said, "You have your car set up to sleep in? Why? In case I fire you and you're homeless on the street?"

Theo lost it. No matter the situation, he always got it when Marc said something totally outlandish, and he was laughing so hard he ended up wiping his eyes. It took him a minute to get things under control. "Actually, no, but that's not a bad backup plan. I take off some weekends and head down the coast. If I don't want to hunt for a motel, I just spend the night on the beach in the back of my car."

"Now that we've got that cleared up . . ." Marc grabbed Mandy's hand and he actually felt like smiling. "That sounds like an excellent idea. Thank you."

It was almost completely dark when Theo and Ted returned more than an hour later with everything Marc and Mandy could possibly need for a night on top of a rugged hill. Ted helped Mandy set up a small folding table and a couple of chairs on a level spot near the car, and then he carefully set a battery-powered lantern in the center of the table. "For ambience," he said. "Also helps you find your food when you're eating. Theo said there are a couple of flashlights in the car as well." He glanced toward the portable restroom set a bit farther away. "I guess I erred in not getting a portable potty with outdoor lighting."

Mandy laughed at that. He'd found one with its own water supply so they could at least wash up with a convenient water source. The lake was a long way down a rubble-strewn hillside.

"I imagine we'll survive, though I'm glad to have the lantern and flashlights. I hadn't thought about needing light." Mandy reached for the cooler filled with dinner. "Of course, it was still daylight when we were discussing this." She was really glad she'd decided to wear jeans and hiking boots, and had tied a sweatshirt around her waist. She'd already thrown it on over her lightweight T-shirt.

Once they had the table set up, she and Ted walked back to the car while Theo helped Marc put together a bed in the back of his car. With a mattress designed to fill the cargo area now covered with a sheet and the comforter and pillows off Marc and Mandy's bed from the cottage, it looked more than adequate. As exhausted as she was, Mandy was already looking forward to crawling into bed. She and Marc had been up and down the steep hill at least a dozen times. She had no idea how JD had maintained the pace she kept, following after her hyperactive dog.

It was almost entirely dark and the men didn't stay long. With a promise to lock the gate behind them, they drove away in Marc's Tesla. Marc and Mandy sat down to their dinner. She put the meal Cassie had prepared for them on their plates—thick, roast beef sandwiches and homemade potato salad—while Marc opened a bottle of Cassie's Tangled Vines Red. He poured wine for both of them.

Cassie had packed real glasses, good linen napkins, and paper plates that didn't leak. It was all good, and absolutely beautiful out here on this lonely hilltop. Mandy was so glad she and Marc had decided to stay here, though there really hadn't been any other choice.

She'd felt a sense of Marc's mom ever since the first

time they'd come out here, as if, like Marc said, she approved of his search. How could she not?

Marc held his glass up to Mandy's. "I want to make a toast," he said. "To closure in one life, and new beginnings in another."

She stared into his eyes, and instead of the sadness she feared, they practically sparkled with joy. "To new beginnings," she said, tapping the rim of her glass to his and then taking a sip.

Marc took a swallow of his wine, but before she could say anything, he was out of his chair and down on one knee beside her. "Mandy?" He reached for her hands.

She hadn't expected this. Not here, not tonight, and yet it felt as if his timing couldn't have been better. Her hands were trembling when she put them in his.

Marc, though, was perfectly calm, his grasp strong and sure, his eyes perfectly focused on Mandy. He looked down at their clasped hands for a moment, and then once again focused entirely on Mandy. "I was serious when I told you I wanted a do over. As much as I loved you before when I asked you to marry me, I had no idea what real love felt like. Now I know so much more. I think I've always loved you, but I had no idea how much more those feelings would grow as the days flew by. As we get to know each other better. I figure that in about, oh, say fifty years or more, I'll finally have this figured out, but I know one very important truth. I don't want to live without you in my life. Not ever. Will you marry me, Mandy? Will you be my wife as long as we're both around to draw a breath?"

She slipped out of the chair and knelt on the rocky ground in front of him. "Of course I will. I love you, Marcus Reed. I always have. I always will."

He reached into his pocket and pulled out a black velvet box. The ring inside was every dream Mandy had ever had should this moment come to be. A traditional yellow gold band with a single exquisite diamond in the center. It wasn't horribly huge, but it wasn't at all tiny.

As far as Mandy was concerned, her ring—like their love—was absolutely perfect.

They finished their dinner, wrapped up the trash, stuck it back in the small cooler, and left that on the floor in the front of the car. There was an old crocheted afghan that Theo had thrown over their bed in case it got cold tonight, but Marc pulled it off and they set their chairs away from the table, close enough together where they could bundle the afghan around themselves and see for miles.

Mandy was more interested in what was right in front of her. She couldn't stop looking at her ring. Even with the lantern and flashlights turned off, and barely a quarter moon in the sky, there was enough starlight for the diamond to sparkle. She snuggled close to Marc, still gazing at her ring.

"I wasn't sure if you were the diamond type," he said, which told her he hadn't paid much attention to the nighttime view. "You rarely wear jewelry of any kind other than earrings, and those are usually yellow gold. If you don't like the design, you're more than welcome to . . ."

"No. Not ever." She leaned close and kissed his cheek, which by now was a bit bristly. "While I love Lola and Kaz's rings, they're not at all what I would choose for myself." She held up her sparkly ring finger. "This is it. Exactly it. I don't think there's anything more beautiful than a solitaire. Thank you for knowing me better than you think you do."

He wrapped his hand around her ring finger and kissed her fingertip. "I'm looking forward to a lifetime of getting to know you even better."

"I like the sound of that." She tried to bite back a yawn and failed miserably. "What time is it?"

He glanced at his watch. "After ten. It's been a long day." He brushed a kiss across her forehead. "Ready to go back to our luxury suite?"

"I am." She stood, grabbed her flashlight, and handed her half of the afghan to him. "After I visit the facilities."

The two of them fit perfectly in the bed in the back of Theo's little crossover car, one Mandy told Theo looked like a sports car playing dress-up as an SUV. Mandy had fallen asleep almost immediately. Marc lay there long after, thinking of his mother, of all she'd missed in his life. Knowing that she would have loved Mandy. He was feeling her presence almost as if she were physically nearby, looking over them.

Coyotes howled, not all that far away, and he'd heard an owl hooting earlier. Mandy turned toward his side and snuggled close, and Marc slowly tuned out the outside world, tuned out the thoughts that had been floating through his head, and all the other little things that generally kept him awake. It wasn't long before he slept.

He should have known he'd dream about his mother, camping out here on the site of her illicit burial so many years ago. If there were such a thing as spirits, hers must have been restless all these years while the truth lay hidden.

The truth would be out there for all to know once her remains had been recovered and DNA testing was able to determine her identity. Marc had no doubt they'd found her. His memories had been there for a reason, to help give her peace, and finding that remnant of her blanket was all the proof he'd needed.

She came to him tonight, walking out of a moonlit

haze and sitting beside him on the shoulder of that big piece of serpentine with the tree growing out of the side. He didn't remember leaving Mandy and walking over here, but that's when he realized his mother wasn't really here, there wasn't enough of a moon tonight to backlight her, and he was still asleep beside Mandy.

Which meant he was dreaming his mother. She shook her head sadly, and he could have sworn he felt her caress when she reached out and touched the side of his face.

Not true, Marcus. I'm as real as your memories, as real as your love for Mandy. Thank you so much for finding me. For not giving up. I knew you would come. I've been with you ever since that night, though it was hard when you didn't believe what I'd told you all along, that I would always love you. I'm sorry your father tried so hard to turn you against me, but you're not him. You're a good man, and I knew that one day you would realize what he'd done.

You have one more thing to do tonight, my son. One very important thing. He's coming. I don't know how, or what he thinks he can do, but you and Mandy won't be safe as long as he's alive. Be alert, Marcus. Don't let him win. Please, hurry. You need to wake up.

Wide eyed, Marc sat straight up in their makeshift bed.

Mandy came awake beside him, rubbing her eyes, frowning. "What's going on? What happened?"

He shook his head, feeling more than a little bit rattled, definitely disoriented. "I don't know. Nightmare, I guess. I was dreaming that my mother was here, that she was talking to me. Then she warned me my father was coming and she told me to wake up." He shook his head. "Man, that was just bizarre."

He started to lie back down, and then thought better

of it. Feeling more than a little bit foolish, he put his finger to his lips. "I might sound like I'm certifiable, but, just to be on the safe side . . ." Quietly he opened the hatchback on the car. Theo had disabled the interior light so it wouldn't bother them, and for that he was thankful.

Mandy was fully awake now, slipping into her jeans, pulling on her boots. Whispering, she said, "I'm going to go use the restroom."

"Okay. I'm just going to look around. Shake off the freaky feeling I've been talking to a ghost."

"That can certainly mess up a good night's sleep." She kissed him. "Be careful."

He watched her walk toward the restroom, the small beam of the flashlight barely showing when she was a few yards away. The serpentine rock with the oak tree was on the other side of the dirt road. He'd peed on it once before, no reason he couldn't use it tonight.

He'd just zipped up his jeans and turned to go back to the car when he heard a car coming down Rockpile Road. There was so little traffic out here this time of night that he climbed up on top of the big rock to see which way it was headed.

It was moving south, slowly, headed back toward the valley. He recognized the older farm truck, one he'd seen out here before, but as the driver went by the entryway to Jeb Barton's property, light glinted off a vehicle parked alongside the road, outside the locked gate. Marc only got a short glimpse, but it appeared to be a silvery gray Lexus.

One that looked an awful lot like the car his father drove.

CHAPTER 16

The sharp jangle of his cell phone brought Ted out of a sound sleep. Theo grumbled and rolled over, so Ted grabbed the phone and went out into the kitchen area of the small apartment to answer the call. "Robinson here."

"Ted! Thank goodness I got you. It's Jerry Russo. I'm in Santa Rosa, but I just now got a call from the deputy sent to pick up Steven Reed at the San Ysidro border crossing. There's been a major fuck up. Reed was released Saturday from the Tijuana jail, not held to be deported on Tuesday as ordered, but we weren't notified. We have no idea where he is, but there's a real stench to this whole thing. I'm worried about Marc but I haven't been able to reach him. My calls keep going to voicemail. Tried Mandy's cell. Same thing."

"They're up at the site. Damn, I've had a really bad feeling all day, and Marc thought he saw his father's car in town yesterday. I told him the bastard was still locked up. I'll grab Theo and we'll get up there as soon as we can. Takes about fifteen minutes, but I'll give you a call once as we arrive."

"Good. I just dropped a prisoner off here at the jail.

We're shorthanded up there tonight, so I'll head that way myself. Keep me in the loop."

Ted ended the call and flipped on a light. Yelled at Theo as he shoved his legs into his jeans. "Theo. Wake up. Marc's dad is loose and no one knows where he is. Somehow the bastard got out of jail Saturday, so he's had plenty of time to make it up here." He finished dressing as Theo shot out of bed.

"Shit." Theo was already throwing on clothes.

Ted slipped his shoulder holster on with his 9mm Glock, grabbed his watch and the fob to the Tesla, and raced Theo to the cottage where the Tesla was hooked up to the charger. Ted got it unplugged while Theo got in and started the car. Ted slipped into the passenger seat.

"I'm going to try calling Marc again. Damn, I've got a really bad feeling about this. He told me he thought he saw his dad's car on Sunday, but when he called the sheriff's office, they said Reed was still in jail. I guess no one got the word to them."

"What kind of car?" Theo pulled up to the locked gate.

"A silver Lexus." Ted jumped out, unlocked the gate and then closed and locked it as soon as Theo drove through. Just in case Reed decided to come here. "Marc really needs to invest in an electric gate," he said, frustrated with anything slowing them down. But what if Marc was, right now, fighting for his life? An electric gate was suddenly a very small matter. Grumbling, he hooked his seatbelt and punched in Marc's number.

A phone rang inside the console. "Holy fuck. His phone's in here. He left it charging."

"Try Mandy's."

He hit Mandy's number.

A phone beneath him chimed. He reached under the

seat, pulled out Mandy's purse, and looked hopelessly at Theo. "We have no way to contact them. Hurry."

Theo punched it. Ted hoped like hell the car had charged enough.

Mandy stepped out of the portable bathroom and set her flashlight on the paper towel dispenser while she washed her hands at the small attached sink. Once she was done, she grabbed a couple of towels and wiped her hands, poked the used towels into the waste receptacle, and then grabbed the flashlight. As she turned to go back to the car, she heard something off to her left. Startled, she turned with the flashlight and glanced toward the sound.

The attack came from behind. A large hand covered her mouth. A muscular arm snaked around her waist and lifted her off the ground. Kicking her feet, glad she was wearing the heavy hiking boots, she connected with what felt like a man's knee. He cursed. She twisted and turned like a wild thing, spurred by panic and a fierce anger unlike anything she'd ever known. His hand was still over her mouth, but she felt the fatty part at the base of his thumb against her lips. She opened her mouth and bit down. Hard.

He cursed and pulled his hand free, but not before she tasted blood. It should have nauseated her—instead, it empowered her. He tightened his one-armed grip around her waist, but she brought her heel up between his legs—hard—and connected with soft tissue.

"Marc!" Her cry was almost drowned out by Reed's curses, but at least her assailant had lost his grip on her when she nailed him. She ended up on her hands and knees in the dirt. Freedom was mere inches away as she scrabbled for balance, shoved herself to her feet, slipped in loose gravel and went down on one knee.

You can do this Mandy. Don't let him win.

The pain knocked the breath from her lungs but the voice in her head gave her courage. She shoved forward again. Too late! He had a hand around her ankle and pulled, hard. She went down on her chest, her chin bouncing off the ground. She cried out as he landed on top of her, threw himself across her back, forced the air from her lungs. His arm went around her neck, tightened. He put more pressure against her throat, cutting off her air. Lights flashed behind her eyes and she thought of Marc's mom, dead and buried all these years because this bastard had strangled her.

She was not going to die. There was no way in hell she'd ever put Marc through anything that awful. With that thought in mind, she went limp. Let him think she was unconscious. She was already close enough, but while he was gloating, she'd think of something.

Silently, Theo pulled in ahead of the silver Lexus—one of the benefits of driving an all-electric car. Ted was out of the vehicle in a heartbeat, weapon drawn, heart pounding. Their phones were set to vibrate, and Ted had turned off both Marc and Mandy's phones, but he'd gotten off a call to Jerry Russo the moment they spotted what had to be Steven Reed's car. With luck, Reed wouldn't have heard them pull in—if he was close to Marc and Mandy, the sound of the Tesla's tires rolling slowly over gravel on the shoulder of the road should have blended in with any ambient noise.

But how in the hell had Reed known to come here? Supposedly he'd been locked up for more than three weeks—Ted didn't think they'd even confirmed a date to search up here at that point.

Except Marc had let his father know he suspected him of murder, had told him about Rockpile Road. Which meant that Reed probably had gone by the house in San Francisco, and when he realized no one was there, he knew exactly where to look for his son—at the same place where he'd buried Marc's mother.

A scream cut the night. Mandy! She'd cried out for Marc, which meant Reed had to have one of them. Theo took off like a shot with Ted on his heels. They went over the locked gate and raced down the dirt road toward the kids' impromptu campsite.

Marc crouched low behind a patch of deer brush. No phone, no gun, and that son of a bitch had Mandy. It was so frickin' dark he couldn't really tell what was going on, but there was no way in hell he was going to let Reed hurt her again.

But getting himself killed wouldn't do either of them any good. He could barely make out the darker shadow that was his father, about halfway between Theo's car and the portable bathroom. He was dragging Mandy, so either she was unconscious or faking it. Knowing Mandy, he hoped like hell she was faking, but it appeared his father was limping, so maybe she'd gotten in a blow of some kind.

He moved closer, staying behind whatever brush he could find until he was barely six feet from the man. His eyes had adjusted as well as they were going to, and he fingered the flashlight in his hand. It wasn't very heavy, so it wouldn't make much of a weapon, but it was a bright sucker. If he could get close enough to blind Reed, he might have a chance.

Except he was positive the man was armed. No way he would have come after them without a weapon. Marc moved a little closer. Reed was mumbling about something, but he couldn't make out any intelligible words beyond the occasional curse.

Faintly, in the distance, he caught the sound of a

siren. Make that multiple sirens. Were they headed this way, or maybe to a fire somewhere? Except there was no reason for anyone to be looking for them up here, and there was no way to call for help. He'd realized right after Ted and Theo left that their phones were still in the Tesla. He hadn't told Mandy—hadn't wanted to make her nervous.

The sirens grew closer. He wished he knew the sounds of the different sirens, which were the sheriff's department, which ones belonged to fire, but they were definitely coming closer.

Would that make Reed nervous? Maybe not as attentive to his surroundings?

"Damn you!"

That was Mandy!

Marc grabbed the flashlight and turned it on full force, shining it directly at his father's eyes. Reed dropped Mandy and covered his eyes with his left hand, pulled his right arm up and fired without aiming, shooting toward the light. Except Marc wasn't there. The flashlight lay on the ground and Mandy was rolling to one side. His father fired wildly in all directions. Marc ducked down as a bullet whizzed by much too close to his ear.

Then he circled around in the opposite direction Mandy was moving as his father spun around, firing wildly. The moment Reed aimed in Mandy's direction, Marc jumped. He tackled his father from the left and knocked him to the ground, but the bastard didn't drop the gun. Reaching around his back, Marc got hold of his wrist and banged his arm against the rocky surface, but somehow his father twisted and managed to throw him.

Scrambling, still holding on to Reed's wrist, it quickly turned into a matter of brute strength. Fired by fear and whatever craziness drove him, Marc's father used his greater weight to pin Marc on his back. He wrapped his fingers across the front of Marc's throat, squeezing the breath from his lungs as Marc struggled to hang on to his father's gun arm.

But Reed was gaining—at least until Mandy raced back into the fight and kicked him in the side of the head. Momentarily stunned, he loosened his grip. Marc rolled free, gasping for air while Mandy went for the gun.

Reed pulled his arm out of her reach and lurched to his feet, winded, struggling to stay upright, but still hanging on to the gun in his hand. He held it and raised it slowly. "Which one first?" he asked. "Or does it really matter, since you're both going to die?"

Mandy turned and looked at Marc, and there was so much love in her eyes. Love and courage, and anger that his father might actually win this one. That was not going to happen. Marc felt a surge of strength and shot forward from his position on the ground, barreling against his father's knees, taking him down.

As he jumped, a light flared and a single shot rang out. The gun had been pointed at Mandy, but his father was the one on the ground. Steven Reed was not moving. Marc pushed himself away from his father's body as Mandy threw herself against him, holding him close and crying. Kissing his face over and over. Loving on him for all she was worth.

Ted and Theo raced across the open area, both of them with weapons drawn. Ted knelt and checked for Steven Reed's pulse, while Theo went down on his knees in the dirt and pulled Marc and Mandy into his arms, hugging them like there was no tomorrow.

"I was so afraid that bastard was going to win, but we couldn't see to shoot. It was so damned dark until we got that bright flash. Damn, I'm so glad you kids are okay." Theo's voice shook, and the emotion spilled over onto Marc.

"He's dead, Theo." Ted helped Mandy stand and then hugged her. "You okay?"

"I am. Thank you. We had no idea you were here."

Ted held his hand out to Marc and hauled him easily to his feet. Then he wrapped Marc in a hug as well.

"How'd you manage to see him?" Marc asked. "Was that a laser I saw, that bright flash before you fired?" He reached for Theo, took his hand and tugged.

Theo stood and brushed the dirt off his butt. "You mean that wasn't you? I thought you turned your flashlight on him again. The first time we weren't in position to get off a shot, and then it was too damned dark."

The sirens stilled as the sheriff's department cars pulled up along the road in front of the gate.

Ted was still staring at Reed's body. "At first I thought it was my imagination. I was trying to aim at what I thought was Steve Reed, but I couldn't see him. We could hear you guys fighting. Theo and I were both afraid to fire."

"Until that light flared," Theo added. "Lit him up like a strobe light, and Ted got off the shot."

"Center of his forehead. We were a good twenty yards away, Theo. I don't think I've ever made a shot that perfectly. It sort of defies logic, ya know?"

Marc stared at his father's body. He searched inside himself for any sense of grief, for sadness at the man's death. This was, after all, his father. He should feel something, shouldn't he? Something other than relief that Ted had been the one to pull the trigger? Because Marc couldn't deny that he'd thought about it, long and hard. He knew he had enough money to make his father go away—permanently—but he wasn't a killer. Tonight though, when Steven Reed pointed his gun at Mandy, Marc's only thought had been that the man had to die.

And Ted Robinson, one of the best men Marc knew, had been the instrument of his father's death. It was going to take a while to come to terms with this, with the fact that he didn't have to be on the lookout for Steven Reed ever again. With the fact he felt absolutely no remorse, no guilt at all that the man was dead. He had a feeling that lack of guilt wasn't going to change. His father had to die. It was the only way he could ensure Mandy's safety, that he could find justice for his mother. The only way to give her peace. She'd wanted her husband dead because she wanted her child safe.

He understood that. Better now, after the way things had happened tonight.

Abruptly, he turned away and focused on Ted and Theo. "I think I can explain the light, but neither of you are going to believe it. And it can't possibly go in any report, but the deputies are here now, so I'll wait and explain later. But, to put it bluntly, I believe we had a little otherworldly help."

He tightened his grasp around Mandy and held her tight. Right now, all he really wanted to do was go back to the cottage and bury himself deep inside her—and effectively consign Steven Reed and whatever demons drove him to the past.

It was almost daybreak before they got back to the cottage. Mandy grabbed her purse from under the front seat and Marc took his phone off the charger. Mandy was reaching for the front door when Nate stepped out of his house next door. Farmer's hours. He was ready to begin his day as theirs was finally drawing to a close.

Marc waved at Nate and kissed Mandy. "Babe, go

ahead and get your shower. I need to fill Nate in on what happened."

She returned his kiss and sent him on his way. Marc was still so wired, she doubted he'd go back to sleep at all this morning. She, on the other hand, was ready to fold. Her chin was a bloody mess, her knee hurt like the blazes, and all she wanted to do was sleep.

She hoped Ted or Theo remembered to drop the blankets and pillows off. She and Marc had totally forgotten to get them out of Theo's car.

No matter. There were extras in the hall closet. With that thought in mind, she went into the bathroom, stripped off her clothes, and made the mistake of looking in the mirror before she got into the shower.

She was a mess. Her chin was scraped raw and the raw part was filled with grit. There was blood on her neck and her hair was filthy and still had twigs in it. She glanced at her knee, which had swollen up like a grapefruit. At least that explained why she'd been limping. Even her throat was bruised. Enough of the visuals. Maybe if she washed the blood off, she wouldn't hurt as bad.

Looking at the sparkling diamond on her left hand helped.

She stayed in the shower much longer than normal, but there was a powerful need to wash Steven Reed's touch off of her, even more than the dirt and grime. The man was foul. Or had been. She refused to think of him as Marc's father. Marc was his mother's son, and Elizabeth Marchand Reed was a woman to be proud of.

Steven Reed wasn't anything anymore, beyond a bad memory.

She wondered how Marc felt about his father's death.

He hated the man, but had he loved him when he was little? Needed his approval the way most kids needed their parents' approval? She and Lola had dealt with that need where their mother was concerned years ago when they'd made a conscious decision to be there for each other, and while her mother was a flake and, as of the last time they saw her, an occasional drug user, she wasn't a killer.

Mandy really needed to call Lola. But not yet.

She stepped out of the shower and toweled herself dry, pulled on her green bathrobe, and stepped into the bedroom. Marc was tucking the blankets in after making up the bed.

He stood and stared at her, almost . . . almost as if he thought she might be angry?

"Are you okay?" She walked around the bed and looped her arms over his shoulders. Then she kissed him.

Marc glanced away. So not like him. But then he closed his eyes, sighed, and turned to Mandy. Cupped her face in his hands and kissed her softly, careful of the abrasions on her chin.

"He hurt you," he said, voice broken, emotions so raw, so close to the surface in every word he spoke. "I'm so sorry, Mandy. I never, ever wanted him to hurt you. I didn't protect you, and I will never forgive myself."

He wrapped his arms around her and held her close. She felt the steady thud of his heart against her cheek, wanted to stay like this forever. Of course, she was ready to fall asleep on her feet, but still . . . "S'okay." She smiled, even though it made her chin hurt. "You were there for me, you risked your life for me, and I wasn't about to let him kill me, either. He's dead, Marc. He's not going to hurt anyone again."

"Thank goodness."

"Actually." She kissed him. Just a quick kiss as a reminder of what they had. Still had, but came too close to losing. "A lot of the thanks goes to your mother."

His eyes went wide. Then he frowned. "Oh?"

"She woke you up. That wasn't just a dream. And when your father grabbed me, I heard a voice in my head and I know it was her. She said, 'You can do this, Mandy. Don't let him win.' I heard her, clear as if she stood in front of me and encouraged me, and maybe I've never really heard her voice, but I knew it was your mom. And then the light that flashed, the one that lit up your dad so Ted could get the shot? You admitted yourself that you thought it was your mother's doing. In fact, we still need to explain that to Ted and Theo, but . . ." She sighed and rested against him, loving the soft thumping of his heart against her ear, the solid strength of his arms holding her. "What you've done, Marc . . ."

"What we've done," he said. "We've done this together, but you're right. What we've done will let her rest. Finally. Hopefully she'll find peace."

She leaned away and took hold of his hand. "Get a shower. You'll feel better. Then come to bed. If I'm asleep, wake me up. I want to make love with you. I love you so much, and after last night . . ." She shuddered. "I realized just how close I came to losing you. I have never been so pissed off in my life, to think that man could take away the best thing that's ever happened to me. I wasn't going to let him."

"You put up one hell of a fight. I was terrified, and so proud of you. When I saw him dragging you across the dirt, for a split second I was afraid you were unconscious, but then I realized that no, you were just letting him think that. Damn, Mandy. You make me so proud."

Mandy was still awake when Marc crawled into bed beside her. He was relieved, because he honestly didn't know if he'd be able to wake her, knowing how exhausted she had to be. And sore, too. His father had hurt her; he was certain she was hurting a lot worse than she admitted.

The sky outside was growing light, and they both needed sleep, but he needed Mandy more than sleep. More than air. When she rolled toward him and pulled him close, he sighed against her throat, running kisses across her collarbone, over the curve of her breast. He trailed his hand over her thigh, slipped his fingers between her legs and stroked through her slick folds.

Her fingers dug into his shoulders; her body arched against his, her voice a harsh whisper in his ear. "Just you, Marc. Only you. I need to feel you inside me." She was wet and hot, and she wanted him. As receptive as she was, her body always so ready for his, she made him feel as if he could do anything, be anyone. Be the right man for Mandy.

She claimed she'd been ready for him for years. He liked hearing that. Loved knowing Mandy felt the same about him as he did about her. There was always the perception when he slid inside her that he was coming home—home to Mandy, to their future.

This time it was that and so much more. He'd come so close to losing her that every touch was intensified, every cry, every whimper, every exclamation filled with even more meaning. She clung to him as he drove deep, his body oversensitized this very first time inside her without protection. The way she felt inside was intense—her heat, hotter, the clench of her muscles stronger, the rippling strength of her inner muscles making their lovemaking that much more immediate. He wasn't sure if it was the lack of the condom, or the fact they'd come much too close to losing this, to losing everything. Whatever it was, it was damned good.

Marc called everyone before he set up the video chat and told them to log in ASAP, that he and Mandy had a lot to tell them. Ted and Theo were already up and having coffee at Nate and Cassie's. They brought their cups and the four of them walked across the yard to the cottage. Ted had his laptop, and set it on the table across from Marc's while Theo walked around the table to where Marc and Mandy were sipping their coffee.

"Good morning." Theo kissed Mandy's cheek. Then he turned, grabbed Marc, and gave him a noogie.

"Hey, what was that for?" Laughing, Marc broke loose from Theo's light hold. "I'm your boss. Respect, man! Respect! Be nice to me."

Theo planted his hands on his hips and glared at Marc. If it hadn't been for the sparkle in his eyes, Marc might have thought he was actually mad at him. "I had nightmares last night. Don't you ever scare me like that again. Do you know how close we were to not being there on time?"

Marc's laughter died. "I know. We can never repay you and Ted, but you know what? My nightmares are gone, and I think yours will go away pretty fast. We're all here, and we're all safe. And Theo, I have no intention of ever scaring anyone like that again—especially Mandy. Me, either. Being scared shitless is highly overrated. Not fun."

"That's good to know." Ted refilled his coffee cup at the carafe on the counter. "Ya know, Marc, when you hired me, you said I'd never be bored. May I admit, in front of witnesses, that you are most definitely a man of your word? Now cut it out, okay? Enough is enough."

"Gotcha. Hey, they should be checking in. We need to tell the others what happened before it hits the papers."

Mandy sighed and leaned against him. "Haven't we played this game before?"

"Yes, but that was a different story, a different shooting, and we're not doing anything like this ever again."

"Gotcha."

Nate and Cassie pulled up chairs behind Marc and Mandy. Theo and Ted sat in front of Ted's computer on the opposite side of the table just as Ben and Lola came online, joining in from Ben's office at Reed Industries. Jake and Kaz came online a few seconds later, both of them sitting in the rumpled sheets of their bed, still looking half asleep. Jake was bare-chested, and Kaz had on a form-fitting knit maxi dress. Even with her hair pointing in all directions, she was absolutely gorgeous.

Almost but not quite as beautiful as Mandy.

"Good morning. Sorry if we woke you guys, Jake and Kaz." Marc glanced at the group sitting around and behind him. "Looks like we're all in the frame. Can everyone see Ben, Lola, Jake, Kaz, Theo, Ted, Nate, Cassie, and Mandy and me? Good. I'm actually not quite sure where to start, but I'll begin with the most important part of the story—Ted was a damned smart hire on my part. He and Theo saved Mandy and me last night when my father attacked us out at my mother's burial site. And yes, the dog got solid hits on her remains, and there's a recovery team headed out there today. My father is dead, the rest of us are alive and basically uninjured, though Mandy got . . ." His voice broke, and he was blinking back tears he hadn't expected. He took a deep breath, held tightly to her hand, and got himself under control. "Mandy got banged up but she'll be okay."

Mandy stuck her face in front of the camera on the computer and pointed to her bruised face and scabbed-over chin. "I promise to heal before the wedding, Kaz. Honest! I really don't want to screw up the pictures."

Marc kissed her cheek. "Thank you for that visual display, Ms. Monroe. Anyway, I know you've heard this before, but we wanted to tell you the story before it hit the newspapers."

He was really proud of himself for getting through it so far without falling apart, but halfway through the tale he realized that the enormity of what had almost happened to them as well as what actually did happen was finally sinking in. His voice broke, he paused and took a deep, settling breath. That's when Mandy squeezed his hand and went on from her point of view.

Then Ted and Theo jumped in. "Neither of us could get a shot," Theo said. "It was so dark up there that we were going more on the sound of their fighting than an actual visual."

"And then," Ted added, "there was a bright flash of light. It illuminated Steven Reed's face perfectly."

"At which point Ted got off a perfect shot and dropped Mr. Reed before he could shoot Mandy." Theo turned to Marc. "You were going to explain that light, Marc. What was it?"

Mandy squeezed his hand, and a sense of calm came over him. "It was my mother, Theo. It started when she came to me in a dream and told me my father was coming. She woke me up from a sound sleep, and I'm sure that's the only reason we were awake in time to keep my father from being able to sneak up on the car and murder us while we slept. Honestly, at first I just thought it was a nightmare, but I decided to look around while Mandy headed over to use the portable rest-room. An old truck went by on the road and the lights flashed off of a silver Lexus that looked just like my father's car parked by the locked gate to the property. Probably the same car I thought I saw on Sunday, since I didn't know until later that he'd been released from that jail in Tijuana before the deputy arrived to collect him."

"When he caught me by the restroom," Mandy said, "Marc was working his way back to our campsite, but it was really dark and he couldn't use his flashlight. I was trying to get away from Steven and we were struggling, but I heard a voice as clear as day saying, 'You can do this, Mandy. Don't let him win.'"

"The same words I heard in my dream," Marc added. "'Don't let him win.' I knew it was my mother's voice, but I didn't realize at the time it was more than a dream. It was her warning me. Warning us."

Mandy nodded in agreement. "Then things just got totally out of control and we were both struggling with Steven at different times. We had no idea that Ted and Theo were anywhere close."

Mandy glanced at Marc, and he picked up the thread. "I had a really bright halogen flashlight and I aimed it at Reed's . . ." He glanced at Mandy, and suddenly it made sense, why she'd called him Steven. ". . . at Steven's eyes, and blinded him, but he started shooting his gun in all directions. I heard a bullet whiz by my ear and I didn't even think; I tackled him and took him down. We struggled, but he was heavier, and so freaked out it made him stronger than me. I had a good grip on his gun hand, but he was on top of me with his hand wrapped around my throat. I was afraid I was going to lose consciousness. That's when Mandy kicked him in the head and he lost the gun."

"We both scrambled for the gun," she said, "but Steven got to it first and he aimed it at me and asked which one of us wanted to die first." She looked at Marc and her eyes sparkled with tears. "And then Marc dove at his father and took him down."

Marc clutched her hand and held on. She would always be his lifeline. Always. "Just as I hit him, out of nowhere there was a bright flash that lit up his face like a strobe light. We heard the sound of a gunshot, and he went down. And Mandy and I were both okay."

"You're saying that flash was . . . ?" Ted was no longer looking at his laptop screen. He stared over the top of it, looking directly at Marc.

Marc nodded. "If you recall, the flashlight I dropped was pointing toward you and Theo, essentially blinding both of you, right?"

Theo nodded and turned to Ted. "He's right."

"I think that flash of light was somehow generated by my mother. The sense of her had been really strong all day long, almost a feeling of approval whenever Bones got a new hit on her remains. Then the dream and Mandy's encouragement—it had to be her. I don't think there's anything that will convince us differently."

Mandy smiled at Marc and kissed him. "And, for what it's worth, I refuse to refer to that man as Mr. Reed, which is why I called him Steven, and that's because I'm going to be Mrs. Reed before too long, and I don't want any association with him at all. Only with this Mr. Reed." She held up her left hand and flashed her ring.

The congratulations had hardly died down when there was a knock on the door. Ted got up to answer it. JD and Bones stood on the front porch. "I sure hope you have some coffee in here," she said. "Because it turns out there isn't any at my place." She glanced around Ted as he waved her in and smiled at Mandy and Marc. "I was hoping you two were back from the site. How'd it go last night?"

No one said a word, though Marc noticed they were all staring at him, as if waiting for him to go through the entire story again. Not yet. He glanced at Mandy.

She smiled at him, kissed him quickly, and then pushed herself away from the computer. "Hey, JD! Good to see you. Tell you what . . . how about I just make another pot?" She smiled at JD and leaned over to pet Bones. "A big one."

CHAPTER 17

Marc, Mandy, JD, and Bones sat under a temporary shade not far from the edge of the slide. A crew was slowly working through all the areas Bones had found and JD had marked. So far, quite a few human remains had been recovered at each of the dog's hits, and it appeared that they would most likely find the entire skeleton.

Tests were already being done to determine the DNA and identity, but Marc knew exactly what they would find. He knew who was out there. She'd told him, quite clearly.

It was an odd feeling, thinking of his mother as a skeleton, but after last night he knew that what they found here today was nothing more than bones. His mother was so much more—she had always been more than the mere physical shell. He and Mandy had no doubt they'd connected with . . . something. Someone. Whatever his mother had been, her essence, her energy? No way to be sure, but she'd saved them. He felt very lucky to have experienced her touch.

Very lucky to be alive.

"Marc, I want to thank you for letting me be here today." JD had seemed surprised that they'd wanted her along, though after hearing the story of what had happened last night, she'd really seemed pleased when they'd invited her to come with them.

"If not for you and Bones, we wouldn't have found her this quickly. I was hoping you'd want to come and see the wonderful thing your crazy beast here has done for my family." He hung on to Mandy's hand while he rubbed between Bones' ears, loving the fact that, finally, he really did have a family. The sense of his mother was strong today, either in his imagination or in her spirit's need to be here for this recovery, along with Mandy, Marc, JD, and Bones.

"Usually, we just go and do our job and then leave." JD shrugged. "We sometimes hear the results when we're called in to testify or read about it in the paper. This is the first time I've actually gotten to know the people we've helped the way I have here." She laughed. "It can be a depressing job, even when you're solving a horrible mystery or finding someone in order to give a family closure, but I always know that closure comes with a price. They can't pretend anymore that their loved one might be coming home."

"I think most people have come to that conclusion by the time you and Bones are called in, even though they don't consciously admit it." Marc's own feelings had been leaning that way when they started this search. "Closure is pretty important. At least it has been for me, because along with closure has come some much-needed answers." Marc stared at nothing, remembering the way he'd felt about his mother for most of his life. "I told you that I was raised to believe she'd deserted me.

That she didn't love me. Now I know she loved me more than anything. No way in hell would she ever have deserted me."

JD sat quietly for a moment before covering Marc's hand with hers. "After what you and Mandy told me, she still hasn't. She was here for you last night. You're very lucky, you know. You have unquestionable proof that she really did love you, that she's done everything she could to let you know that." She glanced around Marc and smiled at Mandy. "Think about it, Mandy. She's going to be your mother-in-law, and she must approve of you or she never would have helped you get away from that jerk."

Mandy chuckled. "I hadn't thought about it that way, but you're right. Thanks for the insight."

It wasn't much later that Deputy Russo joined them under the shade to let them know the team was through, that it appeared they had everything. "Very little was scattered, but your dog is really good, Ms. Stirling. From the position of the bones not with the first find, it appears we've got everything. Marc, once DNA tests are done, we'll release the remains to the funeral home of your choice so you can make arrangements. I'm really sorry for your loss, but thankful that you finally know what really happened."

"Thanks, Jerry. Credit goes to JD and Bones. And thank you as well. You've been really helpful. Do the folks in Marin know what happened? I forgot to call the chief."

"Not a problem. I called this morning first thing and emailed the preliminary report, so they have a copy. I think you folks can go back home, at least for now. We'll be in touch."

They got JD and Bones on the plane back to Butte and then headed home to San Francisco. Ted and Theo had gone earlier in the morning. Marc was anxious to get back, to find comfort in the work and the daily routines that had been his saving grace for years.

They made a quick stop in Marin to speak to the chief of police and then Marc turned the driving over to Mandy and called Alden Chung. The therapist was free that afternoon and invited Marc and Mandy to stop at his office.

His words stayed with Marc long after their visit ended. "It is difficult to disprove what we don't understand," Dr. Chung had said. "And there's no reason to disagree with the validity of something without proof. I would suggest you take your mother's visit as a blessing, hold her close, and treasure that very special connection."

It was almost five by the time they got to the house on Twenty-third. Jake and Kaz were at the unit next door, checking out the new wood flooring throughout the house.

"We get our furniture tomorrow!" Kaz gave Mandy a hug and grinned at Marc. "This is just so cool! Thank you!" She kissed Marc, grabbed Mandy's arm, and dragged her down the hallway to check out the master bedroom. Marc watched them go before turning to Jake.

"Are you guys okay with the remodel?"

Jake merely stared at him and shook his head.

When Marc frowned—he had absolutely no idea what Jake was thinking—Jake laughed.

"Idiot," he said, though Marc thought he said it nicely. "My girl's ecstatic, the unit is ideal, and there's a perfect room in the basement beside the garage for a workroom. What's not to love, and why are you even worrying about this? Crap, man, you've had a traumatic few months. Maybe it's time to think about yourself for a while. You and Mandy."

Marc stared down the hallway where the girls had disappeared. He heard them talking; Kaz's excitement was off the charts. Mandy sounded more reserved, but no less happy. "You're right, you know." He turned to Jake, his oldest and closest friend through so many years, so many highs and lows in both their lives. "We've earned this time, this chance to be happy. I never expected to find love, not like this. Did you?"

Jake laughed. "Are you kidding?" He glanced toward the sound of laughter. "She's perfect, Marc. Everything I could ever want, so much better than I could have imagined. I wouldn't even know her if not for you. You've always come through for me, even when you weren't planning to. That's a skill, man. A valuable skill."

They were still tossing insults back and forth over the way their lives were turning out when Ben and Lola showed up. Lola immediately went looking for Kaz and Mandy, but Ben walked up to Marc and hugged him. "Don't you ever do that to me again."

"Do what?" Marc's mind was spinning. What the hell had he done to Ben?

"Scare the crap out of me or my fiancée. We got off that online chat and Lola broke down sobbing. It took forever to calm her down, and by the time she had it under control, I wasn't in much better shape." He glared at Marc a moment longer and then punched him lightly in the shoulder. "Ya know, I've had about twenty years without any family to worry about. It was a hell of a lot less stressful."

He glanced at Jake and grinned. "What about you, bro? Is it as good for you as it is for me?"

Jake merely nodded. "I think this calls for a beer," he said. Marc and Ben agreed, and followed him into the newly remodeled kitchen. The old round oak kitchen table with all six chairs from the other unit fit perfectly in this kitchen.

A few minutes later, Kaz walked into the room and grabbed a bottle of white wine out of the refrigerator. She handed the bottle and a corkscrew to Jake and went in search of wine glasses. They'd already moved some of the necessities into the unit. Not a word was exchanged. Jake continued talking to the guys, opened the bottle, and handed it to Kaz. She kissed him on the cheek, waved to Marc and Ben, and headed out of the room.

After she was gone, Jake glanced at Marc and Ben and shrugged. "We've already reached a point where I think we're reading each other's minds. Isn't she amazing?"

Marc held up his empty beer. Ben lifted his at the same time. Laughing, Jake took the empties and grabbed new ones. Marc glanced at Ben. "Not nearly as amazing as we are."

Mandy, Lola, and Kaz toasted Mandy's engagement, Lola and Ben's engagement, and Kaz's upcoming wedding. Mandy took a sip of her wine. "Only eleven more days, Kaz. You guys ready?"

Kaz nodded. "We are. Everything has come together so well it makes me nervous, especially with our track record. Do you realize how much crap all of us have had to go through to get our guys?"

Lola looked pensive. "We've all faced risk, things that could have ended up very badly, and in every case we've made it through. Not only have we survived, we've seen our men take really brave, dangerous actions to save us. There's not one of us who has to doubt how our guys feel about us, and they have no reason to doubt us."

"Exactly." Kaz stared into her glass. "The wedding and all . . . that's just a party to celebrate. I already feel married to Jake. I know him better than I've ever known anyone, including you guys. It's very humbling, having a man you've cried with, laughed with . . ." She glanced up and her eyes were twinkling. "One you've been pee-your-pants scared absolutely to death with."

"There is that." Mandy thought of those moments when Steven Reed had his gun pointed at her and she knew Marc was going to go for it. She really hadn't expected either of them to make it out alive. "I never imagined what it would be like to face death, to know if I'd have the courage to fight. I learned that I do, that I can risk everything to save what matters to me. Marc matters. So damned much. I want to get married right away. I really don't want to waste any more time."

"Me, either." Lola grabbed her hand. "Want to go to the justice of the peace this week, if the guys will go along? I don't need a big wedding. I just need Ben."

"Um, ladies?" Kaz raised her hand. "I've got a suggestion. Instead of being bridesmaids, why don't you guys be brides? With me? We could all get married together, if the guys go along with it. So many of the people who are coming to Jake's and my wedding would probably be going to yours as well, and we can add the ones you want who aren't on my guest list."

Lola glanced at Mandy, wide-eyed, before looking at Kaz. "You're sure? That's a huge change in plans for you. Why don't you take a night to think about it? A big decision like that involves Jake and needs his input."

"And Ben and Marc." Mandy laughed. "Though knowing these three, I imagine anything that gets them out of planning a wedding will work. I know I've had my share working on stuff for Kaz and Jake while Ms. World Traveler was jaunting around Italy with her famous photographer." She grabbed Lola's hand and Kaz's and held on. "I think it's about the coolest idea I've ever heard, Kaz, and really generous of you. Let's go for it!"

"I don't know, Jake. A wedding is a pretty big deal for a woman. Are you certain Kaz wants to share her day?"

Jake merely shrugged. "I dunno, Marc, but personally, there's nothing I'd like more than to share it with both my brothers. What about you, Ben?"

"It works for me, but only if Lola and Kaz agree." He glanced at Marc. "And Mandy, of course. I mean, it could certainly make for one hell of a party."

"Hey."

Marc glanced up as Mandy walked in, trailed by Kaz and Lola. She leaned over and gave him a kiss and then plopped down in his lap. "What's up with you three?" Marc asked. Then he leaned around Mandy and smiled at Kaz and Lola. "And why do all of you look like you're up to no good?"

Kaz rolled her eyes. "He's good, Mandy. Scary good." She straddled Jake's lap while Lola snuggled up to Ben. Looping her arms over Jake's shoulders, Kaz kissed him and then glanced toward Marc. "Well, Marc," she said, "we were just talking about how Jake and I have this beautiful wedding all planned, and you guys are all just as engaged as we are, and wondered if you would like to share it with us? Of course, only if Jake's okay with it and . . ." She leaned back as Jake laughed. "What?"

"Merely that great minds think alike. I just suggested that to the guys."

Kaz turned and smiled at Lola and Mandy. "See? He's right. Great minds do think alike. So that's it. We're set. Now you two have exactly ten—make that nine—days to get a wedding dress and invite the folks you want to invite. We'll have to bump up the amount of food, but wine shouldn't be a problem." She looked over her shoulder at Marc. "Right?"

"Right."

"And as long as everyone is okay with jazzy bluegrass, the music should work just fine. Now, ladies, I'm doing the traditional bride bit with my dad walking me down the aisle and turning me over to Jake. Got a man you can bring for dad duty?"

Lola raised her hand. "I call dibs on Theo."

"That's good, because I want Ted." Mandy leaned back and looked upside down at Marc. "Is that okay with you?"

"As long as he doesn't object to being daddy for a day, I think it's a great idea." He thought about it for a moment, about Ted's part in their family. "Personally, I think he'll be honored that you'd ask him."

Mandy crawled into bed beside Marc and curled up close against his long, lean body. So much has happened over the past month that it doesn't seem possible that's all it's been."

"We've most definitely crammed an awful lot into the past few weeks." Marc pulled her closer, until she was draped across his chest. "Can we slow down now, maybe take some time to get to know each other a bit better?"

She snorted and then buried her face against his chest.

"You snorted. What's that for?"

"I think we know each other, Marc, though I definitely want to spend the rest of my life getting to know you better. You okay with that?"

"I think I can handle it. I'm actually looking forward to getting back to the office and a regular schedule. I've missed doing normal stuff with you, Mandy. I've even missed work. I really love what I do. I hope you'll have as good a time with the coffee shop. Theo's got the paperwork all drawn up so we can approach the women's center that you three have selected. I'm going to be looking into my mother's inheritance tomorrow, but from what Theo has learned, it makes my income look paltry. I'm thinking we might want to spread it out over multiple charities, including some in wine country, but we've got plenty of time to think about it."

Mandy propped herself up on her elbows on his chest. "Is this the nerd's version of pillow talk? Because I don't know whether to be turned on and panting or insulted and giggling." She leaned close and licked one nipple.

Marc groaned. She licked the other, and then caught it between her teeth. This time it was more of a whimper, but that worked. She tugged and he arched his back, at which point she trapped his erection between her thighs and began kissing her way down his body. It didn't take her long at all to find what she was looking for, to take him in her mouth, to savor the taste and texture of the man she loved more than she thought possible. She'd promised him forever and she really loved the sound of that.

She took him as far as she could without going past the point of no return. When she raised her head, it was to find Marc watching her. He was smiling, but clearly he was struggling to hang on to control. With a single kiss to the tip of his erection, she crawled up his body until she was kneeling over him with her hands planted on his shoulders. "I love you, Marcus Jerome Reed. I love you so much it absolutely fills me up."

She barely had time to register the devilish glint in his eyes before he'd flipped her over and trapped her beneath him. "That's good," he said. "Because I want to fill you up even more." He nipped at her breasts, nuzzled the sensitive skin along her ribs, and then knelt between her thighs and lifted her to his mouth.

She loved the way his big hands palmed her buttocks, the soft flicks of his tongue against her moist sex, the way he knew exactly what she loved. This was a man who paid attention to all the little things that mattered, the way she shivered when he used his tongue and lips, even his teeth to bring her to the edge, the way he reminded her with every look, every word, every act, just how important she was in his life.

He took Mandy to her peak and over, and before she'd had time to come down completely, he did it again. But this time he was there, filling her with the length and strength of him, pressing deep as he made love to her, holding her close, reminding her once again just how very much he loved her.

They invited Ted and Theo for dinner. Lola had stuck a pot roast in the crock pot before going to work, and once they got home, Mandy fixed a big platter of roasted veggies. Kaz brought dessert—with a flourish. She waltzed through the door, and took a bow.

Jake held a hand up for silence. "I am pleased to announce Her Royal Highness, Kaz, the queen of store-bought gourmet pies." He bowed with a flourish and added, "With ice cream."

"Thank you. Yo, minion." She gestured at Jake. "Ask Lola where she wants this."

"So, I'm a minion now?" Grumbling, he took the two pie boxes and the ice cream and put everything away for later.

The dinner, as always, was a success, but for Mandy, the most memorable time of the night came once Queen Kaz served dessert. When everyone had a plate, Jake poured glasses of deep red port wine from the Tangled

Vines half of Intimate Wines—Cassie and Nate's engagement gift to Lola and Ben and Mandy and Marc.

Mandy tapped the side of her glass with a spoon and stood. "Ted and Theo, Lola and I have a favor to ask of the two of you. We figured we'd soften you up with Kaz's gooey dessert first. So if you're wondering, yes, this is part of our scheme. The thing is, we never had father figures in our lives, and we're coming up to an event on the twentieth of August that truly begs for the presence of a father."

Mandy grabbed hold of Ted's hand and Lola took Theo's, the plan being that if they held on tight enough, the guys couldn't escape. "We realize that neither of you are old enough to be our fathers, but you are both men we love and admire." She glanced at Lola.

Who was losing her battle at fighting back tears. Lola sniffed, looked at Theo, and shrugged. "I'll get through this. Just give me a minute." Then she laughed and shot a quick glance at Ben. He gave her a thumbs up signal and she nodded. "The thing is, Theo, and Ted . . ." She sucked in a deep breath. "Mandy and I would really appreciate it if you would be the men to walk us down the aisle at the wedding. It means you have to wear the tux and look debonair and sexy, but we don't think that's beyond either of you guys."

"I would be honored." Theo stood up, walked around the table and gave Lola a kiss. "Honored and very proud." He held his arms wide and she hugged him as Ted reached for Mandy and gave her a hug and a kiss.

"Thank you," he said, sounding every bit as emotional as Lola. Blinking back tears, he held Mandy close and glanced over the top of her head at Marc. "And thank you as well, Marc. You told me once you figured you'd have to build your own family because yours sucked. We know your mom was actually a pretty special lady, and every person in this room is just as amazing. Thank you for inviting me to be part of this wonderful clan. Mandy? Asking me to be such an important part of your special day just makes everything even more perfect."

Healdsburg, CA—August 20

They'd gotten a room in Healdsburg at a beautiful up-scale hotel for their first night as husband and wife. As it turned out, Jake and Kaz were in one just down the street, a place they'd stayed in during that first photo shoot where they'd fallen in love. Ben and Lola had chosen yet another beautiful hotel in town.

"Other than the paparazzi, that went well." Marc stripped off his tux jacket and the white shirt and bow-tie. Kicked off his shoes, toed off his socks, and sighed his relief. He'd been wearing what Mandy called his "grown up clothes" much too long today. Walking over to the small table by the window, he poured a couple of glasses of port he'd asked the concierge to have waiting for them.

Tangled Vines. The manager had been interested in the winery, knew some of their history, and after tasting a glass from the bottle Marc had given to the man, had said he'd be ordering it for the hotel. They already carried Intimate wines. Marc liked doing what he could to push sales of the wines that Nate and Cassie made in tandem with his.

It was important to keep his vineyard manager and winemaker happy.

Mandy stepped out of the bathroom and Marc almost swallowed his tongue. Gone was the simple wedding gown. Instead, she wore a shimmering white nightgown that appeared almost translucent, backlit as she was by the brighter lights in the bathroom. She paused in the doorway, turned and flipped off the lights. The shadows of her long legs still showed through the silky fabric.

"Honestly?" She smiled that smile that was for him alone. "The paparazzi weren't all that irritating, once you sent out waiters with glasses of wine and platters of chicken satay and egg rolls. I wonder if they'll mention the bribery?"

"Hopefully not, though none of them were rude or pushy. They were just doing their jobs. Besides, it's good advertising for Jake and Kaz. Bet Kaz's Q score goes through the roof."

Mandy laughed at that. "Did you know that a couple of weeks ago Kaz had to ask Lola what a Q score was? She asked me, but I didn't know, either. She's really famous, which is hard to get used to. What's neat though is that I heard her dad telling her today how proud he was of her and admitting he'd been wrong to try and force her into business."

"What did Kaz say to that? And you look absolutely amazing in that . . . wow! I have no words for what that gown is called. It's certainly not suitable for public."

"Don't worry. You're the only public who's gonna see me in this." She curtsied. "And Kaz said she told her father she was really glad he'd pushed her into business school, because she and Jake can both read all the contracts they're dealing with and not worry they're misunderstanding anything. That's pretty important."

"It is. I'm glad I took as many business classes as I did. Did you notice how glassy-eyed Ben looked at the wedding? Do you think it finally hit him today that he's now a married man?"

"Actually, it hit him today that he's going to be a daddy."

"Holy shit. Really?" He sat down at the table. Not that the news hit him all that hard, but . . . well, maybe it did.

"Yes. Really. Lola told him she's pregnant just before they went to bed last night. She's not sure when it happened, but she's suspected for the past couple of weeks. She went to the doctor last week to make sure, but she didn't want to say anything to Ben or anyone else with the wedding coming up. She figured Ben's got enough on his plate right now."

Marc laughed. And, admittedly, felt a little jealous. "How'd he take it?"

Mandy sat across the little table from him and stared into her glass of port. "Lola said he cried and said it was the most perfect gift she could ever give him. I think Ben will be a terrific dad. It's going to change things, that's for sure."

"We'll need to add a playground in the backyard." A big one, because Lola and Ben's offspring wasn't going to be the only child in this group. He couldn't wait for the time when he and Mandy could plan their own family.

"I think we've got time. At least a couple of years."

"Do you want to wait that long?"

"No, silly. Not us. Babies aren't born wanting to play on the jungle gym. It'll be at least that long until theirs is ready to play. Which reminds me," she added. "Ted was right."

"Ted's always right," Marc tapped the crystal lip of his goblet of dark port to hers and took a sip. "That's why I hired him." He wrapped his hand around hers. "So, what is Ted right about now?"

"Well, it could be when he told me I was the most beautiful bride today."

"He nailed it with that observation." He had, too. Mandy had been absolutely steal-your-breath gorgeous in her simple white gown, though the almost see-through nightgown she wore now was a close second. "What else?"

Mandy reached across the small table and took Marc's hand. "When he said he'd never felt as much love in one place as he did today. That it wasn't just us, but the people we'd invited—a lot of the same ones he'd had at his dinner right before he went back to Virginia, remember? That was really fun. He said it was the perfect wedding, joining together couples who had been tested by fire and had come through it stronger and better than ever."

"Ted would know. He's been tested as well."

Mandy smiled. "And he's passed. With flying colors. He told me tonight he's never been in love before, but that he realized this week just how much he loves Theo, that Theo had really helped him embrace who he is, the fact he's gay. He said the best part of all was how much fun they had together. I don't think Ted's had much fun in his life."

Marc thought about that for a moment. "Ya know, if this software gig runs out, I could probably make a living as a matchmaker. Nate and Cassie. Jake and Kaz. Lola and Ben. You and me, and now Ted and Theo. Damn, wife. I'm good!"

"I like that." Mandy set her glass aside, stood and walked around the small table. She straddled his lap and rested her arms on his shoulders.

He slipped his hands around her waist, rested them on the slight curve of her hips. "Like what? That I'm good?" He really loved teasing her.

"No, silly. Wife." She kissed him. "You called me your wife, and I love the sound of it. Almost as much as I love knowing you're my husband."

Her eyes welled with tears. They couldn't have tears,

not on their wedding night. He slipped his arms beneath her bottom and lifted her against his chest. She wrapped her legs around his waist. "No tears, Mrs. Reed." He walked the short steps to their bed where he sat with Mandy still hanging on. "I think it's time that we consummate this marriage, don't you?"

"I thought you'd never make your move, Mr. Reed. I was getting worried. I know your record."

"Okay. So I was a slow starter." He kissed her, and it was a long time before he came up for air. "Are you going to hold that against me forever?"

Laughing, she fell back against the thick down comforter. "Probably. I have a feeling I'm going to take a lot of convincing. You'd better get started."

EPILOGUE

Marc had found a beautiful plot beneath a tree at the same Marin cemetery where the woman and child killed in Ben and Jake's accident so long ago were buried. His mother's remains now lay beneath verdant green grass with a plot of purple iris planted in a bordered garden around the headstone.

The memorial service had been somber but at the same time, joyful. All those closest to him had come— even Nate and Cassie with their newborn son, Nathanial Marcus Dunagan.

Marc had sensed his mother's spirit close by, felt her approval. He thought she really approved of what they'd done with Steven Reed's body. Donating it to science had seemed like a good alternative to burying him. Better the man do some good after his life than forever remain a reminder of all the hate he'd fostered and the misery he'd caused.

There'd been no hate in his mother. He knew there was a part of him that would always miss her, would always miss what they might have shared. She would forever be an empty spot in his heart. A spot that Mandy was filling more every day.

He was thinking of his mother now as he signed the papers establishing an endowment with a portion of his mother's trust designated as the principal financial donor. The endowment itself was named in honor of the mother and son who had died, as well as his mother, Elizabeth Marchand Reed.

And of course there was Bett's Place, the coffee shop that Mandy had recently opened with a crew made up entirely of women from this same shelter, the place they had gathered today to sign the final papers on the endowment that would ensure its survival as a viable safety net for abused women and their children.

Ben was the next to sign, and then Jake. Their attorney went over the signatures and then rose and spoke to the members of the press in attendance. Marc had been surprised at the amount of publicity this had garnered, but it appeared it was rare when a truly huge sum of money was put into an endowment bestowed in perpetuity to honor and help victims of domestic abuse.

Once the formalities were observed and the needed words spoken, it was time to get back to work—Marc to his office, and Mandy to the coffee shop. They'd left Theo watching the office and Ted keeping an eye on the women working in the shop. They were never without a guard, and there had been a couple of incidents where the presence of guards had kept things calm. Mandy's suggestions for bulletproof glass and a safe room had been heeded—but luckily not yet needed.

He stood and tugged Mandy lightly to her feet, turned to Ben and Lola, Kaz and Jake. "You ready?"

They all got into Jake's big Escalade. He glanced at Lola with her slight baby bump and laughed. "Hey, Jake?

Thought about getting a bus? This rig isn't going to work forever, you know. The family's growing."

"When the family gets too big for this rig, you're all going to have to start using your own cars."

Kaz poked his arm. "Spoilsport." Then she turned to look at the rest of the group. "Don't worry. I'll work on him. I'm thinking bus, you know, like the ones that haul people to casinos? Jake could wear a cute little cap, and those buses have bathrooms. I like that!"

Marc tucked Mandy close against his side amid the laughter, and enjoyed the ride back to the office. It was all good. And every time he thought it couldn't possibly get any better, Mandy made a liar out of him.

Life was good and getting better all the time.